# THE ARAMEUS CHRONICLE

## The Girl From Avignon

Bradley S Compton
Praveen V Arla

Library of Congress Control Number: 2017931107

ISBN: 978-0-9897544-4-6

Printed in the United States of America

www.hollandbrownbooks.com

www.arameuschronicle.com

First Edition, First Printing

# THE ARAMEUS CHRONICLE

## The Girl From Avignon

# Chapter One
## An Unexpected Meeting

No matter how many years passed, waiting rooms remained the same. Printed periodicals were long gone, but there was no difference between reading garbage from a magazine and reading garbage from a qubit. Ansley surveyed the room looking at the unlined faces of the bored Nephites going through their weekly ritual. Trying to guess their ages based on mannerisms, he could easily tell who was born before the rise of Arameus from those born in its domed cities.

He looked down at his feet, feeling weakened by the journey from Beladero and shamed by his dependence on the treatments. The one positive was that there were no children present. In the recesses of his mind, he recalled days spent in a doctor's office, annoyed by the whining of sick children. These were fond recollections.

"Ansley Brightmore," droned the receptionist.

He approached the woman, who didn't deign to make eye contact with him, and was amused at the fact that even in Capitol City receptionists were irritated by their jobs. At least that hadn't changed.

"Hold out your wrist," she said. Ansley obliged and she scanned the chip imbedded underneath the skin. "You're approved. Room 14."

He heard the grinding of locks as she buzzed him in.

"It truly was a pleasure," smiled Ansley, moving past.

Walking down the hall, he observed the Nephites receiving their treatments, each in a room of white, attended by a nurse dressed in white, and the sterility of the environment pressed on him. Finding Room 14, he entered, taking his seat in the already reclined chair. As he settled in, a familiar face entered.

"Good to see you, Gertie!" exclaimed Ansley. "Always nice to see a familiar face."

The plump, mild-mannered woman forced a weak smile before taking the bedside seat and pulling up his records on the console.

"You haven't been here in five weeks, Professor Brightmore. That is far too long to go between treatments."

"I apologize, Nurse Gertrude. I would think all these years would have afforded us some informality. How many years have I been coming to Room 14 now? Aren't I a VIP?"

"Hold out your arm," she said with no inflection in her voice. The mechanical appendage descending from the ceiling pricked the vein in the crease of his arm, drawing out blood before applying a clotting agent. The nurse stared at the console, ignoring the procedure.

"Does it say I'm dying, Gertie?" he asked in jest.

She frowned at him before turning back to her work and shaking her head. "This isn't good. Your records show your chronological age as 254 years, 6 months, and 11 days. However your biological age is now reading as 34 years."

"Sounds like I'm aging well. What's the problem?"

"Professor, you can't miss treatments. Your biological breakdown will accelerate given your true age. You have to come weekly. I'm recommending a double dose of nanocytes. I will be back to fill out your exit papers."

The nurse inserted an intravenous catheter into his

wrist, programming the precise amount of fluids he was to receive before leaving the room. Ansley leaned his head back and closed his eyes, feeling the nanocytes course through his body. Within two pumps of his heart, they were distributed, and he felt a euphoric release of the tension in his muscles and a reprieve from his weariness. In free moments like these, his mind always went to her. Her laugh, her touch, her scent, the feeling of her silky black hair against his body, stationary moments brought him the most pain. He roused himself from reverie, pushing the memories deep within. Focusing on the IV, he counted the pulses as the artificial blood surged into his body. Finally, the nurse returned.

"Well, Professor, I have your blood work. Your blood alcohol level was at 0.26. I added an antidote to the serum. You should be sober now."

Of course, Ansley laughed to himself. She only came to him in moments of sobriety. He would need a drink after this.

"Gertie, you are a buzzkill. Why do you always do this to me?"

She sat in a chair and rolled to his side, placing her hand on his. Giving it a gentle squeeze, she looked at him, eyes filled with compassion.

"Ansley, I see a lot of the older ones come in, just like you. They feel depressed. Many have substance abuse issues. This isn't the first time you have come here with a high blood alcohol level. We have treatment for that. Is there anything you would like to talk about?"

Ansley stood, taking the IV from his arm. "I admit this, Gertie. I like booze." He stared at her, defiant, before walking to the door.

"Wait, Professor," she said before he left. "There's more. People have begun to notice your lack of treatments. Your biological age is now at 34, even with today's treatments. You should read at 30, yet your continued failure to show up has aged you four years. We can't get those back, Ansley. And your blood work showed more than alcohol. It showed Sikyon flu. We don't have the flu in the dome. How did it come to be in your system?"

Ansley stopped at the door and smiled back at Gertie. "I'm sure you'll figure it out." He disappeared down the hall.

Left alone, Nurse Gertrude contemplated the information before her. It told of a man who had not led the life of a proper Nephite. It showed a man on the verge of being deemed a deviant. She looked out the window to the Central Tower looming large above the center of the dome, took a nervous breath, and deleted the information.

\*\*\*

Ansley left the nanocyte treatment center annoyed at the clarity in his brain. His hawk was parked at his apartment and thus he was forced to go on foot. Trying to not think about her, he lifted his head and threw back his shoulders, adopting a confident gait to fend off the melancholy. Having been absent from the recent proceedings of the Institute, he headed toward the Eastern Tower, knowing he would be late to the Tuesday talks, where young professors showcased their work. Perhaps high-minded pursuits were in order to ease his mind.

Arriving at campus, Ansley walked across the quad toward the auditorium. He knew he would enter through the back, and as an elder professor, would have to take his place in the front, but still it was better to be seen. Careful opening the door so as not to disturb the speaker, the old Professor allowed his eyes to adjust to the darkness before looking to the light emanating from the screen in the front. Moving down the stairs, he inelegantly found his place among the founding members of the Institute.

Taking a seat, Ansley glanced to his left and right, noting the glares from his colleagues. A lesser man would have felt judged, but a scientist of his caliber found their stares laughable. Sober for once, and in his scientific element, he was the smartest man in the room and everyone knew it. Settling in to listen to the speaker, the name on the screen was shocking: *Arian Cyannah*. Glancing at the title of the talk, Ansley shook his head. He had even chosen her field, or at least, it had been chosen for him.

"This is what I'm proposing," continued the speaker.

"If we can one day attach a bot at the synthesis phase of cellular mitosis, then we can eradicate the need for continuous nanocyte treatments. Thank you."

An awkward silence followed and Arian waited for the standard applause. There was a pause, slight but noticeable, before the members of the Institute showed lackluster appreciation. The young professor lost all confidence in that moment.

"I will now open the floor for questions," said Arian. The dryness in his mouth was palpable but the water bottle was ten feet away. It wouldn't seem proper to go for it now and he didn't wish to appear desperate. He knew his talk was weak and had attempted to get it pushed back for weeks. Due to lack of results, most of it had revolved around potential experiments, an issue that would be exploited by the old guard. Stomach fluttering, he awaited the onslaught that was sure to come. Professor Miller was the first to raise his hand.

"Yes, Professor," Arian said.

"You claim that by attaching this bot to raw DNA, you can bypass the need for nanocytes, yet I see nothing in your talk to substantiate this. You can't even attach the bot. How can you make such claims?"

Arian was staggered by the question, unable to think. His mind was blank as he stared out at the great scientists. Before he could speak, Professor Somorjai chimed in.

"We're getting ahead of ourselves, Dr. Miller. The boy can't even tell us the physics of the attachment. How do you propose to achieve this feat to begin with? Go to the board and show me how the physics will work."

Arian wanted to be anywhere but where he was. His greatest weakness was in physics and he had hoped to avoid the subject. Now blood was in the water and the Institute's hierarchy loved to watch the young professors squirm. Trying to draw forth a thought, anything, he walked to the board.

Nothing came to mind. He grabbed an eraser and wiped away the chalk from a previous talk, nearly choking on the dust coming off the rough surface.

Arian started drawing a nascent DNA strand but froze, unable to continue. He understood biology but had no deep grasp of the physics involved, hoping to leave the equations to others. Then the laughter started behind him. Not an open laughter, but periodic stifled guffaws. That was worse. He dropped his hands to his side, still holding the chalk, a resigned look in his eyes.

"Dr. Cyannah," continued Professor Somorjai, "I'm waiting for my proof."

"Shut the fuck up," said Ansley, standing from his seat and walking toward the speaker. "I know all of you assholes, and none of you can do what you ask of the kid."

The old Professor reached for the chalk dangling between Arian's fingers. "Watch this, kid," he whispered.

Ansley began scribbling equations on the board describing the forces and free energies necessary for the attachment. Given a few days to study his writings, the other professors would be able to follow. When he finished, he turned to the crowd and spoke.

"What Arian is trying to say is that when DNA replicates, information is lost with each generation of cell division. The strand is longer than necessary to account for the loss, but eventually aging occurs. By introducing a bot during this phase, we can store the information that would previously be lost, and thus prevent biological aging. Basically, he is saying that the nanocyte treatments will soon be a thing of the past."

Ansley stopped, shocked by his own statement and stared at the young professor. He walked toward the kid, leaning in to whisper.

"You've started something big here. Let's get out in front of it."

Realizing a hushed crowd was still looking on, Ansley faced them. This was the one venue in which he was always comfortable.

"Any questions?" he asked, staring down the formerly confident professors in the front. No one raised their hands or spoke.

Ansley remained standing in place as the members of the audience filed out. Professor Somorjai approached them, his face red with rage.

"The Institute will hear about this Brightmore, you can count on that." He walked away shaking his head in disgust.

Ansley turned to Arian, who was now gathering his things.

"You know, kid, I probably did you more harm than good with that stunt. I apologize, but I've just always hated how they tear down our young faculty in public."

Arian still seemed dazed and perspiration dripped from his forehead. He managed to nod.

"Don't get too down on yourself," continued Ansley. "At my first public talk, I spent most of it making jokes to cover my lack of useable data. We all have to start somewhere. Look at me now, the most hated and respected man in the Institute."

This elicited a slight smile from Arian.

"Give yourself a couple of days. You'll bounce back. I must admit, my interest was piqued by my explanation of your work. If what I said is true, your work will garner the interest of the Overseers themselves. That might not be a good thing."

Arian faced Ansley now, disbelieving the ego of the man. "You heard one sentence of my talk, Professor, yet you presume to explain it to my peers."

"I thought I did a better job than you." Noticing the blush coming over Arian's face, Ansley retracted. "Sorry. That was a low blow."

"What did you mean when you said the Overseers would be interested in my work? Why would they care?"

Ansley smiled at the naivety of the question. The kid's mother had the same innocent view of the world before the purges. "This isn't a good place to talk. These walls have ears.

How about meeting for a drink tomorrow evening? I'd like to hear more about your research and give you some advice I've learned the hard way."

Arian couldn't refuse an invitation from Professor Ansley Brightmore and accepted. "Sure. I'd love to hear more of your insights." The words rang hollow to the ears of both men.

"Good," said Ansley, unfazed. "I know a quaint place in the southern district where we can speak in private. The Devonshire Pub. I will see you there at seven."

With a slight bow of his head, Ansley turned to exit, leaving Arian alone in the auditorium with his dejected thoughts.

\*\*\*

Arian left work early the following day to change before meeting Ansley at the Devonshire. He resided in the eastern district, just across the Arymides River that surrounded the Central Isle and used the hawk system to get to the southern district. Throwing his leg over the bike, he typed in the coordinates of the pub and the centrally automated system chose his route, analyzing current traffic conditions among other factors.

The system routed him across the East Bridge to the Central Isle, past the marble columned expanse of the Institute, before taking him south past the Southern Tower and the monument district. The ease of travel led to unwelcome thoughts. One day removed from the disastrous talk, he had noticed the averted eyes of his colleagues and could sense their pity. Professor Brightmore hadn't made it any easier with his interruption. Freezing in front of the crowd was embarrassing enough, but being shown up was altogether worse. Nonetheless, Ansley's mention of the Overseers had grabbed his attention. It would be unwise to ignore the advice of a man of his age and experience.

Just across the South Bridge, his hawk turned into a docking station, where it would be charged for his return trip. The district to the south of the Central Isle was filled with pubs, restaurants, and casinos. It was the playground for bored Nephites, many of whom spent their overlong lives in an alcoholic haze.

Still, this district contained the same towering buildings, intricately carved facades, and stunning artwork as every other corner of the Capitol City dome. Arian walked the avenue, admiring the change of scenery. Being young and born in the Capitol City nurseries, he had spent little time in this region of the city. Most of his time had been spent amongst his peers in the youth dormitories and it was only recently, upon his rise to assistant professor at the age of 28 that he had received his own living accommodations. Arriving at the unadorned façade of the Devonshire Pub, he peered in the window and saw that only one patron, Ansley, was seated at the bar.

Arian entered and took the seat next to the old Professor, who was smoking a cigarette and drinking bourbon neat. Without looking over at Arian, he spoke to the bartender, a large man with tanned skin. Black stubble speckled with grey lined his jaw and matched the hair on his head. Age lines surrounded his eyes, and his face was pock marked. He was a Natural Born, not uncommon for a worker in the city, but Arian had never been comfortable in their presence. Their lack of breeding showed in their uncouth manners, and he found their aged bodies to be not only unappealing, but a hindrance to his appetite.

"The kid will have the same, Eddie," said Ansley. "He just got dangled before the sharks."

The Professor had been here for some time as indicated by his slurred speech and dark tone, both absent the previous day. The bartender poured the drink and placed it before Arian. Lifting the glass, he took a sip and began coughing as the harsh liquor burned his throat and lips.

"You'll get used to it," said the old Professor, still not looking at him. "Bourbon is a man's drink, a scientist's drink. Kid, this is Eduardo. Eduardo, this is the kid."

Nodding at the Natural Born man, Arian turned to

Ansley. "I'm not a kid, you know. I'm an assistant professor."

"You're all kids to me. But that's not what I mean."

He slid over the silver cigarette case in front of him. It was high quality and engraved, but Arian noticed that it was warped and discolored on the edges.

"What's this? I don't smoke."

Ansley sighed, pulling out a pocket watch, opening it before quickly shutting it again. "That's your mother's cigarette case. I took it from her body while the heat still cooked her flesh. I gave it to her as a gift when she made full professor all those years ago." He grabbed the silver case, removed a cigarette and lit it, drawing deep while staring into space.

Unsure of how to respond, Arian took another drink of the stout liquor. He was becoming accustomed to the burn now, but he still took small sips. After what he deemed an adequate amount of time, he broached the subject again.

"I realize now that you have an attachment to my genetic mother and that is why you chose to intervene during my talk. You need to understand, though, I have no mother. I was born of the Arameus Empire, created from the genetic material of fallen Nephites dead long before I was born. I don't know them, nor do I care to. I've never understood why the old guard is so sentimental for the past."

Ansley slammed his fist onto the bar, startling Arian. "It doesn't matter how you feel. Your thoughts are given to you from birth. The fact remains that you are of your mother, a woman I loved, and a woman who was taken from me when the worthless masters of this society chose to eliminate those who aided in its construction."

Ansley paused, realizing he had overreacted. Taking a breath, he continued. "You speak so casually of Nephites, as if you are part of a superior race. It's a class distinction, nothing more. Do you think you're that different from those outside the domes? Have you even been outside of Capitol City?" Noticing the blank stare, Ansley added, "I thought not."

Arian stared at the old Professor, dumbfounded by his

treasonous rant. "With all due respect," he said, "you have benefitted from the Overseers' vision more than most. Who are you to lecture to me about living as a Nephite?"

"I have as much to do with it as the Overseers' themselves. In the beginning, we saw it as a social experiment. At last we would have a scientific society and teach the world a better way to live. It was nothing more than a power grab."

"I'm sorry you feel that way," answered Arian.

They sat in silence, drinking. Ansley shook his glass at Eduardo, who re-filled it. Not wanting to be outmatched, Arian choked down what remained in his own glass and shook the empty contents at the large Natural Born bartender.

"Can I help you?" Eduardo spoke in a deep baritone.

"Umm... I'd like another too?" Even as the words left his lips, Arian felt weak, which didn't sit well with him in the presence of a non-Nephite.

Eduardo looked to Ansley, who nodded in approval. The bartender refilled the drink.

Ansley was a patient, experienced man and knew when to wait. He was content to sit and drink in silence; waiting for the question he knew was coming. Finally, Arian spoke.

"I haven't been able to shake something you said yesterday. What did you mean when you said the Overseers would be interested in my work and that wasn't necessarily a good thing?"

Ansley shrugged his shoulders, still looking down at his drink. "I don't know, kid. It seems to me that eliminating the need for nanotreatments takes away all their power. I can't imagine they would like it unless they could use it to their advantage."

"I don't understand why that would be an issue," said Arian.

Ansley sighed, turning to the kid. "You wouldn't have even asked the question if you weren't concerned at their attention. That seems an odd way to think in a utopia if you consider it. And I will give you one more item to think on. Give me access to your research files." Noticing Arian's shocked response, he added quickly, "I'm not trying to steal your work. I'd like to propose a collaboration."

"That's an unusual request," answered Arian. "I would have to submit a proposal to the Institute, since they own the work."

"I'd rather you not," answered Ansley, standing and motioning for the bartender. "Put the drinks on my tab."

"You never pay your tab, Professor," responded Eduardo.

Ignoring this remark, he addressed Arian again. "Suit yourself, kid. I expect someone from above the Institute will contact you soon regardless. If you feel uncomfortable, please reach out to me. I have experience with such matters." Ansley turned and left the bar without another word.

***

Finished cleaning and with the last patron gone, Eduardo was ready to begin the journey to the Natural Born worker camps set up outside the dome. His nieces would be asleep, but he looked forward each night to glancing in on them. One day, they would be recruited for tasks within Capitol City, but for now, they were unburdened by the future. Just as he reached the front door to turn the lock, it exploded inward, striking him in the forehead and knocking him from his feet.

Three Imperial guards rushed into the pub, lifting him up and slamming him into the adjacent wall. He was a big man, strong enough to fight them off, but that would be foolish. He let them hold him. A fourth man entered, clothed in a white robe, garnished with an Imperial purple sash. His face showed the lines of a man of sixty, but that would be foolish to assume of a Nephite. Long white hair flowed down past his collar.

"Let him know I mean business," said the man.

While two of the guards held him, the third struck Eduardo hard in the gut with the butt of his gun. As he dropped to his knees, the guard followed it up with a strike to the head.

Eduardo fell to the floor, his mind hazy from the blow and the burgeoning concussion.

"Lift him to his feet," said the man with flowing white hair, only vaguely visible from his blurred vision.

"Can you talk?

"Yes," stammered Eduardo.

"Good. My name is Consulate Tiberius Septus. You do not want to hear my name or see me again, is that understood?"

Eduardo nodded.

"Ansley Brightmore frequents this bar, does he not?"

Eduardo made no motion. A nod from the consulate and the third guard struck the Natural Born man again, hard in the solar plexus. Falling to his knees, Eduardo coughed for some time, finding it difficult to catch his breath. Kneeling down to the man, Tiberius grabbed him by the hair, lifting his head so that they were face to face.

"We know Brightmore frequents this bar. We have been monitoring him for some time. I have nowhere to be. Do you? I will know every word that was uttered between them or you are in for a very long night."

# Chapter Two
# The Lonely Woman

The light streaming through the window illuminated Kaiya's flawless features as her head rested on the pillow. She heard the shuffling of footsteps, a door closing, and then she was alone. Rising, she let the intricately threaded white blankets slip from her naked body. She stood, walking to the semi-circular looking glass and admiring her perfection.

This was a daily ritual for her. It was reassuring to see the beautiful image staring back from the optical world, in stark contrast to the shame and ugliness she felt inside. Upon confirming that she was still aesthetically pleasing, she turned away from the mirror. Kaiya would return to it many times throughout the day.

She walked to the window, letting the yellow sunlight wash over her body. The UV radiation was removed by the shielding dome and thus the light lacked that familiar burning sensation. She missed the feel of raw sunlight. It had been eighteen years since she entered Capitol City as a consort for Consulate Tiberius Septus. He had taken her from a life of servitude and poverty in the far away domed-city of Sikyon.

Despite the luxuries she enjoyed in the lush mansion, it was a prison. Being improper for a Natural Born such as herself to cohabitate with a high-ranking Nephite, she was kept out of view. When he did allow her to accompany him around town, it was under the guise of a servant acting as a personal assistant. He was always careful not to be too affectionate. She had no friends in the city and her days were spent alone, waiting for Tiberius to return.

She walked to her dressing table, sampling a couple of fresh grapes that had been placed there by her handmaiden Gallia. It was strange to think that she, who had lived in in servitude on a large plantation, now had servants of her own. The grapes were sweet, but nothing like the grappa she had eaten as a child. That was the only part of her former life that she remembered with fondness. She slipped a light blue gown over her head and exited the bedroom. Tiberius allowed her to keep her own quarters, although he spent many nights in her bed.

She continued down the long hallway past the servants' room toward the stairs. The marble felt cold on her bare feet. As she passed the room, both Gallia and Idalia, the two full-time maids, rushed out to meet her.

"Can we get you anything, my lady?" asked Gallia, her accent thick.

"I'm fine," Kaiya responded in her disarming quiet manner. Rarely speaking above a whisper, the high-pitched tone of her voice was surprising from such a radiant woman. It was the voice of a small girl. "Perhaps I will take breakfast in the courtyard."

"We will have it prepared immediately, my lady," responded Idalia, rushing off toward the kitchen area.

"Will you join me, Gallia? It would be nice to have some company."

"Of course, my lady." The two women continued down the hall.

The Capitol City dome had been designed around the

massive Central Tower. At a height of over three hundred stories, it was visible from thirty miles outside the city. It was from this building that the burgeoning empire of Arameus was run. It contained most of the offices of the high officials, along with the Parliament and the private quarters of the four Supreme Overseers. Surrounding this tower and located at the exact four points of a compass were the North, East, South, and West Towers. Still massive at one hundred and fifty floors each, they were dwarfed by the Central Tower. Roads leading away from there were met with cross streets at measured intervals so as to form concentric circles radiating outward. A beautiful blue river marked the boundaries of the Central Isle. Known as the Arymides, it was not a true river, but a man-made and self-contained channel. It created separation between the residential districts and the island. Checkpoints ensured that only authorized Nephites and Natural Born servants could access the main seat of power for all of Arameus. Pleasure cruises operated on the blue waters, allowing the wealthy Nephites to dine as they circled the island.

Tiberius Septus' manor was located on the West Bank of the Arymides. Gallia and Kaiya exited the back entrance onto the cobbled courtyard that overlooked the river. Large privacy walls rose on either side so that they were only visible from the river itself, were a boat to pass. The two women took a seat at a table on the balcony above the river, waiting for breakfast. Kaiya looked out over the Central Isle, her gaze floating up, high above the city, to the four spires at the top of the Central Tower.

"It seems so strange," she said, almost to herself, "that the four old men in that tower have dictated the events of my entire life."

"Do not speak such things, my lady," said Gallia. "There are always ears present."

She was right, of course. Not to mention that Tiberius was also in the tower, surely carrying out some sort of important government business. He had brought her here, taking her away from the horrors of her former life. For that, at least, she should be thankful.

"Tell me of your life, Gallia."

"My life is of no interest to you, Kaiya. I am no one."

"Please. I have been here for years and yet I know nothing of you. You act as if I am one of them. I am no Nephite. I'm just a woman with no name."

Gallia looked at Kaiya, affected by the heartfelt words. Her look softened and she obliged.

"I live just beyond the eastern walls of the dome in the free city of Mardonia. We are all poor, but we are free to raise our families. Most of us work as servants within Capitol City, although many are farmers who sell their crops both to our own and to the Nephite traders in the eastern market at the entrance to the dome."

"Mardonia sounds lovely. I too am from a farming town. And what of family? Are you married?"

"I was… to a wonderful man. His name was Hector. We made three strong boys together before he was taken from me by the flu that struck ten years ago. We could not afford the medicine from the Capitol City doctors. Afterward, I needed a way to provide for my family. With no husband, I had no need to worry about the sterilizations that are required by dome workers. I undertook them willingly and have been in the service of Consulate Septus ever since. He has been a kind master and lets me keep decent hours so I can return home to my children. I can hope for nothing more."

For any other woman, this story would have evoked emotion and necessitated comforting words, but Kaiya was not any other woman. She had seen and experienced too much hardship in her life to be moved by those of another. Despite her youthful appearance, she was at least twenty years older than Gallia, who appeared to be somewhere close to forty. Tiberius had been giving Kaiya the nano-treatments for years. It wouldn't do for his prized consort to age.

Idalia arrived with breakfast. The servant placed the

plate of mixed fruit and assorted grains before Kaiya, along with a carafe of wine.

"Thank you," said Kaiya. Turning to Gallia, she added, "Please leave me now. I wish to be alone.

The servants exited, leaving Kaiya alone with her thoughts. She picked at the fruit, not really hungry. She never had much of an appetite, as evidenced by her thin frame. Letting her thoughts wander, they settled on Gallia's mention of children. The idea horrified her. What if the child were a girl? What if she were beautiful? That fear had long eliminated the possibility from her mind, which was strange since she might be the only fertile woman in Capitol City.

Wishing to avoid scandal, Tiberius had bypassed all official measures when bringing her to the city. A man in his position could do such things. It would not be politically beneficial to be seen cohabitating with a Natural Born. By avoiding the official immigration measures, she had also avoided the sterilizations. This had proven to be a problem for her on multiple occasions, when she missed her monthly cycle. Always resourceful, she managed to terminate the pregnancies without alerting Tiberius. She did not want to jeopardize her position in this household and Tiberius was content with the thought that she was unable to conceive.

Again, her eyes found the Central Isle. She had been there many times over the years as an assistant. Had she risen as far as she would? Could she shed the label of Natural Born and forever become a Nephite? This prospect seemed impossible just days ago, but recent developments had changed everything.

Tiberius had mentioned it in passing during pillow talk. The Overseers were monitoring the movements of a man named Ansley Brightmore, curious about his activities since removing himself from the greater scientific community. While this failed to register as an issue of national security to Kaiya, Tiberius impressed upon her the importance that scientific supremacy occupied within Nephite society. It was brought to the Overseers' attention that Professor Brightmore had interrupted the talk of a promising young professor, creating a stir, and potentially uncovering a damaging flaw in the power structure. Making matters more complicated, Brightmore met with the same scientist the following evening, a worrisome development. Tiberius was offered a high honor from the Overseers: the task of contacting the young scientist, a man named Arian Cyannah, and enlisting him as a spy for the Security Council of Arameus. Wishing to keep himself distant from anything that could be perceived as intrigue, Tiberius enlisted Kaiya to contact the young professor, hoping her feminine charms would win his allegiance.

Many would have deemed this an insulting task, but not a woman like Kaiya. Her wiles were her weapon from childhood, her protection from a cruel world. This time, however, Tiberius had promised to use her service to the empire as a way to legitimize her in society. She could be made a true Nephite and no longer have to hide in the shadows of her mansion prison. She would be free to pursue all of the things that had been denied, free to restore the name of her family and forget her horrendous past.

All she had to do was seduce one more man. She needed only to convince him to befriend the Professor by sharing his research. One more seduction and she could be a citizen of Capitol City.

She stood, taking a last glance at the Central Tower before heading back into the house, this time toward Tiberius' personal quarters. He had given her both the code to enter his bedroom and the code to use a spare qubit to contact Arian's office under the guise of an Institute employee. She was ready for the task and prepared to make a new life for herself. Perhaps as a Nephite, she could even be Tiberius' wife. She entered his room, full of confidence about her new mission.

Men were always so easy.

# Chapter Three
## Appreciate the Finer Things

The weekend refreshed Arian's mind and body and he awoke Monday morning eager to get back to work. His apartment occupied the top two floors of a thirty-five-story complex in the eastern end of Capitol City. It was before dawn and the red night sun hung over the horizon when he finished dressing and headed to the lab.

Arian stepped into the lift, descending to the garage below the building. He walked to port 35, which was designated for his vehicle. Pulling out his qubit and hitting a button, the sleek black bike, known as a hawk, rose from within the floor. Placing his leg over the seat and straddling the vehicle, his weight and bio signals were instantly recognized and the electric bike buzzed with life, locking his ankles in place. He opened the center console and typed in the coordinates that corresponded to his laboratory, located just outside of the East Tower on the Central Isle. Placing his hands on the handlebars, the hawk shot forward to the ramp leading to the street.

The morning route had become so ritualistic that he often arrived at the cybernetics lab with no memory of the journey. These were his most valued times, where he was alone with his thoughts and able to contemplate the ideas he had been formulating without the pressures of the lab setting. It didn't hurt that the Institute was beautiful. Artificial waterfalls, streams, and small trees dotted his path, and the glass dome that covered the city prevented any bad weather from affecting his commute.

His hawk directed him into his docking station at the front of Laboratory 432. A mile further beyond the East Tower, the majestic Central Tower showed where the true power was quartered. Docking, he walked the short distance to the elegant glass entrance to the lab areas. Seemingly within the glass itself, the words flashed upon his approach.

"Institute of Bio-cybernetics– Restricted"

Arian placed his hand on the sensor, and was immediately recognized. The door opened vertically. "Welcome, Doctor Cyannah," Athena's voice boomed as his qubit linked to the lab mainframe.

Walking down the massive hallway, he found himself struck, as he often did, by the expansiveness of the architecture. "The Institute does know how to create an inspiring workplace," he thought to himself. Entering his office, he noticed the flashing blue light emanating from the desk indicating a message. Placing his finger on the crystal surface, the inbox activated as he sat down.

Passively scrolling through the messages that had built up over the weekend, he ignored the offers of speaking engagements, dinners, and questions from stressed out students. He stopped on an encrypted hologram message marked "Office of the Institute - Science Directives."

"That's weird," he said aloud, placing his thumb on the recognition crystal.

A stream of colorful light filled the room as the form of the most beautiful woman Arian had ever seen took shape. Her voice was high. She sounded almost childlike, but had a directness of speech and demeanor that made Arian feel uneasy.

"The Institute has taken an interest in you lately, Dr. Cyannah," the nameless woman began. "While we're satisfied with the progress of your research, the senior directors have been made aware of your meeting with Ansley Brightmore. We need to get together and discuss the direction of your research as well as your future interactions with Professor Brightmore. I would like to get together at the West Tower this Friday night. I will be at the Four Corners restaurant at 7 p.m. This is a mandatory meeting."

The hologram disappeared and erased from his inbox. Arian sat back in his chair, uneasy. He had met with the old Professor three nights past and reported the man's controversial opinions to his superiors the next day. He had expected that from his end, at least, that would be the end of it. The woman in the message troubled him more. He had never seen her around the Institute. Was she from the Central Tower? Despite his misgivings about the message and its ominous tone, Arian couldn't say he was too disappointed about meeting the beautiful female from the hologram.

The rest of the week passed without another word from the enigmatic woman. Arian occupied himself in his world of science, directing students and exploring possible new paths in his research. Since the Institute was founded, science had become much less collaborative. Arian was only given access to developments within his own field and was mostly unaware of further advances in physics and chemistry. His knowledge of these fields was taken from what was considered to be scientific canon from the days before the rise of the Arameus Empire. This was why Professor Brightmore's request had been so unorthodox. Ansley was credited with having a hand in both the quantum computing revolution and particle-field theory. It made no sense that the two men would ever share data. Of course, Arian knew that Ansley had matured as a scientist long ago, when collaboration was the norm in science, leading to many breakthroughs, the nanocyte treatments being chief among them. He couldn't imagine what a man with well over two hundred years of mastery in these fields could be thinking.

The world had changed around Ansley. True, this was a world that Ansley had helped create, but he had not been able to control it. That task had fallen to the wealthy, and ultimately, the Overseers. Ambition and science were not comfortable bedfellows. Arian should have empathized with him. As a fellow scientist who had risen to heights that all young scientists now coveted, it must be difficult to deal with an Institute that had no further use for him. Arian was from a different world, however. He had been raised in the Capitol City nurseries along with his fellow Nephites and was firmly indoctrinated with the power structure of Arameus and the need to work within this framework to rise in society. It was for this reason that he was concerned about his meeting with the strange and beautiful woman.

As the week passed, Arian's apprehension grew and by Friday, it took all his effort to focus on work. Despite his best efforts at focusing on his student's presentation, his mind couldn't leave the meeting with Professor Brightmore. Wondering what protocols he had breached, he dreaded the upcoming dinner meeting.

"Um… Dr. Cyannah? Do you have any comments?" stammered Matthew Conway. Conway was an idiot, but Arian should have been listening. Having no idea what the student had just presented, he voiced a standard criticism every experienced scientist could draw from when unsure of what to say.

"Conway, have you considered the issues involving the boundary conditions of your simulation? By my calculations, the long range electrical forces are not going to be dampened given the size of your simulation box, and all of your results are bunk until you incorporate an Ewald Summation to correctly express the interactions."

The student looked confused and a little scared. "Yes, Dr. Cyannah," he muttered as he shuffled out of the office.

"I'm finished seeing students for the day, Athena," said Arian. He looked at his qubit. It was 6:30, time to meet the strange woman. He walked down the arched hallway and stepped out into the fading yellow sun. Finding his hawk, he typed in the proper coordinates and headed off to the West Tower. Arian closed his eyes, allowing the air to flow over his face. He had never been invited to the West Tower and the excitement was getting the best of him, despite his reservations. Athena's voice boomed from the qubit, disturbing his thoughts. He had arrived.

"Your escort approaches."

"Continue path."

Two men pulled up on either side of him. They were hosts for the Four Corners. "Going to dine at the West Tower?" the left host asked.

"Yes," answered Arian, feeling significant. They arrived at the veranda of the prestigious Four Corners, the best restaurant in Capitol City. As he stepped off his bike, the two men had him place his hawk in valet mode so that they could manually park. He was met by the hostess and ushered past the lobby into a luxurious domed atrium, the rising red sunlight streaming through glass onto the privileged and rich. A beautiful blue stream flowed beneath tables that were suspended by a clear polymer that was used in much of the architecture within the dome. The water was funneled from and returned to the Arymides River. The hostess ushered him toward the back of the restaurant.

"She's at the back table," the hostess said.

"The back table? Can you be more specific? I don't even know who I'm meeting."

"Just go through that door, Professor Cyannah."

"How do you know my name?"

"Professor, just keep walking that way."

Moving up a flight of stairs, he entered a private room, walking past two well dressed, yet powerfully built men on either side of the door. He saw her sitting at a table in the corner of the room alone, the image of a goddess. Her entire being struck him like a fist to the gut: eyes, lips, and breasts. Perfect. Her reddish-auburn hair fell gently on her naked shoulders. She wore a black evening dress, offset by her creamy white, slightly freckled skin. Her appearance was so piercing and beautiful that Arian lost all semblance of confidence.

"Dr. Cyannah. I'm pleased to make your acquaintance. My name is Kaiya. Please have a seat," she said. He recognized the voice. It was the same high, meek voice from the hologram. Arian examined the table layout and noticed there were three seats as opposed to two. That was odd for a pre-planned dinner at a restaurant as nice as the Four Corners. He debated which seat to take before deciding on the one across from her, leaving the seat to her side empty.

"I hope you don't mind but I ordered for you. They have a wonderful lamb scalencia with a mint sauce. I thought you would enjoy it." Arian was taken aback by this liberty she took, but he was in no position to question her at this point. He just wanted to know what this was all about. The waiter approached with a bottle of wine. It was a Sagittarian, bottled only in Avignon, and it was expensive. The man poured a small glass for her to approve. She smelled it, gave it a taste, and replied, "Very good. Perhaps a glass for my guest?"

"Thank you," replied Arian. His palms were sweating. He didn't typically feel nervous around women, but this one was different.

"I don't often get ordered for on dates," Arian said. He lifted his glass in a toast. She looked to her glass, unimpressed, and made no movement. "Of course we will be drinking to the Institute," he said, unabashed. She stared at him unblinking, betraying no emotion. Her hand moved slowly to her own, and never lowering her eyes from him, she drank, suppressing a laugh.

"A date? You are a confident one, aren't you? Nevertheless, to the Institute, I suppose." She drank again and motioned for the waiter to refresh her glass.

"And to Professor Brightmore, I assume?" he retorted with sarcasm evident in his tone. This made her twitch. Winking, he added, "I gathered from your message that my report to the Institute of the encounter did not go unnoticed."

"You appear to gather a lot, Arian. That is a very attractive quality, although it is a quality that can bring you trouble around here." She sat back and observed him before adding, "I would expect that a man of your caliber wouldn't shy away from a little trouble." She smiled.

The hot red blood rushing to his face was apparent to Kaiya. She looked down and nibbled at her lamb, which had just arrived. Embarrassed, Arian ate as well. The awkward silence stretched before them as they drank wine and measured one another across the table.

"I'm curious," said Arian finally. "Why exactly have you invited me here?"

"This is an interesting concept to me. It isn't often Nephites question a request from the Institute. Most of you tend to be honored that they even know who you are."

Kaiya took another drink of wine. Every movement she made was smooth and graceful, almost calculated. Arian was finding it difficult to focus on the conversation. She was intoxicating. Or was that the wine? Over the smell of mint and wine and lamb, he sensed her perfume. It was a light citrus, but all he could smell was sex.

"I think it would be proper for me to give you some background first. We at the Institute have been monitoring Professor Brightmore's movements for some time. We have strong evidence that he is an operative for the Centauri. Our agents have concluded that he is working on something big and hiding his research from the Institute. I believe that he may have shared some of these details with you during your meeting."

"Wait. I hope you aren't implying that I'm having some sort of secret Centauri meetings with that old bastard. I met him for a drink. I'm not going to turn down an invitation to meet with the Institute's most famous scientific mind."

"You're cute when you get defensive. But save your protestations for a time when they're better suited. No one is accusing you of anything. I just want to know if Professor Brightmore gave you any insight into what he is working on. He has become quite incorrigible and is no longer filing his weekly reports."

"There isn't much to tell. He seemed interested more in my genetic mother than my work. He knew her before she died. "

"I see," she answered.

Arian finished off his glass of wine, and glancing down at Kaiya's diminishing glass, motioned to the waiter. Turning back to Kaiya, he leaned in close, whispering, "I have to be honest, I find you quite enticing, and I think we could both use a couple of stiffer drinks." Kaiya rolled her eyes but said nothing to protest. If anything, she seemed bored by him.

The waiter arrived at the table and to Arian's surprise, Kaiya announced, "Four Agave shots, please." Arian gazed at her with a perplexed look. The waiter took the order and nodded toward the bartender. Kaiya leaned in close this time, whispering, "In my opinion, you need a couple of strong drinks."

Arian examined the woman in front of him. The kind of woman that would order two shots for herself was a woman with which he was unaccustomed. Not to mention that he had never been a heavy drinker. She had a confidence about her, like she knew something he didn't. Kaiya gave him a coy look. His revelry was broken by a set of bronzed arms entering his vision, setting down the four silver snifters.

"I assume you know Eduardo," Kaiya stated matter-of-factly.

Shock and disbelief filled his entire being and his stomach clenched into knots. Now he was worried. While he knew no crimes were committed, he also knew that he had not been truthful with Kaiya. Professor Brightmore's treasonous comments circled in his thoughts.

"I see you have multiple sources of employment, Eduardo. Good for you."

"I do what my employers request of me," replied the dark-skinned man. "Enjoy your shots."

"Please have a seat, Eduardo. I think you have something to add to this conversation," Kaiya opened, in a voice so sweet it was poison.

Eduardo took the seat next to her and Arian knew that he had been set up from the start. He grabbed one of the silver snifters, drained it, and felt the blood in his veins grow warm. Setting down the glass, he grabbed the other snifter in front of him and repeated the action. Kaiya looked at Eduardo, slid one of the snifters in front of her to her right, and the two of them matched the ritual.

"We have a dilemma here, my young professor," Kaiya began. "Your account of the night with Professor Brightmore doesn't seem to match Eduardo's. Would you care to enlighten us? I'm sure the board of the Institute would be more than curious about these discrepancies."

Arian shifted his glance between Eduardo and Kaiya. What he said next was crucial, but he didn't know what was expected from him.

"I had some drinks with the old Professor. He attended my talk and was interested in my work. He's under the impression that there may be consequences I haven't considered. I disagreed and went home. That's all."

Kaiya looked to Eduardo. "Is this true?"

Eduardo spoke gruffly, in short sentences. His voice had no hints of the smooth baritone from their previous encounter. Examining him closer than before, Arian could see he was a hard man.

"Somewhat. He ain't lying about the drinks. But he isn't saying everything either."

This was not the speech of the man that Arian had met at the bar. He seemed less refined. His voice had a chilling quality to it. It was that of a man who cared not whether any of them lived or died.

"So what are you misrepresenting to us, Dr. Cyannah?" Kaiya returned. "What are you not telling me? Keep in mind that Eduardo has already given me a full report of your conversation."

"Thank you, Eduardo," said Arian, shooting a stern look at the man. For the first time he noticed that his face was swollen, deep bruises noticeable beneath concealer. "I met Professor Brightmore for drinks. I was flattered he wanted to meet with me. Who wouldn't be?" Arian stated. "He implied that the Overseers would not be pleased with certain implications of my work unless they could twist it in an ulterior way. Then we parted ways."

"Is this an accurate depiction of what you witnessed Eduardo?" questioned Kaiya.

Eduardo studied Arian long and hard, almost too long. It was disconcerting, but also a bit strange. Arian made note of it.

"It's accurate," he replied.

"Are you happy with his account then?" asked Kaiya.

"I am."

"Then leave us Eduardo, I have private business with our deceptive young professor."

Eduardo stood, lumbering, and Arian noticed his sheer size. He was at least six foot five, with broad shoulders and a strong build. He glared at Arian, his shadow encompassing the table.

"Be careful," he said in a cryptic voice before walking away. Arian returned his attention to Kaiya.

"What does the Institute want me to do?" he asked.

"What we want is simple. We know you are a loyal citizen of the empire; otherwise we wouldn't be talking this evening. Loyalty is a quality that both the Institute and government of Arameus do not overlook. All we require from you is a change of heart." She looked down at the table, and then looked up at him, her large brown eyes filled with hope.

"What do you mean a change of heart?" His voice was much sterner than he intended. He couldn't help but notice her flinch and instantly regretted his tone.

"Please, Arian, just message him back," she replied. "Tell him you share his concerns about the motives of the Overseers. Become his confidante. Share small details of your work with him to gain his trust and then find out what he's working on."

"So you want me to spy on the Institute's greatest scientist? Is that right?" His tone was much more agreeable this time.

Kaiya seemed exasperated. "The Institute wants you to report on his activities. I don't want anything from you. This is a minor request for a patriot such as you. I think this could be a very lucrative career opportunity if you take advantage, as I expect a man of your makeup will."

Arian twisted the empty glass between his fingers. It wasn't every day that an opportunity such as this arose, and if the Institute was interested in Ansley's doings, it was his duty to oblige. Even though he should have felt honored, he felt a little dirty. Nevertheless, he looked into her beautiful brown eyes and said, "I will do whatever you require of me."

"Good," she answered brightly. "I want you to message him tomorrow. Tell him you have reconsidered his proposal and would like to have another meeting. Go to his favorite bar, the Devonshire Pub. Eduardo will be waiting."

Thinking back to the Natural Born man's powerful grip, Arian could think of no place in Capitol City he would least like to revisit.

"Perhaps I will bring him here. Wine him and dine him."

"As you wish," returned Kaiya. She looked down at a jeweled watch on her wrist. Arian found it strange that she didn't carry a qubit. "I think we have accomplished everything we can at this meeting. I must be going."

Arian stood as she did.  She moved around the table to his side, standing on her tiptoes to plant the softest kiss on his cheek.  Arian looked at her, full of surprise.

"You have such lovely eyes," she stated, her manner confident and direct.  She sauntered off, her perfume seeming to linger, floating on the air.  His exhalation was an estuary, a mixing of her otherworldly scent and his own breath.  It would be days before her aroma left his nose.

# Chapter Four
## An Interrupted Card Game

"Give me another one, Eddie," Ansley said in a slurred voice. "Put it on my tab."

"I'm not sure you need another one, Professor," replied Eduardo, his concern evident.

"Damn it, Eddie, who are you to tell me how much to drink? It isn't like I'm getting any older. Pour it up!"

"This'll be your last one. I'll pour two. We'll take it together. I can't keep giving you top shelf drinks on your tab. The manager knows you never pay it."

"I thought you were the manager, Eddie."

"That's right, and you don't pay." Despite his protests, the large man poured the two shots.

"Thanks, Eddie. It's good to know people still respect their elders." They clinked glasses and drained the contents. Ansley lit a cigarette, took a drag, and looked back to Eduardo. "You know, as sad as it is, I think you're my best friend. Perhaps I should take you to the card game tonight."

"You know you shouldn't be going to that card game,

Professor, and besides, they don't let non-Nephites in the casino unless it's to work." Eduardo moved toward Ansley and put a sympathetic hand on his shoulder. "You're drunk and you already owe them. Go home. Sleep it off. There is always another card game."

"Ah, but Eddie, what you don't understand is that every card game I sit out is credits I leave behind." He stood, waivered, and then sat back down. "Let me try that again." This time he had more success at standing and without another word, he exited the bar.

As he stepped onto the marbled pavement that made up the streets of the Southern pub district, a dim red glow washed over his face, cast by the night sun. The casino wasn't more than a few blocks away, which was the main reason he frequented the Devonshire. He felt most at home among the seedier members of Capitol City. Navigating the curving avenue, he was dwarfed by the identical buildings rising on either side of him, distinguishable only by their ornate gold leaf statues and marble relief sculptures. As he rounded the circus, the casino filled his vision with gaudy flashing lights seemingly out of place in the surrounding splendor.

Entering the casino, he moved his shoulders back and added a bounce to his step. Winking at the hostess, Doris, he added a winning smile to his demeanor. The casino always brought about this change. It was a happy place for Ansley. Ignoring the jingling and flashing of the slot machines and the mechanical people operating them, he angled toward the high limit poker room.

Poker was a game with no house odds, just gamblers playing against gamblers, in a game run by gamblers. The casino's only stake was in the exit taxes they levied on those who won. As Ansley approached the hostess of the room, he gave her a friendly and familiar greeting.

"Hello Sharie," his affection for her evident in his voice. "I trust you're having a fine evening. I, too, will be having a fine evening after I teach these young men how the game is played."

Sharie was beautiful, dark and seductive, like all high limit hostesses. Only the best specimens from the Natural Born were chosen to work the high limit games, entertaining the Nephites, oftentimes in more ways than beverage service. Glancing at Professor Brightmore, she returned the greeting in a cold tone.

"Hello, Professor. I didn't expect to see you around here after last weekend.

"I had a few too many drinks with one of those young Institute hot shots, not to mention bad luck from the cards. I expect tonight will go better," returned the Professor.

Sharie leaned, whispering in his ear, "There have been auditors from the Central Tower asking a lot of questions about our books." Discreetly she slipped a rolled up piece of paper into his hand. He nodded to her in acknowledgement and walked away to the restroom where he could examine its contents. Entering a stall, he unrolled the paper, revealing a handwritten note.

*The casino is aware of fund transfer discrepancies*
*We need another revenue source*
*The other members of the Counsel of Elders grow impatient*
*They want to know how long until the Iris is complete*

Wadding up the paper, he flushed it down the toilet. Let them grow impatient. A project of this magnitude had never been attempted in the history of the world. Of course, it would take time and be expensive. He would not rush. Far too much was at stake and far too many people had lost their lives already. He did fear for Sharie though. She would be the first investigated if they found the books were off. All crimes committed by Natural Born within a domed city of the Empire were met with death. He would have to find a safe place for her. Now was not the time to think about it though. His head was spinning from alcohol and he wanted to gamble.

Heading back to the card room, he gave Sharie a nod of

acknowledgement. She looked disappointed, as if expecting more, but unhooked the golden clasp and allowed him to pass. Entering the room, the Professor was overwhelmed by the thick smell of cigar smoke, brandy, and perfume from the Natural Born women. Eleven men sat around the console, their faces bathed in the radiant blue light coming from the touch screens on which their cards appeared. Looking down at the console, even as drunk as he was, he couldn't help but notice the community cards before the players and his head swam with probabilities and calculations that these men couldn't fathom.

The table chatter ceased upon his approach, ten heads turning toward him in unison. Only the man in front of Ansley abstained from turning as it would have been beneath him. Seeing the elaborate purple robes that clothed him, as well as the long white hair, the Professor recognized Consulate Tiberius Septus. A bodyguard behind the Consulate leaned down and whispered into his ear. The man raised his cigar to his mouth, taking a deep puff. The smoke filled the space in front of him.

"I see the great Professor has decided to give more credits to his superior. So generous of him. I have always felt that the Central Tower overpays our fellow Nephites in the Institute, and I see you are in agreement, being so eager to give it back."

"You're a terrible card player, with all due respect. You played the odds wrong every time last week and should have lost. You got lucky." Ansley felt he could have answered the Consulate with a better, more snarky comment, but the alcohol coursing through his veins prevented him from engaging in wittier repartee.

The other men around the table, a mixture of Institute employees and low level Central Tower officials sat in stunned silence. Tiberius broke the icy awkwardness.

"This is a high stakes game. I assume you can provide the minimum five thousand credit buy-in? Or are you hoping that Sharie will allow you to play with house credits again? Hmm? Sharie, how long does the house plan to extend credit to this drunk?'"

Sharie moved behind Ansley, whispering in his ear. "I'm sorry, Professor, but you've exceeded your thirty day credit limit and I can't allow you to be staked until you settle the debt."

Despite her discretion, the other men and women in the room had heard the hostess and a few laughed, while others looked away embarrassed. Blood rushed to Ansley's face and there was no way to hide his shame. The Consulate laughed, cold and dismissive.

"How fortunate for the table that the genius is too broke to take our credits!" Tiberius turned around for the first time and looked Ansley in the eyes, his expression filled with accusation. "What happens to all of your money anyway? Spending it on some Natural Born whore outside the dome? Funding Centauri separatists?"

The old physicists' nerves calmed and he walked over to Tiberius. The Consulate raised his hand to his bodyguard allowing him to pass.

"Well, Tiberius, I usually spend it on booze, although tonight I'm drinking on the house." He leaned over, grabbed the brandy snifter in front of the seated man, and drank the entire glass.

In an instant he was thrown, first to the ground, then onto the shoulders of the giant bodyguard. The casino was stirring hours later, as patrons recounted in shocked disbelief how they witnessed Professor Ansley Brightmore being carried to the casino door and tossed into the streets of Capitol City.

Given the potential for embarrassment that this fiasco could cause and the possible political ramifications, Tiberius thought it prudent to leave the casino following Ansley's removal. Escorted by two guards, he was ushered into his vehicle, a large cab that could seat six members of a party, though it still traveled on the same lines as the hawks. One of the guards typed in the coordinates to his mansion on the banks of the Arymides. They escorted him through the gates before retiring for the night to their own homes on the other side of the city.

As Tiberius entered his chambers, his servants unclasped the purple robe that wrapped around his torso, removing it, along with his boots, black pants, and undergarments.

"Is she here?" he asked the servants.

"In the bedroom, your Honor, as you requested," replied Gallia, his head chamber maid.

"Good. You may leave for the night. I need you here first thing in the morning to upload my notes for the Parliamentary proceedings in three days."

"As you wish." Gallia and the other two servants bowed and exited.

Entering the bedroom, he walked naked to the bed, examining the beautiful, petite woman sleeping. Bathed in the dull red glow of the night sun, Kaiya seemed unreal. She stirred as he pulled down the covers and moved beside her.

"How did your gambling go, my dear," she uttered sleepily. "I trust you won again?"

"Of course I won. If these idiots know what is good for them, I will always win."

"You're a remarkable man, my love," returned Kaiya, her voice flat.

Tiberius rubbed a finger along her stomach as she turned toward him, exposing her nakedness. "I saw the Professor tonight. He didn't fare so well."

"Arian?"

"No, my dear, not your spy. Professor Brightmore. I had the washed up beggar removed from the casino. I'm no longer going to allow our game to be defiled by that crazy drunk. He's working with the Centauri, I'm now sure of it."

"Why do you suspect him of being Centauri?" Kaiya asked in earnest.

"That is my concern, not yours. You just need to get

this young professor to find out what he's up to and get as close to him as possible. I trust you can handle this endeavor?"

Kaiya rubbed his cheek. "It's already taken care of, my dear. I met him two nights ago at the Four Corners. He didn't seem willing at first, but I brought Eduardo to the table and he was spooked. He will do as you wish."

Tiberius moved his hand away from her stomach and gave her a sharp annoyed look.

"Why was I not informed of this? You can't move freely around Capitol City, even with my protection. You should not have had the meeting at the Four Corners. How did you get my table?"

Kaiya was frightened.

"I knew you were busy, my love. I wanted to surprise you and show you I could handle things like this. I called Maria at the restaurant and requested your table. She's met me enough times. I thought it would lend gravity to our request."

"You take too many liberties. Even with my ability to pull strings and allow you to pass as an assistant, if you keep too high of a profile, people will ask questions. If you must know why we are interested in Professor Brightmore, it is because we have informants indicating that he is leaving the city somehow and going into the outside zones. The informants believe he has influence with your kind, although they don't know in what capacity. Unorganized, they pose no threat, but when led by one with the mental capacities of Brightmore..."

Kaiya grabbed his hand and placed it back on her soft, flat stomach.

"Well then, shouldn't you be interested in what I found out from Arian?" she asked, her voice soft and high, taking on a girlish quality.

Tiberius' face softened, his hand sliding to her breast. "And what did you find, my sweet," he whispered, kissing her neck between each word.

She allowed his hand to stay where it was, but her body

45

tensed. This time, it was she who was annoyed at how flippant he was with her. She gained control of herself. She could never betray emotion in front of the Consulate other than that of loving sweetness.

"He's working on something. Arian and Eduardo don't know what, but it sounds big, and for whatever reason, he's taken an interest in Arian's research. It's all over my head, though. You know I wasn't educated like one of you."

Tiberius gave her a polite smile, but his face showed concern. What could this be? His mind flashed between a thousand different scenarios, all implausible. What would a particle physicist need from a bio-cybernetics guy? What could the connection be? The idea of a scientific collaboration made him uneasy. They were dangerous and forbidden by the Overseers of Arameus. Could the old drunk be trying to create some sort of bio-weapon? That could be the only explanation. Of course, the dome covering the city protected it from all forms of radiation, but if Brightmore had secret ways into the city of which the guards were unaware and was able to introduce a specially designed bio-organism, great harm could be brought to the citizens of Capitol City, even with the nanocytes.

"You did well, Kaiya," he said after a moment. "The Overseers will be pleased with my findings. It's unfortunate that you are Natural Born," he mused aloud. "If you were of better birth, I think you would be capable of great things."

Kaiya climbed on top of him, pressing her firm body against his and kissed him, teasing his nose, then his upper lip. He was overwhelmed by her smell. It drove him crazy with desire. He was powerless before the raw sex that she represented.

"My love, you are always too sweet to me," she said, as she moved him into her.

## Chapter Five
## The Unannounced Guest

*Bodies were thrown through the air with hellish force.
Charred flesh smoldered, falling off the bones of fresh-made
corpses. All sound was gone except for a persistent ringing.
Stumbling, his body was numb. Palms finding pavement,
he steadied himself, eyes open, yet only seeing the white
light burned into his retinas. Choking on black smoke and
reaching for her hand, his hearing returned, and the sound
of the afflicted was horrendous. Explosions in the distance
punctuated the crash of falling marble. Feeling around the
immediate area for her body, his hand found hers, and the ash
that had been her flesh fell from bone. Following the path from
her hand to her chest, he felt no movement. Blinking rapidly
to restore vision, the white light faded and was replaced by a
bald, blackened face.*

Ansley awoke breathless, his shirt soaked through with
sweat. It took him a minute to realize where he was and that
he was not a part of the horrible scene. It was a nightmare he
often had. The alcohol helped, as on many nights he passed

out into a dreamless oblivion. Last night had not been one of them. The yellow day sun was painful to his eyes as it shone through the windows of his office. He had gone there in his inebriated state and fallen asleep at his desk. Pins and needles emanated from his right arm down into his fingertips. He lifted his head off the console and the throbbing arm, allowing the blood to painfully rush back to the extremity of his hand. Wiping the sleep from his eyes, he rubbed his temples, and noticed the empty bottle of Tegave on his desk. Trying to recall the previous night, he forced himself to push the recurring nightmare into the back of his mind where it resided, waiting in the depths of his soul for a moment of weakness to present itself.

The first memory that came stabbing back was his disgrace in front of the Consulate. Even in his state of dehydration and hangover, the embarrassment overwhelmed him. But why was he in his office? Looking around his disheveled workspace, it became obvious he had been searching for his hidden bottle. It made sense. A man with no credits could afford no booze. Remembering his interaction with Tiberius again, he grew angry. How could he be so foolish? He was drawing attention to himself and more importantly, to his finances. His alcoholism was undermining his plans.

"Esther! Do I have any messages!" he screamed at his desk.

The hologram of an indistinct female form filled his vision. Sad as it was, this was one of the few common, and calming, companions of his life.

"Professor," the monotonous voice chided, "you know you never have messages." The hologram paused. "However, you must turn around to notice you are flashing blue."

Ansley hated artificial intelligence.

"Play the damn message!" he shouted.

To his bewilderment, a hologram of Arian filled his vision. Head throbbing, mouth dry, and stomach churning,

Ansley beheld the figure before him.

"Professor, I hope all is well with you. I've given some thought to what you said and must admit that I am troubled by some of the implications. My schedule is busy with my new role as an assistant professor, but I think that we should have another meeting. How about the Four Corners? Let's say... Wednesday night at eight in the evening."

Ansley felt his nausea subside as he listened to the message. This was promising. The kid was willing to hear him out. Perhaps he was more than a mindless Nephite. If Ansley could convince him of the righteousness of his cause, Arian would be compelled to contribute his groundbreaking work. The young professor had filled him with a hope he hadn't felt in years and he was excited about completing and implementing his theories. This could be the last stage of a quest he had begun over eighty years ago, although for the last fifty years, he had been on his own. His mind went to her. After all these years he could still conjure her image without trouble.

"I'm coming, my love," he whispered to himself.

***

Time seemed slower than usual as Arian's day crept along. It should have been an exciting day as his students were making startling progress. He had been chasing an elusive dream for some time and it now seemed within his grasp. The holy grail of cybernetics was to create a bot that could control a cell's reproduction at the most fundamental level. It would not only eliminate the need for continuous nano-treatments, but also make the body more reactive on its own. A bot attached to a chromosome could govern the replication in an intelligent way given the advances in A.I., not to mention that it could be controlled from a remote source and given updates in coding that could be implemented in the organism. He had the technology for the bots in place. The only issue was attaching it to a living cell.

In spite of this, Arian found his thoughts elsewhere. On the verge of the greatest scientific breakthrough of his generation, if generation was still a valid term, he found himself worrying about his meeting with Professor Brightmore. He received no reply to his invitation. With any luck, the man had drowned himself in alcohol, relieving him of this burden given to him by the Institute. Arian often imagined how he would be perceived in a few hundred years, and knew deep down that he would not be one of those old scientists who became marginalized by lack of continuing ingenuity and outdated views.

Arian didn't relish the idea of spying on one of the scientific treasures of the Institute. That wasn't to say that he was unwilling to go through with his agreement with Kaiya. It was a rare opportunity to be courted by a higher up from the Institute, despite the fact that it had been done in secrecy by a mysterious woman. The rewards could be great if he could give them what they wanted. The possibility of unlimited funding, promotion to full Professor, even a future in Institute or Central Tower politics flashed in his head. Perhaps he would even have his own private table at the Four Corners, and why not? He had earned it. Or he would when his work became public knowledge.

Sitting in his office, he looked over Conway's latest report with feigned interest. Apprehension about the dinner meeting and the vague dirty feeling that permeated his body told him that he was wasting his time. He decided to head home and change for the evening. Grabbing his cloak, he instructed Athena to inform his students he would return in the morning.

At his building, he docked his hawk and took the elevator to his penthouse apartment. Stepping from the lift into the lobby area, he placed his thumb on the crystal adorning his door. The recognition software blinked before Athena's voice spoke in a confused tone.

"Professor, I thought you had already arrived? You entered the house ten minutes ago."

"No," Arian replied annoyed. "I left the office ten minutes ago." In spite of his life's work, Arian hated A.I.

"Of course. Shall I contact Technical Services about a possible software issue?"

Perplexed, tired, and in no mood to have a conversation with a machine, Arian impatiently waited as the glass doors opened, allowing him entrance into his hallway atrium.

"If this is you, professor, then I am unaware of who is sitting in your living room."

"A person in my living room?" Arian muttered to himself. He was concerned now. He rushed through the atrium to find Professor Brightmore seated at his bar, helping himself to a glass of champagne. Agitated, he stormed toward Ansley.

"How did you get in here?" he demanded.

"Relax, kid. Four Corners isn't my style. Also, this wasn't always your home. These apartments used to house my old friend Professor Chandler. We were very close. But that's not how I gained entry. You have to remember, my young friend, I am capable of coming up with unique solutions to problems. In this case, my problem was how to enter into your home." Ansley flashed a smug smile at Arian. For a second, he thought Arian might attack him. Arian, however, composed himself.

"Our meeting is at the Four Corners. To what do I owe this intrusion?"

"Again, I say, relax. Would you like a drink?" Ansley held up the open champagne bottle. This annoyed Arian immensely, but he remained calm, at least, as calm as could be expected.

"With all due respect, I'm going to repeat myself. Why are you here?"

"Oh, you know, we had our meeting scheduled, but I realized I hate the Four Corners. I appreciate the offer, kid. I can only assume that the cost of that restaurant would be high for a young man in your situation. However, I try to not dine with assholes, and the Four Corners would really cramp my style."

"Okay," replied Arian. "So you decided to enter my home uninvited instead."

Ansley stepped down from his barstool, offering Arian a previously unseen glass of champagne.

"I poured this for you earlier," he stated, matter-of-factly. Walking toward the center of the den, he pulled a small half egg-shaped device from his pocket. "Athena," he said, as he placed the device on the center table, "thanks for amazing hospitality. May I ask one more thing of you?"

"Of course, Professor," she replied.

"What are the chances that an old physicist can get a table at The Four Corners tonight?"

"Let me link into the system and check for you."

"We already have a table," interjected Arian. "Idiot."

"C'mon kid, you're falling behind." Ansley placed the small half egg device on the table and, just as Athena began to respond, pressed a button on the top. The half shell opened.

"Professor, our database indicates that…" The sound of white noise filled the room and Athena disappeared.

Ansley clicked the button a second time and the device removed even the white noise.

"What the hell are you doing?" demanded Arian. "What the fuck is that!"

"You know, kid, I've been a little out of the public eye for the last thirty years or so. The Institute no longer trusts or values a man like me. However, a scientist of my considerable intellect tends to keep a few tricks close to the chest. I have a question for you. Has anyone from the government approached you?"

"First of all, I'm not a damn kid," replied Arian forcefully. Stating this aloud, however, made him feel childish. "And, no, I haven't been approached by anyone about you. Why would I be?"

"That was the question I was asking you," replied

Ansley in a glib tone.

"I'm afraid I don't follow you."

"I took the liberty of scanning your apartment while awaiting your arrival. The exorbitant amount of information being streamed from this place shows that somebody is interested in what you're doing. Put bluntly, you're being bugged."

Concern washed over Arian's face. He sipped his champagne, hoping the old Professor hadn't noticed. Looking around the open atrium that made up his den area, he felt violated.

"But why would anyone listen to me in my private quarters? I have to admit, I find this unsettling."

Seeming tired, Ansley moved to the half-circular white sofa at the center of the room, sinking down onto it. Looking up at Arian, he replied, "I think I am to blame for that. I haven't exactly been on good terms with the Institute or those criminals in the Central Tower. I'm afraid your agreeing to meet with me has brought undue trouble upon yourself. I am very sorry for that. I will understand if you want to disassociate yourself from me."

Relieved that the Professor was not onto his mission and unaware of his meeting with Kaiya, Arian relaxed a little. He knew he had Ansley now.

"To be frank, I agree. How could you get me wrapped up in whatever problems you have with the powers that be?"

"Do you know what happens to us when we are no longer needed, Arian?" asked Ansley. "Do you know what happens when your work or your views are no longer deemed an asset to the Institute? Do you know what happened to my good friend Professor Chandler who used to sit with me in this very room?"

"Professor Chandler died in an accident," answered Arian. "An unfortunate lab explosion ended his life, if I remember correctly. Not a bad deal overall, in my opinion. He lived for over two hundred years in perpetual youth. Even we within the dome must die eventually. You can't stop accidents. Statistical fluctuations will occur."

"However, you can cause accidents," Ansley answered with a trace of sadness in his voice.

"What are you implying... that the Institute kills off its own prestigious members?"

"So naïve, however, I said nothing of the Institute. Perpetual youth can be annoying to those trying to create the perfect society." Ansley drained his glass, shaking his head. He was agitated now. Sitting in the room where he had shared so many wonderful discussions with Professor Chandler had him upset, as did the subject of this conversation. His mind drifted to her, as it so often did. They had shared memories here as well. Many parties to welcome the Red Sun's New Year had ended in private kisses on the balconies above.

"You question the wisdom of our Overseers as if you owe them nothing. They have provided you with unending youth, wealth, security, and the funds to pursue all of your research. They have ended disease, pain, suffering, and created the perfect society we have strived for since the beginning of time." Now Arian was worked up. He loved the Institute. He loved his life. And he loved Arameus and the Overseers who had guided its creation. He was no longer concerned with Kaiya or his mission. "I think you should leave. And take your fucking egg with you."

Ansley lowered his eyes and, taking the last sips from the glass of champagne, rose. Despite his youthful looks, he seemed old.

"I understand," he said. Glancing at the egg, he walked across the atrium to the entry hallway and paused as if searching for something to say. He had a strange longing in his eyes that Arian found unnerving but deeply human.

"You have your mother's features. You told me you have no curiosity about your genetic parents, but do you know anything about them?"

Caught off-guard, Arian had no reply. His mind was

blank. It was a shocking question, especially among Nephites. It was a question that stirred deep unresolved feelings in him.

"I know the same about my parents, as you do of yours, Professor," he replied after a long lapse. "I know their histories and their accomplishments."

"I knew my parents, Arian. They raised me. My mother loved me. My father played with me. We were a family. But what do you know of your parents… the real them. The people they were?"

"Nothing."

"May I stay a bit longer?" asked Ansley. "We have a lot to talk about."

Arian paused, conflicted. He had lost his temper, which he regretted, and moreover, he had lost sight of the mission given to him by the Institute. However, these were only fleeting regrets, as at a much deeper level, he felt a nakedness and vulnerability to which he was unaccustomed. Self-control and self-assuredness were central to Arian's character, and he never experienced doubt. He had been born with a path set before him, and he had followed it without question with a zeal that bespoke of his massive ambition. Ansley's mention of his parents had piqued his interest, and he wanted to know more.

"Please… come in. You're invited this time."

Without hesitation, and with no apparent memory of the awkwardness of the past few moments, Ansley stalked past Arian toward the wet bar.

"Do you have anything real to drink here? I'm sick of that sparkling grape juice you forced on me."

"That bottle cost… ugh, never mind," Arian responded, realizing there was no point bringing up that he had never offered his expensive champagne to Ansley. "Fine. Athena, open the upper shelf of the liquor cabinet. Apparently our guest requires only the finest," he continued, with more than a hint of sarcasm.

"That's not happening, kid, I thought you were smart," replied Ansley as he made a head motion toward the egg, still open on the table. "Don't worry. In my day, we could open our own liquor cabinets." He stepped on a footstool and rummaged around before pulling out an unopened bottle of Tegave. "There!" he exclaimed, satisfied. "Now we have some talking juice."

Arian shook his head with an amused smile. "I don't even feel like this is my place."

"Good," replied Ansley. "It isn't. It's owned by the Overseers, as is everything else in this world. Now let's at least get some good use out of this mini-mansion and move to the balcony. This room stifles me." Arian could do nothing else but follow the old Professor up the spiral staircase and out the door to the east balcony.

As was everything else in this designer city, the balcony was breathtaking. Situated on the 35th floor of the complex, it was one of the few apartments that had an unobstructed view of the city. The balcony itself was made of a clear polymer, including the floor, and it extended out from the building, allowing a vertigo- inducing view of the massive drop below. Ansley removed two glasses from his pockets and placed them on a patio table, pouring liberally into each glass. Tegave was a spirit best consumed warm, allowing the volatile aromatics in the solution to breathe and the palate to better appreciate the complex richness of the flavors. Handing a glass to Arian, Ansley picked up his own drink, raised it, and uttered almost to himself, "To second chances," as he clinked the other glass.

He walked to the balcony and leaned on his elbows, his drink held over the long precipice below. As he expected, Arian followed him to the ledge, assuming a similar posture. For a moment, they both stood in silence, sipping their drinks and taking in the view. They could just make out the edge of the dome at the far end of the city. It had been constructed of the same polymer as the balcony, both for strength and to prevent the harmful ultraviolet rays of the red and yellow suns, which of course, were a major contributor to the aging of the skin.

"Do you ever come out here, Arian?" Ansley asked,

breaking their reverie.

"Why do you ask?"

"You just don't seem to be a man who enjoys taking in a good view."

Puzzled, Arian said nothing. Ansley was looking at him so earnestly that he could no longer contain himself, and burst into uncomfortable laughter.

"What the hell are you talking about? You are one strange man."

Ansley chuckled. He pulled out a cigarette and lit it. Ansley knew he was acting strange, but he felt good, almost giddy. It could have been the alcohol, for he had drank copious amounts awaiting Arian's arrival, but for once, he didn't feel his high spirits were related to distilled spirits. It was this place. Being back on this balcony brought back so many good memories of times long passed, and friends long deceased. It brought back memories of the wind in her hair and stolen kisses in the dark. It brought back true memories of youth, not this false youth he now inhabited, but real youth, full of promise, doubt, dreams, and desire. Now his young body was plagued with an old mind. A mind filled with regret and loss. The unfulfilled dreams of his past defined the prison that was the present.

But up on this balcony, high above the beautiful city, Ansley was happy. For once, the only negative tinge he felt in his being was a gnawing guilt, ever so slight, of bringing Arian into his world and robbing him of his own youthful naiveté. He took a long last drawl from his cigarette and threw it off the balcony. As it fell from the dizzying height, the butt initially flashed a brilliant red-orange as the rush of oxygen hit it, but the color diminished as it continued to drop, and was eventually snuffed out to darkness.

"Would you like to hear something even more strange?"

"Well, I assumed you brought me out here to tell me something interesting? I guess something strange would qualify."

Ansley pulled out another cigarette, lit it, and said almost shyly, "The last time I stood on this balcony, I was with Padma."

"Padma?"

"Your mother. You don't even know her name," Ansley replied, shaking his head ruefully.

"My mother's name was Lakshmi Dasai. I at least know that."

"It's true, that was your mother's official name recorded by the Institute and taught to you, but her closest of friends called her Padma. And she was an absolute joy to be around. A treasure."

Arian felt queasy and unable to stand. Draining his glass, he moved away from the balcony to the patio table, where he sat and poured another drink. He was still for a moment, studying the brown liquid within, his brow furrowed in contemplation.

"I understand that you had a relationship with my genetic mother, but I don't see its relevance."

"I knew your father as well. Richard was my best friend. I've often felt that the Overseer's choice to use his sperm with your mother's egg was a direct shot at me. You see, Padma and I were together from our time at university until her death, almost one hundred and eighty years later."

Arian took a moment, sipping his drink and looking out over the city. As Arian surveyed the horizon, he found it to be quite tranquil. He was surprised he hadn't spent more time here. Perhaps he was not a man who took time to admire a good view.

"I understand you feel compelled to tell me that you were my genetic mother's lover, but that's kind of a weird thing to tell someone. I suppose you see me in some twisted way as a long lost son?"

"I assure you, my reasons are scientific. It will all make sense in time."

"Well, since you are here, you might as well tell me

about her."

Ansley walked toward the table, taking the seat across from Arian.

"May I?" he asked, looking toward the Tegave bottle. Arian waved his hand flippantly, in an uninviting invitation, before running his hand through his jet-black hair. Re-filling his glass and drinking deeply, Ansley exhaled the aromatics and began.

"Your mother was lovely. The most beautiful woman I have ever known. She was funny and quirky and had a special energy about her that made everyone around feel safe and at ease, an energy I haven't encountered in another in nearly two hundred and fifty years of living. I haven't been the same since she died. I will never be the same. She would have loved you."

Arian dipped his forefinger into his glass, swirling it, allowing the alcohol to cool the flesh. He was silent, content to contemplate the clear floor beneath. A loving mother was a foreign concept to him.

"And my father?"

"Brilliant. We were classmates at University, roommates and best friends, as well as collaborative colleagues. We were both at the forefront of our fields and ultra-competitive. We challenged each other to be better. We were among the first chosen for the extended youth experiments. They wanted to preserve our talents. They gave us nonsense about how losing the most prestigious members of society had always been the downfall of civilization. It didn't hurt that your mother and Richard had a hand in creating the nano-treatments. I'm afraid they had as much to do with this tyrannical society as anyone. When the experiments were successful, it brought hope to the world. There would be an end to death. But only the richest members of society could afford the treatments. Coming on the tail of the great financial collapse, there were few who could. Ultimately, they established a new class of people independent of wealth, at least in their minds. They saw it as a rebirth of society and called us Nephites. They had made better people. It was only then that I heard the term Natural Born introduced."

"I'm glad that you were so fond of my genetic parents, but I'm afraid that I am a child of the empire. All Nephites are my family. My only sense of pride from your comments comes from sharing DNA with people who helped create Arameus," Arian answered. "But you seem as if you regret it all. You would have been dead hundreds of years ago had it not been for the vision of our Overseers. Your greatest work would have never happened. You wouldn't even be a memory. You would only be some footnote in a history book."

Glaring at Arian as if he were only a foolish boy, he took a breath and responded icily. "Boy, you don't get it. Your mother, father, and I were Natural Born as were your precious Overseers. I came from nothing, yet rose to greatness. The next great mind born into the world is likely going to die an uneducated Natural Born, working in some mine outside of the domes. You were created from genetic material harvested from your long dead parents to fill a position specifically created for you. This is not the natural order of things."

Silence fell between them. Arian didn't know what to think, and Ansley wondered if he had pushed too hard too soon. The kid had no concept of social equality. And how could he? The two suns were almost below the horizon on opposite sides of the city, the yellow sun setting, while the red sun rose. Ansley realized the egg was still distorting the qubits and time was scarce. His device could only scatter the signal feed for so long.

"I have never heard such an eloquent statement about the unfairness inherent in our stations. It is all quite radical to me." What would have previously offended Arian had actually intrigued him in his current state, diminished by alcohol.

"Arian, I assure you, you were born into this world as a slave. Even your genetics were chosen before your birth. You have never had a single choice in your entire life, which will be long."

"So I don't have choices?" interjected Arian.

"You always have a choice, Arian. But at what point have you decided your own path? At what point did you choose to be a cyber-genetic engineer? This was the path you were set on when they chose to create a zygote from Padma and Richard. You are their slave just as they enslaved your mother, father, and I through our own wrong choices. Let's just say this, if I were a betting man, which I am, I would have bet all of my credits that you would end up exactly where you are today at the date of your birth."

Arian was annoyed and had heard enough of Ansley's rant. There was truth to it, which stung, and Arian wanted nothing more than to expose him to Kaiya for the ungrateful traitor that he was.

"You are very good at weaving a sad tale of your former life with my mother and father, but to me, you sound like a man who regrets his current place in a world he helped create. And you need me for something, so just come clean. What do you really want from me?"

"To be honest, kid, I'm not sure. As far as you're concerned, I'm a washed up scientist, my better days behind me. Would you even believe me if I told you I was on the path to my greatest discovery?"

"And that would be?"

"Oh, that's top secret. It would be treasonous to tell you." Ansley laughed out loud, though Arian failed to get the joke. "I'm only kidding. Have you ever heard of the Amasarsi boson?"

"I must confess," replied Arian, "that particle physics was never among my strongest courses, but I am aware of it. I believe it is the hypothetical particle predicted by the Standard Model of particle physics. It is speculated to be the fundamental particle that gives mass to other particles such as quarks and electrons. I've never seen any evidence that backs this theory."

"That is correct, essentially," replied Ansley, impressed. "However, I am sure you are not aware that the same mathematics that predicts the existence of the Amasarsi boson also predicts that if we ever succeed at creating one in an accelerator, a secondary particle known as an Amasarsi singlet will be created at the same time. These massless singlets would exist in a fifth dimension, outside of time, giving them the ability to move both forward and backward, thus reappearing in either the future or the past."

"Obviously, I am not aware. I see you have not given up all semblance of being a physicist, but I repeat my initial question. What do you want from me?"

Ansley pulled the last two cigarettes from his case and threw one across the table to Arian. Not knowing why, Arian accepted. Ansley lit his own cigarette, stood up, and drained his glass, throwing the lighter on the table within Arian's reach. Taking a long drag, he turned his head toward the city, letting another uncomfortable moment pass between them. He questioned internally whether he trusted the kid before deciding to expose himself.

"Simply put, kid, it's like this. You are as much a slave as everyone else outside of the domes. I hate this world we created, but I must admit, it has allowed me to complete my greatest work yet. I need you. And what we create together will not be used to make slaves of men. It will be used to free them."

# Chapter Six
## The High Parliament of Arameus

Other than the elevator attendant, Tiberius was alone in the lift as he ascended to the 135th floor of the Central Tower. The Central Tower was the tallest building in Capitol City by a factor of two, reaching the top of the dome itself, where the Overseers' kept their residences. Halfway to the top of the towering structure, the Parliamentary chambers occupied an eight-story expanse, which bulged from the Tower to nearly twice the width of the other floors. It was essentially a giant stadium built into the center of a skyscraper.

He ignored the attendant as he exited and walked down an expansive tunnel toward one of the designated entryways, his hard-soled sandals reverberating. He arrived at a massive archway that opened into the bright white Thasos marbled hallway that led to the Parliament Chamber of Arameus. This walk was designed for grandeur and would make any man feel humbled, even a man such as Tiberius.

Though he had been through this corridor a thousand times, the nervousness was always there. The sense of purpose and importance of being involved in something so great as governing the world had always overwhelmed him. Tiberius had been born into luxury and lived it his entire life, but the Overseers' empire of perpetual youth had reinvented society. Among the Nephites, they were as gods. Entering the Parliament chamber in the grand Central Tower of Capitol City was as close to a religious experience as Tiberius Septus would ever know.

Arriving at his destination, two guards in ornate Imperial armor opened the doors. Armor was as outdated as manual entrances, but it was all part of the pomp and procedure that made being a Consulate special. He took a deep breath, readying himself for what was to occur, before entering.

Tiberius was overwhelmed by the dull roar created by thousands of far-flung Consulates from all over the empire arguing their cases and attempting to make beneficial political alliances before the proceedings began. He looked down from the top of the bowl at the hundreds of alcoves that each represented a province of the empire and descended downward toward a central platform in the center of the bowl's lowest point. This was where the Overseers would sit, in full view of the Parliament. Being an important Consulate from Capitol City, Tiberius was low in the bowl and few members were closer to the Overseers. He descended the steep stairs, passing his less important colleagues on his way to his own alcove. The raised dais in the center of the bowl, which would seat the Overseers, remained empty. When he entered his alcove, his aides were already in place.

"Welcome, your honor," Thaddeus greeted warmly. "The proceedings are about to begin. You are third to speak. A great honor, sir." Thaddeus was his most trusted advisor and a great ally. He was loyal and had no ambitions of his own. His family had served as principal advisors to the Septus family for three centuries and would happily serve for another three. Loyalty was rare and went a long way in the higher circles of the empire.

A servant offered a bottle of water, which Tiberius accepted to wet his parched throat. As he sipped the cooling liquid, trumpets heralded the entrance of the Overseers. Cloaked in the Imperial Purple, the four white haired Overseers walked into the lowest level of the bowl. Each walked from a separate entrance, adorned with the jewel-encrusted insignia of the Overseer's noble family. Silence engulfed the auditorium as every Consulate, aide, and servant stood in reverence. As was custom, the Overseers took their positions in unison before turning a solemn face to the large words carved in marble above them, as they chanted, "Peace. Unity. Prosperity. Order."

The rest of the Parliament repeated the words with dogmatic fervor. "Peace. Unity. Prosperity. Order." Then all Consulates threw their right hands to their left shoulder, embracing it as they forcefully lifted their right elbows toward the carved words in a stiff, somber salute. The expansive bowl seemed to rumble, thundering with the sound of hundreds of Consulates shuffling to take their seats, followed by a hushed silence as they turned their collective gaze toward the Supreme Overseers of Arameus. The Overseers allowed their majesty to wash over the adoring audience before being seated. The Speaker of the Parliament, Demetrius Gracchus, stepped forward to a podium and called Parliament into session.

Entering the semicircular podium, it lit up with hundreds of white lights and rose to his armpits before closing behind him, forming a scaled miniature model of the circular bowl of Parliament. Each of the lights represented an alcove occupied by a Consulate and his staff. During debates, when a consulate wished to, or was called upon to speak, the Speaker would touch the light corresponding to that particular Consulate, and a high resolution image would stream from the alcove to a space directly before the Overseers, allowing them, as well as the rest of Parliament, to view and hear the speaker. For those who were too far from the lower bowl, or who wished to watch in a bit more comfort, all alcoves were equipped with screens displaying the same stream.

Grabbing his over-sized, symbolic gavel, the Speaker tapped three times, the hits echoing through the auditorium, before announcing in a stiff, formal, artificially enhanced voice, "We hereby call into session the two thousand three hundred and forty seventh session of the great Parliament of the United Cities of Arameus. In these hallowed halls, we shall tell no lies, let no personal matters interfere, and always labor as we have for these two hundred and twenty-four years of peace and prosperity to justly govern the people of our world." Another three hits with the gavel ended the opening formalities.

"For our first order of business, we wish to discuss a report from the consulate from District Four of the city of Pathos. The Overseers call Consulate Iulius Van Arsdale, chair of the Committee on Worldwide Natural Born Affairs, to report on their interim findings." Reaching to his upper right, the Speaker touched the white light representing the Consulate's alcove, and the image of his standing figure materialized on the platform in front of the Overseers.

"Esteemed Overseers," began Iulius in the well practiced cadence of an experienced orator, "I am, as always, humbled to be in the presence of your wisdom and benevolence."

Tiberius rolled his eyes and flashed a knowing smile to Thaddeus, who returned a wink. Iulius and Tiberius had been schoolmates countless years ago when they were young, before Arameus was created. However, Iulius now inhabited the city of Pathos, thousands of miles west of Capitol City. With beautiful black sandy beaches and blue waters to the west, it was flanked on all remaining sides by large mountains, covered with evergreens and capped in snow. It was a paradise on its own, and was the only city that didn't require a dome. The local Natural Born remained in the city as workers, and its primary function was as a vacation escape for other Nephites. This was ironic to Tiberius, since the head of the Committee on Worldwide Natural Born Affairs had almost no real dealings with the Natural Born outside of Pathos.

"However," Iulius continued, "I have the unfortunate task of being the bearer of somewhat distressing news. Unrest amongst the workers inhabiting the broad world outside of our wonderful cities continues to grow. There seems to be a certain uniformity of opinion developing. It is almost as if they have unionized around a central governing body."

Isolated murmurs were heard throughout the bowl. Iulius paused briefly as the Overseers conferred, before relaying a message to the Speaker.

"But how can it be that the Natural Born are able to unionize across the world?" the Speaker asked. "They have no press, they are illiterate, and they have no way to communicate across the lands to one another."

"I believe they are being organized from within our own hallowed cities. I believe that certain Nephites within the domes are conspiring with the low-born rebels known as the Centauri to spread discord and organize the masses into a formidable foe."

Iulius looked around nervously as the hall was now buzzing with dissenting voices. The Speaker's podium seemed to light up all at once with many Consulates wishing to speak their reservations. Again, the Overseers conferred, and again, the Speaker relayed their words.

"We will take no dissenting opinions at this time and will continue with the report from the committee chair." Iulius' hologram took on an otherworldly glare, as all of the alcoves lit up in red, the Parliamentary sign for silence.

"Thank you. As I was saying, esteemed colleagues, we have strong evidence to back our claims. I'm sure all of you have experienced the labor stoppages outside your respective cities. I'm sure you have also seen an increase in violence from the workers within your walls on Nephites. Productivity reports have shown that our workers are 25% less effective worldwide. And none of us can ignore the Centauri's assassinations of our society's founding members. Have you all forgotten the bombings that took down our world's greatest minds? We have been dealing with this Centauri problem for seventy years. And I know my colleagues from the Capitol City will never forget the Blood Sun Day attacks fifty years ago where ten simultaneous explosions destroyed almost the entire founding generation of the Institute."

The crowd remained silent due to the alcoves' red lights, but Iulius noticed that many were nodding their heads in solemn agreement. Tiberius was impressed with his friend. He was handling himself well and working the crowd into a silent frenzy. This was politics. If anyone knew this, it was Tiberius. Iulius, himself, seemed to be feeding off this energy, working his voice up and down like an actor, adding gravity to his points.

"And, of course, I would be remiss to not mention that we also lost three members of Parliament on that terrible day, yet we sit here today in our alcoves, ignoring the threat that continues to grow just outside our domes and inviting future attacks on the pillars of our society."

"How long will we sit idly by? It is time for us to act, is it not? It is time for us to crush this miniature rebellion and show the Natural Born that our charity does have limits. We saved them from worldwide famine and this is their expression of gratitude? I would expect nothing less from these low-birthed vermin. We need to send a message that there is justice in our generosity. It is time for us to seek out and destroy the Centuari!"

Despite the red lights that illuminated the bowl, the consulates erupted in a cheer. Everyone in the building stood within their alcove and clapped. Even Tiberius was overcome, and in spite of the reserve he usually displayed, not even he was able to control his jubilation. Only the Overseers and Speaker remained unmoved in the bottom of the bowl, seemingly unaware of the fanfare occurring around them.

As the applause subsided and the consulates took their seats, the Speaker again spoke in his booming monotone voice.

"Your points are well-taken and will be considered and debated by this great body. I understand you have another member of your committee to call to speak?"

"Yes, Speaker. I call Consulate Marcus Pentus from the Seventh District of Capitol City to the platform. He has been working with us on the issues plaguing this city and is more familiar with its intricacies than me."

"Thank you, Consulate," replied the Speaker, and with two brief touches of the white lights on the podium before him, the image of Iulius disappeared and was replaced by the tall black-haired figure of Marcus Pentus.

"Esteemed consulates and Overseeers, I'm afraid that Iulius is not exaggerating the difficulties facing our empire. We have it on good authority that within Capitol City, there is a well-organized system of Natural Born citizens smuggling money and technology to the Centauri outside the domes. We also have information that sympathetic Nephites are collaborating with this ring both on the inside, as well as on the outside to make sure the rebels are funded and unified. We believe that this is the source of the newfound collective interest in worker rights amongst all the lowborn throughout our lands." Marcus paused, awaiting a response. A few lights on the Speaker's podium blinked.

Receiving an approving nod from the Overseers, the Speaker announced, "We will open the floor for discussion. We recognize Consulate Addis Adrachi from the Fifth District of Alexandria. The hologram of Marcus Pentus shifted a few feet to the right as the form of Consulate Adrachi materialized before the Overseers.

"These are serious charges you bring forth, Consulate Pentus," Addis began gravely. "Accusing our own citizens of working with the drivel that resides on the perimeter of our cities is more than ludicrous. Why would anyone living in luxury risk his life in a treasonous attempt to help a group of traitors?" Addis shook his head as he spoke, looking up to the other consulates incredulously, as if the idea was unfathomable.

"Of course I agree with the sheer nonsense of the scenario," responded Marcus in a measured tone. "And I can't speculate as to their reasons, only that we have strong evidence to support our claims."

"And what evidence do you have?" Addis demanded, his voice rising. "You have presented nothing in support of these findings."

"For one, our audits have shown four straight years of a negative credit balance in the city. Large amounts of credits are leaving unaccounted for and on a semi-regular basis. Also, there have been glitches in our security monitoring systems. There are periods of time where the closed circuit information streamed from strategic monitoring positions disappears. The Centauri have found a way to mask their actions whenever they wish. This would explain how ten explosions could be organized and detonated without us having even a hint of information about it."

Again the hall buzzed. More lights flickered on the Speaker's podium. None were given the opportunity to speak, however, as the Overseer seated on the far left raised himself from his chair. All voices in the bowl ceased at once, and a nervous silence fell over the crowd.

It was Marco Luccio. The Overseer by far appeared to be the oldest man in all of Arameus. His bright purple robes and gold Imperial standard stood in stark contrast to the white pallor his skin had acquired in his long years before technology had stopped his aging. Even standing upright he would have only reached a height of 5'8", but his stooped posture left him a mere 5'2". As he began to speak, his voice quivered weakly, yet behind the wavering tones was the confidence and assuredness of a man who had wielded near unlimited power his entire life.

"If these reports you present are indeed true, we should all be quite alarmed," he began in halting, labored breaths. "I will not have us quibble over points that long ago should have been decided upon. The uneducated masses have long suckled from the tit of the wealth we generate. We will no longer sit idly by while our hallowed institutions are threatened by those who desire class warfare and deal in terror." He paused, leaning forward on the dais to catch his breath before continuing. The audience listened with rapt concern, hanging on each word, though many worried at the unprecedented expenditure of the old man's energy. "I ask not for further evidence but for action. Tell us no more, Marcus, of what you know, but of what you plan to do."

The Overseer slowly returned to his seated position with the help of two aides who rushed over. The three Overseers to his right seemed to not even have noticed that he had spoken at all as they made no movements and stared ahead as if bored. It was as if they had expected this and nothing had happened that was not part of the plan from the beginning. Marcus seemed equally prepared in his polished response.

"Your Graces, we have anticipated this need for action and have implemented a plan that we believe will bring these dark schemes to light. I call the Under Secretary of Intelligence for Capitol City, Consulate Tiberius Septus."

Although he had known for two days he would be called to speak and was well prepared, the anticipation made his stomach queasy and his bowels turn. Adding to his apprehension were the Overseer's unexpected remarks. This was rare, and a great honor, but it also added a sense of urgency. He took another gulp of water, handed the bottle to Thaddeus, and rose in his alcove, walking toward the motion body scanner that would project his image before the Parliament.

"I think I speak for our entire governing body when I say that your words are both wise and true, Your Grace," he said, addressing the Overseer on the far left. "We have for some time been tracking the movements of high-ranking members of the Institute of Technology. Our methods have included the audio monitoring mentioned by my colleague Consulate Pentus. In our extensive monitoring, only one of the subjects has exhibited the brief information blackout periods, making us deaf to the subject's conversations." He paused, taking a breath and allowing his words to sink in.

"We believed this made the subject a viable suspect, and I had some of my most trusted intelligence officers integrated throughout the man's life. Not wanting to prematurely damn one of our respected citizens, I will protect the subject's anonymity. However, I will allow that the suspect is a professor of the High Institute."

"We have learned much from our spies. It appears the professor is attempting to recruit other scientists to some unknown project. He has been unsuccessful in this pursuit until recently." Tiberius stopped and allowed a smile to creep over his lips. Looking at the panel of Overseers, he beamed as he continued. "I am proud to say that, through our intelligence efforts, we were able identify one of the scientists he was attempting to recruit and have managed to turn him into an informant. We have encouraged continued meetings and soon expect to discover the secrets of the Centauri."

Clasping his fingers together and resting his palms on his stomach, Tiberius seemed pleased with himself. He awaited the response of his peers. It was Consulate Adrachi, whose image still remained beside him, who spoke first.

"If what you tell us is true, you have done very well. If I may ask you to speculate, do you have any thoughts as to what the professor is working on… why he needs other scientists?"

"My thoughts, Consulate Adrachi, are that he is attempting to develop some sort of sophisticated weapon that can bypass our defenses and detonate within the Capitol City and other domes as well. If my hunches are correct, this suspect could be behind the Blood Sun Day, and I believe in my heart that he is aiming for something much larger and more destructive this time."

On cue, the body of consulates erupted in outrage. The anger hanging over the room was palpable, and the Speaker had to remove his gavel and strike it multiple times before order was restored.

The Overseers again consulted with the Speaker, and he returned to his podium, stating, "We are pleased with this report, Consulate Septus, and all of the resources you require shall be at your disposal. Rid us of the Centauri plague that has been festering all these years and Arameus will owe you a great debt of gratitude. We are sure that a man of your lineage will do no less."

"I am honored by your confidence," replied Tiberius, bowing to the Overseers as the images of him, Addis, and Marcus disappeared from the platform.

# Chapter Seven
# The Cheshire Pub

Tiberius should have been tired as he walked down the avenue toward the Cheshire Pub, but he was still energized from the morning's Parliamentary session. It had gone better than he could have hoped, and Tiberius knew that if he could succeed in thwarting whatever plot the Centauri were undertaking, then he would distinguish himself before his colleagues and, more importantly, the Overseers. His thoughts went back to his father, who had now been dead for hundreds of years. Never the type to heap praise upon his son, he would likely find something to criticize. Nevertheless, Tiberius was in good spirits. He had shed his heavy formal robes for a simple pair of slacks and a white collared shirt. Taking his hawk to the entrance of the Southern District, he had chosen to walk from there, whistling to himself and admiring the architecture.

He arrived at the corner of the avenue and the squared low front of the Cheshire Pub. This was the first pub in Capitol City and a place where many great writers and scientists had come to work over the years. What it lacked in accouterments, it more than made up for in prestige. It poured old style warm ale and served simplistic fried food but provided the sense of being in an academic's living room. He felt even more excited as he approached the entrance, for he knew his old friend Iulius would be waiting inside. Tiberius couldn't recall the last time they had been together socially, but regardless of the passing years, they always met as if they had left one another yesterday.

The pub was dark and he was overwhelmed with the smell of stale beer, urine, and fried fish. He never had understood why a pub in Capitol City should smell like this, but it was part of the charm nonetheless. The pub's real attraction was its system of private alcoves, each with a fire at the end, surrounded by a semicircular couch. There were no hostesses at the Cheshire, and Tiberius was forced to peek into each alcove looking for his friend. Arriving at the sixth on the right, he heard the familiar voice of the famed orator.

"Tiberius, you old bastard, have you solved the mystery of the Centauri yet?"

"Old? I remain now, as I was on the day of my birth, three months your junior, although I am your senior in all other affairs." With a sly wink and an arrogant grin, Tiberius entered. In the dancing light emanating from the flames in the fireplace, he could make out the outline of two females seated on the couch. "I didn't expect company, Iulius, but it's always welcome. Please, introduce me to your friends."

"This is my new friend Kaiya. I believe you're familiar with her." Iulius turned to Tiberius, smiling mischievously. "I think I'm in love." Tiberius felt a jolt, a mixture of anger and jealousy. He was angry with Kaiya for once again stepping out too far and betraying his trust and jealous that Iulius was now coveting his private treasure.

"Still wearing your emotions on your sleeve, I see. Relax, old friend, and say hello to the beautiful Katrina." Hardly noticing the other woman in the alcove, Tiberius inclined his head in acknowledgment, still attempting to control his rage at Kaiya's impropriety. Trying to look as natural as possible, he walked around the couch to the front of the fire. "To be honest," continued Iulius unabashed, "I was surprised you wanted to meet here. It has been a long time since I have been able to share your social company outside of a casino."

"Tonight wasn't a good night for the casino," replied Tiberius quietly.

"More shocking words have never come from you, my friend. Perhaps a man is never too old to change." Ignoring Iulius' subtle jibes, Tiberius signaled for a waitress as she walked by.

"Four blue sun shots for my friends and I, please. Charge this bastard on the couch." He shot a glaring look at Kaiya before softening and turning toward his friend. "You look good, Iulius. And you spoke well today."

"And you spoke as well as could be expected. Stop looking so damn apprehensive," he added, noticing Tiberius' glower. "I got hold of your maid and asked if you had anyone 'special'. She speaks well of you and clearly I have my own." He pulled Katrina close to him and kissed her neck roughly. She giggled, but in her eyes, there was no laughter. Kaiya sat, prim, proper, and unaffected. She nodded at him and spoke in her soft, girlish voice.

"Are you going to sit, darling?"

He glanced at Iulius, a man who in his youth had chosen celibacy to make sure his work was never disturbed. Now he was publicly groping a Natural Born woman. Tiberius felt there was no more need to keep up appearances. He took the seat next to Kaiya and leaned back uncomfortably. He wasn't so much bothered by her presence, but by the fact that she had made herself known to another consulate. He had told her again and again to keep a low profile, yet here she was out in society, chatting up one his oldest friends as if it were nothing.

The waitress arrived with the shots, placing them on the table before them. She began to take her leave but was stopped by Tiberius, who announced, "Two ales for my friend and I, if you don't mind," and looking at the women, continued, "and something more palatable for the ladies." Iulius laughed aloud, and Tiberius shot him a devilish smile. "If we are drinking, then let us drink, old friend!"

"I see you haven't lost a step," replied Iulius.

"I see you have gained a step or two," Tiberius shot back, motioning his head toward Katrina.

"This lovely lady? I picked her up awhile back on a trip to Parliament. She's fun. My years in Pathos have taught me to appreciate all the finer things you used to rave about back in University. I picked up this little lowborn beauty on a tip from the bartender at my hotel. She's a little pricey, but is quite pleasant company and well worth it. I call her my little Natty."

"Natty?"

"It's what we call the cute Natural Born girls in Pathos. I believe she comes from the same province as your little Kaiya." Tiberius' eyes narrowed.

"Province?"

"Oh c'mon, Tiberius, you used to be the crazy one. Don't think I haven't noticed the large vaccination scar on her arm. She wasn't born in the domes and certainly isn't from our generation. We knew every person who took the first treatments. It's okay, you're amongst friends."

Kaiya kept her gaze on Iulius but leaned toward Tiberius, placing her hand softly on his chest.

"Tiberius is always so image conscious, Consulate. I'm sure you know how it is." She giggled, turning her head to gaze up at Tiberius. "And where did you get your scar," she asked Iulius in a playful tone, her eyes never leaving her own man.

Iulius' hand shot up to the light pink scar that moved jaggedly along his left cheek from the corner of his eye to the area between his mouth and nose. Rubbing it softly, Iulius answered almost to himself, "You would think that after all these years this wretched thing would have softened." He perked up a little, removing his hand and replying directly to Kaiya, "It always tends to redden when I drink. I have Tiberius to thank for this beautiful addition to my face. But Katrina doesn't seem to mind, do you?"

"I think it's sexy, darling," Katrina replied.

"Of course you do. Anyway, as I was saying, Tiberius gave this to me during our second year in university. My competitive friend never understood the meaning of a friendly co-ed game of Patolli. Here we all were, going half speed for the women, and Tiberius blind sides me in the back of the head with a dodger. I fell from my glider and split my face on the surface below."

"My dear has a scar as well," Kaiya interjected, "a little one on his lower back." She smiled.

"This is inappropriate talk," began Tiberius before being cut off.

"It would have been bigger if I had been stronger," Iulius proudly announced. "That was my revenge. We went to the pub later that evening and, still stewing from my new injury, I took it upon myself to hit big bad Tiberius in the back with a chair. I just wanted to knock him down and let him know I wasn't beaten. We all looked up to Tiberius, you see. However, the wood splintered and exposed a screw, which gave him a scar of his own, though it was a mild revenge at best."

"You were so short, Iulius, I wouldn't have seen it coming if I had been facing you," said Tiberius, laughing and rolling his eyes in an exaggerated fashion. "It's damn good to see you."

"And you as well. Now let's take these shots. The ales are here!" Iulius exclaimed as the waitress reappeared.

As they grabbed their blue-hued shots, Tiberius raised his and announced, "To the Capitol City Gliders!" Kaiya and Katrina raised their own glasses in answer before draining them as well. Iulius, however, remained unmoved.

"Oh no, no, my friend, you can't possibly think I will drink to your overrated team. I'm disappointed in you ladies as well. Clearly my Pathos Pirates will take the Four Roses Cup once again this year. West Coast Patolli has been dominant for fifty years. To the Pirates!" he announced to himself, drinking down his own shot. Placing it on the table, he turned to Tiberius, lowering his voice, "We have more pressing things to discuss than old school-day injuries and women. Do you really believe you have an insight into the Centauri? Knowing you, I am assuming this is just politics as usual."

Tiberius glanced at Kaiya, but this was unnoticed by Iulius. Despite this being his oldest friend, Tiberius didn't trust him. You learned that early in public life, especially when the politics and lifetimes spanned hundreds of years. These long years had already born witness to the metamorphosis of Iulius from a meek, celibate bookworm to the formidable political foe who now stood before him, taking up with a lowborn whore. Friends were never friends forever and after all this time, how could he trust that the man before him hadn't changed in other ways? The great men of Arameus tended to fluctuate between adolescence and maturity. Fifty years of doing the right thing almost always led to a complete reversal. Men would feel they weren't living the lives they had been blessed with and would inevitably turn to a life of leisure, which would again reverse in time.

The only constant Tiberius could be sure of was that men were always drawn to money, power, and women, and no amount of age, even his own two hundred and eighty-seven years, would ever change that. After the death of his wife before the nano-evolution, Tiberius had expected to find a woman to spend his unending years with. The women of Arameus, however, were prone to the same massive changes in behavior over time as the men, thus guaranteeing an end to traditional monogamy. This is why he preferred to be with Natural Born women like Kaiya. Their lives were fleeting and they weren't prone to the same periods of regression as those within the domed cities. They appreciated the time that they had, and theirs was the love that can only be shared by those who know it is limited.

"Of course it is always politics, Iulius. That is the life we have chosen. I may have exaggerated my knowledge of the Centauri, but you know me, I always have another card to play. I have been setting up a system of Natural Born loyal to me for some time. I do believe we're closing in."

"Should we be talking about such things in front of the ladies?" inquired Iulius. "It lacks a certain sense of decorum, even for you."

"You are right, my friend." Tiberius looked from his friend to his companion. "Katrina, why don't you go smoke? We have to talk about some things you probably shouldn't hear."

"Of course, Consulate," Katrina responded, grabbing her purse and heading out of the alcove without a hint of defiance.

"And the charming Kaiya?" asked Iulius.

"She can stay."

"I see this vixen has truly won you over. This is unexpected from a man such as you."

"She has earned my trust, yes," replied Tiberius. Looking to the floor, he added, "That doesn't mean I have lost my wits. I know who and what she is, but regardless, I trust her and she has become a valuable ally to me. And you can keep your reservations to yourself, Iulius. I am still your senior consulate and will have no judgment from you. She stays, your whore leaves."

Tension filled the alcove, and to break the uncomfortable silence, Tiberius pulled out two Sagittarian cigars, offering one to his friend.

"I'm sorry for being so crass with you, but these are trying times and I don't know who to trust. I don't know Katrina and had to take extra precautions. We aren't as familiar with the Natural Born here as you are in Pathos, but Kaiya has earned her place."

Iulius lit his cigar, slowly rotating it to ensure a uniform burn. Then he laughed.

"This one really has got you on the hook, huh?"

"I do what he requires of me," responded Kaiya.

"Oh, I'm sure. But what is it that he requires of you? What makes you move against your own people?"

"I have no people. I have only myself."

"This is a good way of thinking to be sure. In the end,

a person can only count on his or herself. But our world does contain certain, how do I say this, inequities. Being born to the worker's class, I would think you would be a little more sympathetic to their plight. The Centauri are, after all, working to eliminate the current hierarchy and begin anew on equal footing."

"They are terrorists, Iulius, nothing more," interjected Tiberius. "They have no organized goals other than death and destruction."

"And as I said, I am loyal to myself," Kaiya added. "Tiberius takes good care of me, and although I may not have been born into your class, I have attained certain luxuries, and considering the alternative, I am happy with my choices."

Tiberius gazed down at her lovingly. She returned his gaze, smiling at him and placing her hand on his knee. Her eyes, icy blue, beautiful, betrayed no emotion.

"I will tell you, Iulius, in confidence, what it is we are working on," Tiberius broke in, taking a long drawl from his cigar and slowly exhaling the smoke.

"I am on eggshells in anticipation."

"Funny. But what I am going to tell you cannot leave this alcove under any circumstance. I need your word that you will never repeat this to anyone. Spies are everywhere, on both sides, and any leak could jeopardize everything."

Iulius looked at Tiberius seriously, responding, "You have my word, old friend," before adding, in a lighter tone, "the Cheshire Pub shall be my vault."

Tiberius seemed pleased.

"Good, then I won't waste your time and will get straight to the point. We have had tails on Professor Ansley Brightmore for some time. We have infiltrated nearly every aspect of his life. We have detailed knowledge of credit laundering at casinos, as well as information distortions in our bugging devices when he is around. I have good reason to believe he was behind the bombings on Blood Sun Day that killed the founders of the Institute, his own friends and colleagues. I also believe he is leading the Centauri and organizing the workers across the world. We just don't know how he is evading us and what his ultimate goals are."

"These are heavy charges against an academic giant. You better be able to back them up," replied Iulius.

Tiberius reclined on the couch, pleased, and placed his arm around Kaiya.

"For one, our academic giant is a drunk and a murderer, and two, that's where this beautiful specimen comes into play."

"How so?"

This time it was Kaiya who responded.

"Professor Brightmore has been attempting to lure a young professor from the Institute to his cause. He has something planned. We aren't sure what it is, but we believe it is the key to the Centauri's long-term goals. As it happens, this young professor seems to find something… alluring about me." She smiled at Iulius.

Tiberius cut her off, adding, "Anyway, this young professor she speaks of is the child of Richard Cyannah and Lakshmi Dasai. He goes by Arian and works in the same field as his parents. He is now our man on the inside. He is gaining the Professor's confidence, and I expect that we shall soon have infiltrated the inner circle of the Centauri."

"Impressive," responded Iulius. "You have been busy."

"Indeed I have, and it won't stop there. Once Arian has infiltrated the Centauri, I plan on carrying out similar strategies in all of the domed cities, including Pathos. Being without a dome, your citizens are more vulnerable than most. I will identify suspected sympathizers across the land and infiltrate the satellite cells. We will eradicate this virus of dissent from the inside."

"I will drink to that," Iulius replied, raising his beer to his lips. "We could find good use for Kaiya in Pathos," he added, eyeing her body.

"Kaiya will not be coming to Pathos! Her talents are best saved for Capitol City. I shall assign you whom I see fit. It will be one of my own men, of course." Tiberius eyed Iulius for a few seconds before adding in a much more jovial tone, "Call your girl back in, you dumb bastard, I am done with business for the evening."

# Chapter Eight
## Fire in the Night

Stepping out of Arian's apartment building into the artificially cooled night air of the dome, Ansley felt the effects of the alcohol. The inebriation served to relieve him of the burdens he had lived with for well over fifty years. Along with the false relaxation came a false sense of confidence, and the old Professor decided he would have a few more drinks at Eduardo's place, the Devonshire, before heading down to the casino. Having left his hawk at home to avoid being tracked to Arian's, he walked a few blocks to the corner of a random avenue and pulled his qubit from his pocket.

"Esther."

"Yes, Professor," answered the monotonous voice of a mature woman.

"Call me a cab."

"Right away, Professor."

It was less than two minutes before the automated transport locked onto his qubit and arrived at the corner. Stepping into the vehicle, he spoke his final destination aloud and set off on the transportation grid toward the Devonshire

Pub.  Ansley watched the city fly past as he sat reflecting on his conversation with Arian.  He knew he was getting the kid in over his head.  None involved could fathom just how far he was planning to go, not the Overseers and not Tiberius.  In his drunken haze, Ansley allowed himself a moment to gloat.  He was, after all, the greatest scientific mind in the world, and if his plans came to fruition, all players in the game would become obsolete and Padma would be avenged.

His thoughts turned dark as he reflected on the loss of Padma.  She had not been beautiful, but was sweet, smart, and quirky, three traits that made her more than exquisite.  He needed a distraction to take his mind off her.  These reflections never yielded any good and often led to flashbacks and nightmares of that hellish night.  Arriving at the Devonshire, he couldn't exit the cab fast enough as he bounded toward the bar, seeking another soothing drink.  He slammed his hand down on the counter, announcing his arrival.

"Eduardo, you beautiful man, give me a double agave on the rocks, please."

The barman knew Ansley was drunk from experience and could tell from his false bravado that he was in one of his moods.  Without a word, he poured the drink, sitting it in front of the old Professor, who drained the glass in one swig and held it out for more.  Still silent, Eduardo obliged, only this time, he caught Ansley's eye and motioned with his head toward the end of the bar.  Following the motion, he looked over and noticed Anabelle seated alone, sipping a glass of wine and staring back at him coldly.

"Make that two, Eddie.  I've got a girl to talk to."

Ansley walked over to the woman, engulfing her in a long embrace.

"I've missed you," he lied.

"You aren't good at calling, are you?" she asked.  "You smell like a fucking brewery."

"I'm afraid I have over-imbibed, my dear, but my smell I cannot help."  Anabelle was beautiful and Ansley wanted her, if only to ease the pain he was feeling inside, but he knew not to indulge his desires. He had been down that road before and beautiful and unstable was never a healthy combination. But then again... she was pretty, and a night with company might be long overdue.

"Here's your drink, Professor... and one for the lady."

"Thank you, Eduardo, Anabelle always looks better after a few drinks."

Anabelle smacked him hard on his left shoulder. He began to recall why she annoyed him.

"You're an asshole," she said in mock anger, sliding his drink toward him while picking up her own. She drained it in one swallow, the stain of agave still fresh on her lips. Ansley mimicked her action, allowing himself to feel the liquor burn all the way down his throat and esophagus. Without warning Anabelle grabbed the breast of his shirt and pulled him into a kiss. As she released his black shirt, she gripped his bottom lip with her teeth, biting softly. He could taste the sweetness of the agave on her lips. Hesitating, he took a step back, considering his next move. Padma she was not, but Ansley needed someone tonight. Anabelle would do. In spite of his age, his nano- treatments made him strong, and he grabbed her around her narrow hips, lifting her from her seat and throwing her aggressively against the wall, kissing her. Ansley didn't often succumb to moments of weakness but, drunk and tired, he deserved a reprieve from the problems of the world.

"Excuse me, Professor! Excuse me! You can't do that here," Eduardo repeated in the background. Annoyed, Ansley kept his gaze on Anabelle, replying instead to her.

"Let's get out of here, honey, and head to friendlier confines. Put them on my tab, Eduardo," he said as he grabbed her hand and led her out the door, leaving the barman standing puzzled.

"Where are we going?" she asked as he opened the door.

"Let's go gamble, sweetheart," he replied. "I know how you love the action."

"I assumed the friendlier confines would be your

bedroom. You know I can be a very good friend."

"In time, my dear. A few thousand more credits on my qubit always increases my appetites."

"Then by all means, we should go to the casino. I want you to be hungry."

The night was spinning out of control. Ansley and Anabelle stumbled down the street, arms interlocked. While it didn't feel right, it did feel nice. It was freeing to let go of his burdens and allow the night to take him where it did. It felt good to not care.

The casino was only a few blocks from the Devonshire Pub, and as they rounded the corner, the flashing lights of the entrance came into view down the street. Ansley picked up the pace, forcing Anabelle to follow suit. His heart was pumping as the adrenalin coursed through his body. The few moments before he entered the casino were the only times Ansley ever noticed his heartbeat.

"I'm getting excited ba…"

A violent flash broke through the night.

*Bodies were thrown through the air with hellish force. Charred flesh smoldered, falling off the bones of fresh-made corpses. All sound was gone except for a persistent ringing. Stumbling, his body was numb. Palms finding pavement, he steadied himself, eyes open, yet only seeing the white light burned into his retinas. Choking on black smoke and reaching for her hand, his hearing returned, and the sound of the afflicted was horrendous. Explosions in the distance punctuated the crash of falling marble. Feeling around the immediate area for her body, his hand found hers, and the ash that had been her flesh fell from bone. Following the path from her hand to her chest, he felt no movement. Blinking rapidly to restore vision, the white light faded and was replaced by a bald, blackened face.*

The familiar vision left his mind and Ansley regained his bearings, finding reality just as grim. Their bodies had been thrown backward five feet. Ears ringing, Ansley stumbled to his feet and searched the ground for Anabelle, shaking with apprehension. He found her a few feet to his left, struggling to regain her footing. Rushing over to her, he grabbed her by her arms, helping to steady her.

"Are you okay?" he thought he said, although it didn't register in his ears. Her mouth moved, but the sound escaped him. He pulled her into the brick face of the storefront and held her, attempting to regain composure.

As the ringing in his ears subsided, he looked down the street toward what had been the casino, but was now a ruin of fire and ash. Thick black smoke poured out of the front before being sucked down into the dome's filtration system. Bodies and gore littered the street. The air was filled with the pungent odor of cooked meat. His hearing now returned, he spoke to Anabelle.

"Are you okay?"

"Yes, I think so," she responded, visibly shaken. Leaning against the wall, she sank to the ground. "How can this be happening again?" she muttered.

"I've got to go help," Ansley responded, ignoring her question and looking around the storefront. He ran toward a clothing store two doors away. Finding it closed, he kicked in the glass door, adding yet another alarm to the myriad of chaotic sounds on the street. Clearing out the glass, he hurried through the opening, grabbing the first piece of linen garment he found. Holding it over his mouth and nose, he bounded back out the door toward what was left of the casino.

Coming to the smoldering ruin, Ansley heard the cries of the injured and dying as they writhed in pain. The fire bathed the area in a hellish orange. Holding the linen over his mouth, he searched the ruins, looking for a way to help. The fire response team had yet to arrive, but many of the local constables of the pub district were attempting to quarantine the area and restore order. Looking into the now open front of the casino, Ansley saw the full scope of the explosion. The entire second floor and the marble staircases leading to it had collapsed to the ground. Rubble filled the lobby. Searching, Ansley found a familiar doorman, who despite a gaping wound in his shoulder seemed otherwise coherent.

"Santiago, where is Sharie?" The man stared ahead, unresponsive. Grabbing him by the collar and shaking him into cognition, he again demanded, "Santiago, where is Sharie!" Santiago lifted his trembling arm and pointed into the inferno.

"Damn," the Professor whispered before rushing inside. The heat was intense, but bearable, as most of the tinder for the fire was on the perimeter of the building. Water poured from the sprinkler systems above, warmed by the heat of the flames, yet still cool by comparison to the air temperature. Rushing through the atrium and dodging the rubble, he veered right toward the high limit poker rooms.

The arched entrance was partially collapsed and, stepping over a ruined column, his eyes fell upon a room full of smoldering bodies, some in Imperial robes, some in the garb of the Institute, but most were dressed in the common clothing of the Natural Born. Running to the hostess area, he lifted the shattered podium, dropping it at first as the wood burned his hands. Being prepared this time, he quickly threw the podium aside to reveal the body of a woman he had once known as Doris.

"Oh fuck, oh fuck!" he thought as he moved past her, searching for his friend. He found her a few feet away.

Sharie was almost beyond recognition. Large chunks of burned skin, hair, and flesh were intertwined and hung loosely from her face. Her right eye socket was caved in and the eye was gone. He had to read her plastic nametag to be sure of her identity. Ansley put his ear to her mouth and nose and heard sharp, shallow breaths. She was dying, but was still alive. Placing the linen cloth over her face, he swept her tiny frame into his arms and rushed back over the ruined column toward the street. The smoke was affecting him, making him woozy, though he pressed on. Rushing out of the inferno and back to the open air, he felt her stir in his arms. Ansley laid her on the cobbled street, oblivious to the chaos going on around him.

"Sharie. Honey, it's Ansley. I'm here. I'm so sorry."

She opened her remaining eye, fixing it upon his face. He cradled her head in his arms, comforting her, tears streaming down his face. Sharie lifted her arm to her chest and pulled a gold locket from the remains of her shirt. Clicking a button on the back, a flash drive ejected from the bottom. Ansley grabbed it, placing it into his front pocket as he continued to cradle her.

"My family," she whispered. "Please keep them. Please keep them safe."

"Always, Sharie," he muttered back. "I will make sure they are taken care of."

And for the second time in the long life of Ansley Brightmore, a burned woman died in his arms. He remained in the street, amongst the ruins and the bodies, clutching her for some time. It could have been five minutes or it could have been an hour. He would never be able to say. He was stirred from his mourning by the commotion of the arriving emergency crews.

Looking back down at the dead woman still in his arms, Ansley kissed her softly on her forehead and whispered, "I swear to keep your family safe." Gently laying her head on the pavement, he took a deep breath, stood, and walked away from the scene. It would be better if he weren't around when the authorities began asking questions. Walking back the way he came, he felt dazed, unable to comprehend what had occurred, and he wasn't sure whether he wanted to anyway. Right now, all he wanted was to hold the pain at arm's length. As he came to the storefront where Anabelle still stood, she grabbed his arm, attempting to stop him.

"Ansley, honey, are you alright? What happened?"

"Go home, Anabelle," he replied. This night was over.

# Chapter Nine
# Aftermath

In the weeks following the bombing at the casino, life in Capitol City slowed to a crawl. All places where people gathered in numbers, such as clubs, restaurants, and even the Institute itself, were closed while security officials swept the city in search of other planted explosives or clues about the culprit of the unprompted attack. All citizens seemed to agree that it was yet another in a long history of attacks by the Natural Born terrorist organization known as the Centauri. The lack of ability to work and the somber mood of the city left Arian in sour spirits. This was compounded by the fact that he hadn't heard from Professor Brightmore since that night, which was strange given all of the personal details the man had shared about Arian's mother and his hinting at some grand plan. With no other way to pass the time, Arian was content to lounge on his sofa in the atrium watching the nonstop 33-hour coverage of the bombing. He was unshaven and hadn't showered in days as he lazed around his apartments with no reason to leave.

Staring at the holograms flashing over his glass table, he watched in a daze as a mildly attractive reporter recounted the latest events.

*"This is Sophie Mayeaux for Capitol 11, giving you the latest on the Cardinal Street Tragedy. It seems our most recent reports indicate that Natural Born workers from outside the dome orchestrated the recent suicide attack that took five of our revered Consulates."*

"She is kind of hot in a strange way," Arian thought to himself. "Athena! What do you think? Is this news chick hot?"

"Do you require something, Arian?" returned the automated voice of his qubit.

"Oh shut up."

"Of course, Arian."

Contemplating his half empty martini, he couldn't decide whether it was worth it to lean forward and pick it up, as even this simple task required too much exertion on his part. Arian was bored, unmotivated, and unsure how he should spend the rest of his day. He turned his attention back to the news.

*"The Parliament is again engaged in intense debates over the new controversial bill known as the Natural Born registry, which will require all workers from outside the dome to submit to a series of background checks and cross examinations in order to ensure all who work within the city can be known to be free of Centauri involvement. Those cleared would be allowed to work within the dome, provided they carry a card at all times containing their pertinent information, as well as have a tracking chip implanted in their wrist by which all movements can be monitored by Capitol City authorities. The author of the bill, Tiberius Septus, is scheduled to address the Parliament this afternoon."*

"Athena… I'm bored! Make something happen!"

"What would you like me to do, Arian? Would you like me to pull up your research on your tablet?"

"No. I don't know… Order me some food or something."

"Would you like your usual order Shiang Xi noodles

from Le Venetian?"

"I don't care. Sure. Make it extra spicy and have them send a bottle of Sagittarian wine. I'm thirsty and this martini is too far away."

"Right away, Arian." Athena's voice disappeared, and she was likely already communicating with the computer system at Le Venetian.

Sagittarian wine wasn't his typical order due to its exorbitant price tag. He had only tasted it once and that had been at the dinner with Kaiya. He was surprised how concerned he was with her lack of contact since the attack. He hardly knew her and his meeting with the Professor had given rise to doubts about their collective mission. Despite having only met her once, Arian was smitten with her. He felt conflicted, pulled in two directions by her and Ansley. Trying to ignore these unsettling thoughts, he turned his attention back to the holograms dancing before him. Fire and ash littered his atrium, along with rubble and sounds of terror. The news was, once again, reshowing the live footage taken in the wake of the bombing.

"How many times do I have to watch this? Play some damn Patolli highlights!" He knew that all Patolli matches had been cancelled, even in the other domed cities, in solemn solidarity with Capitol City.

"Athena, pull up the Patolli rankings." His request was met with silence. She was still ordering the food. He needed to upgrade his qubit. The lack of multi-tasking ability was annoying, particularly when he was at the lab. He picked up the tablet next to him and accessed the rankings manually. There had been no change in the last few weeks, and since he pulled them up every day, he knew them top to bottom. Still, it made him feel good to see that Capitol City was in second place, behind only Pathos in the quest for the Four Roses Cup. After a few moments, Athena responded.

"Accessing the rankings."

"Never mind," Arian shouted irritably. "I'm watching the news."

The images of fire and death were now absent, along with the mildly attractive reporter Sophie Mayeaux, and were replaced by the Special Representative for the Natural Born, Habimana Muteteli. His thick accent bespoke of his origins on the distant isles of the Sentwali Sea, but he was a Nephite, born and raised.

"...of these proceedings. Of course most of those who inhabit the Natural Born zones around our domes are hard-working honest people, just looking to provide for their families. They abhor violence and wish for the perpetrators to be apprehended and justice to be served for the brutal murders of not only our esteemed Consulates, but also many of their Natural Born brethren who showed up to their jobs at the casino that night, just trying to put food on their tables."

"And how do you believe the Natural Born will respond to the new Natural Born Registry Bill proposed by Consulate Septus and widely believed to pass without much resistance?" Sophie's voice inquired from off camera.

"I believe they will be very pleased with the bill. Why should they not be? They have nothing to hide. They expect the new tracking systems will provide them with more security from the violent Centauri that threaten not only the stability of our society, but also their own personal safety. They know that our governing body has their best interests at heart, and they feel good knowing our Overseers care enough to take a personal interest in their well-being, just as they take an interest in the well-being of the Nephites within the domes."

"What a jackass," Arian thought to himself. As if the lowborn would be happy about being branded and tracked like cattle. Would they next start tracking even members of the dome? Uneasiness settled upon him as he realized that, in a way, they already were tracking their own members, and he was the tracking device. The spinsters at the Central Tower were effective at framing their power grabs as a caring government protecting its people. Terrorist attacks by the Centauri always seemed beneficial for Parliament's goals.

"Arian, you have a visitor at the door. I assume it is

your food," Athena's voice rang out, breaking his revelry. Standing up for the first time in hours, his legs felt weak from lack of use, and as he headed toward the door to retrieve his meal, he realized that he needed to pee. Picking up his qubit to pay the deliveryman, he entered the marbled foyer, placed his feet into his slippers, and pushed the button that opened the door.

He was shocked to find, not a deliveryman, but a demure looking Kaiya awaiting him. Her auburn hair was pulled into a taut ponytail that started high on the back of her head and extended down past her shoulders. She was wearing a black fitted coat, buttoned to just above her stomach, revealing a nearly see-through white lace evening dress underneath. In the late afternoon light, he noticed for the first time the sprinkling of freckles on her creamy white skin. His shock turned to embarrassment as he realized how he must appear to her. His skin was oily, his hair unkempt, and he had the funk that only days of wallowing on a couch without showering can give you. She was gripping the tote of food delicately in her left hand and holding the wine in her right.

"I came up the elevator with your deliveryman and thought I might offer a more appetizing view." She thrust the bottle of wine forward to him. "I see you enjoyed the Sagittarian wine we shared at dinner. Are you going to invite me in?" she asked, her high voice a barely audible whisper. Speechless and dumbfounded, Arian could manage only to step aside to allow her entry, taking the wine from her as she passed.

As she entered the foyer, she slipped her arms out of her coat, letting it fall, as if expecting Arian to be there to take it. He was. Hanging it on the rack in the corner, he turned back to find her facing him. His jaw dropped as he beheld her form, backlit by the sunlight streaming through the glass ceiling of the atrium. Her skin was even more visible beneath the white lace of her dress in this light. The material covered her from just above her breast to midway down her thigh. Black leather boots covered her lower legs to the knee. Her soft, rounded shoulders and long regal neck were exposed. She was beautiful.

Feeling vulnerable and exposed, not to mention having to relieve his bladder, Arian nervously excused himself.

"Please, have a seat in the atrium. I have something to take care of that won't take long. Feel free to open the wine. Athena, please access the wine glasses."

Rushing down the hall, he let out a sigh as the restroom door shut behind him, happy to be hidden from her gaze. Looking into the mirror above the sink, his worst suspicions were confirmed as the man looking back at him had oily hair going in every direction, bright red eyes with bags underneath, not to mention he was wearing his bed clothes. Moving to the toilet, he relieved himself and tried to regain his composure. He laughed out loud as his ego began to restore itself.

"What the hell is your problem?" he asked the face in the mirror. "You, a Nephite and one of the Institute's most promising young professors, are bothered by the presence of a beautiful woman? He relaxed at this realization, yet still, he threw water on his face and hair, and exited looking better, his ego and self-assuredness restored as well. He found Kaiya sitting on a stool at the bar, legs crossed, hands folded in her lap, the wine unopened.

"Shall I pour us a glass?" he asked

"I thought you would never ask. I'm thirsty and we have much to discuss."

He walked to the end of the bar where Athena had raised the clean glasses. Grabbing two along with a corkscrew, he opened the wine and poured two generous portions, the pungent smell of the contents filling the room. They swirled the wine in their glasses, taking a moment to breathe in the rich earthy tones.

"This wine reminds me of home," she said, breaking the silence. "I'm from the Sagittarian region of Avignon."

Arian was caught off guard by the implications of this statement and was not able to hide his shock, though he quickly recovered.

"I had no idea," he said. "Then you are Natural Born? When did you come to Capitol City?"

"You are very perceptive. I came some years ago, more than I care to admit. Age takes on more meaning for those of us born outside the domes." She sipped her wine, a perfect example of grace and elegance. Somehow Arian, despite his privileged upbringing, felt barbaric around her as he gulped his own.

He mulled over her reply, trying to understand how a Natural Born could be in a position of power at the Institute. He ignored his reservations, not wishing to offend the beautiful woman sharing wine in his atrium.

"I see. And what did your family do in Avignon?" he inquired.

"My father managed a vineyard outside the domed city of Sikyon. The vineyard was owned by the family of Flavius Decimus. As you may or may not be aware, it is Decimus who produces all the Sagittarian wine enjoyed throughout Arameus. I grew up smelling the very earth feeding the grappa that produced this vintage. My father worked hard, but ultimately was a slave. Being endowed with certain assets others found desirable, I was able to gain access to many of the luxuries those born in your position take for granted.

She was quiet as she looked down into her glass, swirling the wine gently. She seemed vulnerable. Not knowing how to respond, and not relating to the struggles of the lower class, Arian remained silent.

"However," she continued after a moment, "you see me here, and I have managed to rise in my own way. I will never go back to what I was before. I am completely loyal to the vision of the Overseers and their mission to create a perfect society."

"That much is clear. Still, I wonder at your motivations."

"A lady must keep her secrets, Arian, surely you know that. Or has a woman never stolen your heart?" she asked in a playful tone, making brief eye contact.

"My work keeps me busy enough. I've never had much time for personal relationships. I was the youngest graduate of the Institute of Science, as well as the youngest assistant professor. I received the Overseers Grant for Biotechnology at the age of twenty-five. I have been told that my path was determined before my birth and I have not strayed from it. When my work is complete, I will find time for other indulgences. Time, as you know, is a commodity in which I am incredibly wealthy."

"I am aware of your resume, Arian. Ansley would not have approached you if you did not possess prodigious skill. However, the pursuits of the body are quite different from the pursuits of the mind. Surely you must feel... certain urges for human companionship." Kaiya looked at him, bringing her fingers to her chest, just below the neck, caressing her skin.

Arian stood next to her, watching her reflection in the mirror over the bar. Feeling the warm blood rushing to his face, he was forced to turn his gaze, sipping his wine, allowing its tart sweetness to roll over his tongue.

"Why are you here, Kaiya?" he asked. "I'm tired of these games."

"I like a man that who's forceful and knows what he wants," she replied, smiling.

"Just answer the question."

"Well, I had entertained the thought of making this a social visit, but since I can see you're in a serious mood, let me show you something." She pulled a flash drive from inside of her left boot and held it out to Arian. "Of course, I have no qubit so you will have to play this on yours," she said, looking embarrassed for the first time since he had known her.

Taking the drive from her and placing it into a port on his qubit, Arian ordered Athena to play the hologram. The room was once again filled with smoke and fire, as he found himself in the midst of the bombing at the casino. This time, however, the hologram zoomed in on a man holding a severely burned woman in his arms. The image wasn't clear, but Arian recognized the man to be Ansley Brightmore.

The audio feed had been disrupted during the bombing, but it was clear they were speaking to one another. It was also clear that Ansley had great affection for the dying woman. The video feed cut and the hologram disappeared.

"That's strange," Arian mused. "I wasn't aware that Ansley was present at the bombing, though it's not surprising. I've heard he goes to that casino four nights a week. Perhaps this explains why I haven't heard from him. Is he okay?"

"He's fine," replied Kaiya. "And this woman he seems so attached to?"

"Of course he would have friends there. It was his second home."

"I want you to look closer. Have your qubit play the hologram again. This time zoom in four times at the one minute and twenty second mark."

Arian complied, and again his atrium was engulfed in flames, and again he saw the Professor with the dying worker. At the allotted time, the hologram zoomed in on the woman's chest just as she extracted what appeared to be a drive from a locket on her neck. She passed it to the Professor and the video cut.

"What was that?" Arian asked.

"We don't know. But we want you to find out. We pulled this video from the local security cameras outside the casino. The woman's name was Sharie. She was a hostess for the high limit poker room and in charge of taking in and paying out credits. We believe she has been central in a credit-laundering scheme that's been funneling money to Centauri terrorists. You need to find out why Ansley was with this woman, and you need to find out what is on that drive. Whatever it is, it's clearly important enough to risk entering a burning building."

Arian sat, dumbfounded by the information he was hearing, wondering himself what was going on. It seemed impossible that the man sharing drinks and memories of his parents could be caught up with the terrorists. That had been the same night as the bombing. The thought sent chills down his spine. He was struck by a peculiar thought.

"Why would the Institute care about a money-laundering scheme or terrorists? What does any of this have to do with our University?" Arian demanded, glaring at Kaiya.

"I'm afraid I haven't been forthright with you, Arian," Kaiya answered, returning his gaze.

"What do you mean?"

"I mean only that the people that I represent go far above the Institute."

"Who are you?"

"I am no one important. But believe me and take this to heart, the people I represent are extremely powerful and not to be crossed. You must do exactly as I say."

"Why should I believe you? You have misrepresented yourself from the beginning. Why should I trust a Natural Born woman who can't even state her purpose?"

Kaiya stood, taking Arian by his hand. In spite of his confusion and rising anger, his stomach fluttered with nervous anticipation. She pulled him to his feet and led him to the couch at the center of the atrium, sitting on it and pulling him down beside her. Before he could speak, she thrust her head forward, kissing him softly on the lips. Her lips were moist, tantalizing, and her smell, a blend of musk and citrus, triggered an increased heart rate. As far as Arian was concerned, Ansley and the Centauri were now a million miles away.

Pulling her head back, she remained within inches of his lips and whispered, "I need your trust, Arian. If not for the welfare of Arameus or for the people I represent, then do it for me."

"What do they want of me?"

"Do everything that Ansley asks of you. Gain his trust. There is no saving him at this point, so ease your conscience. We need to know what he is working on, and we need to know what is on that drive. It could be the key to defeating the Centauri."

"For you, I will do all of this, but I must know, for whom am I gathering this information?"

"As I said, a woman must always keep her secrets, but when this is over, you will have your explanation."

He leaned in again in an attempt to kiss her, but she was already on her feet, heading toward the foyer. Rising to follow, he caught her by the arm as she grabbed her coat, spinning her around.

"You're just going to leave?"

"I have to go now, Arian," she replied. "I shouldn't be here and I have other engagements tonight. We will talk again."

Pressing the button that opened the door, she exited and was gone, leaving Arian standing alone in the foyer. Confusing as it all was, all he could think about was the feeling of her soft, wet lips upon his own.

# Chapter Ten
# Marco Luccio

Tiberius stood on the platform rising above the city until he reached Level 314. This was the highest level of the Central Tower that the members of Parliament could access. The lift was large and circular, with a red sofa in the center, radiating outward and embroidered with the Imperial eagle. At Level 314, it was as if the platform was merely part of the floor of a much larger room, also circular. Light from the yellow day sun filled the room from all directions. At this height, the view of the city would have been stunning had Tiberius been of a mind to enjoy such things.

At the portions of the room corresponding to North, East, South, and West on a compass, there were ornately patterned gold doors, each emblazoned with the family crest of the Overseer with which they were associated. Jewels punctuated the beautiful carvings, gleaming in the sunlight. The northern door was covered in emeralds, the green sequoia heralding the family of Vladymir Romanov. To the west, red rubies outlined the scorpion of the Medici family. To the east, the blue sapphires of the venerable Paulo Dominiccio outlined the griffin that had long represented his family. Tiberius turned south toward his destination, facing the diamond encrusted two-headed serpent of Marco Luccio. Unconsciously, he grabbed his own family crest, hanging from his neck, his fingers rubbing the medallion's grooves, feeling awed, yet inspired by the spectacle before him. Stepping from the platform, he was chided by a secretary for Overseer Luccio, stationed just to the right of his door.

"Please step back, Consulate, and have a seat on the sofa behind you. The Overseer will see you shortly. Would you like a beverage while you wait?"

"No, thank you, I am fine," Tiberius replied, in spite of the dryness in his throat. He took a few steps back, abashed, seating himself on the red sofa. A man such as him was not accustomed to waiting, but then again, he was not accustomed to having a private meeting with an Overseer either. To say this was a great honor would be a disservice to what it truly was. It was an opportunity, and Tiberius was well aware of the practice of making those below you wait before a meeting. He sat, nervously toying with the medallion around his neck, which felt tighter than when he had entered. The secretary looked down at the console before her, oblivious to his presence. He could see that the secretaries for the other Overseers were equally unimpressed with him. After a few moments, a red light began flashing from the desk of Overseer Luccio's assistant.

"The Overseer will see you now," she said without looking up. The gold door creaked as it lifted upward, revealing a beautiful lift, as ornate as the door that had obscured it. As he walked past the desk of the secretary, she cleared her throat politely, bringing him to a halt.

"Consulate, our scanner shows you still are in possession of your qubit. I'm afraid you will have to leave that with us."

Looking to the guards at the door, Tiberius relinquished his qubit, feeling naked without it. He was apprehensive at leaving it with one who worked for the

Overseers given the sensitive personal information it contained, but had no choice. Moving past the secretary, he walked toward the now open door, feeling better as the guards on both sides moved, allowing him to pass.

Entering the lift, Tiberius was in unknown territory. The top of the Central Tower consisted of ten stories, the last five of which were comprised of four independent spires that housed the Overseers. The five floors below the spires served as office space for their staff. Tiberius was headed to the top floor of the southern spire. He had been invited to the home office of Marco Luccio. The elevator slowed to a stop, and Tiberius stood in nervous anticipation of what awaited him on the other side.

As the door slowly rose, he was overwhelmed by the smell of jasmine. The floral odor hung thick but fresh in the air. Stepping out, he was struck by the grandeur of his surroundings. The walls were comprised of thick white marble with large rectangular windows, from the floor to the 40 foot vaulted ceiling, placed intermittently around the room. Four skylights angled the light of the yellow day sun to a bronze emblem on the floor in the center of the room. The diamond serpent eyes reflected the sunlight, sparkling with a thousand rainbows. As his eyes adjusted to the brilliance of the light, Tiberius was able to see that the jewels etched out the pattern of a two-headed snake choking the Imperial eagle.

To the left of the jeweled emblem, at the far end of the room, four long steps rose from the marble floor leading to the carved oak desk of the Overseer, currently unoccupied. Tiberius took a few steps forward, unsure of what do before a fit of coughing caught his attention. Two nurses were attending to an old, sickly man in a portable hospital bed. Monitors were all around him, and an IV fed a clear solution into his arm. Tiberius felt embarrassed, as if he had stumbled upon something he wasn't supposed to witness.

"Tiberius? Is that you?" rasped the feeble voice of Marco Luccio. "Come here, my boy."

Feeling relieved, but still apprehensive, Tiberius walked

to his bedside.

"You may take a break, ladies. I'm sure I can survive a few minutes without you," Marco said to the nurses, motioning them off. He began laughing, as if at some private joke, a horrible cough-like sound emanating deep from within his emaciated chest. "Have a seat, Tiberius," he said, moving his wrinkled, spotted hand to a button on the railing of his bed. A chair rose from the floor. Tiberius paused, transfixed by the living corpse, before walking to the chair and sitting down. He had never been this close to an Overseer.

"You look well, your grace," Tiberius began. He instantly regretted the lie.

"Come now, Consulate. I didn't look well two hundred years ago, but I appreciate the sentiment. Your father was a liar as well. You do know he was a business associate of mine, long ago, before all this. It's a shame he didn't live long enough to receive the treatments." A coughing spell overcame him, and it was some moments before he was able to speak again. "Then again," he continued, his tone adopting an air of reflection, "perhaps it was a blessing for him. Eternal youth. Who wouldn't sign up for that? Eternal old age, however, is quite a different matter. It's a shame the technology can't yet reverse aging completely."

"Your continued leadership is an inspiration, your grace," Tiberius replied. "It's your wisdom and experience that has led us to this utopian society we now enjoy."

"That is kind, Tiberius. You have done your family proud. The Septus name is a large burden for a man to carry, and much was expected of you. You have not disappointed. I know the casino assignment was a tough one to carry out, but you handled it brilliantly. It was an unfortunate yet necessary evil. Part of maintaining balance is making difficult decisions. By cutting the funding to our enemies, they will become weak and fragmented. It is only a matter of time before we have them in our grasp."

"I must say, your grace, I was alarmed at the news that five of my fellow consulates were in the casino. I was given to understand that the building would be void of Nephites that night. The thought that our actions brought about their demise has haunted my dreams."

"Everything was as it should have been. You were given to understand what you needed to understand and nothing more. The five consulates who died that night were, in my opinion and that of the other Overseers, enemies of the state. Their incessant liberal agenda and constant crusading for the lowborn scum made them a liability to our fragile peace. In a land where men no longer die naturally, sometimes they must be removed unnaturally. But let your conscience ease, my son. These actions were warranted."

"But how could they be, your grace?" asked Tiberius. He knew he needed to tread carefully and maintain his temper, but the shock of knowing that the government had assassinated five of its members had overcome him. "These men were from great families. They were my colleagues. Killing low born terrorists plotting to destroy us is one matter, but killing peers over political differences is quite another."

Marco again laughed that wretched laugh. It sounded like a death rattle.

"Don't act as if you are a naïve boy. Your father was naïve as well. For all of his great talents, he never had the stomach to make the hard decisions. He sought the favor of the public, to the detriment of his own interests, I might add. When Luccio Holdings staged the takeover of Nanosoft, do you think they just handed us the keys to the kingdom? They held the knowledge that would end death, but they didn't recognize what they had. It isn't scientists and thinkers who build societies. It is the ambition and acumen of our businessmen and the greed of mankind. We created the wealth and industry that fund this perfect world you now inhabit. It is the natural law. Everything in the world exists at the expense of something else. The lion feeds on the gazelle. The eagle hunts the snake, though not according to my seal. A man must carve out a spot for himself in the world, and in filling that place, must necessarily deny that position to another. No man would choose to be the gazelle if given the choice to be a lion. WE ARE THE LIONS!" he screamed, his voice gaining a vigor and fervor Tiberius didn't expect the frail body was capable of producing.

Not surprisingly, Tiberius found himself not only calmed, but also moved by the wise words of the exalted Overseer. He leaned in closer to the man, over the railing of the bed, in eager anticipation of the wisdom Marco Luccio could teach him.

"Don't ever forget what you are, my boy," he continued, softer and more subdued. Reaching his gnarled hand out, he grabbed the medallion that was now hanging out of Tiberius' robes, drawing him closer. His stomach churned as the hot, putrid breath of the old man filled his nostrils. "As a Septus you were born a lion. But never forget that anyone outside that dome would take that from you without hesitation. It is the actions of the Overseers that keep you a lion."

"Thank you, your grace. I see the truth and wisdom in your words. They have eased my concerns. I apologize for having doubt in your vision."

"It is nothing, my boy. It's only human to feel empathy. If you didn't question the validity of your actions, you would not be a man worthy of your titles. And your actions at the casino have shown that you are not your father. You are not a man who shies away from tough decisions."

"Your grace is too kind to me. If I may be so bold, I have spent my life seeking the love of the people that we govern, but now I understand that to govern requires an almost cutthroat commitment to the goals of society as a whole. I believe I understand now that I can maintain the façade of being a man of the people, while serving our own greater vision as the Overseers see fit. Your guidance has never led us astray. I am enlightened by your words."

"I am proud of you today. I have never fully trusted you before, but I find my doubts alleviated. We've decided to create a special security department to oversee all of our domed cities. We would like you to take charge of this endeavor, which, as I'm sure you have ascertained, will be known only to the Overseers and those who work for you. You will have anything you need at your disposal and access to all our information. Understand that this position is a great honor for you. You will be the Chief Security Officer of Arameus, with powers to arrest and bestow justice on whom you see fit… upon consultation with me, of course."

"I… I don't know what to say," Tiberius stammered, tears filling his eyes.

"Don't say anything. My secretary will give you a special transponder when you leave. It is a direct line to me, as I will be your only contact. The transponder will give you access to an account we have created for this project, which I trust, you will find more than adequate to hire the agents you need."

"I will not fail you, your grace," responded Tiberius in a solemn tone.

"See that you don't. Your purpose is to root out and destroy our enemies, wherever they are, whether in the Institute, in our own Parliament, or outside the dome."

"I will destroy the Centauri," Tiberius promised.

"Good," Marco replied, chuckling to himself. "Now go. I must rest."

Tiberius stood, bowed slightly, and turned toward the lift, his chest swelling with pride. He had only gone a few steps before he heard the voice of the Overseer again.

"And Tiberius?"

"Yes, your grace," he replied, turning back toward the bed.

"See that you end your little tryst with that lowborn whore. I believe they call her Kaiya? We can't have our head of security sharing a bed with a Natural Born. Your former colleague Horace Greely could attest to that… or at least he would be able to if he weren't killed in that unfortunate explosion at the casino. We had it on good authority that he was sharing his bed with a lowborn hostess named Sharie. As it turns out, she had her own agendas."

Tiberius' heart sank and his knees nearly buckled. How could he possibly know about Kaiya? He began to speak, but stopped himself, bowing again, before exiting the room.

Marco closed his eyes, trying to rest as he heard the door to the lift shut, but his brain, the one thing that had never aged, was racing. Deception upon deception, his mind was a forest. He thought of his visit with Iulius a few weeks prior. These Consulates were all the same with their whores. He had given Iulius the same warning he had given Tiberius, but this advice had been ignored. Now it was time deal with Iulius. It was a shame, really. So much wasted potential.

He opened his eyes as the two nurses re-entered the room. Pulling the IV from his arm, the priceless nanocyte solution spilled to the floor. Lowering the railing, Marco rose and stepped down from the bed. He allowed himself a moment to enjoy the coldness of the marble floor as his feet touched the ground before stepping forward into his newly placed slippers. He extended his arm, as one of the nurses guided the thick sleeve of his purple Imperial robes over the shoulder, and around the other arm.

Without a word, he walked forward over the jeweled sigil, feeling the warmth of the sun on his face as he moved. The nanocyte treatment restored his vigor, and he no longer seemed as frail. Moving up the marble stairs, past his carved desk, he stood at the window, looking down on his exquisite city. The hunger in his gaze bespoke of his massive ambition.

# Chapter Eleven
## Science and Intrigue

Arian sat at his desk puzzling over the data he had just been handed by his young student Matthew Conway. It felt good to be back at work after the month-long closing of government buildings. Science was Arian's life, and being in the labs of the Institute was the only place he was truly happy. It was more stimulating than watching the newscasters replay the explosion again. He was concerned that the break might put his research behind, but that couldn't be further from the truth. If the data he was looking at was accurate, it could be a monumental breakthrough, even if he didn't yet understand the full implications.

The fact that there was data at all was what shocked Arian. On the night of the explosion, Conway had set up an overnight experiment in which he attempted to attach a nanobot to the gene that controls up-activation of telomerase. The goal of the experiment was to determine whether it was possible to hijack a cell at certain points of its reproductive cycle, allowing the programming of the nanobot to override the chemical instructions transcribed within the DNA. In theory, this was simple enough. The real question for Arian was whether the cell would respond to the commands of the bot, and moreover, how would the second-generation cell be affected.

Being an assistant professor of bio-cybernetics, Arian's primary interest was the interfacing of an artificial nanobot with a biological substrate. Conway, however, had his own interests. Truthfully, he should have been assigned to the Institute's Anti-Aging division, for that was what seemed to captivate him. However, the Institute had deemed that he should work under Arian in cybernetics to complete his doctorate, and the Institute's word was law in academia.

Aging had ceased to be a concern some time ago, and thus Arian had never taken much interest in the mechanics of it, though he understood the general theory. He was actually one of the few in Arameus who did, as it was one of the most guarded secrets by the Overseers. They understood that those that controlled the secrets of immortality controlled the world. Being employed in the field of cybernetics, Arian had to be educated in the modern biological machinery of the Nephite. As a student, he had hated having his scientific passions governed by his research advisor, so he allowed his students the liberty to pursue their own interests. He hadn't thought much of it when Conway had introduced the idea of a secondary bot, programmed with the exact DNA sequence of the cell on which they were attempting to attach the primary nanobot.

His idea was intriguing. The role of the secondary bot, which he had loosely coined a "bio-bot," would be to scan the freshly copied DNA sequence during the S-phase of the cell cycle as the primary cell entered into mitosis. If the sequence was copied incorrectly, or mutations had occurred, the bio-bot would transmit a signal to the primary nanobot, which would signal the secondary cell to undergo apoptosis, or auto-cell death, upon completion of cell division. The primary cell would then begin its reproductive cycle again.

This was an interesting concept to Arian, so he allowed Conway to introduce the bio-bots into the experiments. His main concern was interfacing the primary nanobot into the cell cycle and Conway's ideas would not interfere with this goal. However, the results in front of him defied all logic.

He was staring at evidence of hundreds upon hundreds of cellular reproductions, followed by hundreds upon hundreds of cell suicides in the resulting second-generation. This was evidence of a successful attachment and an indication that the bio-bots were indeed communicating with the primary nanobot, which was triggering cell death. But why would the cell have incorrectly sequenced the DNA so many times? Had the nanobot interfaced at the wrong gene and disrupted the S phase? There had been only one successful cell division during his three-week absence from the lab. Upon sequencing the DNA of the second-generation cell, Conway had found, to his complete surprise, that the sequences no longer matched. It was utterly impossible to believe, but during cell division, the second-generation cell had "inherited" an extraordinary amount of extra genetic information.

Arian rubbed his temples, deep in thought, moving his hands to the back of his neck and allowing them to rest there. Obviously the kid must have screwed something up. He continued to stare at the data, hoping to make some connection he had previously missed. He was interrupted by a knock. Looking out the door, he saw JiYeon Ku, one of his female graduate students standing there, papers in hand.

"What do you need, Ku?" he demanded, perhaps too harshly.

"Professor, I wanted to discuss the next steps for our nanotube auto-assembly research. Some of my simulations have completed during the break."

Arian took a deep breath, annoyed. He knew he should meet with her, but his mind was occupied with Conway's results and he didn't want to be disturbed.

"I'm sorry, JiYeon, but I'm busy now. Can we set up a meeting for tomorrow afternoon?"

"Of course, professor. I'm sorry to disturb you," she replied, with an obvious tone of dejection. She shuffled off with her head down. Returning to his meditations, he was again interrupted by the sound of knocking.

"JiYeon, I told you I'm busy. What about that did you not understand!"

"Are you always this rude to your students?" Ansley's voice answered. "Not exactly a good way to be as a young faculty member."

Shocked, Arian was at a loss for words. The visit was so unexpected, he didn't know how to react, although by now, he should have been used to Ansley's unannounced intrusions. Remembering his conversation with Kaiya, and thus his mission, he quickly forgot about his research troubles and hit a button on his desk, allowing the door to slide open. For the first time since the night of the bombing, Arian beheld Ansley Brightmore as he sauntered in. There were bags under his eyes, his clothes were wrinkled, and he carried himself with an air of aloofness, as if detached from the world around him.

"You're not drunk. That's strange," Arian said sarcastically.

"No. I'm not. I'm working."

"Well, I was working, but now I'm talking to you," replied Arian. "To what do I owe this distraction?"

"Tsk, Tsk, Arian. Not only are you rude to your young students, but to your elders as well? As your senior professor, I should take offense, but I don't think I will. Being offended is a luxury of the young. If you don't get blown up, you will realize that someday."

"I saw you."

"I see you now."

"No. I mean I saw you on the news… at the explosion." Arian knew it was a lie, but he hoped that the Professor would believe it. It would be uncomfortable to have to explain the truth.

"Not a surprise, kid. I frequent that casino. I was in the vicinity and I tried to help. You should congratulate me. I'm a hero. I should have been interviewed by Sophie."

Arian studied Ansley for second. He was acting strange, even for the old

Professor. "I wasn't aware that anyone was saved."

"No one was saved, although not through any lack of effort on my part. I didn't find the response of our emergency services to be all that timely. However, my heroism isn't defined by whom I was able to save, but what I was able to save."

Arian's heart skipped a beat as adrenaline rushed through his veins. Could it be this easy? Was Ansley just going to stroll into his office unannounced and give him the information Kaiya requested?

"And what exactly were you able to save?" Arian asked, attempting to sound nonchalant.

"I'll make a deal with you, kid," Ansley replied, smiling. It was more of a smirk than a smile. "Discuss with me these results that puzzle you so and I will answer any questions you have about the night at the casino."

"Again, you ask about my research. You have never made it clear what my role is in this proposed collaboration. Why do you care about my research anyway?"

Ignoring Arian, Ansley pulled a cigarette from the misshapen silver case and lit it. Taking a long drawl, he spoke. "Aren't you going to offer me a drink?"

"Fine," said Arian, standing and walking to the cabinet behind his desk. He removed two glasses and filled them with Tegave. Turning back with the glasses, he began again, "I'm glad to see you left that fucking egg-thing at home."

"Oh! Good call, Arian. I knew I could trust you," Ansley replied jovially as he pulled the egg-shaped device from his pocket. Flipping the switch on the top, there was a brief flickering of the lights in the room as all electromagnetic signals were disturbed. It was evident that the old Professor was toying with him.

"My graduate student has stumbled upon something," Arian began, retaking his seat behind the desk, "but I'm afraid the results have left me puzzled."

"As they should," replied Ansley. "All those unsuccessful attempts to attach the nanobot to the gene and upon achieving success, you find the successive generations have an altered genetic sequence."

"How could you know of this?" asked Arian, the shock evident in his voice. He was beginning to fear what it was Ansley was hiding. The old Professor dismissed him with a wave of the hand before continuing.

"Your mistake, my young friend, is that you discounted the other variable in this experiment. The secondary bot introduced by your student, responsible for ensuring the successful replication of the DNA, what was its purpose?"

"By ensuring only perfect genetic replication, it would prevent the adverse effects of an aging cell and the loss of the telomere. It would ensure that no cancerous cells are created. In doing so, we could create biological immortality without the need for the nano treatments."

Arian stopped to consider his statement. Saying it aloud, he realized just how groundbreaking this discovery could be. The secondary bot was the key to preventing damaged cells from procreating. The primary nanobot received signals from the secondary bot. His entire scientific career devoted to attaching a nanobot to a cell during division, and a graduate student had found the key.

"You're a fool, Arian," said Ansley, breaking him from his reverie.

"How so?"

"You are a fool to think that the Overseers would for one second give up control of the nano-treatments and thus the source of their power because of a mere scientific breakthrough. Perhaps not a fool, but naïve. You still don't understand what's happened here."

"And that is?" shot back Arian.

"When I entered this office, you were troubled, and I can only assume that it is due to the new genetic information coded in the successive generations of cells. You failed to grasp the role of the secondary bot. This bio-bot was scanning the primary cell in order to determine whether the secondary cell was biologically perfect, only you failed to consider that it was also scanning the nanobot attached to the substrate itself. This secondary bot is a very powerful computer, equipped with the most sophisticated artificial intelligence software in all of Arameus. It killed every cell produced until it was able to reproduce the perfect code according to the nanobot's scans."

"I'm afraid I don't follow," responded Arian.

"The secondary bot has created, genetically, a biological transmitter that acts just as the artificial nanobot you initially attached."

"I don't understand."

"Think of a beehive, Arian. There are thousands of individuals acting as one super-organism through the transmission of pheromones. This is what the bio-bot has created within the secondary generation of cells. It has coded for a veritable super-organism of cells, all in contact with one another, governing subsequent reproduction for the good of the host."

"If what you say is true," replied Arian, "then we have made the greatest discovery in the history of mankind. We can make a better man."

"You foolish, foolish boy," said Ansley, shaking his head in disbelief. "I respect your optimism, but lament your lack of a basic grasp of the regime under which we toil. Nothing you do occurs in a vacuum. Any advance in science is twisted to suit their own selfish desires and place a heavier boot on the neck of every citizen of this world."

Arian finished his drink. His head throbbed, as it was all too much to take in. His thoughts raced back to Kaiya and her request. Who was this man before him, and why did he know more of Conway's results than he himself?

"How do you know this?" he asked, anger and fear evident in his voice.

"Why would you question my actions at the casino?" retorted Ansley, full of confidence. "We all have our secrets, don't we?" he added, with a knowing smile.

Arian's heart raced as he searched for a solution. Did Ansley know about Kaiya? Were they both being manipulated by the same shadowy group? He had to respond to avoid giving Ansley the upper hand, so he reacted rashly, succumbing to his impulsive nature.

"I have discussed my results with you, now it is your turn to answer my questions. What is the object you obtained at the casino on the night of the explosion?"

Ansley glanced to his right as the lights flickered.

"You seem to have some knowledge as it is, but my time is limited. First tell me, what do you desire from your research?"

Without hesitation, Arian answered.

"I desire to use technology to take control of the cell cycle and create a better man. People view cybernetics as some grandiose experiment in design. The design already exists in the human body. I only wish to push it in a controlled direction. We can be so much more."

"Good," replied Ansley. "Very good... That's exactly what I need from you."

"So what did you retrieve from the casino?" Arian asked.

"Another time, my friend. The flickering of your lights tells me that my, what do you call it... oh yeah, fucking egg, is about to lose its effectiveness."

There was a knock at the door drawing their attention to the left. Four distraught students stood huddled together.

"I see your students are disoriented. I'm afraid my device may have interfered with some of their experiments. Anyway," Ansley continued, standing while placing the egg back into the pocket of his coat, "we shall continue this another time. Have a good night."

He exited the office with the same jovial step with which he had entered. As he left, a stream of students poured into Arian's office, leaving him with little time to contemplate his shock and disdain over how the meeting had ended.

As Ansley exited the labs, he was relieved. Arian knew more than he was letting on, but Ansley did as well. Feeling the egg underneath his coat, he knew he now had access to all the files in the office. Wins had been few and far between recently, and it felt nice to have something go his way. He picked up his pace as he angled toward Eduardo's bar. He deserved a drink.

Walking toward the bar, a thought occurred to him that stopped him in his tracks. Perhaps it was time to take a chance. He had been playing it safe for far too long and the recent bombings indicated the Overseers were closing in on his plans. He pulled out his qubit and flipped open the cover.

"Athena, contact Arian."

"Right away, sir."

After a few seconds, he heard Arian's voice.

"What do you need now?" He sounded perturbed, and a bit tired.

"Come to the Devonshire on week's end."

"Why?"

"Because, you were kind enough to help me out today, and I want to repay you. I have four tickets to the Gliders game. As one of the most senior professors in the Institute, you aren't going to get better seats unless you go with a consulate. I assume you're a Patolli fan."

"Hell yeah, I'm a Patolli fan!"

"Good. Come to the game with me. It will be fun. Bring a date."

Arian thought for a moment. While Professor Brightmore would not have been his first choice to attend a game with, free tickets were free tickets.

"Alright," he replied. "I'm in. I will meet you at the Devonshire at noon."

As Arian ended the transmission, Ansley continued toward his destination. He assumed he would see Anabelle at her familiar perch at the end of the bar.

"I guess I need a date," he thought to himself. "Damn."

# Chapter Twelve
## The Capitol City Gliders

The rest of the week passed quickly for Arian, a blur of research, meetings, and data. His students were advancing in their projects and a young professor could ask for nothing more. Still, he and Conway were no closer to explaining how they had achieved their strange results. He set Matthew on the task of recreating the experiments in hopes the reproducibility would give him further confirmation. As the week came to an end, the issue was no more tractable, though he solved the riddle of finding a date for the game. In his imagination, Kaiya was on his arm, but this was not feasible, not only because he had no clue how to contact her, but also because she was Natural Born. He considered bringing a graduate student, but that wouldn't reflect well on him. In the end, he decided upon a colleague and friend, Dr. Alexandra De Rosia. She was attractive and smart, but being raised together in the Institute from the time they were young children, she could never be a romantic interest for him.

Since their offices were adjacent to one another, they met there, deciding to take a public transport to the southern district. Alexandra chattered the entire way and it was evident that she was excited at the idea of attending a Patolli match with Professor Brightmore. Arian found this amusing. If she only knew what the Institute believed of the man, she would not be so impressed.

They arrived at the bar and Arian held the door for her as a gentleman should. Entering the dimly lit pub, Ansley, who was already standing at the bar beside a woman he had never before seen, spotted him.

"Over here, Arian!" he shouted, motioning to the stools beside him. "And who is your breathtaking friend?" The woman to Ansley's right looked back toward Alexandra, annoyance evident on her face, before giving him a punch in the arm.

"Professor Brightmore," Arian replied, "this is my good friend and colleague, Dr. Alexandra De Rosia."

Alexandra extended her hand to Ansley, saying, "Professor, it is a great honor to meet you. Please call me Alex."

"A lovely name to be sure. And you may call me Ansley."

A brief awkward moment passed between them, as Arian and Alex looked at Ansley, waiting for him to introduce his date. When he didn't, Arian took the initiative.

"And who might your friend be?"

"I'm sorry," Ansley answered, "where are my manners?" He turned to Eduardo and ordered four pints of Capitol City Ale and four shots. Turning back, he added, "And this is my friend Anabelle Marie Aster."

Looking her over, Arian noted that she had a distinctive look. She wasn't quite beautiful, although her face was pretty. She seemed to possess a fierce independence and spirit, indicated by her unruly brown hair and the large, white and black leopard print bag hanging from her shoulder. When she looked back at Arian, wildness evident in her eyes, she made him uncomfortable.

"Aster?" asked Alex. "Are you part of the Aster family?"

"I am," answered Anabelle, pleased. "My father is Consulate John J. Aster, former chair of Nanosoft."

"Oh my!" replied Alex, clearly impressed. Her voice seemed to raise an entire octave as she continued speaking. "I had no idea we would be hanging out with an Aster today. I have to tell you. I love your bag, so cute."

"Well they seem to be hitting it off," Ansley said turning to Arian, bored by the exchange. "So, have you had any luck with your research problem?" he asked, handing Arian one of the ales.

Arian's face faded to white. He shot a nervous glance toward Eduardo who was listening intently. Was the Professor unaware that the bartender was working with Kaiya?

"I have had little success," he muttered.

"Relax, Arian. We're amongst friends, right Eddie?"

"I like to consider myself your friend," Eduardo answered in his accented voice. He glared at Arian. It was a warning. The large Natural Born man made him ill at ease.

"See…we are all friends. Eddie, can you grab us a few of your favorite tapas to munch on before the game? We have to let this alcohol settle on something." Eduardo nodded and hurried away to the kitchen. "Anyway, I think I can help shed some light on your little problem. I think I can help shed some light on a lot of things."

"How could you?" Arian asked in disbelief.

"Well, that is a conversation for another day. Shall we take these shots, ladies?"

Anabelle was in the middle of explaining her new line of handbags to Alex, and both ignored him.

"Ladies," Ansley said, even louder. "Shots?"

"Oh, hell yeah," Anabelle responded in a cheery voice. "To Ansley, for giving us these awesome tickets!" she said, draining her shot as her companions drank their own. Then whispering to Alex, she added, "My father's box would have been a much better choice, but he despises Ansley. Perhaps that's why I like him. You know they are the same age."

Introductions and niceties aside, the next two hours were filled with small talk, drinking, and eating. The girls talked of fashion and dome gossip as all upper echelon Nephite women did, while Arian and Ansley traded statistics and analyzed the upcoming match. It was going to be a good one, with the visiting top ranked Pathos Pirates coming in to challenge the Capitol City Gliders. With the bill, Ansley ordered four last shots before they headed to the game. As Eduardo placed the bill on the bar, Ansley and Arian placed their hands upon it simultaneously.

"You've been a good sport, kid. Let me get this one," said Ansley. Arian removed his hand and nodded in acceptance. Ansley raised his glass in another toast. "To Arian. This kid has real talent. He can go far, and I expect he will." They all drained their glasses. He put his hand on Arian's shoulder and added in a whisper, "If you manage to avoid the vultures." Arian looked back into his eyes and saw there was no hint of humor. "Eddie….put it on my tab."

"Don't close that yet, Eddie," an unfamiliar voice came from behind.

Confused, Ansley turned and found a tall, good-looking man standing behind him, wearing an oversized sombrero that had clearly been pulled from a wall decoration. The old Professor stared at the man, unable to respond. The man looked down at him, a hint of amusement mixed with arrogance on his face.

"Relax. My name is Jackson Price. My friends and I are fixing to go on a pretty big journey. I figured a rich guy like you wouldn't mind buying us a round of going away shots." The good-looking man chuckled and winked at the girls. Ansley stuttered, feeling self-conscious and trying to find the words to respond before Anabelle saved him the trouble.

"Oh come on Ansley, you cheap-ass," she chimed in. "If you aren't going to buy this gorgeous man a round of shots then I will." She eyed Jackson, looking him up and down.

Having no choice, Ansley told Eduardo to add the extra shots to his tab. The charismatic stranger grabbed them with a wink before returning to his table without a word of gratitude. As he walked away, he slapped Arian on the butt, not troubling to look back at the bewildered young professor. The bill being paid, Ansley grumpily turned to his companions.

"Let's go."

As they stood to leave, Alex rushed over to Arian, grabbing him around the waist. "I can't believe we're going to a game with Anabelle Aster," she squealed. "Did you know she runs the CC boutique a few blocks from here? Anabelle says she is going to bring me there and give me a makeover. I'm so glad you brought me," Alex added, nuzzling closer. Arian didn't know how to react to this affection, but it made him feel strange. Exiting the bar onto the cobbled street, he noticed Anabelle wrap her arms around Ansley's left arm, rising on her toes to give him a kiss on the cheek though he quickly jerked away. She seemed undisturbed by the lack of reciprocity. At least Arian wasn't the only one on a date with a woman in which he had no interest.

They headed toward the South Tower, already buzzed. It was a pleasant day, as all were within the climate-controlled dome, made even more so by the lack of clouds in the sky outside and the bright yellow sunlight streaming through. They walked together, laughing and joking with one another as if they were old friends. Ansley was amused that alcohol had a way of cementing friendships quickly. Coming upon the avenue that led to the South Tower, they joined a large influx of fellow Nephites heading toward the stadium.

A green space comprised the courtyard of the expansive tower, flanked by monuments to the men who contributed to the creation of Arameus. Each tower had its own monuments, highlighting the great men of the Empire, the largest belonging to the Overseers. The South Tower honored Paulo Dominiccio. His likeness was in a marble columned temple with no walls, his statue seated on a throne overlooking the green, the griffin of his family crest carved into the palisade.

"The monument to my father is at the West Tower," Anabelle explained to Alex, who despite having taken field trips to the monuments as a school girl, still seemed impressed. "Of course, our crest is the wolf. I think that is much more striking than a griffin," she continued.

"My monument is in the lobby of the fucking Institute," Ansley replied sourly, to no one in particular. "In my younger days, monuments were for the dead."

"Yeah, but your monument is surrounded by twenty other scientists, and most of them are dead!" responded Anabelle, eliciting a laugh from both Alex and Arian.

They walked on, toward the escalators that brought people from the green into the stadium built below the tower. It was one of the great engineering marvels of all the existing domes. The ground floor of the tower had a clear floor that provided a glimpse into the 90,000-seat Patolli stadium below. Initially constructed as a shelter that could harbor most of the city's important citizens in a time of crisis, as the dome's security increased and violence outside subsided, it was converted into the greatest stadium in all of the domed cities. It had been a strong political move, showing their strength and confidence.

Ansley stopped as they neared the descending escalator. "We should smoke. You can't smoke in the stadium."

"Yuck," said Alex. "I think smoking is disgusting."

"I'll take one," said Anabelle.

"Me too," said Arian.

"You are out-voted my dear," replied Ansley, "but you are correct. It is disgusting."

Finishing their cigarettes, they stepped onto the escalator, crowding into the mass of elite citizens, most garbed in the red and gold of the Capitol City Gliders, with a few of the more well-to-do citizens from Pathos, who had made the trip, garbed in purple. Descending under the clear floor of the tower, they entered the expansive vault below. From the escalator, they walked into the lobby of the stadium's top floor and were ushered into lines to have their tickets checked. Bypassing the masses, Ansley guided them to the VIP check-in, where a scan of his qubit gained entry for all four. Alex turned to Arian as they passed through the arched entryway to the stadium, her eyes wide.

"I can't believe we just got to skip the line like that," she exclaimed. "I've never been to a Patolli match. You have to help me with the rules." Arian seemed disheartened by the prospect, but Anabelle, overhearing her, jumped in before he could respond.

"Oh, honey, it isn't about the game, it's about the tasty men."

When they walked through the archway, the stadium came into full view. They were standing on a platform at the very top, with the lights that illuminated the field just below them. Half of the lights were lit with a bright red glow, while the lights across the field displayed the purple of the Pathos Pirates. Ten stories below, in the center of the bowl, the beautiful green of the turf field spread out before them.

"This way," motioned Ansley, leading them to an elevator that would take them to his box at the third lowest level of the bowl, eight stories down.

Ansley pressed the number 2 on the elevator, electing to take them first to the bar area outside of the suites. He needed a few more drinks before going to his box. His companions readily agreed to this, particularly Alex, who seemed excited by the prospect of meeting other famous people. Arian couldn't blame her. Despite his cool outward appearance, he was excited as well.

Whispering into Alex's ear, he said, "This is pretty damn awesome, huh?"

"Yes!" she squealed.

As the doors to the elevator opened, Ansley turned to them all and asked, "Ready to meet the assholes?" Anabelle laughed the loudest.

They entered an elegant room, the centerpiece being an

ornately carved rectangular bar, lit up in red. The lighting was much more subtle than in the general stadium seating, and the patrons around it were dressed in evening attire. Interspersed throughout the room, the consulates were identifiable by their white robes. Soft music set a calmer mood than the apprehensive cacophony of voices in the stadium. They walked to the bar and Ansley ordered two glasses of Claremont Whiskey on the rocks for him and Arian, and two glasses of Sagittarian wine for the ladies. Even he was influenced by the pomp of his surroundings. As they sipped their spirits, the girls and Arian scanned the room.

"Oh my!" exclaimed Alex. "Is that Henri Gerard?"

Ansley looked over and saw the famed film director holding court before a group of six admirers.

"You don't know, Henri?" Anabelle asked, feigning shock. "Well, come on girl, I will introduce you."

"Are you serious?"

"Of course…Henri and I had quite the affair after University."

Anabelle grabbed her hand, rushing off, leaving Arian and Ansley no other alternative than to follow. As they walked, Arian grabbed Ansley aside.

"You and Anabelle Aster?" he asked, puzzled.

"Long story," responded Ansley.

"Hey, I'm not judging. Good for you. You landed a famous socialite."

"I'm not 'with' Anabelle," Ansley snapped, stalking off toward the women. They found them conversing with Henri, his former group of admirers annoyed by the intrusion. Anabelle was rambling on about some trip they had taken in the past together, as Henri smiled in faux politeness. Turning toward Alex, he seemed to notice her for the first time.

"I would hate to interrupt our fond recollections, my dear Aster," he interjected, "but you have not introduced me to your lovely friend."

"Oh," responded Anabelle, with a hint of

embarrassment, "this is my new friend Alex. I'm sorry, I mean, Dr. Alexandra De Rosia."

"Dr. De Rosia, the pleasure is all mine. Tell me, my dear, are you descended from the De Rosia clan of the Terragona region? You have their elegant look about you and high cheek bones."

Blushing, Alex was unable to contain a giggle as she answered him.

"I am a distant cousin. I can trace my lineage to theirs, although I have never met them."

"Of course, my dear, of course. It is a shame you never considered acting. I could have made you a star."

Listening to the conversation, Arian felt a tinge of jealousy. He harbored no feelings for Alex, and perhaps it was just wounded pride at how quickly she had jumped at this famous man. Surveying Henri, Arian found him to be a short, large nosed man with a prominent brow that made him appear ape-like. In his arrogance there was a certain charm that Arian could not deny.

Anabelle, however, had turned her attentions back to Ansley who was paying her no more mind than he had before. Arian joined them, still not understanding his feelings about the encounter. Ansley gave him a knowing pat on the shoulder, but said nothing, motioning to his empty glass. In unspoken agreement, the three of them headed back to the bar, leaving Alex with Henri. The bar was filling up and they found a line for drinks when they arrived. They waited in silence, Arian annoyed at Alex leaving him, Anabelle annoyed at Henri's indifference to her, and Ansley annoyed at everyone in the room due to his lack of alcohol. When their turn arrived, it was Anabelle who took the lead.

"I'm finished with wine boys. Let's do shots," she announced, ordering three double shots of a strong anise-flavored liqueur. She shot hers immediately and kissed Ansley on the mouth before turning to kiss Arian affectionately on the cheek. The two men exchanged confused glances before

Arian shrugged his shoulders, as if to deny culpability. Ansley laughed, scooping up his own glass and toasting to the Gliders as he and Arian clinked drinks and downed the dark liquid.

"It looks like I have two dates now," she continued, a wild rasp creeping into her voice.

"Three more doubles," Arian exclaimed in response. Upon receiving them, he raised his own glass, "To Anabelle's two dates!" They all laughed as they again drained the dark contents. They were becoming drunk. Now it was Ansley's turn.

"Three double Claremont Whiskeys on the rocks!" he said, looking back at the line of annoyed customers who were still waiting for them to move. "We will have a drink for you guys," he said to the crowd.

Grabbing their drinks and turning, Ansley bumped into a robed patron, spilling part of the man's drink on his arm.

"Excuse me, sir, I apologize profusely," said the old Professor.

Looking up, he was confronted by the bronzed face and long white hair of Tiberius Septus and he immediately regretted the apology. The consulate was standing with a petite, yet elegant woman.

"I see you are in un-rare form," boomed the deep, polished voice of Tiberius, "drunk as usual. I haven't seen you here in some time. I expected you would retire to a life of solitude without your beloved casino."

"Ah, Tiberius, but I seem to recall that you were a regular there as well. It appears you and the casino had some sort of falling out," answered Ansley, accusation evident in his voice. "But I digress," he continued more composed. "I would be rude not to introduce you to my colleague. This is Dr. Ari..." his voice trailed off as he turned to Arian and saw that his face had gone white and he was staring slack-jawed at the woman with Tiberius.

"This is Assistant Professor Arian Cyannah," Tiberius continued Ansley's words, though directed at Arian himself. "I have followed your career closely, my dear boy. I knew your father Richard before his unfortunate demise. The Institute seems to believe you have a bright future." Turning to Ansley, he added, "The Institute engineered a perfect match between your mother and father."

Arian stumbled over a greeting and shook hands with Tiberius, his gaze never leaving the woman by his side.

"Thank you, Consulate. I am honored by your kind words," he managed to say.

"Of course my boy, of course, and Anabelle Aster," Tiberius continued, a smug smile on his face. "Is your distinguished father aware of the company you are keeping these days? I would hate to inform him you are still behaving inappropriately for one of your stock." Anabelle didn't answer him, choosing to look at the floor red-faced.

"Well, Tiberius," Ansley replied for her, "you seem to know all of us, but I have not had the pleasure of meeting your lovely companion."

"And you will not, Brightmore. Who are you to presume an introduction from me?"

"I am Kaiya," his companion responded in a quiet, yet defiant voice. "It is a pleasure to meet you, Professor Brightmore. I have heard much of your accomplishments, although I am afraid I am not schooled in the sciences to have a proper appreciation for them." She turned to Arian. "It is nice to make your acquaintance as well, Dr. Cyannah. If what Tiberius says is true, you should be very proud."

Arian took her hand, giving it a half-hearted shake. He felt deflated and overwhelmed by this unexpected meeting and the presence of the consulate. Tiberius cut them all off.

"We have all been well met, it seems. Kaiya, let's head to our suite. I'm sure Brightmore needs to get upstairs to his box for the game."

"Actually, Tiberius, my name is Professor Brightmore. I believe I have earned that title."

"And you will address me as Consulate Septus,"

responded Tiberius with indignation.

"A well-earned title, I'm sure," answered Ansley. Turning to his downtrodden companions, he added, "Would you guys like to go to the locker rooms before the game? I know a few of the players and am always welcome." Anabelle perked up, forgetting the previous insult.

"I would love to go to the locker rooms. So many exquisite Natural Born men," she said looking at both Ansley and Arian.

"I'm afraid it is we who must be taking leave of you, Consulate," Ansley said, looking Tiberius in the eye as if challenging him.

"Of course," Tiberius replied, his tone cordial. "I know you enjoy your time among the Natural Born." Kaiya gave Tiberius a harsh look that didn't escape Ansley, as they took their leave. The bar was emptying as the beginning of the match approached.

"I told you guys," Ansley smiled, "everyone is an asshole down here. Let's go to our seats. We can go to the locker room another time. I don't want to miss the beginning of the game."

Disappointed, Anabelle followed him to the elevator while a still dejected Arian shuffled behind. The opening ceremonies were coming to an end as they entered the box. The crowd was noisy, buzzing in anticipation of the upcoming game between two top-ranked Patolli teams. The colors and pageantry seemed to re-invigorate both Anabelle and Ansley.

When they were seated, Anabelle turned to Arian with the type of concern only a woman can give.

"Are you upset about Alex? Cheer up. She wasn't that great, and Henri pulls that stuff with everyone." She placed her hand on Arian's thigh, looking into his eyes.

"She's right, kid. Cheer up. We're at the Pathos-Capitol City game!" Squatting beside Arian, Ansley put his arm around him and added, "Hey, did you place your bet yet?"

"I don't gamble," replied Arian.

"Oh, have a little fun. The spread is Capitol City by 3.5. It's a lock. I know my Gliders. Bet it!"

Reluctantly, Arian pulled out his qubit, thinking it over. What did he have to lose? He was already having a miserable day.

"Should I bet fifty credits?" he asked.

"You should if you aren't a man. I bet two thousand credits," Ansley responded.

"Fine, two thousand credits," Arian muttered, still depressed. As he placed his bet, he considered Ansley before secretly changing his bet to Pathos. He had seen enough of the old Professor to know better than to trust his betting instincts. "Alright, my first ever bet is in."

"Oh, hell yeah!" Ansley exclaimed. "I might make a man of you yet." He turned to the box attendant. "Three ales, please. My friends and I are going to party!"

The entire stadium went dark other than the dimmed lights within the boxes themselves. Spotlights illuminated large gates at opposite ends of the field. A pyrotechnic explosion erupted beside the gates as they were thrust open and the players for each team flew toward midfield on gliders. Heavily armored, the participants appeared more ready for battle than for a sporting event. The crowd cheered as the starting nine from each team met at midfield, while the reserves glided down to field level on either side, joining their coaches who were seated on the benches. At centerfield a pedestal rose 20 feet in the air to the same plane the starting players occupied. Resting on the top was the game ball, a prolate spheroid known as a Patolli. Forming a box like perimeter around the center circle, four additional pedestals rose from the field to a height of 10 feet on which rested the spherical dodgers. The lead official was at the center of the field, giving the captain of each team a few pre-game warnings. The energy of the crowd was tangible, and Ansley wanted to explode with excitement.

"I don't understand Patolli, Ansley," Anabelle said in a child-like whine. "Explain it to me."

"Are you kidding me?" demanded an incredulous Ansley. "You've been here a thousand times. You were raised in that luxury suite below."

"I know. But I never really watched the game. It was always about the men and the celebrities and the parties in the suite. Your box is cute, but I don't see any celebrities or men or parties."

Arian chuckled aloud at this, prompting Ansley to blush.

"I knew you should have invited Henri to sit with us, Ansley," Arian said. "Now Anabelle will have no one to entertain her."

He and Ansley both laughed at this, and Anabelle looked away annoyed.

"Fine," Ansley relented. "What do you need to know?"

"Well…" she chirped happily, "I just need you to explain what they are doing during the game. I know they need to get that silver ball in the center to the end zone. I get that." She crinkled her nose as she tried to think. Ansley found this to be irresistible.

"And I understand that the other guys throw those dodgers at each other to eliminate the guys from the other team. That's it."

"A good start," Arian condescended. He was in no mood to hear her annoying questions. She stuck her tongue out at him. It might be the booze, but Ansley was finding her to be quite adorable.

"Let's just watch the game," said Ansley, ignoring Arian. He leaned in to reassure her. "When you don't understand something, just ask." She rubbed her head against his.

The crowd was now silent in anticipation as the lead official blew his whistle signaling the start of the contest. The Patolli was launched in the air by cannon within the pedestal, which lowered back to its spot below the field. As the ball shot up, the four pedestals holding the dodgers also retreated slowly into the ground. The players launched into action. Four men from each side, the forwards, angled their gliders upward in pursuit of the Patolli, while another four from each side raced downward in pursuit of the descending dodgers. The remaining player on each team retreated backward toward their respective end zones. It would be their task to defend the goal.

As was typical, the Pathos enforcers charged at the two dodgers closest to them. Three of the four enforcers for Capitol City mimicked this on their side. However, Jabari Stoudamyre, the star enforcer for the gliders, headed straight past the dodgers to those sought by the Pathos players. Just as a Pathos enforcer was about to grab a dodger, the dark-skinned, well-muscled Jabari slammed into him at full speed, knocking him from his glider and sending him hurtling to the grass field ten feet below, where he lay motionless for a few seconds before standing and carrying his glider to the sideline. Jabari circled back to the black leather dodger, scooping it in his left hand and firing it at the next nearest Pathos enforcer, its golden seams sparkling in the stadium lights. The dodger struck the defender square in the chest, sending him to join his teammate on the sideline. Jabari followed the trajectory of the dodger and scooped it from the ground almost as soon as it landed on the field.

Ten feet above, on another plane of action, Kadeem Hardison, lead forward for Capitol City, had obtained the Patolli, and was gliding from side to side, searching for an open teammate to pass the ball. Ansley jumped up and down in the box. He grabbed Arian by the shoulder, shaking him violently.

"Ten seconds in and they are already down two players! Nine players to seven, I like our odds to score!"

"I don't understand," said Anabelle. "Why did the one guy have to leave the field? He wasn't hit with a dodger."

"Yeah, but he got knocked off his glider," responded Ansley without taking his eyes off of the action. "He has to sit until possession changes."

"Okay," Anabelle said unconvinced.

The enforcers joined the main action on the plane twenty feet above the field. Kadeem was now gliding backwards toward his own goal in an attempt to avoid an oncoming Pathos defender. Finding an opening, he launched a perfect spiral seventeen yards ahead to an open Kenyon Dieng who arched his torso as he made the catch, narrowly avoiding a well-aimed dodger. His forward progress halted at the 33-yard line in Pathos territory as he searched for a way to advance the ball. A beam of light shot from one side of the field to the other, marking the newly formed line of scrimmage for the crowd. Two Pathos players converged on Kenyon, who flipped the ball five yards back to Kadeem who was charging forward, following the action. Just as the ball left his hands, a dodger caught him square in the back, knocking him from his glider and sending him crashing to the ground twenty feet below. Ansley was close enough to hear the audible snapping of the bone, as Kenyon's leg fractured. Medics rushed to the field, carrying him to the sideline, as the play above continued.

"Fuck!" screamed Ansley and Arian in unison, drawing looks from fans in adjoining boxes. The Pathos contingent roared with approval at the injury. Kadeem again halted as a new line of scrimmage formed at the 38-yard line.

"I don't understand. Why are they going backward?" asked Anabelle.

"There was no way to advance the ball," answered Ansley. "He was going to get knocked off his glider."

"There was only one guy in front of him," she responded. "Why didn't he try to beat him and score?"

"You can't be serious!" Arian interjected. "You can only advance the ball in the air. How can you not know that?"

"C'mon, Arian, give her a break. She is busy being cute."

Anabelle gave Ansley a half smile, mischief in her eyes. Ansley winked and finished his ale.

"Drink up friends! We're at a Patolli match!" He

ordered three more, indifferent to whether his companions needed one or not.

On the field, the frenzied play continued. A Pathos defender flew toward Kadeem, attempting to knock him from his glider but was intercepted by a dodger-less Jabari. The impact knocked both to the ground, and they landed with a thud a few feet apart. Cursing, Jabari and his opponent headed to their respective benches. Just as he was climbing over the wall, Jabari looked up to see Kadeem connect with Peyton Rodrigo in the end zone for an amazing score. The crowd exploded as fireworks went off at the top of the stadium. The seven Capitol City players still on gliders flew toward the end zone to celebrate

"1-0," shouted Ansley at Arian. "We're on our way to covering the spread."

Arian had never seen Ansley so happy. It was a welcome change from the sour man he was used to dealing with. This was an Ansley he was growing to like. The excitement was short-lived, however, as all nine players returned to the field for the change of possession, minus Kenyon, who was replaced by a second string forward. Pathos managed to score just as fast, and on the ensuing Capitol City possession, Kadeem was knocked from his glider with the Patolli, leading to a turnover. Within minutes, Pathos took the lead, 2-1.

As the first half expired, Pathos had a comfortable 9-6 lead and Ansley sat in the box with a dejected look on his face, his apparent zest for life wavering. An all-female acrobat team came onto the field to perform during the intermission.

"I don't want to watch these little girls flip around," stated Anabelle in a high-minded voice. "I'm going back to the bar."

When neither Ansley nor Arian made a move to follow or acknowledge her plan, she stood and exited the box, muttering something about finding Alex to liven up the game. Ansley and Arian sat together in silence for a few moments, soaking in the sights and sounds of the halftime show and sipping their drinks. Finally, Ansley stood and lit a cigarette, offering one to Arian.

"We can't smoke in here," said Arian, bewildered.

"Whatever. I'm Ansley Brightmore. What are they going to do?"

Still apprehensive but wanting to smoke, Arian took the cigarette and stood with his companion. Looking down at the suite level below, Ansley spotted Henri in a box in front of Tiberius' suite, whispering something in a woman's ear.

"I don't think Anabelle will have any luck finding Alex."

"Why?" asked Arian, his lack of concern evident.

"Because she is right there with our director friend," Ansley replied pointing below.

"So she is."

They watched in silence as Tiberius and his young companion Kaiya returned to the box from the accompanying suite. Turning to speak to Arian, Ansley saw his brow furrow and darkness pass over his face. Not knowing what to say, Ansley contemplated him for a moment.

"You really have a thing for Alex, don't you, kid?"

"I don't give a fuck about Alex."

Arian was feeling drunk at this point, and his inhibitions were diminishing by the minute. Ansley studied him, remembering the interaction with Tiberius before the game.

"Do you know that woman with Tiberius?"

"Of course not. How could I?" Arian responded with too much force.

"I see. Be careful about people in the suites below us, especially those who associate with Tiberius Septus. He is a powerful and dangerous man. No one who would choose to befriend him should be trusted under any circumstance. So I ask you again, are you in contact with any of those you know to be associates of Tiberius?"

"No!" exclaimed Arian. "You're the great Professor Brightmore. I run in humbler circles by far."

"Alright, alright, I believe you. That woman with Tiberius is beautiful, though. If I were a younger man, I would love to know her. Have you seen her around Capitol City or the Institute?"

"No," Arian responded.

"I didn't think so. You can recognize a Nephite from the tract marks in the arm from the nano-treatments. She has the marks, though they are subtle, too subtle to have received a lifetime of treatments. Also, did you notice the freckles on her nose? I'm sure you did. They indicate someone who has lived outside of the dome and has been exposed to the rays of the yellow day sun when not protected by our polymer. I picked up a slight accent from her as well. She hides it, but I expect that she comes from somewhere in the vicinity of Sikyon."

"You presume a lot," Arian said uneasily.

"I perceive a lot. There is a difference, you know." Ansley placed his hand on Arian's shoulder in a paternal gesture. "Relax, kid. This world we live in doesn't make a lot of sense. We live in a sterile environment that emphasizes perfection and achievement while minimizing emotions such as love, grief, and sadness. I find it ironic that we use the term 'natural' to describe the citizens our society suppresses. In my experience, succumbing to the innate emotions that make us vulnerable produces supernatural results. You may live a thousand 'natural' lifetimes, kid, but if you never allow yourself to love and sacrifice for that which you choose to love, then you may as well have never lived at all."

Arian nodded, his gaze never leaving Kaiya. Ansley continued his reflections. Arian was unsure whether the old Professor was speaking to him or himself.

"Trust me, kid. I've lived longer than any man of my generation should have, and when you get to my age, you occupy a world of regret, a world of loss. I had my chance at love, and that was stolen from me… stolen by this perfect world you now are finding your place in. I can never, ever, no matter how many lifetimes I still may live, get back what I lost when your mother was murdered." Ansley slammed his glass on the counter at the front of the box, shattering it, its cool contents mixing with the crimson blood now dripping from his hands. "When Padma was murdered... I find it difficult still, after all these years to speak her name. I would trade it all for ten more years with her. I apologize for speaking so bluntly about your mother, but as you are well aware, she was more of a friend to me than a mother to you. What I'm getting at is that no matter how long your life may seem to you, opportunities to find love like that remain fleeting. They remain once in a lifetime, to be cliché. If you think you can find that, then don't let it pass you. You don't want to live as an immortal with an eternity of regret."

Arian looked at Ansley, feeling as if he should say something, affected by the stirring words. He began to respond but was interrupted by Anabelle's return.

"I hope you boys didn't miss me too much. You will never believe who I ran into!"

Ansley looked at Arian, rolled his eyes, and turned to Anabelle, laughing. "And who did you meet, my dear?" he asked, taking her into his arms. As he pulled away, Anabelle noticed the blood dripping from his hand.

"Oh my, baby, what happened to your hand?" she asked, bewildered.

"Don't worry about it, beautiful, it's nothing," Ansley responded.

"Do you want me to kiss it?" she asked, sweetly.

"Kiss it here," said Ansley, pointing to his cheek. The wetness of her kiss felt nice on his skin, and he allowed the feeling to linger. "So who did you meet, you beautiful, beautiful girl?"

"Oh, you will never believe it," she responded excitedly, concern for his hand all but gone. "I met Angelese Gracie, the famous opera singer. She was sooooo pretty.

Actually, I didn't really like her outfit, but that can be fixed. I gave her my card. She is coming into the boutique for a fitting. And you will never believe who she was meeting."

"Who?" Arian asked impatiently.

"You'll be happy to know she was going to meet our friend, Henri Gerard. I expect Alex will be back with us soon."

She crinkled her nose, happy about the good news she was delivering. Arian seemed unimpressed, not the reaction expected by Anabelle, who lost a bit of her fervor. Fireworks erupted again from the end zones and the players at last flew back onto the field.

"The second half is starting!" Ansley exclaimed. "We are a second half team," he announced, grabbing Arian on the shoulder roughly. "We will win our bet yet!"

Looking at the monitor in the box and studying the first half statistics, Arian was unconvinced, though gladly, since he had bet against Capitol City.

"I don't know Ansley," he began, "Pathos outgained us by two hundred yards in the first half. It would seem they have a decided advantage."

"Ah, that's nothing kid. When you have watched as much Patolli as I have, you know that it is a second half game. The team that makes the best adjustments comes out on top. You would do well to learn that. The same thing holds true in life."

As the second half began, it seemed as if Ansley's prediction would prove to be true. An early interception by Jabari led to a quick score for Capitol City. They followed this up with a massive body check from Mao Lin to Pathos' lead forward, Patrick Pitt. The hit sent Pitt off his glider to the ground, eliminating him from the possession and setting up a twenty-five yard scoring pass from Kadeem Hardison, cutting the lead to one point at 9-8.

Unfortunately for the Capitol City fans, and Ansley in particular, that was the last score for the gliders. Kadeem was taken out by a dodger to the back that led to a concussion upon hitting the ground below, and even Jabari Stoudamyre was forced to exit the game with a sprained knee. When the final whistle sounded, the Pathos Pirates were awarded a comfortable and well-deserved 19-8 victory. The match had not even been close.

"Oh well," said Ansley, his speech slurred from drink, "you win some, you lose some. I'm sorry I convinced you to bet, kid. You should never go with me on any bet. I'm bad luck."

"It's okay," Arian lied. "I will gladly lose if I get to have fun like this."

They stumbled toward the entrance of the box. Ansley put his arm around Anabelle, who looked up at him smiling.

"You are being a little sweetheart tonight, Ansley. What has gotten into you?" she asked.

"My darling, you become more beautiful with every drink."

She slapped him playfully. Arian shook his head, amazed at the transformative properties of alcohol. They exited the stadium, a mass of people moving like cattle, ushered between the bottlenecks defined by the narrow doors. Once again on the great lawn, surrounded by monuments to the past, the fresh air made them all the more drunk. Ansley removed his arm from Anabelle and placed it on Arian's shoulder.

"I had a blast with you today, and look, your young lady has returned."

Not knowing what he was referring to, Arian looked up, expecting Kaiya. He was disappointed when confronted by Alex.

"There you are! You will not believe the time I've had. I was in the box with Tiberius Septus. What an incredible host. He asked a lot of questions about you guys too! Henri took such good care of me. He gave me his card. He said he is going to get me in for a preliminary shoot to see if I work well with the camera. Angelese Gracie interrupted us. Can you believe that? I told her I knew you, Anabelle, and she wants me at the fitting as well. This has been the best day!"

Arian looked at Ansley, who seemed to have tuned out the shrill female. He found Anabelle's gaze and they both burst out in laughter. It had been a ridiculous day, and Arian was ready to go home. He had more money than he had begun the day with, but less pride.

"Let's go, Alex. I need to be in the lab tomorrow."

"Of course," she responded.

"Then I guess we should take our leave of you," Arian said to Ansley and Anabelle. "I really appreciate the gesture, Ansley. I had a wonderful time."

"Anytime, kid." Ansley placed his arm around Anabelle's waist, pulling her closer.

"Mm…I like this new you," she said, leaning her head into his chest.

"Let's go back to my place tonight. I don't want to be alone."

"I thought you would never ask," Anabelle answered. "I've missed you."

As they walked off, arm in arm, Ansley stopped and turned back.

"Arian come here for a sec," he yelled.

Arian and Alex reluctantly turned, walking halfway to meet him. Ansley pulled a cigarette pack from his pocket and opened it.

"I have two left. I thought you might be able to use one as much as me." Handing Arian one of the cigarettes, he lit them both.

"That's such a gross habit," Alex said.

"Shut up," Arian snapped.

As Ansley turned to walk away, he stopped short again.

"One more thing, kid," he said, pulling an object from his pocket and flipping it between his fingers. "I believe I owe you this."

He tossed the item to Arian. Examining the burned object between his fingers, he realized it was a flash drive.

"Maybe you can gain more knowledge from it than I could," Ansley said, as he turned away with Anabelle, disappearing into the crowd.

# Chapter Thirteen
# The Flash Drive

The first thing Arian noticed the following morning was that he was alone in his bed. This was a welcome realization as he recalled Alex's advances the previous evening. He would have hated to make an alcohol-influenced mistake with someone he had known for so long and for whom he held the deepest respect. Still, he thought, it could have been nice. Shaking off these thoughts, driven by fatigue and the leftover impurities, he rolled over and grabbed the bottle of Revive he had placed on his nightstand. He opened it, tossed his head back, and allowed the sugary, fortified liquid to wash down his throat.

The stimulant's effects were instantaneous, and his mind cleared. Suddenly frantic, he searched the pockets on the clothes he had failed to remove the night before. It wasn't there. Had he imagined it? He jumped from his bed, searching the sheets and carpeted floor for the object. Had Ansley really given him the flash drive? It all seemed so muddled now, even with the Revive. Rushing from his bedroom and down the spiral staircase to the atrium, his eyes found the desired object.

He hadn't imagined it. There it was, sitting on the glass table in the center of the room.

He picked up the drive and contemplated it. Things had seemed so easy when he was plotting with Kaiya before, hoping to take down a possible terrorist, a member of the Centauri. It was different now. This was Ansley, his friend and his mother's closest confidante. How could a man who rushed into the fire at the casino to save a hostess be the enemy? He had been kind to Arian, and those Ansley despised displayed a level of arrogance that Arian himself disliked. And above all, Ansley had been honest with him. That much could not be said for Kaiya. He had been operating under the misconception that he was working for the Institute to investigate a possible terrorist in their midst. This had been agreeable to Arian, as he had hoped it would advance his career. However, meeting Kaiya with Tiberius Septus had destroyed what little trust he had for her.

His feelings of betrayal were two-fold. For one, he was not working for the Institute, but for a far more powerful employer, and that thought alone scared him. Second, and more important, he felt embarrassed. He had been captivated by Kaiya and thought about her constantly, but the chance meeting at the Patolli match had showed him how much he mattered. She was with Tiberius Septus and any thoughts Arian had entertained about the two of them must be forgotten. The Professor had chosen to hand over his flash drive, but why should Arian turn it over to Kaiya? They were trying to destroy his new friend. Could he turn the drive over to such a deceitful woman and possibly implicate the old Professor? There was much to think about.

At the lab, Arian was bombarded with student inquiries. Matthew Conway's meeting request stood out the most, as he was interested to see his student's progress over the weekend. Looking down at the console, he saw that the lab was filled with markers tracking his graduate students. Touching the marker representing Conway, the lab map disappeared and was replaced by his student's personal information. Touching the

"Call" button, he heard Matthew's voice almost instantly.

"Yes, professor?"

"I understand you wanted to speak with me," began Arian. "You have results?"

"Yes, professor, I do, although I don't yet understand them."

"Very good. Come to my office immediately. I am curious to see what you have found."

"Of course, professor. Right away." Within moments the young student was standing before him, placing the data on Arian's desk. Arian began flipping through the pages.

"It happened again. I was able to introduce the bio-bot that was coded with the cell's DNA sequence and network it with the nanobot monitoring disease and foreign bodies. Again, there is evidence of hundreds of auto cell deaths before we get the second-generation cell. And again, the second generation cell is…changed."

"How is it changed?" demanded Arian, barely able to contain his excitement.

"It has the extra information coded in the DNA. There seems to be new genetic material in the cell."

"But how can that be?"

"I'm not sure, professor, but there's more. This time the second generation cell continued to divide, without the hundreds of cell deaths, and all of the new cells had the same extra material coded in the DNA."

"Are the new cells continuing to carry out their metabolism normally, unaffected by the new material coded in the DNA?"

"Not exactly…"

"What do you mean?" asked Arian, perplexed.

"I connected to the nanobot remotely to run some basic diagnostics and try to figure out why the bio-bots are allowing these to live. The next generation cells are not only thriving, they are all behaving as if they have their own bio-bots and are networking back with the parent nanobot."

Arian stared at him, not knowing what to say. It wasn't often that he was scientifically dumbfounded, but there was no explanation for how new genetic material could be introduced to the cell and it continue to behave normally. He needed to come up with an experiment that would shed more light on these results.

"You've done well, Matthew. I'm proud of you," Arian said, causing Matthew to smile brightly. "Continue to monitor the experiment. I need some time to consider what you have told me. There must be something we are missing."

"Thank you, professor. I will be sure to report any further developments as they arise," Matthew said. The student exited and Arian spent the next few hours puzzling over the data. His stomach rumbled reminding him he needed to eat. A change of scenery might help invigorate his mind. Reaching in his desk, he pulled a protein bar out and headed for a nearby park, his fingers fondling the flash drive hidden in his left pocket as he walked.

"Athena, office lockdown in ten seconds." The inside of the room flashed red, counting down the seconds until the office would be sealed, and the motion sensors activated. He exited the building toward the adjacent park.

Once there, he found his familiar bench by the lake and sat, allowing himself a moment to take in the scenery. The afternoon sun shone down through the dome onto the rippling water, scattering the rays in all directions. Ducks swam and fought, dunking their heads below in search of food. Small, sculpted dogwoods dotted the horizon around the lake. He marveled at the ducks, splashing the day away, carefree, with no worry other than obtaining their next meal. He had never watched them before. He envied them in a way. He often ate lunch here alone, using the quiet to organize his thoughts, but today the park was a welcome refuge from the sterile world within the dome. It was a slice of nature hidden amongst the marbled buildings.

Arian knew he should be working, but he had no

motivation. He removed the flash drive and turned it in his fingers. It was charred from the fire that had stolen the life from Ansley's friend. The thought had a chilling effect on him. It must be important, yet he had no clue what information it could contain. As if struck by sudden inspiration, he pulled out his qubit and inserted the drive. The screen flashed the word, "Connecting". After attempting to read the files contained within, Athena informed him that the drive was too corrupted. He laughed to himself. All the scheming in the world wouldn't help Tiberius obtain the information he so desperately sought. Ansley would have known the drive was ruined.

He placed his qubit, with the flash drive still connected, onto the bench beside him and continued to ponder the lake. He was startled from his reverie as two hands shot from behind him and covered his eyes. He was about to spring up to confront the person when he heard her barely audible, high-pitched voice.

"Guess who?"

He allowed himself a few seconds to calm down before answering, his heart pounding. Her hands were soft and warm. They smelled of tangerines.

"I know who this is," he responded in a flat tone. "But I apparently know nothing about you. Tiberius Septus? A little strange considering you kissed me when we last parted. Had I known I was kissing Consulate Septus' errand girl, I wouldn't have been so eager to reciprocate." He was angry, and no Natural Born daughter of a grape farmer was going to make a fool of him.

She removed her hands and walked to the front of the bench, but Arian kept his gaze straight ahead, neglecting to glance at her.

"May I sit?" she asked, her voice proud, but there was nonetheless a hint of sadness in it.

"This is a public park," Arian responded. "You are free to sit where you like, although I was under the impression that this city was for Nephites." Even as the sentence left his lips, Arian felt embarrassed, even ashamed, although he didn't know why.

She sat next to him, folding her hands in her lap and putting her feet together in an elegant pose.

"I understand why you are angry," she said softly, looking down at her hands. "But what we are doing is sensitive. I couldn't just run up and say hello. You were with Ansley."

"And does Tiberius know?"

"Does Tiberius know what?"

"Does Tiberius know that you and I have been in contact? Does he know you have been to my apartment?"

"Of course he knows. He is the one who gathered the information about your initial meeting with Ansley. He is the one who sent me to gain your trust and get you to work for him, though he doesn't know the exact details of where we meet and what takes place. Tiberius is a busy man, much too busy to concern himself with the small details of our operation and my daily life."

"I'm not sure he would be happy to learn that you kissed me. I know I'm not."

Kaiya sighed. "Very little concerns a man that wields the power that Tiberius wields. He seeks only results and is threatened by nothing. And as you said, I am no Nephite. I am more of a convenient distraction to Tiberius than a companion, a pretty girl he can flaunt in front of his fellow consulates."

Arian felt the shame from his previous comment return. They sat in silence, allowing their discomfort to hang thickly in the air. She reached over and placed her hand on top of his, clasping it between her slender fingers. His first inclination was to pull away, but as he turned to look at her hand, he saw her in the corner of his eye for the first time since she had arrived, and all animosity faded away. In profile, her high cheekbones and soft skin created an impressive silhouette, and her expression betrayed a vulnerability he had never before seen. It made her even more beautiful. He had never seen her in the full daylight, and the sun illuminated the perfection of her lineless, creamy white skin, dotted with freckles. She seemed more human and less ethereal.

He felt compelled to speak.

"I apologize for what I said about the park being for Nephites only. It was out of line. I feel strange emotions for you. Obviously your intelligence on me tells you that I have led a partner-less life. But your natural beauty compliments this scenery far better than any of my engineered colleagues could."

Kaiya glanced at Arian, looking away nervously before allowing her eyes to drift back to him. A hint of a smile formed on her pursed lips but she remained silent. Her demeanor drove Arian wild with lust, and he wanted nothing more than to kiss her again. A few minutes passed before either of them spoke. They were content to sit on the bench, holding hands, basking in what was now turning into the late afternoon sun. It was Arian who broke the silence.

"What does Tiberius plan to do with Ansley?"

Kaiya measured her words carefully.

"Arian, you must be able to separate our mission and your personal feelings for Ansley. He is a dangerous man. Tiberius is convinced that he is leading the Centauri and that he was behind the bombings at the Institute all those years ago and more recently at the casino. His heart is filled with hatred for the world the Overseers have created and he seeks to destroy it."

"I can't believe that," responded Arian. "You don't know him as I do. He loved my mother. Why would he choose to murder his fellow scientists, his companions, and his colleagues? Tiberius must be wrong."

Kaiya squeezed his hand tighter.

"Ansley is a brilliant man, Arian, with a focused mind. It is not out of the realm of possibility that he has scouted you and is using things he learned to gain control of your emotions. You, as a scientist, should be aware of the lengths a man will go to when he fully believes his ideals are correct. Do not let him fool you."

"But how do I fit into all this plotting and politics? We are playing a game with stakes far higher than I was led to believe."

"Tiberius thinks that Ansley trusts you. He needs you for something, and that something could be very dangerous to our way of life. We must know what Ansley is planning if we have any hope to stop him."

Her passion was evident, but Arian found something troubling about her argument.

"You say he is dangerous to 'our way of life' but is it lost on you that this is not your way of life? You are a Natural Born. It seems odd you would have no sympathy for the plight of your brethren, no matter how twisted their methods."

"Those are dangerous words, Arian. Do not let Ansley pollute your mind with rhetoric. Regardless of whether you are able to help us, he will be stopped as well as the Centauri. The Overseers have seen to it that the net is nearly drawn. And about my loyalties, do not pretend to know me. My father was taken from me at the age of twelve by the flu that swept through our region. Of course, those in the domes were protected from its ravages. I vowed that I would rise in whatever capacity I could. Daughters of Natural Born farmers are not blessed with many opportunities in this world but I was beautiful, and this was not unnoticed by the leaders of Sikyon. I was taken into the house of a noble in that domed city. I was essentially a whore, but I was alive. Through my travels with him, I met Tiberius and was brought here where I have remained. He took me away from horrors you could not imagine. I am fifty-two years old, Arian, and look at me. I don't look a day over twenty. Tiberius gives me the same nano-treatments you receive. My loyalty is to myself, as should yours be."

Arian gasped at this new knowledge. He had underestimated how long she had been receiving nano-treatments. It was illegal, but then again, nothing was impossible for a man like Tiberius.

"I apologize again for presuming to understand your life. You have seen many more hardships than I, and it is not my place to question your allegiances."

They again sat in silence, this time with a shared intimacy that was lacking before. She removed her hand from his and placed it on the qubit between them. Tensing up, he grabbed it, removing it from her reach.

"You have the flash drive," she said, almost in a whisper. "If you don't wish to turn it over to me, I will understand your reasons, but trust me when I say that Tiberius will find out somehow. He has his ways. I will not be able to protect you if he finds out you have betrayed our operation. I'm not even sure I will be able to protect myself."

These last words struck Arian. The thought of harm to him, while concerning, was not enough to break his will. However, if harm were to come to her, he could never live with himself. He pulled the charred flash drive from his qubit and paused. The knowledge that the files were corrupted and unusable made the decision an easy one. He could give the drive to Kaiya without harming her or seeming to be an accomplice to Ansley. It was the perfect scenario. He let the drive fall from his fingers into her hand.

"You did well," she said. "And you made the right decision."

"It was easier than you think," he replied, flashing her a smug smile. "I've checked it. The files cannot be recovered."

Kaiya laughed at this. "Of course the hardware will be faulty from the fire, silly, but the information is still intact. I assure you, Tiberius will be able to access it all."

Arian's heart dropped as he realized he had just handed over a gift from a friend that would likely incriminate him and lead to his demise. He looked at Kaiya, again feeling betrayed.

"Don't be troubled," she whispered. "You are doing what you must and it will save lives, the most important of which is yours, at least as far as I'm concerned." They stood looking at one another awkwardly before saying brief goodbyes and walking away in opposite directions.

Arian felt horrible about handing over the drive, so much so that he bypassed his office altogether and headed home. Regardless of the motives for the transaction, which he felt were honorable, he couldn't shake the feeling that he had betrayed his new friend. He pictured the old Professor being arrested and carried away like a criminal and the thought made him sick. He carried this feeling all the way home.

When he arrived, he opened a bottle of Tegave and drank from it with no glass. Hours passed as day turned to night, but he couldn't shake his feelings of guilt. He replayed the Patolli match he attended with Ansley over and over again in his head, remembering his new friend's love for gambling and competition and drinking. The man did know how to live. He smiled at the memory. He placed the cork back into the half finished Tegave bottle and stood to head to bed. This was a problem that would have to wait until morning. As he walked toward the stairs, Athena's voice rang out.

"Arian, you have a visitor."

A visitor? Who would be coming at this hour? Feeling the effects of the alcohol, he stumbled toward the entrance. Hitting the button that opened the door, his jaw dropped as Kaiya entered, letting her thick black coat fall to reveal the white lace lingerie beneath. She eyed him, mischief evident in her seductive gaze. Without saying a word, she walked into the corridor and pulled the clasp in the back allowing the garment to fall to her ankles. Beholding her pale naked body for the first time, Arian felt as if he were looking at a goddess.

# Chapter Fourteen
## Torrijas for Two

*Bodies were thrown through the air with hellish force. Charred flesh smoldered, falling off the bones of fresh-made corpses. All sound was gone except for a persistent ringing. Stumbling, his body was numb. Palms finding pavement, he steadied himself, eyes open, yet only seeing the white light burned into his retinas. Choking on black smoke and reaching for her hand, his hearing returned, and the sound of the afflicted was horrendous. Explosions in the distance punctuated the crash of falling marble. Feeling around the immediate area for her body, his hand found hers, and the ash that had been her flesh fell from bone. Following the path from her hand to her chest, he felt no movement. Blinking rapidly to restore vision, the white light faded and was replaced by a bald, blackened face.*

*"Padma," he whispered, cradling her smoldering head in his arms. The heat emanating from her burned his skin, yet it was nothing. He stroked what remained of her face, the charred flesh falling away.*

*"I love you, Padma. Please don't leave me alone.*

*I can't do this without you."*

*She was silent. He sat there rocking her. Her breathing diminished until it ceased, her heart too weak to beat again, leaving the burned shell of his former lover.*

"Padma!" screamed Ansley, waking in the darkness of his bedroom, soaked in sweat and breathing heavily. He looked around before regaining sense of his surroundings. Moving to the edge of the bed, he held his head in his hands and tried to let the anxiety fade. The terrifying memory haunted his nights and unsettled his mornings. The booze kept the dreams at bay but never away. He only saw her as she was in those final moments, a charred corpse.

"Not Padma, silly. Anabelle." The unexpected voice startled him. "Are you having a nightmare, honey?" She placed her hand on his back to comfort him. "Wow!" she exclaimed. "You're drenched."

Ansley tried to allow his eyes to adjust to the darkness. Finding this impossible, he told Esther to draw the shades. Mid-morning light streamed into the room, revealing the figure of Anabelle Aster lying on her side with her head propped on her elbow, wrapped in the dark blue sheet. She was looking at him quizzically.

"Anabelle?" was all he could manage to say.

"Did you expect someone else? This Padma woman perhaps? You weren't looking for Padma last night."

Her constant perkiness and sheer strength of personality had always been what attracted Ansley to her. However in this moment, her company was unwanted and her presence shocking. He rubbed his eyes, trying to recall the previous night, and wondered how drunk he had gotten. It wasn't the first time he had awoken next to Anabelle. It wasn't even the twentieth, but he had given that up, as it never filled the void the way he hoped it would.

"No, of course not. I just had a bad dream. I'm sorry I woke you."

"Come here, baby," she said, raising the sheet to let him in. Her exposed nakedness confirmed his suspicions of what had occurred, and for the first time he noticed his own nakedness. Reluctantly, he crawled toward her, allowing her to enclose his body within the sheet, her warmth a comfort to him. "What did you dream about?" she asked in a whisper.

"It was nothing. A memory from the past."

"I can make it better," she said, pulling him closer. His hand found the curve of her hip. Feeling her lithe body, her form reminded him of Padma in a strange way. Overwhelmed by this notion, he embraced her fully and ran his fingers through her hair. Padma had had the most beautiful black hair, thick and wild. He opened himself to the intimacy he so longed for, kissing her neck softly. Padma had always smelled of lavender. He could taste its floral bitterness on his lips. His hands moved to her back, caressing the individual vertebrae with the tips of his fingers. She had loved to be massaged. He used to spend hours each night massaging her back and discussing their research.

He moved on top of her and their bodies became one. Opening his eyes, he drank deeply from her exotic, foreign beauty. Her almond shaped green eyes stared back at him, as if imploring him to action. *But what action did she want?* She seemed terrified. As he gazed at her face it melted, skin and flesh dripping off the bone, revealing the skull. "Why did you let this happen to me?" the skull spoke, its sickening mandible flapping as the exposed muscle burned away.

"What the hell!" He screamed, jumping away from her and falling off the bed, still attempting to scoot away even as he hit the floor. Anabelle, who appeared equally afraid, replaced the accusing skull of his dead lover. She looked at him with concern, her brown eyes glistening with tears.

"What's going on, Ansley? You're scaring me."

"I don't know," he replied truthfully. "I just need a minute. Please excuse me." He walked to the bathroom on the other side of the room and shut the door. Leaning over the sink, he looked at himself in the mirror. Dark circles encompassed his eyes, but the rest of his face was a ghastly white. He splashed cool water on himself to regain composure. Nightmares of Padma had haunted him for fifty years, but they had never manifested themselves in this manner. He truly believed he was making love to her, which made the hallucination that followed all the more disturbing. The doctors at the Institute had suggested that he be medicated for this condition, but he trusted nothing from them. Furthermore, it was inevitable as a mind reached the age that his had, it would be affected by multiple traumatic events. He emerged from the bathroom to find Anabelle standing at the foot of the bed, attempting to zip the back of her dress.

"I don't know what's going on with you, Ansley, but you are seriously fucked up," she said, fear giving way to anger.

Walking over to her, he gently clutched her shoulder, feeling her body tense. "Let me help you with that," he said, adopting a soothing tone. Ansley zipped her dress. "I don't know what came over me, but I don't want to be alone right now. Please allow me to make you breakfast."

She remained motionless for a moment, before her body and demeanor loosened. Looking at his face and seeing the sincerity within, she sighed. "Ansley, you are damn lucky that I find you so interesting."

Laughing to himself, Ansley walked her down the stairs to the personal kitchen area adjacent to the atrium.

"Sit here and I will make us a couple of café con leches. I have found that after a night of drinking this is what you need." He was making an effort to be overly accommodating, as he felt bad for causing her to cry, particularly after sleeping with her.

"That would be nice," she responded flatly.

"Good. Have you ever visited the Castilla-La Mancha region of Espialleros?"

"Of course I have. My father has many interests in the domed city of Lucentum. I've been there many times."

160

"Well, my dear, you are in for a real treat then, because I assure you, the domes are the same no matter where they're constructed, but you happen to be sitting at the table of a very old and experienced traveler who had the pleasure of visiting this region before we sterilized the world. Let me introduce you to the simple joy of Torrijas."

"What is that?" she asked, crinkling her nose in excitement. Ansley was glad to see her mood soften.

"My dear, it is wonderful. It is bread soaked in milk, sugar, and egg, and fried in olive oil. It is completely decadent, and happens to be my other cure for a hangover. They take about two hours to prepare. Here is your café con leche."

"Two hours?" she almost screamed. "I don't have two hours to wait for French toast. I have to get to my boutique."

"No worries. I prepared it a few days ago. I will have Esther heat it for us and we'll have it in ten minutes. I assume you'd like a cigarette with your coffee?" He removed his cigarettes and tossed her one, along with the lighter. She lit it and passed the lighter back to him, allowing him to light his own. He sipped his coffee and surveyed her over the rim. Perhaps it was still his guilt over the events of the morning, but he felt a certain fleeting affection for her.

"We make an odd pair, don't we?" he observed.

"What?" she replied with mock scorn. "A washed up scientist with a penchant for pissing off the government and a disgraced heiress, known more for high profile affairs than accomplishments? I suppose."

They laughed together at this strange juxtaposition. Moments like this had become rare in Ansley's life over the last fifty years and he allowed himself to enjoy the light banter. They talked and laughed and his dark thoughts were forgotten. He had devoted his life to his private endeavors for so long that it had been some time since he had opened himself to a new relationship. Perhaps it was his budding friendship with Arian that was driving this change, but looking across the table at Anabelle, he could imagine himself being with her.

"Your breakfast is ready, Ansley," Esther's voice interrupted, destroying the peaceful reverie.

"Ah," said Ansley, walking to the warming console and watching as the two freshly heated dishes rose from within.

"Don't forget to use the oven mitts," again came Esther's chiding voice. "The dishes are hot." The drawers containing the mitts opened on her request. Ansley removed the mitts and grabbed the dishes from the warmer.

"Breakfast is served." As he placed Anabelle's portion before her, she seemed displeased.

"Is there a problem?" asked Ansley.

"I wouldn't call it a problem," she replied hesitantly.

"Then what is it?"

"My nanny always used to make a smiley face with the syrup," she said with a straight face, before erupting into laughter.

"Come here," he said, grabbing her by the hand and leading her to the couch in the atrium. She looked at him quizzically as he pulled her by the waist toward him and kissed her. For the first time, he truly made love to Anabelle, for her, as she was. Padma would never return. Ansley had loved her and he had lost her, but this was Anabelle Aster, and she was wonderful.

As the door closed behind her, Ansley was sad to see her go. He could still smell her in the atrium, her pungent scent hanging heavily in the air. He sat on the couch feeling happy for once. Perhaps there was still a reason after all these hard years to live and enjoy life. Were all of his plans worth it? Ansley's light musings were interrupted as his qubit lit up with activity.

"An unknown caller is on your secure line, Professor," Esther's voice echoed through the atrium. Pulling out an earpiece from a drawer on the center table, Ansley connected it to his qubit.

"Let it through."

"Professor, we need to meet. Manuel has been arrested

along with his crew in the outer regions near Abilene. It was a new security team from Capitol City. They intercepted the shipment."

"Do you know where they took them, Eddie?"

"No, but I'm working on it. Perhaps the detainment center down south. Our intelligence is incomplete, but I lost contact with Manny at the checkpoint. Local farmers informed us they saw an Imperial unit trap the caravan. They knew they were coming, Ansley."

"Where are you, Eduardo? Are you safe?"

"Yes. I'm in the basement of the Devonshire."

"Is it possible, Eddie? Could there have been echo information on that drive?"

"I don't think so. I had it scrubbed by our best. It seems impossible that there could be any useable info on it."

"I don't like this. It seems wrong. Someone is sending us a message. We have a spy in our midst. We have to be careful."

"Professor, there's something else."

"What?"

"It's Richard. His health is failing fast and he's requested you come to the caves. He's not sure the task can be completed. We need you, Ansley."

"Damn! It's too soon. We aren't ready. Give him the last of our nanocyte stores. We have to buy more time."

"I'm afraid we don't have time, Ansley. We must move forward with our plans."

Ansley paused. Looking around the room, he considered the life he could have with Anabelle, allowing a moment to mourn for what could never be. He had chosen a path and good men had dedicated their lives to his cause, to him personally, and he would never abandon them. Resolute and with renewed fire, Ansley responded to Eduardo.

"Contact Jabari. It's time we take Arian out of the dome."

"We'll need a few weeks to set it up," responded

Eduardo. "With this new tracking system on the Natural Born about to go into effect, things are getting pretty tight around here. People are afraid."

"I understand, Eddie," Ansley responded. "Take your time and be safe."

# Chapter Fifteen
## Pathos

"Is something troubling you, my love? You seem distant." Tiberius was concerned Kaiya may be feeling overwhelmed by the mission. A person of her birth status was ill-equipped for the pressures of the Capitol. This, and the grim warning from Marco Luccio, is why he had sent her to Pathos. Still, that fire within her that he loved had cooled to a dim flicker.

Kaiya turned over on the bed to face him, brown eyes betraying no emotion. He could discern nothing from her gaze, but then, when had he ever been able to read her?

"You read me too well, my dear," she responded. "I hate it here. These sea folk are unlike anyone I have met. They are shallower than the people in the capitol. And this salty air is ruining my complexion!"

Tiberius was kind in his response. "My darling, I had to send you here, for your safety as well as for mine. We could no longer be together in the Capitol. It was forbidden by the Overseers themselves."

Kaiya furrowed her brow, unconvinced.

"I don't feel right about what we're doing to Arian. He seems nice. And Ansley seems nice as well. How could they be traitors?"

"It's not your place, nor mine, to question the motives of the Overseers. They have their reasons, which I am sure are just and right. Rest easy now my love. Your part is over. You were able to get the drive that I believe will infiltrate the inner workings of the Centauri. Don't trouble yourself, so. Nice means nothing."

"But you are always nice to me," she added, arching her back and moving over him.

"Between the sheets, I am as kind as any man, but in the political arena, I am sure you are aware, I am as deadly as a snake."

"Yes, but you are my deadly snake," Kaiya said seductively.

"Of course, my dear. Now let's get out of this bed and meet the day. It isn't often I get to enjoy what Pathos has to offer."

He rose from the bed in the bungalow that Iulius had provided for Kaiya. It made Tiberius uneasy to be sheltering her in Pathos knowing the Overseers' displeasure at his friend's relationship with a Natural Born. Looking out the window at the ocean, waves crashing onto the rocky shore, he felt too far away for it to matter. He decided to take a shower. True, the bungalow didn't offer the bathing comforts he was accustomed to, but he couldn't complain about his beachside lodgings.

As he exited the bathroom, he found Kaiya waiting for him in the hallway, dressed in a fiery red bikini, holding two beach towels.

"Don't you need to shower?" he asked.

"I shower in the ocean," was her response as she grabbed him by the hand and led him out the door.

Outside the bungalow, Tiberius took a deep breath of fresh sea air. It was the only city of Arameus that wasn't covered by a dome. Set in a bay that was surrounded by a mountain range, Pathos' only entrance was a heavily guarded tunnel drilled by the government some two hundred years ago. It was the Nephites' playground. Rental bungalows dotted the beach landscape, with the permanent residences and official buildings built into the mountainside. The contrast between natural, rugged beauty and sculpted marble and glass was breathtaking, even for a man such as Tiberius. The government had spared no expense in planning this world. Walking along the boardwalk toward the beach, he felt more relaxed than he had in fifty years, his stress melting away in the presence of such awe-inspiring architecture and geology.

The most striking element was the warmth of the yellow day sun on his body. It seemed to literally cook his skin, which, after being protected from UV rays by the domes for all these years, had almost no pigment. The night before, he had been so red he needed to call in a burn cream from the local pharmacy, which returned his skin to its white brilliance. In the distant past, he would have been worried that these rays caused long term damage to his skin, making him age, but even this would be remedied when he returned to Capitol City and received his nanocyte injections.

Tiberius set the two beach towels onto the black volcanic sand as Kaiya bounded into the waves. He laughed to himself as a large one knocked her down, submerging her. She jumped back out of the water and turned to him, waving and laughing. It was a shame that the two of them could never be officially together. She made him happy. What was the purpose of wielding all this power if he could not be with the one who made him feel this way? In that sense, he had no power at all. This thought troubled him, and he put it away. He was not a man who dwelled on negative things.

As Kaiya splashed in the waves, a Natural Born living a Nephite fantasy, he settled down on a towel and allowed the yellow day sun to warm his face. As the surf crashed on the beach, he was lulled into a state of relaxation. Tiberius entered the void between sleep and cognizance, where time became confused. He was occupying a world of abstract visions, half real and half fantasy. In his dream, he was climbing a pyramid, trying to reach Kaiya, but no matter how high he climbed, she was always out of reach. She seemed so powerful, as though by reaching her, anything would be possible. As he got close, the pyramid, then his entire world collapsed, everything sucked down into blackness, as though it no longer existed.

A sharp vibration startled him awake. Opening his eyes, it took him a minute to re-orient himself. Realizing where he was, he reached to the pocket of his shorts and found the transponder that the Overseer, Marco Luccio, had given him when he received his promotion. He looked to Kaiya and found her still playing in the surf.

"Damn," he thought to himself, bolting upright. Of course he had to answer, but they knew he was on vacation. Did they know whom he was with? Composing himself quickly, he placed the transponder to his ear. "Your Grace, to what do I owe this unexpected pleasure?"

"Pleasure indeed," intoned Overseer Luccio in his decrepit voice. "Are you able to speak freely, Tiberius?"

Tiberius looked around the beach and, finding no one within hearing range, answered in the affirmative.

"Good. I can't say I approve of this vacation, my son, but your choice of location may prove beneficial to our plans."

"How do you mean, your Grace?" responded Tiberius.

"In time. First we must make pleasantries. How are you finding your stay? Is Pathos as pleasurable as we designed it to be?

"It is exceedingly so, your Grace."

"I'm glad to hear that, truly. If I recall, the women in Pathos are quite nice as well. Have you found an opportunity to sample the local offerings?"

Tiberius hesitated.

Laughing, Marco didn't give him a chance to respond.

"I guess Avignon has its own offerings."

Tiberius only managed to utter a guttural "Uh," before

Marco cut him off.

"Relax, Tiberius. I have an assignment for you, one that is perfectly suited to your present scenery."

"I will do anything. What is it?"

"I am aware you are staying in a bungalow owned by your fellow consulate Iulius Van Arsdale."

Tiberius felt his skin crawl at this statement. Of course the Overseer would know. How could he not?

"I need you to send a man from Pathos on a mission in the name of the Special Parliamentary Security Division. I know he is an old friend of yours. Do you trust him to carry out such a mission?"

"Yes, I do," responded Tiberius. "I would trust him with anything."

In his head, Tiberius thought over the changes he had seen in his friend when they had met at the Cheshire Pub. This worried him, but he still felt confident that his oldest friend would not disappoint him.

"I'm pleased to hear this because our mission must begin immediately. We have received some interesting information from an informant in the coal mines 300 miles east of the paradise you currently inhabit. There is evidence that a large quantity of mined coal is being lost. Our sources suggest this could be one of the ways the Centauri are powering their operations."

"But why would we need to send a consulate to deal with a group of rebellious miners?"

"This is a valid question. The mine is loosely governed by us, but is predominantly run by Don Gravano. His family has proven difficult in the past, but they wield great power in the outlying districts, amongst the Natural Born. Sending a consulate will be both a show of respect to his power and a threat of ours. Obviously he would not be so foolish as to shun a Consulate of Arameus."

"Then send me. My mere name inspires fear amongst those outside our cities. Should I not be the one to meet with this Don Gravano?"

"Your loyalty is inspiring and worthy, Tiberius, but Gravano is a dangerous man and would be more accepting of a man from his own region. Yet as the head of the Security Division, I leave the final decision to you."

"I understand, Your Grace. What shall I have Iulius do?"

Tiberius listened as Overseer Luccio detailed the plan while he watched Kaiya ride wave after wave with her youthful body. He was relieved when Marco ended the encounter just as she rushed up the beach toward him.

"I've changed my mind about Pathos," she declared, tackling him to the towel and kissing him on the lips. "Maybe it got better because you're here."

"I'm glad you're having fun," he answered half-heartedly, his clothes dampening from the water dripping off her body.

"I'm having so much fun. Who were you talking to?"

"No one important," he replied. "Just business from the Capitol."

"Always working."

"Indeed. Baby, I'm going to need you to do lunch by yourself. I have business with Iulius this afternoon."

Frowning, Kaiya stared at Tiberius, searching his eyes for information before responding, "Is everything alright, my love?"

"Of course, dear, but I must leave immediately." Tiberius kissed her before standing and walking down the beach, leaving Kaiya to watch him disappear from view.

On Luccio's orders, he was to go to a cabana located on the highest peak overlooking the city. It housed an exclusive restaurant and bar patronized by Pathos' elite. He walked to the closest station that housed the high-speed magnetic vehicles the public used to travel within the city.

He found a representative for Luccio waiting for him. Dressed in a brown tunic, his broach identified him. Depicting a snake strangling an eagle, the official Luccio family crest showed this was a dangerous man. He was well tanned, with thinning blonde hair and an air of danger. Introducing himself only as Siva, Tiberius found the man's utter lack of regard for his station distasteful.

As they entered the private, unmanned vehicle, Siva typed in the coordinates of their destination. The console then asked for security clearance. Siva lost a bit of his mystique as he turned to Tiberius. As soon as Tiberius finished punching the final number, the car shot off at a high speed, leaving the beach behind and entering the main part of the city. It took sharp turns without slowing, and Tiberius more than once found himself thrown around the interior before deciding to grab two handrails. This drew a disdainful laugh from Siva. As they approached the eastern mountains, they connected with a track that lifted them up over the city and into the sky, so high that Tiberius felt his ears pop from the pressure change. At their destination, the car stopped abruptly, nearly throwing him again.

Tiberius was overwhelmed by the view of Pathos from the mountaintop. The marbled city spilled down the mountain to the black-sand beach and brilliant blue water, which opened into the expansive ocean. He would have to bring Kaiya here before leaving. Of anyone, she would appreciate the panoramic view. Siva grabbed him by the arm and steered him toward the open-air restaurant. The simplicity of the architecture was surprising, but Tiberius assumed that the designers had not wanted to compete with the natural beauty of the surroundings.

They entered a square bar covered by a thatch-roofed hut with grills to the side for preparing the food of the region's original inhabitants. He could smell a mixture of pork, pineapple, salty air, and pine trees. There was one man seated at the bar, wearing the traditional robes of a member of Parliament, whom Tiberius immediately knew to be Iulius. How could he have gotten here already?

Iulius turned to him, revealing the familiar scar on his

left cheek, and his weasel-like face.

"Tiberius, old friend!" he said cheerfully. "I see you've met my new friend Siva."

Tiberius was surprised by the greeting, as it was his understanding that the choice of Iulius for this mission had been his alone. He didn't let the unsettled feeling growing within show.

"I can see by the redness of your scar that you have been drinking without me," he answered with equal warmth. "And how do you know Siva?" he added.

"He came to me this morning on behalf of Overseer Luccio and said I should be here at this hour, that you might have a request for me."

Shooting Siva a glance, Tiberius took a seat next to his friend and Iulius continued.

"Your constant rise has never surprised me, Tiberius, but to be selected as Chief Security Officer of Arameus by an Overseer, I could have never expected you to reach these heights."

Looking back to Siva, who held his distance, Tiberius spoke in a lower tone.

"I thank you, my friend. Your kind words humble me."

"You have never felt humble in your life," Iulius retorted, laughing. "Get us a round of Tegave, bartender! Where did the bartender go? Siva, grab us a couple of drinks!" When Siva didn't respond, Iulius merely shrugged at Tiberius.

"You should take it easy, Iulius, you have important business to conduct today," said Tiberius in a measured tone.

"And what exactly is the business?" inquired Iulius.

After Tiberius recounted Marco Luccio's story of the coal and the meeting with Don Gravano, Iulius waved him off with a flippant hand.

"I will have no problem dealing with a low-born coal gangster. This is my district, Tiberius, and I command the respect of the people in the outer regions. I will have them do whatever the Capitol wishes. I don't understand why we allow these gangsters to wield so much power in the Natural Born world. So what deal am I to make with this Gravano?"

"The Capitol wishes that you deliver surveillance equipment to the Don and impress upon him the importance of stopping any leakages of coal from the government owned mines. The Capitol has already informed Gravano of your arrival and provided you with a small bribe to pay him with the expectation that his men will come down on any perceived misconduct with a heavy hand," answered Tiberius.

"Simple enough. When do I leave, and how am I to travel? Of course, I will need my security detail."

It was Siva who responded from behind.

"We have arranged for a Capitol Raven to arrive upon my request. It waits nearby with your cargo, your security team, and a woman whom the Overseers thought may provide you with comfort on your journey."

"Great. Call them," commanded Iulius.

Siva whispered something into a transponder on his wrist and within moments the hulking black ship appeared over the mountains to the north, rising first on jet turbines underneath before switching to jets in the back that propelled it forward at such speeds it reached them in less than a minute. The ship came to an abrupt stop as its forward thrusters fired and its lower turbines eased it onto the landing pad.

"I'm riding in style, Tiberius," said Iulius, full of excitement. "Soon I will be more important than you!" He stood from his stool and embraced his old friend.

"Be careful, Iuli," warned Tiberius.

"It is time," said Siva, grabbing Iulius by the arm and leading him toward the Raven. Tiberius was uneasy as he watched them walk away and enter the transport. Something about Siva rubbed him the wrong way. It was of no real concern though. Iulius was a capable politician, and he would have his security detail along with him. Tiberius turned back to the bar and ordered a drink from the bartender, who had appeared as Siva exited. He might as well enjoy the view.

As Iulius boarded the Raven, he was greeted by his security detail, comprised of his closest friends. Soon after, his eyes found Katrina.

"My little Natty," he cried, running to her and sweeping her into his arms. "I'm so glad they sent you. I guess our trysts in the Capitol were noticed, and you are my reward for my hard work!"

She greeted him with equal delight, burying her head in his chest.

"Well, obviously, you know my security detail." Iulius' friends gave Katrina polite bows. "This unhappy oaf is Siva." Siva made no acknowledgement of her existence. "I was just thinking when I was given this mission, how great it would be to take you to some of the outer regions."

Their journey was filled with the laughter that flows when old friends and lovers reunite. They looked out the windows admiring the scenery as they soared over the protective mountains of Pathos and out into the red desert that comprised the eastern province. By this time in the late afternoon, the yellow day sun and red night sun were at equal and opposite distances in the sky, bathing them in an orange glow. It was only forty minutes before the red mountains from which they mined the coal came into view. Surrounded by the camps where the miners spent their evenings and a protective fence with guard towers to defend the claim, the mine was an intimidating place. The larger structures and landing pads were outside the fences, where the wealthy Natural Born with interests in the red coal resided when visiting.

As they slowed and descended upon the city that surrounded the mine, the guards and Iulius were excited. It wasn't often that members of Arameus were able to travel to the outside world, other than flying over on trips to other domes. Secretly, Iulius hoped that Don Gravano would take them to a Natural Born restaurant and allow them to sample the local food and drink. Of course, they would need to visit the nanocyte treatment center upon returning to Pathos to protect themselves from any outside germs that they had not been exposed to in their sheltered world. As the Raven came to rest on the landing pad, the doors opened and the exit ramp lowered. Iulius spotted a man who could only be Don Gravano waiting on the other side of a red velvet carpet that extended from the ramp to their welcoming committee.

Don Gravano was a large man, fat even. He was bigger than any man living in Arameus. There, the nanocytes prevented excess fat. This was a man who enjoyed the spoils of his position in this mining community. He was bald on top and tanned by the harsh desert sun. Lavishly dressed in a black suit, with diamond rings gleaming on his fingers, Gravano was flanked by three guards on each side who appeared unarmed.

"Good," Iulius thought to himself. "These men respect authority."

"Leave your arms, men," he announced to his security detail. "This is a friendly meeting. Come, Katrina. Let us go meet our host."

They exited the ramp and walked toward their welcoming committee, Katrina and Iulius in the front, with eight guards trailing on either side of them. Siva exited as well, following far behind. Walking the velvet carpet, they gazed at the buildings on either side, structures made of different colored bricks and brightly painted wood rising to a height of three stories. The terra cotta roofing complemented the walls. They contrasted with the domed cities, and Iulius found them appealing. Balconies, likely from apartments, dotted the sides of the buildings. When they were five feet from Don Gravano, the party came to a halt.

Inclining his head in a sign of respect and humility, Iulius issued the standard formal greeting.

"As a member of the Parliament of Arameus, a representative of Pathos, and a special envoy for our Chief Security Officer, I greet you cordially, Don Gravano."

Don Gravano neither inclined his head nor bothered to speak. He sneered back with such disdain and hate that Iulius was himself speechless. No one treated a man of his rank in this manner. Regaining his composure, he began anew.

"As I was saying, I bring a gift for you as well as a special request from our great Overseer Marco Luccio. I was informed you would be aware of this agreement."

From this distance Iulius could see Gravano's yellow, crooked teeth, exposed by the sneer that had yet to leave his face. The gentle breeze carried his body odor, which stank of sweat and garlic.

"Marco Luccio, you say?" Gravano replied after a long pause, his voice oozing with sarcasm. "I am aware of this man. A great man, this Marco Luccio."

"Good. Then you have been informed of our proposal?"

"Indeed, I am aware of a proposal," Gravano responded. "Marco told me to offer you his condolences."

Iulius was only puzzled for a moment before a loud CRACK startled him. He looked around confused, but found Gravano and his guards hadn't moved. Then he heard Katrina let out a choked scream followed by a sickening gurgling sound. He rushed over to her as she fell to the ground, blood spouting from a gunshot wound to the neck. Looking up at the balcony from which he heard the shot, he heard multiple other shots firing all around, followed by the dull thuds of his guards' bodies hitting the dirt. As he turned to protest to Gravano, he felt a sting in his chest and gazed down to see blood staining his white robes. He felt woozy and collapsed to the ground, reaching for Katrina. As he lay, bleeding to death, he clutched her hand and looked into her pale face, her dead eyes staring into infinity. He felt a shadow cover him and struggled to turn his gaze upward. Siva stood over him with a gun barrel pointed at his face.

"I have your drink, Consulate," was the last thing he heard as Siva smiled for the first time. Then his final vision, the flash of the barrel as he fired.

Leaving his escort to deal with the bodies, Gravano tried to avoid stepping into the pools of blood spilling over the carpet and launch pad as he followed Siva back to the Raven.

As Siva unloaded the large boxes of automatic weapons, flashbangs, and explosives, courtesy of Capitol City, the Don could hardly contain his joy.

\*\*\*

The sky was turning from orange to red before Tiberius decided to leave the cliff top bar. He had enjoyed his time alone with his thoughts, drinks, and the local food, but now he knew Kaiya would be worried, and it appeared that Siva and Iulius might be some time on their mission. Returning to the car by which he had arrived, he programmed the coordinates for the beachfront station.

Walking from the station to the bungalow he shared with Kaiya, he was at peace, happy to be helping Iulius advance in the eyes of the Capitol, but happier still to return to his lover's embrace. Entering the bungalow, he was met by silence, no noises coming from the atrium console or the bedroom. She must be sleeping.

Excited to slide into bed with Kaiya he entered the room, but found it empty. Searching, he found a hastily written note on the bedside table. Lifting it to read, he nearly passed out and had to sit on the bed to keep from falling. He read the note over and over again.

*Tiberius, I'm sorry to have to rush off, but something came up.*
*I have returned to Avignon to keep you safe.*
*I will love you always.*
*-Kaiya*

# Chapter Sixteen
## Revelations Part I

Arian lounged in his atrium, watching Sophie Mayieux's news coverage on his center console. It was a Saturday afternoon in late spring, a wonderful time in Capitol City. The Spring Festival was fast approaching, a time when all the well-to-do Nephites lost their snobbish airs and took a week off to celebrate the changing seasons with costumes, parades, and drunken revelry. Spring and summer had little meaning within the climate-controlled domes, but those in charge made it a point to simulate the seasons that went on outside with different colored lights and slightly varied temperatures. The pastels and mild temperatures of the spring put everyone in the city in the best mood of the year.

Arian, however, was not in a festive mood. A prominent consulate from Pathos was killed, along with his security detail, when their Raven was shot down by a Centauri cell. Parliament had pledged swift justice, pleading with the Nephites to avoid interactions with the Natural Born who worked in the domes. They believed the murder to be an inside job. Keeping true to their word, they had captured the culprits.

A Centauri cell leader named Manuel led the operation. He was apprehended at a checkpoint attempting to smuggle coal stolen from a government-owned mine.

Arian felt uneasy about his relationship with Ansley. Could the things Kaiya said be true? Could his friend be aligned with these murderers? Perhaps handing over the drive had been for the best. These doubts, however, were not the source of his sour mood and lack of motivation in research.

It was Kaiya herself. Thoughts of her consumed him. No matter how he reasoned, he couldn't explain why she had come over and given herself to him that night. It had been two months and he had not heard a word. He felt hurt and used, as if she had merely come over as payment for the flash drive or as a gift from Tiberius Septus for a job well done. But it hadn't felt that way. It was special, at least for him, as if he were living in one of the fantasies that played nightly over the networks. They made love twice that evening, but in the morning she was gone, not bothering to leave a note.

Confusing matters more, Ansley had contacted him this morning for the first time since the Patolli game. Arian speculated that entrusting him with the drive had been a test. He was aware that Ansley, with his egg device and ability break into apartments, would be able to monitor him in some way. A man with his knowledge and technology could be dangerous. However, after this lengthy absence with no mention of the project, Ansley's request was bizarre.

"Arian, the Capitol City Gliders have a bye week. I remember promising you at the match you could meet the team. Today is the day. Be ready by noon and bring anything you want signed. I'm going to introduce you to my good buddy, Jabari," he had said.

Pushing his doubts aside, Arian headed toward the stadium, which was where he and Ansley were to meet. He was disappointed that Ansley hadn't decided on a bar, since he could use a drink, but he knew it was for the better. He didn't want Eduardo's spying ears to be within range. Heading to the door, Arian's eyes fell on the Patolli dodger he removed from his closet earlier in the morning. As an assistant professor at the Institute, he felt more than a little embarrassed at the prospect of arriving at the stadium carrying a dodger as if he were a child, but it wasn't everyday you got a chance to get an autograph from Jabari Stoudamyre. He scooped up the dodger and exited his apartment.

Moving though the city, he could feel the cool, manufactured spring breeze on his face. Here and there, he noticed preparations for the parade that would signify the beginning of the festival. Colorful floats shaped to resemble birds from around the world were being constructed on the closed sections of streets. It wasn't long before Arian spotted the bright green expanse that made up the South Tower's lawn and the columned monument of Paulo Dominiccio.

Being a weekend, the tower was closed and there were ample docking spaces for his hawk. Looking around, he was unsure of what to do, not seeing Ansley anywhere. He walked to the entrance of the tower, trying to gain access to the escalator that led down into the bowels of the stadium. Placing his hand on the sensor, it responded with a red light and refused to open.

Arian reached for his qubit to contact Ansley just as he saw his friend saunter around the corner of the building, one hand in the pocket of his pants, the other raising a cigarette to his mouth.

"There you are," Arian shouted to him. "I was just about to contact you."

Looking amused, Ansley closed the space between them in silence. Stopping in front of Arian, he looked him up and down before bursting out in laughter.

"What's so funny?"

In between guffaws, Ansley was barely able to verbalize his response.

"You look so cute with your little dodger! Maybe we can get the whole team to sign it!"

Arian's face turned bright red.

"I knew this would be a waste of my time." He began to walk off.

"No, no, wait. I was joking." His continued laughter seemed to indicate otherwise. "Seriously, Arian, stop. I have important things to discuss with you today. I was only joking," he finished, finally composed.

"You smoke too much," replied Arian, turning back to him.

"Well, when I was growing up, they used to kill people. Once they freed us from that unfortunate consequence, I never stopped."

"Well, you still stink."

"Indeed," replied Ansley. "Just wait until you smell the locker room. You will be wishing I would light one of these."

Still annoyed, Arian walked back to the tower entrance and stood as if waiting for Ansley to open the door.

"Oh no, no. We won't be entering through there. I don't care to have all the security of Capitol City know what I am up to today. You didn't try to enter that door, did you?"

"No," Arian lied, a bit confused on why it should matter.

"Good. Follow me." Ansley walked back around the side of the building from which he had come and stopped by a service entrance marked "Maintenance." After Ansley knocked on the door twice in succession, then once, then twice more, Arian heard the jingling of locks being turned on the other side and the door was opened. A short, fat, though altogether jolly looking Natural Born man greeted them. He was dressed in all khaki to signify his station as a maintenance man. They were quickly ushered into a darkened corridor that was part of a system used to move workers unseen to wherever their services were required. Once they were within the safety of the corridor, the man relaxed.

"Great to see you, Ansley," he said, wrapping his arms around the old Professor. Arian was shocked to see this sort of familiarity from such a lowly worker.

"Great to see you too, Raul," replied Ansley. "I appreciate you setting up this tour for me and my friend. Look how excited he is. He even brought a Patolli dodger." At this, both Raul and Ansley burst out in laughter, and it was a full minute before either stopped to Arian's irritation.

"All joking aside, this is the kid I have been telling you about. Arian."

Raul studied him before saying, "It is my pleasure to meet you. Hopefully you won't be a disappointment to Ansley." He reached his hand out toward Arian. Arian merely looked at it in disdain until he withdrew it.

Arian wasn't sure what bothered him most, the familiarity with which the Natural Born addressed Ansley, or the condescending way with which he, a Nephite of the highest breeding, had been addressed. Ansley showed similar familiarity with Eduardo, but the best of the Natural Born stock were chosen for customer service, a distinction that mattered. Furthermore, he was confused about how he could disappoint Ansley by taking a tour of the Gliders' locker room. Arian was losing his patience.

Slapping Raul on the back, Ansley said, "I think we should continue on to the locker room." Raul nodded and led the way. Arian followed.

They entered an elevator and rode in silence, down into what must have been the deepest point of the stadium. As the doors opened, Arian found himself looking into the tunnel through which the players entered the arena for the game. Awestruck, he stepped out and was overwhelmed by the vivid green of the field in contrast to the eeriness of the dark empty stadium above. He began to walk in the direction of the field, wishing to run around like a child, but Ansley grabbed him by the shoulder, turning him around.

"This way to the locker room, superstar," he whispered.

They walked under the archway through which the players entered the field and approached a door marked "Gliders Locker Room – Restricted Access." Taking out keys,

Raul unlocked and opened the double doors and stood to the side, allowing Arian and Ansley to pass. Breathless with anticipation, Arian rushed in, but instead of finding a well-lit locker space filled with armored athletes, loud voices, and testosterone, he instead found a dark empty room, lit only by the dim green lights coming from the gliders charging around the wall. There was not a single locker occupied by a body. Arian turned sharply as he heard the doors close behind them and an audible click. Raul had locked them in.

"What the hell," Arian shouted, as he rushed to the doors in the dark, shaking them with all of his might. They would not budge.

"Relax, kid. This is all part of the plan." Ansley's voice came from behind him. It contained a certain menace he had never before noticed.

"What plan? I'm not part of any of your fucking plans, you terrorist!" "Terrorist?" Ansley's voice was calm and chilling. "You know nothing, boy."

"I know you're part of the Centauri. And the government knows it too."

"You must be referring to your trysts with Tiberius' pet. What is her name? Kaiya? You do discredit to yourself if you believe that I haven't known about her and you from the minute she invited you to that restaurant. You think I have survived this long without keeping a close eye on my adversaries?"

"What are you talking about?" Arian asked, turning toward the voice, though he could no longer see Ansley. He had moved into a shadow. "You are the enemy of the state."

"Do you really believe that? If so, then why are you here? Were you really that enthralled with meeting the Gliders? Did you think you could win her affections by turning me over to Tiberius? By giving over the hard drive? Did you expect your love pact would be sealed by my death? You can't honestly be so foolish as to think that Tiberius Septus would just let you walk away with his Natural Born harlot. Handing me over would seal not only your death, but hers as well."

"I…I…" Arian sighed, and slid down the door until he was seated on the floor, his head in his hands. The shadows shifted and Arian saw Ansley standing fifteen feet away, illuminated by the dull green glow. "I don't know what I wanted."

"Let me ask you another question, Arian," said Ansley, his voice taking on a paternal tone. "Why did you not take Raul's hand when he reached out to you a moment ago? Do you consider him to be so far below you? You seemed to have no difficulty touching Kaiya. She is Natural Born. So is he. What makes them so different to you? Is it that she is beautiful and he is ugly? Is that how you distinguish between which of the masses that occupy the world outside these walls is worthy of your affections? I can assure you of this. Raul will never manipulate you and use you for his own ends. I am positive I could not say the same for Kaiya."

"I am a Nephite," replied Arian. "We were bred to be better. We are taught not to interact with those of the natural world."

"I will use your unfortunate upbringing as an excuse for your rude behavior. Were it not for that, I would have killed you for such an offense. You are neither as accomplished nor as valuable as Raul Hernandez. And what of me? I am both naturally born and a Nephite, as were your parents. Are you above us? Would you not embrace them?"

Arian sat unresponsive for several minutes. When he finally responded, he sounded tired.

"You know I don't think I'm better than you. I don't know what to think anymore. Why don't you answer my question? Are you a Centauri?"

For the third time that afternoon, Ansley laughed at Arian.

"You foolish boy, there is no Centauri."

"I don't understand," was all the response Arian could muster.

"I think I have made it abundantly clear by this point my connection to the outside world. I formed these connections with Padma and Richard. Your own mother and father were destroyed on Blood Sun Day. I heard the same thing you hear every time a high-ranking member of Arameus runs afoul of the Overseers. I heard that the Centauri staged another bombing, working from the inside with prominent Nephites. I have never been a man to sit idly around and accept the explanations of others, so I went in search of this Centauri, and I assure you, kid, it doesn't exist."

"What do you want from me?" asked Arian.

"You have been a pawn for those in power during all of this. Honestly, I believe that Kaiya has as well. Maybe even Tiberius. What I want from you in the end is actually quite selfish. However, I don't wish to reveal my ultimate goals to you at this time. Right now, I just want you to stop playing both sides and choose who you trust. Would you rather trust Tiberius or me? You are welcome to return to the city above now and we will never speak of this again. But if you are a man who seeks the truth, and I believe that you are or I never would have contacted you, I think you should come with me now and seek that which I can see you are now believing to be true."

"Come with you where?"

Ansley lifted his qubit from his pocket and said, "Jabari." At the far end of the locker room, a large steel security door began to rise, filling the room with fluorescent light from a newly opened tunnel.

"This is how the players enter the dome for games. Come with me outside the city and I will show you a world you never could have imagined." Ansley reached his hand out to Arian.

Arian's mind was swirling. He thought of meeting Kaiya with Tiberius at the game. He remembered handing over the drive to her on the bench and the smugness she showed at her success. Then he thought of Ansley, drunk on his balcony, reminiscing about his dead mother. With a rush of understanding, Arian knew whom to trust. He reached out and grabbed Ansley's hand.

Yanking Arian to his feet, Ansley pulled him into a tight embrace, whispering in his ear, "If it is a Centauri they want, then I'm going to give it to them."

# Chapter Seventeen
## Revelations Part II

Tiberius was pacing, making it difficult for his servants to wrap him in his dress attire. After much pleading, they were able to convince him to remain still long enough to drape the Imperial purple sash over his white robes. He was nervous. What he was doing was unprecedented. No one demanded a meeting with an Overseer, but after a month of internal debate, he found no other recourse. Kaiya's disappearance needed to be addressed.

He was unsure at first whether her leaving was of her own accord, but it seemed unlikely to him that she would choose to return to Avignon. Her home had always been a place of pain. It wasn't until a few days later that news broke of the death of his old friend Iulius, along with Katrina and his entire security team, at the hands of a Centauri cell.

There had been no reports of the whereabouts of the mysterious Siva, whom he had believed was a representative of Overseer Luccio, nor was there any mention of Don Gravano or the coal mines. In the unlikely scenario that the Raven truly had been shot down, Siva would have been amongst the casualties. This, combined with Kaiya's mysterious disappearance, made him feel as if he had been manipulated into sending his friend to his death, while leaving the woman he loved unprotected.

He had stayed at the bungalow they were sharing for a few days after her departure. Each day he awoke, he expected to find that she had slipped into bed next to him during the night. All of this ended when he heard of Iulius' death. Whatever his emotional state, he no longer felt safe in Pathos. He departed for Capitol City immediately. If ever there was a time to be a valuable asset to the Overseers, now was that time.

Upon his arrival in the Capitol, he had given Thaddeus, his most trusted adviser and friend, the impossible task of accessing the data from the burned flash drive. If Ansley valued this drive enough to risk his own life, it must contain critical information that would aid him in hunting the Centauri. Presenting this information to Overseer Luccio would be a good step in restoring his ties with the leaders of Arameus. The exercise had an air of futility given that he had personally organized the bombing at the casino. The death of his friend Iulius weighed heavy as well, given its unlikely nature. Tiberius felt he might be chasing a ghost. He brushed all these thoughts aside. His place was not to question. His place was to follow orders.

It took a month, but Thaddeus and a team of the finest computer engineers in Capitol City managed to recover the information from the damaged drive. The data was encrypted, and to break the code, Thaddeus was forced to run it through a more powerful central computer. What they found removed any doubts about whether there was a Centauri dedicated to bringing down the government of Arameus. It even eliminated his doubts over whether this terrorist group had the ability take down a Raven. Tiberius found evidence of a vast economic ring, embezzling small amounts of money and resources from all over Arameus. Many of the files naming those involved were corrupted, and those names they were able to recover were dead ends, as the men had died in various ways over the years. All seemed to be funneled to an underground laboratory not far outside Capitol City. There was also a great deal of scientific data which Tiberius himself could not understand, although it seemed to suggest that they were conducting highly technical experiments.

Armed with this information, he requested a private audience with Marco Luccio. Given the recent developments, Luccio was sure to accept. Tiberius had ulterior motives, needing to know the truth about Kaiya and Iulius. More likely to be killed than gain this knowledge, he pushed the issue. One way or another, his internal doubts would cease, although he would prefer answers to death.

Departing in his special transport, he was sure that this would be the last time that he saw his beloved home. At the Central Tower, he showed his credentials and stepped onto the now familiar circular platform in the center of the Tower. Arriving at level 314, he again found himself square with the floor of the circular room that held the offices of the Overseers' secretaries. As before, light from the yellow day sun filled the room from 360 degrees high above Capitol City. He was nearly to the top of the dome itself. Turning to the southern part of the expansive room, he walked toward the diamond encrusted two-headed serpent on the door that led to Marco Luccio's quarters.

The pug-faced female secretary, a Nephite who had been serving the Luccio family since the beginning of Arameus, again asked him to step back to the red sofa in the center of the platform that had formerly been the lift, only this time, she asked for his qubit before he stepped back. It was only a minor difference, but Tiberius noted that on his previous visit, his qubit had only been confiscated upon entering the diamond-encrusted doors to the lift that accessed Luccio's private chambers. Feeling apprehensive, he took a seat on the red sofa.

He waited for almost fifteen minutes, fidgeting and feeling more uncomfortable by the moment. He was startled by a screeching sound from above. Looking up, he was shocked to see a metal hatch in the ceiling opening from a central point and spreading outward until it was the exact size of the platform on which he now resided. Almost immediately, the platform shot upward in a clear shaft, and he watched as he passed the spires that housed the Overseers. Rising twenty stories, the platform became level with a clear polymer floor supported by the spires themselves.

At the highest point in Capitol City, he was in a dome within the dome. A clear floor spread from the top of each of the four spires. Made of the same nearly indestructible polymer that comprised the dome around the city, it held the most wondrous room Tiberius had ever seen. The transparent walls sloped inward meeting at a central point fifty feet above. Where the spires connected, jewel-encrusted doors bearing the insignias of each Overseer signified personal platforms through which each man could gain access to this area from his private quarters.

The room was filled with exotic plants from around the world, both level with the floor and hanging in baskets connected to the dome above. It gave the impression of a massive garden suspended in mid-air. Many strangely dressed people were moving around at the North end of the room. They appeared to be servants, both men and women dressed sparsely. The shirtless males wore only what appeared to be skirts, striking in their bright red color. The women were barely covered, dressed in ornate bikinis, glittering with jewels. They were all standing around a large square table, seated at which he saw the unmistakable figures of Paulo Dominiccio, Pierre de Medici, Vladymir Romanov, and Marco Luccio. He stood, frozen, afraid to disturb a scene he wasn't sure he should have stumbled upon.

Marco Luccio's voice echoed through the domed room. He was obviously in the midst of chewing.

"Tiberius, my son, come join us. We have much to discuss." He raised a cloth napkin to his mouth, wiping it.

Tiberius walked toward the table through the rows of exotic plants, startled as he passed a giant cat from some distant land. It hissed at him from the other side of its cage. He passed many other enclosures filled with animals he could not name from around the world, possibly from other worlds. As he reached the end of the garden, he came to the table. Made of solid gold, it was worth a fortune, not to mention that it was much larger than it had seemed from across the room. The male and female attendants stood at attention ten feet behind, ready to meet any need the great men might have. He realized now that their attire, though aesthetically pleasing, might also have something to do with security, as nothing could be hidden on an almost naked body. This seemed a moot point as he now noticed the eight heavily armed Formaddi, the most highly trained mercenaries in Arameus, surrounding the perimeter. He also observed the familiar Imperial robes, four of them, hanging to the side of the table. The Overseers were dressed down, wearing only short-sleeved shirts and linen trousers.

The array of food on the table was mind-boggling, even for one of Tiberius' wealth. The plates were made of gold as well, complete with goblets ordained with the jeweled seal of the Overseer to which they belonged. Steaming pots of lobster and other sea delicacies long outlawed due to their endangered status stretched before them. Overseer Luccio motioned to a vacant seat beside him, and as he did, a beautiful woman as exotic as the flora and fauna surrounding him placed a gold plate and goblet before it. As Tiberius took the seat, he stole a glance at the other three men at the table. None of them had deigned to look at him and all seemed more concerned with the lunch before them than his presence.

"What do you think of the goblet?" asked Marco.

Noticing it for the first time, Tiberius was shocked to find his own family seal, an archer framed in amethyst. "I…I don't know what to say."

"Then don't say anything." Vladymir Romanov turned to him finally, still chewing, giving him a disdainful look. "I would hate to be bored. You have done that enough with your speeches in Parliament."

Despite the fact that he had just been insulted, Tiberius counted himself lucky. Not many people in Arameus had had the pleasure of being personally addressed by Overseer Romanov.

"Oh, be kind, Vlad," came the thick accented voice of Pierre de Medici. "We have assembled to honor the boy."

"To honor me?" asked Tiberius, hesitating. "I don't understand."

Slapping Tiberius on the back, and leaving his hand on it, it was Marco Luccio who responded.

"My son, you have done well. You have carried out your duties, in spite of having to deal with the unfortunate demise of your good friend Iulius and the departure of your beloved Natural Born whore. What was her name…oh yes, Kaiya, I believe. You have performed admirably and used her to accomplish it as well. That is something that we feel deserves commendation. I must admit, when you ignored my warnings and attempted to hide her in Pathos, I was disappointed. Most of us believed you should be eliminated as a threat."

All of the men at the table laughed at this. Even Vladymir. Tiberius felt empty. He now knew that Kaiya was dead. Looking down at the table to hide his shame, he muttered, "I only did my duty, your grace."

"Ah, but you did your duty well, too well, perhaps. We might need to find a new position for you after this. A man of your talents could be an asset to us. But we will talk business later. Now you should feast. I think I am correct to assume that you have never enjoyed the pleasure of lobster. Eat now. Let us talk of topics more pleasant."

As Marco Luccio spoke, Tiberius couldn't help but notice how much younger he looked than the last time he had seen him. His skin seemed tauter, and it had an earthy tone that was in stark contrast to the pallor it had shown before.

"You look much better than when I last saw you, Your Grace," he said in earnest. "You seem to be in much better health."

194

This again drew a hearty laugh from the men at the table.

"You should have brought this guy a long time ago, Marco. He makes me laugh," said Paulo Dominiccio between guffaws.

"Pay them no mind, Tiberius," advised Marco. "These men have been in power so long they have forgotten what it means to be young and ambitious."

"I am hardly young, your grace."

"This is true, but you will always be young to us. Now eat."

Tiberius had no choice but to oblige. He pulled a steaming lobster from one of the pots before him. Thankfully, it had been pre-cut. He tore a chunk of the soft white meat. It seemed both rubbery and flaky at the same time. Dipping it in the butter sauce, as he had seen the Overseers do, he placed the meat in his mouth. It was succulent and juicy, with hints of butter and lemon. He would have enjoyed the dish more had not the eyes of all four Overseers been upon him. As he continued to eat, the four began to talk amongst themselves.

"So, Pierre, it has been some weeks since we last spoke. How was your trip?" asked Vladymir.

"Every time I visit my home in Vina del Mar, I wonder if I will ever return to Capitol City," responded Pierre with a laugh. "It is my own personal paradise. We just finished the east wing of the house. Maritza and the baby will stay there while the child is young."

"Pierre acquired an island off the southern cape of Marengo," said Marco, turning to Tiberius to fill him in. "He has spent the last fifteen years building his own personal palace there."

"And the baby was healthy?" asked Paulo Dominiccio.

"Another strapping young boy," Pierre announced proudly. "He came out screaming. He will be a strong-willed one, a true Medici. His genetic scans show he will possess great intelligence with an aptitude in mathematics. He is prone to heart disease as is all of my family, but the nano treatments will take care of that."

"Will there be enough women left for him by the time he comes of age?" chided Marco. "How many families do you now have living on the island?" This drew a laugh from the rest of the table.

"I only have five wives in that household," answered Pierre, undeterred. "The other four were not very happy that I gave the east wing to Maritza. Of course, if they don't like it, I can always find a less ideal situation for them."

All at the table laughed except for Tiberius. He was awestruck that he was present for such a candid moment between the men who had shaped Arameus. It had always been rumored that the Overseers had children of their own in the natural way, but it had never been confirmed until now. He felt anger rise within him as he thought of Kaiya. These men had households all over the world with kids that could only be described as Natural Born, and yet he was not allowed the same luxury.

"And how are you talking to me about number of wives?" Pierre continued. "Vladymir could fill an entire dome with his offspring."

"Don't worry," Vlad responded coldly. "I plan on it."

"We should be careful," joked Paulo. "Vlad's children will overthrow us all."

"I plan on it."

Of all the Overseers, Tiberius could easily identify that Vladymir Romanov was the most dangerous. He carried himself with an air of detachment, but his eyes were hard. It was obvious how he could be the man responsible for the greatest military-industrial complex the world had ever known.

"And what about you, Tiberius," began Paulo, "have you ever desired to have children?"

Tiberius was taken aback by this question.

"Relax…He means the question genuinely," reassured Marco.

"In the days before the domes were constructed, I had

hoped to have a large family," answered Tiberius. "As you know, my father had nine children. It was wonderful growing up in a household filled with siblings. I married young and began my political career, but for whatever reason, my wife and I were never able to conceive. When I lost her, I lost all taste for family. By the time I was invited to enter the dome and take the treatments, the forced sterilization seemed of little importance to me. However, as I have aged and my wife's memory grows more and more distant, I have sometimes wondered what a life complete with family would be like."

"I am jealous when I hear you speak of your deceased wife in this way," remarked Paulo genuinely. "I find it quite endearing. My first wife died when I was only forty. I did not receive my first nano-treatment until I was ninety-three years old. By that time, I could no longer even picture her face in my mind without the aid of a photograph. For you to hold on to her memory after all these years is astounding."

Tiberius swallowed hard. The lobster lost all flavor as he realized he had a woman besides his former wife to mourn through the endless years. He would not soon forget Kaiya and the happiness she had brought him.

"Such very sweet sentiments, to be sure," Vladymir said, eyeing Tiberius from across the table. "Of course, I should inform you that the sterilizations, while given to all Nephites, are only effective on the women. Do you think our strict policies against fucking Natural Born women are without cause? Everything we do has a distinct purpose and that is to maintain our control over this world." Vladymir's palm smacked hard on the table in emphasis of this point, rattling the dishes. He stared at Tiberius, his cold gaze surveying him, before continuing. "Surely you are not foolish enough to think that there will not always be unrest outside of our domes. Would you be content to be a lowborn while the Nephites enjoy the fruits of great wealth and eternal youth? This is why we could not have you cohabitating with a Natural Born. Suppose you had conceived a child? He would have no place in Arameus, yet should not the son of Tiberius Septus feel he belongs by your side? This is exactly what we are trying to avoid."

Tiberius shifted in his seat, yet he didn't let his eyes waver from Vladymir. It took all his courage to not look away while the Overseer spoke.

"Every Natural Born female worker that enters a dome is immediately sterilized. We may have been content to allow you to keep your nighttime playmate had you gone through these channels. But you chose to sneak her into Capitol City and bypass our policies, as if we would not find out. We always knew. By our reckoning, she has terminated four pregnancies since entering the dome. That is what she thought of your offspring. And you blatantly ignored Marco's warning to rid yourself of her. If it were up to me alone, you would be dead, but unfortunately the others did not agree. I must confess, I may have been rash in my judgment as your delivery of Ansley's flash drive has proved to be quite beneficial." He paused and motioned to the male servant nearest him. "Boy, bring us six glasses of wine."

Tiberius' throat was dry, not from thirst, but from fear. Overseer Romanov deserved his reputation as an intimidator. It was seconds before the servant returned, placing a glass of wine before each of the Overseers and two glasses before Tiberius. Puzzled, he looked to Vladymir questioningly.

"I feel a bit guilty for my rash opinion of you and for the loss of your pretty little Natural Born. Choose the woman amongst these servants that most pleases you and ask her to join us in this toast."

Tiberius, still confused, obeyed. Looking around, his eyes landed on a smallish dark-skinned woman in the corner. She had coal black, shoulder-length hair and small perfect breasts. What really drew him to her was the fear that was evident in her striking green eyes. He wanted to comfort her, and thus he chose her to join them in the toast.

"What is your name," he asked.

"Sonya," she answered, apprehension evident in her

voice.

"Please join us. You have nothing to fear." Her lip quivered as she stepped forward. Tiberius handed her one of the glasses.

"Good," said Vladymir. "I raise my glass to Tiberius Septus," he began as the others joined him in the act, "may he never disappoint us again."

The five men and Sonya touched glasses and drank. Surveying the room, Tiberius noticed the concern evident on the faces of the other servants. He stood to thank Overseer Romanov for the toast but was interrupted by a terrible gurgling noise. He spun just in time to see Sonya crash forward into the table, before falling to the floor, blood tricking from her mouth. Instinctively, he leaned down, pulling back in revulsion when he saw the distant gaze in her eyes. One of the male servants rushed forward to her, shouting "Sonya!"

He only made it two steps before a loud CRACK rang out behind him and he fell to the ground convulsing from the 240,000 volts pulsing through him. The nameless Formaddi returned his thunder-stick to its holster and stood back in place, as if nothing had occurred.

"You chose the correct glass to give her, Tiberius," said Vladymir, leaning forward in a menacing pose. Seeing the shocked look pass over Tiberius' face, Paulo felt the need to clarify.

"Don't let him frighten you, Tiberius. All the wine served in this room delivers a mild poison. It is no threat to any Nephite. The nanocytes eliminate it. It was originally developed because we had a problem with the servants depleting our wine stores as we traveled."

This made Tiberius even more disgusted. How could they treat life so flippantly?

"You see, Tiberius," said Vlad, "there are only two types of people in this world: those who wield power, and those who submit to it. And would you like to know what real power is? Consider this. That servant knew fully that she would die if she drank that wine and yet she did. Why do you think that is?"

"Because she is afraid of you," answered Tiberius without a second of hesitation.

"Precisely. But fear can only keep a mass populace in check for so long. Fear turns to desperation, and they no longer value their own lives. They live only to bring down those in power. That is what we must prevent. Rebellion. This is the true value of the information you have brought us."

"I don't understand."

"Let me explain," interrupted Marco. "Perhaps I can put a less grim spin on things than our dramatic friend here. From the data you have given us, I am sure you know we have been able to locate a secret lab that the Centauri have been using to conduct illegal experiments. What you may not know is that from the science we were able to retrieve, it is clear they are attempting to streamline the nanocyte production process. We believe their goal is to introduce the treatments to the masses. Their efforts are apparently being guided by a Nephite who we believed to be long dead."

"Would that be so bad?" asked Tiberius.

"It would be catastrophic. The secret to our continued power lies in the fact that we do not die. This continuity of leadership and wisdom maintains solidarity within Arameus. Each generation of the Natural Born must be educated anew. Over time, previous knowledge is forgotten. They must struggle to provide for their families and to survive, thus all attempts at revolution have been fragmented and idealistic. This has led to our comfortable existence. We have never fought a major battle since our inception."

"Were they to find a way to introduce the treatments, even to a small number of Centauri leaders, this advantage would be lost. They would have countless years to find ways to undermine our authority. Now that we know the location of this laboratory, we can destroy it."

"Suppose you do destroy this particular lab. There will

always be another. They will not stop until they unlock our secrets," replied Tiberius.

"Very good," continued Marco. "You are correct in this, but this is where our advantages of extended life make themselves clear. Within the Institute, we have long been working on a way to solve this problem. We need the workers in the natural world to sustain our life, but we also need them to be loyal. It was no coincidence that we asked you to spy on Dr. Arian Cyannah. It is the work of his group that has proved to be the most promising for our goals." Marco allowed himself a coy smile, excited by the news he was about to share. "When it was brought to our attention that Ansley Brightmore was attempting to learn the details of his research, we knew that we were onto something big, and moreover, we knew we had a way to rid ourselves of the troublesome Professor." He leaned back in his chair, crossing his arms, his face full of pride.

"You see," added Vladymir, "one of Arian's students has made a major breakthrough. Ansley has surely ascertained this, although we are not sure whether Arian grasps the implications. If the results are correct, it may be possible to use a semi-sentient bio-bot to manage the synthesis of DNA during cell replication. The bot can be programmed to accept signals from exterior sources. Through this bot, it would be possible to achieve total thought control over a population. This will be the ultimate in biological warfare. We can enslave the population outside the domes. If a person displeases us, we just send a signal to the bots to commit cell suicide and eliminate the threat." Vladymir made a flippant sweeping motion with his hand, brushing away the meaningless lives. "This was the real reason behind the Natural Born registry and tracking program we implemented through Habimana Muteteli. Those outside our domes believe he is representing them. They trust him. Our goal is to use the implantation of the tracking devices as a ruse to infect them with the bio-bots."

"You would make slaves of the entire population of this world?" asked an incredulous Tiberius. He knew he was just as much a part of subjugating the Natural Born as the Overseers were, but slavery seemed a step too far. It offended his sensibilities.

"Look at the larger picture, Tiberius," answered Paulo. "What we are doing will be more humane. We will eliminate their need to rise from their station. They will be content with their work and families. We will take away all their doubts and ambitions. They will exist in a state of perfect harmony, both happy with their lives and fulfilled by their work. The bio-bots will eliminate all sadness. I envy them in a way. They will struggle with none of the higher questions of purpose and existence."

"It is those of us within the domes that will be left to struggle with these questions," added Pierre de Medici.

Tiberius could not deny that it would not be such a bad lot for the Natural Born. However a glance to where the two corpses just fell cast a darker image of this harmonious world. Surely those two servants had entertained their own hopes and dreams. He knew Kaiya would have rather died than be controlled by some bot. She had died anyway. He had never asked her if she had dreams. It didn't seem a proper question to ask a Natural Born woman. Now that he knew of these bio-bots, he wondered if he would have been able to keep her, provided she was controlled.

Vladymir sighed.

"We are not here to convince you of our plans. We do not require your approval. Marco wanted to have you here to celebrate your good work. I grow tired of this meeting and the company of you all. Let's just get on with it."

"What my impatient friend is hinting at," said Marco, in a triumphant tone, "is the reward we agreed upon for your accomplishment. You mentioned that you had in the past entertained thoughts of a family. We agreed to meet with you, in spite of the impertinence of your request, because we want to offer you the highest honor in Arameus. We want to offer you the privilege of having children."

Tiberius was shocked. He had believed a family to be impossible since accepting a place in the dome. Overwhelmed by the prospect, he choked back a sob as emotion overcame him.

Marco clasped his shoulder. "I see it is not lost upon you how great of an honor this is."

"Thank you," was all he could mutter in response.

"We have decided that you should take one of my young daughters as a wife," added Pierre. "She is eighteen years of age and quite beautiful. When your child comes of age, we will give him the governorship of Lucentum. We will make sure it is a boy. We have been displeased with its leadership for some time."

"I am afraid to say it is one of my sons from an earlier marriage," said Marco ruefully. "He was always disappointing, but I believed the responsibility would steady his path. I will place him in one of my households. He will enjoy bedding the Natural Born women."

"Pierre has even been so good as to dedicate one of his island holdings for you and your future family," added Paulo. "There you can build your mansion and live out your dreams. On your island, away from Arameus and the outside world, you will be free to bed whomever you choose, even the Natural Born, but only on the confines of the island."

"Understand that with these honors, you pay a price," said Vladymir sternly. "You will be watched at all times by our men. If you step out of line again, we will not hesitate to eliminate you. If you do as we say, for the betterment of Arameus, then you will prosper and live well.

"I humbly accept," answered Tiberius, tears still welling in his eyes. "I will not disappoint you, nor will I forsake this great honor."

"See that you don't," said Marco. "Now we shall end this meeting. I have matters of personal business to attend to, as I am sure you all do."

The five men stood. Tiberius felt almost as an equal,

though he knew this was not true. Each of the Overseers shook his hand. When he clasped the hand of Vladymir Romanov, the great man whispered in his ear, "I knew your father well. He was a great man. It was unfortunate he did not live to see the nanocyte treatments. I expect the same greatness from a man of your pedigree."

The four Overseers retreated toward the corners of the large room. Unsure of what to do, Tiberius headed back down the row of hanging plants and cages, toward the platform he had used to gain access to the room. Just as he was about to step onto the circular lift, he felt a hand brush against his shoulder.

Turning, he was surprised to find Paulo Dominiccio standing before him. "Your grace?" he asked.

"Please, call me Paulo. I wanted to have a brief word with you in private. In this room, there is no threat of unwanted ears." Paulo extended his hand.

Tiberius took his hand and held it. He noticed for the first time the man's striking blue eyes. Despite the ravages of age that had occurred long before the advent of the treatments, the man retained a soft, sensual quality. He must have been very attractive in his youth. Tiberius found him to be rather beautiful.

"What is it, Paulo?"

"I know you saw some shocking things today. I want you to know that I do not condone the wanton killing of the Natural Born that Vladymir exhibited today. He has a dark soul, coupled with a flair for the dramatic. I hope these unnecessary deaths will be prevented by the implementation of the bio-bots in the future."

"Thank you for that, sir. I mean, Paulo. I did find it shocking. But I am no one to question the actions of an Overseer."

"No, of course not. I just wanted to add something that wasn't mentioned, though I am sure it occupies a large area of your thoughts. Your former lover is not dead."

"What?" asked Tiberius, thinking he misheard the man.

"I know that look. I have lost many a lover. Marco chose not to kill her. He has taken a liking to you. You remind him of how he was before all this. He wanted to scare you and to test your loyalty, but he would not allow Vladymir to have her removed as was his wish."

"Where is she?" asked Tiberius, desperation and elation in his voice, still grasping the man's hand.

"She resides in Avignon, working as a house servant. I am sure this is not the ideal position for her in your eyes, but she lives. I must implore you as a friend to not contact her or respond to any messages you receive. This would prove catastrophic for you. Do as you are told. Marry Pierre's daughter. When you are on your own island, no one will question if you bring her to you. You can have it all. You just have to do as we say."

"I understand," said Tiberius, releasing his hand.

"Good. Fret not, my boy. Good things are in store for you." With this last salutation, Paulo Dominiccio kissed him on his cheek and walked back toward his own spire.

Tiberius watched him for a moment before stepping onto the lift. Twenty floors below, Marco's secretary was ready for him when he arrived, standing in front of him with his qubit in her hand.

"I trust you had a good lunch, Consulate," she said, handing him the device. Before he could respond, the platform again shot downward, 314 floors to the lobby of the Central Tower. Exiting the building, he looked at his qubit for the first time and found it flashing. It was Kaiya. After a painful moment of contemplation, he rejected the call.

"Block all calls from this number," he said aloud. He was acting in both of their best interests. He hoped that one day she would understand.

# Chapter Eighteen
## Beladero

The tunnel stretched for miles as they traversed the underbelly of Capitol City. The walk was made in silence, both men contemplating the conversation that had taken place. Arian was surprised by how far the city expanded outward from the South Tower. It was an hour before they came to another steel vaulted door.

"Well, are you ready?" asked Ansley.

"I'm ready," was Arian's reply. Ansley stepped forward and typed a code into a keypad beside the door. It creaked as hydraulics worked from deep within to lift the massive door from its resting place beneath the floor.

Arian stepped through the opening, past the last walls that made up the base of the dome that covered his home, Capitol City. For the first time in his life, he stood in the direct yellow sunlight, the ultraviolet rays warming his skin. He felt naked and insecure without the safety of his controlled environment, as if he were for the first time exposed. The fact that he had been forced to leave his qubit behind enhanced this feeling.

"We wouldn't want you being tracked outside the city, now would we?" were Ansley's words. He had never considered that his personal qubit could be used as a means for those in power to track him. The thought unnerved him. He felt as if he were stepping off a ledge from which he could not return, yet still he moved forward. Curiosity had taken him over now. He needed answers, and he felt they resided outside the dome with Ansley.

What answers he desired were a mystery even to him. He knew he had been stirred by Ansley's remarks about searching for his mother's killers and finding no Centauri. But more than that, he felt that somehow, by following this path, he would also find the answers to his questions about Kaiya, and as ashamed as he felt about it, this was his main concern.

They were met outside the dome by a towering figure. Rippling muscles, dark skin, and a six foot six inch frame, Jabari struck an intimidating figure.

"Do you still have your dodger?" Ansley's voice whispered from behind.

"Shut up," mumbled Arian.

"Jabari, you big bastard, let me introduce you to Arian Cyannah," announced Ansley, embracing the large man.

Jabari, who dwarfed Ansley, gave him a couple of hard pats on the back and muttered, "Whaddup, whaddup." Then turning his attention to Arian, gave him a sharp head nod. Arian, being unaccustomed to these mannerisms, gave an awkward nod back, feeling self-conscious. "Well let's go, dog. The vehicle's this way." Jabari's massive arm reached around both professors and ushered them to a six-wheeled all-terrain cruiser.

Arian had never seen a vehicle quite like this one. It was painted to resemble the tan, brown, and reddish tones of the high desert that surrounded them. It was open on top and seated four, with re-enforced shocks buffering the six thick tires, designed to drive over large rocks and uneven terrain. Two fuel canisters were attached to the back, which Arian found to be quite primitive. He was surprised combustion engines were still in use.

As they drove away from the city, Arian looked back, dumbstruck by the imposing dome that receded behind him. They were heading into what appeared to be the wilderness, as he could see nothing in any direction but dirt, brush, cacti, and red mountains in the distance. Arian was in the back alone, while Ansley and Jabari occupied the front, with Jabari at the wheel. Leaning forward, Arian whispered in Ansley's ear.

"What?" Ansley yelled over the roaring engine. "I can't hear you."

"I said," screamed Arian, "I thought all the local Natural Born occupied a city right outside our walls."

"That's to the east of the city," yelled Ansley in reply. "Our destination lies to the west, about 70 miles out. There are too many people and too many ears in the worker's settlement. Jabari lives in a city known to its residents as Beladero. People who live their lives independent of the Overseers populate it. It's a good place for us to talk."

Jabari swerved to miss a larger rock, throwing Arian to the other side of the cruiser. Looking up front to his driver, he noticed he had some sort of headphones in and was bobbing his head as if to music. Jabari looked in the rear view mirror and adjusted it to catch Arian's eye.

"Yo, you excited to have some NB cuisine tonight, dog?" Arian looked back confused, and Ansley punched Jabari on the arm, both of them laughing. Arian didn't like feeling so out of his element, and this feeling was exacerbated by their constant demeaning jokes.

After around an hour, Arian saw the tell tale signs of civilization on the horizon. Thick black smoke rose from large towers, which, though foreign to him, could only indicate industry. The community was framed in the shadow of a sharp cliff that rose almost a thousand feet into the air. As they drew closer, he saw the buildings taking form. They had a peculiar shape, as if many white washed clay buildings had been placed on top of one another until they reached four stories in height. At that level, the construction moved inward and formed another four stories, as if creating large steps to the top of the cliff. The roofs were thatched in colorful tile and seemed sturdy enough. It was obviously a large community, and Arian wondered how they obtained water in the middle of this vast desert.

As Arian was leaning forward to ask Jabari and Ansley about the water source, his question was answered. His eyes were drawn upward by a rainbow created from diffracted light to a massive waterfall spilling from the center of the cliff-face and landing somewhere behind the step-like buildings. Engulfing mist moved outward from it and wet the tops of the roofs in front.

"Incredible," he muttered to himself, though Ansley seemed to have heard.

"Within the rock face is a deep cavern containing a reservoir, part of an extended underground cave system that extends east to just beyond Capitol City. The water rained down thousands of years ago, filtering through the mineral rich rock into the aquifer. Pressure has forced it back up into the spring that waters these lands. In the capitol, their wells draw locally from this source. This entire region is sitting atop an underground freshwater sea."

"Amazing," remarked Arian. "Does the Parliament know of this place?"

Ansley laughed. "There are thousands of places like this, my boy, all flourishing outside of the Arameus Empire. Parliament doesn't care. They only care about threats."

Jabari guided the cruiser past the open gates of the city and through the outlying neighborhood streets. Arian had never seen so many children in his life. In Capitol City, as in all the domes, the children were raised in the pediatric nurseries together until they reached school age. From there, they were moved as they aged, from dormitory to dormitory on the East Campus of the Institute until they graduated to University. At this time they were divided up according to aptitude and future profession. But this... this was something different. Children were running free in the streets while disinterested parents enjoyed drinks on their balconies. Boys and girls ran together, throwing fake dodgers to one another in make-believe Patolli matches. They laughed and chattered to each other without a care. Arian wondered if they realized how insignificant they all were. He thought not.

The cruiser came to a stop in a square in the middle of the city. In the center of the square, a large pool of water bubbled, filled by the waterfall before splitting off in eight equidistant directions, radiating outward. Footbridges went over the canals, allowing for pedestrian traffic. Jabari and Ansley exited the vehicle, followed by a puzzled Arian.

"We walk from here," said Jabari, as he headed toward a festive looking storefront on the east side. Ansley put his arm around Arian's shoulder as they followed Jabari.

"I'm sure you are curious about this place," began Ansley. Arian nodded. "The waterfall feeds this central cistern and from here, the water is re-routed through irrigation to various community farms around the city. They are self-sufficient, producing all their own food. The electricity for the city comes from that system of turbines midway up the falls."

Arian gazed up at the massive turbines, which provided power for all these people. He was surprised such a primitive people had been able to maintain such a self-sufficient lifestyle. He thought of the people who slaved outside Capitol City to provide the power and food, wondering why they hadn't found similar means to support themselves. A life of supporting others seemed trivial.

"You have to be glad that we come from a society that has bypassed these base needs and can focus on the beauties and complexities of the universe," he said to Ansley. "What truths am I supposed to learn here?"

Ansley frowned. "If these are your impressions, then you understand nothing of the beauty and complexities of this universe. Loosen up and follow me. I'm sure we will be able to blow your superior mind in time. Right now, however,

Jabari wishes to be a gracious host and show us some of the local cuisine. I suggest you be respectful."

Shrugging, Arian followed across one of the bridges toward the storefront. Pushing through the curtained door, he was stunned by brightness of the interior. It was as if he had left a world of nondescript desert tones and entered another, filled with bright colors. Each wall was painted in contrasting shades of blue, red, and yellow. Ornate chandeliers hung every few feet along the ceiling, emanating a blue hue. Tables filled the front of the restaurant with families dining together in groups of six and seven. Arian felt a tinge of sadness and loss as he saw these people, though he wasn't sure why.

Ansley ushered Arian down a hallway that opened up into a large, semicircular bar, full of festive patrons. The bar overlooked an empty stage area with small cocktail tables. Jabari stood before one of the tables, motioning Ansley to sit as they approached. Ansley and Jabari sat opposite of one another, leaving Arian to take the lone seat facing the stage.

Once they were seated, two nondescript, dark-skinned servers brought water. The rest of the stage area remained empty. Music played over a speaker in the background, the style and language of which Arian had never heard. It seemed up-tempo, with what sounded like guitars and steel drums. All in all, he found it to be pleasing. Arian's disappointment with the water was evident by the look on his face.

"Don't worry, kid. I don't plan on drinking water either. We will have drinks soon enough." Ansley smiled reassuringly. Jabari raised his hand to signal the waitress. Arian's jaw dropped as an elegant woman with long black hair, a tall, shapely body, and olive skin appeared.

Before he could stop himself, Arian blurted out, "If your name is as beautiful as you, I must know it now." Ansley erupted in laughter and Jabari lifted an eyebrow.

With more grace than Arian would have expected from a Natural Born server, she replied, "My name is Daniela." Her thick accent drove Arian crazy. "I see you have met my husband, Jabari." Arian slunk in his chair, unable to meet the gaze of Jabari, who mocking stared him down before bursting out in laughter as well.

"It's all good, dog," Jabari said. "My girl is hot."

Daniela squeezed Arian's shoulder and whispered for the entire table to hear, "My husband's bark is bigger than his bite." This drew a snicker from Ansley and a frown from Jabari. She pretended to not notice her perturbed husband. "I know this is your first time in our wonderful city, so let me suggest what Ansley and Jabari tend to order. Our famous Desert Snake shot to start."

"That would be wonderful," Arian replied, his cheeks still hot with blood.

"Give us a couple of large ales too, baby. We are thirsty from our trip," shouted Jabari after her.

"You're always thirsty," was her only reply as she disappeared behind the bar.

"Desert Snake?" asked Arian.

"It's good," reassured Ansley. "It is booze, you know."

Daniela reappeared with the ales and three Desert Snake shots on a tray. Placing them in front of the three men, she leaned over to Jabari, whispering, "Pace yourself, darling."

Jabari chuckled. "Get out of here, woman." His affection for her was clear.

Ansley was the first to grab his glass and raise it. "I raise a toast to my only two friends, who both happen to be twenty-eight years old. May you each live many more than that."

The three men drained the shots, Arian choking from the high proof.

"Wait," he said between coughs, "you're the same age as me?"

"Does that surprise you?" asked Ansley.

"No. I don't know. I just assumed he was older."

"Of course you do," Ansley said. "You stopped aging at twenty-two. Our big friend, however, has been in direct sunlight his entire life and left to the elements. We all take these drinks together, as I have for hundreds of years, yet I assure you, only Jabari is in danger of an early grave from its poison. Fifty years from now you will still be a young professor in the Institute and this man, a physical specimen to behold, will be wasted away, old and dying. Do you think this is fair, Arian?"

Arian shifted in his chair and grabbed his ale. Jabari spoke before he had a chance.

"That sucks, dog. You're depressing me, Ansley."

"Still, Arian," continued Ansley, "with all of your advantages, do you feel secure? Suppose Jabari wanted to reach across this table and snap both our necks. Would we be able to stop him?"

Looking across the table, Arian felt real fear. Jabari only shook his head and looked down, as if embarrassed.

"Well, if he won't answer, then I will," continued Ansley. "He could kill you and me with ease. Yet despite all of his advantages, he will die, soon in our years, likely from these drinks we have before us, and you will live on forever. Again, I ask, does that seem fair?"

Arian stared into his glass.

"Why do you think it is that he doesn't kill us both? He should. His people have been abandoned by the rich and powerful and left to die outside our domes, yet they thrive without us. We have discovered the secret to eternal life and locked it away from the rest of the world, and yet he harbors us no ill will. To you, he is merely entertainment, but I assure you, he is so much more than that. Why do you think that is?"

And at once Arian knew, and before he could stop himself, he blurted out, "Because he's happy."

"An interesting thought," said Ansley. "Are you happy, Jabari?"

"Who me? Hell yeah I'm happy, dog. Have you seen my girl?" Jabari chugged his ale and slammed the empty glass down onto the table, smiling.

"Are you happy, Arian?" asked Ansley, his gaze penetrating.

Thinking for a moment, Arian laughed and chugged his own ale. Slamming his glass on the table next to Jabari's, he looked at Ansley.

"I see what you're trying to do, and it is a ridiculous premise. Happiness is a meaningless term and unquantifiable. A man is born with a certain disposition and no environmental influences can change that. I am a Nephite, a professor of the Institute, and I love my work. That is enough for any man. And regarding love, I have an eternity to find it, and when I do, I will not lose her as you did."

The comment stung Ansley and his cheeks rose to a warm shade of crimson. Even Jabari seemed uncomfortable. Arian instantly regretted the insult.

Drawing close, Ansley spoke in a low tone, venom in his voice, "I assure you, kid, I have never, for a single instant, lost her. She is always with me." He turned and ordered three more Desert Snake shots and three more ales. The stage area was beginning to fill up and the dull drone of an expectant crowd filled the area. Ansley excused himself to the restroom. Jabari leaned forward to Arian when he was gone.

"That was cold, dog. That was your own mother you just called out."

"Drop the sentimental garbage. I didn't know her and neither did you."

Jabari leaned his large body back in the chair and eyed Arian, judging him with his viper-like eyes.

"It's true that I didn't know your mother. But my people," and he motioned at the other patrons around the restaurant, "they knew her well. It was she and Ansley that built the turbines that provide our electrical power. It was she who designed the irrigation system that has allowed us our independence from your world. Your mother is well regarded here. And let's not forget Arian, one man out, one man in. If your mother never dies then you are never born. I may be your entertainment, but I have seen much more of the world than you."

They sat in silence and drank their refreshed ales. The front of the stage was full now, and Arian watched the primitive band set up their percussion instruments and amplifiers. He was different from most scientists and had always been drawn to art and music. He was excited to hear the band play. Ansley's return disrupted his thoughts. In a gesture of contrition, Arian offered a cigarette, a vice he had taken up since meeting the old Professor. As he went to light it, Jabari grabbed it from his hand.

"They don't smoke inside here," said Ansley. "Lung cancer and emphysema. When you don't have nanocyte treatments, cigarette smoke can be quite harmful. Let's go outside." Jabari released his hand and nodded to Ansley, who guided Arian back through the restaurant and outside.

As they exited the curtained doorway, dusk was breaking over the city. The yellow day sun was settling behind the cliff face as the red night sun broke the opposite horizon. The receding light from the day sun created a strange but beautiful shadow effect across the waterfall. Blue halogen lamps lit the city. Arian attempted to light his cigarette, yet the high desert winds kept snuffing out the flame.

"Here," said Ansley, cuffing his hand around Arian's lighter. "You have to block the wind. We aren't in the dome anymore." Lighting his own, Ansley leaned back against the wall on one foot, studying Arian, waiting for him to speak. After a moment, Arian did.

"So you and my mother built this place together?" he asked.

"We did."

"Why?"

"Why not?"

"You had everything in the dome. Why would you risk it to come out here?"

"I think it would be difficult for one of your upbringing

to understand why we did this. I think it will be even more difficult for me to explain why I brought you out here. But I guess now is as good a time as any for me to make an attempt."

"Well," responded Arian, "you clearly think me incapable of understanding you, yet here I am." He took a long drawl off his cigarette. "I'm listening."

Ansley took a deep breath, looking to the sky for inspiration before beginning.

"Imagine for a moment a world where everyone is born equal. All have the same opportunity to thrive or fail. Some may die young. Some may live long inconsequential, yet happy lives. In this world, everyone has the opportunity to become the leader or the villain. This is how the old world was designed by law. Yet there was another factor. Birthright. Imagine that everyone is entered into a lottery to be the leader of the world, yet those born from better families had more entries in the drawing. Everyone strove, and everyone hoped, and sometimes, the underdog won that lottery against all odds. But no matter how high a man rose or how low a man fell, their paths always converged on that dark road we know as death.

"Now imagine that there is a worldwide economic collapse that only those with the most influence can survive. But they don't merely survive. Prices are low, and they are the only ones with money. They buy up more and more, and their influence increases exponentially. Now, although the law still decrees everyone is equal, the lottery is severely skewed toward those with money, and the cycle continues, growing harsher toward those with no birthrights every pass. This is what happened during my time. The wealth became so concentrated in private hands that the elite rivaled the worldwide governments, and since they owned the private companies that supplied the militaries of the world, the food for the world, and the energy that powered the world, they now had the governments of the world subjugated to their interests.

"The top four companies in the world called a conference in a city that used to be called Patagonia. They controlled all the important economic sectors except for one. Science. That had always been a government-funded enterprise. The four heads decided at that point to hold the economy hostage unless they could gain control of the government's only trump card. Nanosoft."

"But I thought Nanosoft was the pre-cursor to our modern day Institute?" interrupted Arian.

"Precisely," answered Ansley, pleased. "But that was not its intended function. Nanosoft was a company that subsisted almost entirely on donations, both private and from governments worldwide. Its motivations were pure, and it was devoted to wiping out diseases that had plagued mankind since its inception and alleviating poverty worldwide. John J. Aster, Anabelle's father, amassed one of the world's largest fortunes and devoted it to philanthropy. With Nanosoft, he assembled the greatest collection of minds the world had ever seen, your mother, father, and myself included."

"And I am not going to be humble about it, kid. We created wonderful things, the most important of which was your mother and Richard's work on nanocyte technology. We had it in our hands, Arian, the gift of eternal life, a way to stop all pain and suffering, and we were prepared to share it with the world."

"So what happened? How did we end up here?" asked Arian, puzzled.

"The Patagonia Agreement happened."

"The Patagonia Agreement?"

"As I said, the heads of the four most powerful corporations in the world met in Patagonia. No one really knows the details of what occurred at this meeting, but we do know the result. You may recognize the participants of this meeting. Marco Luccio was the chairman of the World Bank and the largest financier in the world. Paulo Dominiccio owned all rights to the mineral mines and refineries on the Ursula moon. This is the source of nearly all the world's energy not created by coal, and much cleaner as well. Dominiccio was a very powerful man. And how do you transport all this energy from the Ursula moon back to our planet? That's where Pierre de Medici made his fortune, specializing in space transport. He had a monopoly on the transportation industry. I have seen you flying around Capitol City on his patented hawks. The most powerful man of them all, Vladymir Romanov, owned Allied Defense Systems. He designed, built, and supplied all of the world's militaries with weapons ranging from bullets to ballistic missiles. Of course, he kept his more cutting edge designs to himself for his own private mercenary armies."

"How can that be? You're saying that the Overseers made a pact to deny eternal life to the world?" interjected Arian.

"I'm saying the men who would become the Overseers met and made a pact to consolidate their power," replied Ansley, his patience waning. The worldwide economy was in shambles. There were food shortages, riots, and protests. The middle class fell into poverty and voiced their concerns over the disproportionate concentrations of wealth. The four entered into an agreement to protect themselves from the masses." Ansley paused, pondering the orange glow at the end of his cigarette. There was a look in his eye, not of sadness, but of resignation.

"They bought all the land in Patagonia and built an impenetrable city from which they could safely continue to wield their power and run their companies," Ansley continued. "This was the first domed city. Marco Luccio financed the project, Paulo Dominiccio provided the energy to run the self-contained ecosystem, and Vladymir Romanov created a state of the art defense system, which included a newly discovered polymer that could withstand a 2-megaton nuclear blast. It is this polymer that covers Capitol City. In case you were wondering, you live in a land that used be known as Patagonia."

Arian felt sick to his stomach. They never studied the history of how Arameus was created at the Institute. There were passing mentions of how the Overseers had brought them from a world of chaotic riots to a world of security, but that was as far as it went. This all seemed so different. Separating themselves from the less fortunate seemed callous.

"You would be killed for sharing this knowledge with me," observed Arian.

"Trust me, they have tried. It turns out that Ansley Brightmore is a greater adversary than they expected. But they can't be seen by Nephites to be murdering their citizens to maintain power, so they created the Centauri as a front to systematically remove those of us who were here from the beginning, cleansing Arameus of all citizens not born in their hatcheries. In this way, they will maintain absolute control of the myth surrounding them. I'm afraid your mother was a victim of one of their cleansings."

Arian's stomach dropped, and he felt a deep rage overtake him. How could the empire murder its citizens? He felt as if his perfect world was crumbling before him and being replaced by something dark and ugly.

"How does Nanosoft fit into all of this?" he asked. "How is it that the nanocyte treatments were not shared with the world?"

Ansley stubbed out his cigarette before replying. "Being among the most powerful and richest men on the planet, they had representatives on the board at Nanosoft. When news came to them of the breakthroughs in nanocyte technology, they wanted to control it. Nanosoft was struggling with an internal ethical debate on how to utilize the treatments. Curing major diseases was a no-brainer, but should they use them to stop aging? It was a radical thought to consider. How would a world function if its citizens didn't age? How would that affect the way we reproduce? It would lead to overpopulation and demand more resources. And what was to be done with the oldest members of society? Could we as scientists overthrow the entire natural order?" He raised his eyebrows.

"However, the Overseers were already advanced in their years and had no time for such debates. Moreover, a population of forever young and healthy members would threaten their power and attempts to create a lasting hold on the world's wealth. They needed the treatments for themselves, and they needed to control the treatments for their survival. When the board decided to use nanocyte treatments only for gravely ill children, the Patagonia Four decided to act. It is not known how they were able to get John Aster to resign as chair of Nanosoft, but many believe it was by kidnapping his beloved only child, Anabelle. She was three years old. She and her father have resided in Patagonia, now Capitol City, ever since. A series of unexplained murders took care of the rest of the board, and Marco Luccio took over as chair of Nanosoft."

"So they began taking the treatments themselves?" Arian asked.

"The nanocyte treatments were never made public, but the Overseers and those in their inner circle received them. All Nanosoft labs were moved to Patagonia, along with their scientists and it was re-named the Institute. To maintain the flow of the nanocytes and other technologies that they now monopolized, they had to provide the staff scientists with treatments as well. Your mother and I were among the first to receive them."

Ansley pulled out two cigarettes and offered one to Arian. "You look like you need this."

Arian nodded, lighting his cigarette, as Ansley spun the story of the past. With each revelation, his own world was torn down, replaced by a devastating new scenario. Mesmerized, he hung on every word from the old Professor, who continued with increasing enthusiasm.

"As it became apparent to the rest of the world what was happening in Patagonia, the richest members of society turned over all their wealth and land holdings to the four men who built the city in exchange for the nanocyte treatments. None were permitted the treatments unless they agreed to reside within the dome. The power and wealth of the entire world shifted to Patagonia, and given the large wealth disparity, governments were no longer solvent and began to collapse, one by one, under the strain of debt. As this continued over many years, the Overseers began to collect the best and brightest of the outside world to add to the diaspora of humanity they were creating. Artists, engineers, models, all deemed worthy were collected and offered eternal youth within the city.

"Outside the dome, there was a power vacuum, and society fell into a feudal state, with the Overseers owning most of the land and factories of the world. They appointed bosses to run their interests in the various regions, often with brutality and violence. Domed cities were constructed around the world, each governed by the new Capitol City. Child bearing was limited due to spatial constraints, a law enforced through a simple immunization administered upon entering the dome.

"DNA samples were taken of each new citizen of the domes. When "unfortunate accidents" occurred, and I assure you, there were many, children were engineered from combinations of this DNA and the zygotes were implanted in the Natural Born foster mothers who give birth in the hatcheries. Actually, it was at this point that the term "Natural Born" came into existence. People born the old way were the Natural Born and those engineered within our domes were Nephites. The creation of the two classes was the true birth of Arameus. As years turned to decades, those outside the domes who remembered the past died, and our current system remained in place."

Arian was silent as he finished his cigarette and looked out over the free city before him.

"And places like this?" he asked.

"Oh, there are many, I'm sure," responded Ansley. "People are resilient and find a way to survive and flourish. These free cities are mostly left alone and ignored by the government as they are no threat."

"If you had the technology for nanocytes, why not give it to the world?" asked Arian.

"It isn't that simple. We had the knowledge, but no access to resources on our own. The Overseers control everything. However, you will find that we have not been idle. Your mother and I began to build something special here, which I hope to show you if you decide to pledge your loyalty to our cause."

Arian needed only seconds to consider.

"My curiosity about what you're up to alone is enough for me to commit to your cause. Looks like I'm joining the Centauri." Against his will, his mind went to Kaiya. He was close to fulfilling her original request.

"That will have to be enough for me to trust you," answered Ansley, giving Arian a curious look. "Let's go in. You have to see this guitar player."

As they re-entered the restaurant, Arian's head was spinning with a thousand different thoughts. The one thought that repeated most often was that he was now part of some type of revolution. While the idea of treason was an uncomfortable subject for him, the idea of being a revolutionary held a certain excitement that he just couldn't shake. He had never done anything to stray from the path that the governing bodies of Arameus had set before him, and because of that, he had always felt that his life was missing something.

Still, he had no idea what this revolution was. All Arian knew of the Centauri was that they killed innocent people in bombings. But if Ansley was correct, and it had been the Overseers the entire time, then what would be the goal of Ansley's Centauri?

His thoughts went to Kaiya. He was in love with her. For whom was he truly an agent? He had sworn allegiance to Ansley, but was that another ruse to infiltrate the cell on behalf of Kaiya? It hadn't felt like that. He meant what he said to Ansley. If the Overseers murdered his mother, he could no longer serve them in good conscience.

He was drawn from his thoughts by a hard slap on the back from Ansley.

"Kid, snap out of it. I know that was a lot to take in, but we are finished with work for the night. B.B. Borkar is playing. Relax."

Arian noticed for the first time the scenes taking place around him. Hundreds of colorfully dressed Natural Born of various races stood shoulder to shoulder in the area surrounding the bar, dancing and cheering. The air was filled with the sweetest sounds Arian had ever heard as drums and horns pounded out bluesy rhythms while a lead guitar hit just the right notes to send chills down his spine. Ansley grabbed his arm and ushered him past the crowds back to the now occupied tables before the stage, finding Jabari sitting by himself, drunker than he had been when they left him.

At the stage, Arian found the source of the guitar. It was the most aged human he had seen in person. Ansley was the oldest human he knew, but appeared to be twenty-four. This man was large and overweight and his skin sagged, forming deep crevices in his face. He was also the darkest man Arian had ever seen in person. He had the same skin tone as Habimana Muteteli, the special representative of the Natural Born. He was wearing a suit made of sequenced material, the lights above reflecting the entire spectrum off him. He sat in a chair at the front of the stage leaning back with a beautifully adorned guitar resting on his lap. His giant foot tapped along with the beat, leading the band.

Then he began to sing. It was his voice that took Arian's breath away. Filled with the rasp and hurts of a thousand lifetimes, he belted out deep from within his stomach the struggles that all the men who occupy this world, no matter how high or low, have in common. His voice made Arian feel like he was a member of this crowd, as if they were all equals.

"This is fucking amazing," he screamed to his companions at the table.

"Yeeaaah," yelled Jabari. "I think our boy likes the blues."

"Why do we not have this music in Capitol City?" he said in Ansley's ear.

Laughing, Ansley slapped him on the back and replied,

"I don't think the Overseers were ever big fans of the music of the lower class. Art like this tended to spawn revolution in centuries past. It tends to make those who are supposed to feel downtrodden get a little more pep in their step and realize they aren't alone."

"Well, I feel like I could take over the damn world right now. Let's get some drinks!"

"Yeah, yeah, now he's talking," yelled Jabari, slamming his fist on the table. "Yo baby, get us another round of ales and Desert Snakes," he screamed across the floor to Daniela.

She frowned at him, motioning in a way that stated, "Get them yourself."

"I'll be right back, dog," said Jabari, jumping up and rushing to the bar.

Ansley and Arian were content to sit and enjoy the music. Arian relaxed and allowed his mind to rest, entranced by the spectacle before him. The music was so raw and open and free. It was everything that he wished he could be. When the song ended, the crowd, including Arian, erupted in applause. As the cheering died down and the musicians tuned their instruments, he leaned over to Ansley.

"Why does Jabari keep calling us 'dog'? Is it some sort of insult against Nephites?"

Ansley waved him off. "You need to stop being so sensitive. It's a slang term popular in the free cities. It's like saying 'buddy'."

Before Arian could respond, his shoulder was grabbed firmly from behind. Looking up, he saw a menacing man towering over him. He had a thick, knotted beard and a deep scar that ran from above where his left eye should have been, down through the socket and onto his cheek. In his good eye, Arian could see that this man meant him nothing but harm.

"What business does a Nephite have in Beladero? You aren't in your fucking dome now, are you? Why shouldn't I break your unnatural little neck?"

Ansley leaned forward and said, "Friend, he is traveling

with me."

"Stay out of this, Ansley," glowered the man. "We tolerate you in Beladero on account of what you've done. Don't confuse that with acceptance."

Arian, trying to make peace, looked up and said, "Dog, we have no problems between us."

"Dog?" The man smirked, turning to the crowd forming around them and announcing, "This little Nephite just called me 'dog'." He clenched his giant fist and hurled it toward Arian's face. Arian closed his eyes in anticipation as he heard the shattering of glass around him. The blow never landed. Opening his eyes he saw that Jabari had caught the approaching fist in mid-air, stopping it with ease. Their tray of drinks was spread about floor. Jabari's expression was contorted with rage as he removed the hand from Arian's shoulder and, whirling the man around, gave him an aggressive shove in the back. The man stumbled five steps, almost falling into another table. Turning back to Jabari defiantly, he was met with the superior man's commanding baritone.

"Keep walking, dog."

Still reluctant, the man turned and slunk off a few steps. He stopped and turned, as if to say something else.

"I said keep walking!" Jabari rushed at him, but Daniela appeared out of nowhere and stepped in between. The man exited the stage area and Daniela ushered Jabari back to the table.

"I will get you more drinks, baby, and someone to clean this up. You just sit here and I don't want to see you fighting with anyone." She leaned down and kissed his cheek before walking around the table and placing a gentle hand on Arian, massaging the shoulder the man had just been squeezing.

"I apologize, honey. Some people have no manners. You won't have any more problems tonight. Relax and enjoy yourself."

Arian didn't think that this would be possible, but after a few assurances from Jabari, a few more Desert Snake shots, and a few more songs from B.B., his head was foggy and his heart was happy again. The rest of the night was spent drinking and hearing stories from Jabari's life. All things considered, it turned out to be a fantastic and informative evening. As the concert drew to a close and lights turned on overhead, Arian knew he was drunk. Ansley reached over and grabbed his arm.

"Come on, my boy. Let's go sleep this off. Jabari will show you to your room for the next few nights."

"My room?" protested Arian. "We aren't going home?"

"We are home, at least for a few days," replied Ansley. "The Spring Festival begins in the morning in the Capitol. No one will expect you anywhere for a week. I didn't choose this time by accident. Our qubits are in the city. As far as the powers that be are concerned, so are we. Besides, I haven't shown you anything of my plans. Tomorrow I'm going to blow your mind."

Too drunk to protest, Arian lumbered off behind Jabari, wondering what adventures a new day would bring.

# Chapter Nineteen
# The Prodigal Daughter

Sunlight streamed through the window, warming Kaiya's face as she awoke in the tiny servant's chamber. The breeze came into the room this time of day, causing the drapes to flow and casting shadows on the floor. The windows were always open in this part of the world, with its mild weather and misting rainfall. She could smell the familiar muskiness of the damp earth. It was on this very soil that her ancestors had bled and sweat for hundreds of years to produce the grappa. Without the grappa, there could be no wine.

The cool air brought out the rich odors of the antique oak furniture that had been passed down through the generations of her family. As a young girl she would have dressed and scurried into her father's room, anxious to wake him. Her mother would not be there, having died bringing Kaiya into the world. Since she had never known her mother, she could not perceive the loss other than in the sadness she saw in her father's eyes. His spirits always improved when gazing upon his daughter, and he never failed to comment on how her beauty would surpass that of her mother, which, according to the other villagers, was really saying something. Kaiya closed her eyes, trying to recall repressed memories from long ago.

*Her family lost the vineyard during the economic collapse, well before her father's time, though they stayed on for generations as tenants of the land. During the economic struggles, the Overseer, Pierre de Medici, gave governorship of the new domed city of Sikyon to select family members. The least of his flock, Flavius Decimus, was given dominion over the fields of Avignon. Though not a Nephite, he was allowed nanocyte treatments, and thus lorded over Kaiya's family for over two hundred years.*

*When her father and brothers were taken by the summer flu, she was orphaned at the age of twelve. In Flavius' mind, he could hardly be blamed. The young orphan was blossoming into a woman right in front of him, while he stayed with his same un-aging wife. She was young, unsoiled, her breasts just beginning to burgeon. When his wife discovered the abuse three years later, she arranged for Kaiya to be taken away to a brothel that specialized in child prostitution. She wanted the woman who seduced her husband to be the whore that she was. At age fifteen, Kaiya was the most sought after prostitute in town.*

She rolled in the bed, surrounding herself in the covers, dreading the moment when she would have to leave their comforting protection, though that time was long past. Standing, she allowed her bare feet to acclimate to the cool wooden floors beneath. Walking to the dressing mirror, she admired her naked reflection in the glass. She was still beautiful. Being without the nanocyte treatments for over a month, she feared her age would catch her, and she would find a woman of fifty-two staring back. Tiberius would never accept her then.

After dressing in the coarse brown servant's dress, she exited the room, walking down the workers' stairs to the kitchen. Moving past the line of cooks and maids, she noticed that none bothered to honor her with a glance. She was no longer one of them, even though she had grown up with them all. She was the master's whore. She didn't blame them, really. They had all aged naturally and looked every bit of their hard years. How could they understand? None of them had been forced to sell their bodies at fifteen. The great beauty everyone praised when she was a girl had turned out to be a curse. There was only one use for beauty in a Natural Born female. All she had ever desired was a way out. She had found it in Tiberius. For all his faults, he had never treated her as a slave.

Exiting the kitchen, she entered the plantation's elegant dining room. The sprawling room had the ability to seat fifty, but currently, only the members of the Decimus family were present. Flavius sat at the head of the table, surrounded by his wife, Lucretia, his three sons and their wives. All of them received the treatments and thus were at least a hundred years of age. This was Flavius' fourth wife, and she was the youngest at the table at one hundred and seven. Entering the dining area carrying a silver coffee pot, Kaiya heard his terrible voice.

"I see our servant has graced us with her presence. I was assuming you would continue to sleep in."

"I apologize, sir." Kaiya's voice was barely audible. "I must have overslept."

"Of course, my dear, why fret?" came Flavius' cold reply. "And why shouldn't you sleep? Obviously you run this plantation."

She walked to the table and began to pour his coffee, tensing as he slid his dry, cold hand up her leg, under her dress, resting in on her inner thigh. Painful memories of him touching her as a girl rushed through her. Shaking, she lost control of her fingers, dropping the coffee pot onto the table and spilling hot black liquid onto the white linen, which then pooled into the lap of Flavius' horrible wife.

Lucretia's voice was shrill. "That whore ruined my dress. How can you let this happen, husband?"

"This insolence will not stand, my love, I assure you. Come, Kaiya, let's see if we can't beat this rebellious streak out of you." Grabbing her by the arm, he dragged her out of the dining room, through the parlor and out the front door. As Flavius yanked her into the morning sunlight, she knew he was taking her to the stables. Entering the cool dim shelter of the old horse barn, he gritted his teeth and spoke from between them.

"If you are to act like an animal, then perhaps you should be beaten like an animal."

Fear rushed through her and would have paralyzed her had he not been dragging her. She had been to the barn before, as a young girl.

"Please... I'm so sorry. I didn't mean to drop it. I just... I don't know. It won't happen again!"

"You're damn right it won't."

He pulled her into the stable to an empty stall reserved for unbroken horses. Chaining her wrists to the wall with a metal brace, he selected a whip from the shelf.

"And this is how I will make sure of that." He let the whip fly. A loud SMACK sounded throughout the stable. It was the sound of skin being ripped from flesh. Kaiya cried out in vain as he rained down, blow after blow, until she collapsed in the dirt and hay, whimpering. Walking up to her quivering body, he lifted her to her feet, ignoring the blood streaming down her body. He ran his finger through the blood before running it up her leg to her inner thigh.

"It's been a long time since I've had you, but you're still beautiful." As he raped her, her mind left, and she was back in the fields with her father and her brothers, running amongst the freshly blooming grappa vines. It was a technique she learned long ago. Anything was better than the horror that was her life. Of all of Sikyon's ruling class that had used her as they wished, she could remember almost nothing from the encounters. Her mind always disappeared into the joys of her youth, when her father was alive to protect her. She had never been naïve, however. Somewhere, deep in her subconscious mind, the horrors were storing up. Within her there was a terrible, vengeful monster waiting to lash out at the world.

As he walked away, leaving her chained and cowering in the corner of the stall, he stopped and looked back, laughing.

"Don't you ever forget, if you breathe a word of this to anyone in the house, I will sell you back into sex slavery in Sikyon." He took a few more steps before adding, "I will send Dante here with a nanocyte treatment for you. I'm not sure these scars on your back will look good for me." He walked to the corner of the stall and rinsed off with water from a trough. Discarding his robes to the ground, he pulled down a fresh set hanging from a hook. It was clear to Kaiya that she was not the only member of the household who was forced to endure this sick ritual.

As she lay upon the ground, wetted with blood, tears, and semen, her thoughts went to Tiberius. He would see through her note. He would come for her and take her from this place as he had twenty years ago. Deep down, however, she knew she had been abandoned. It hadn't been Tiberius who had sent her here. Her exile was a message from the Overseers. A man of his ambition would not fail to recognize this and would adjust his behavior accordingly. Tiberius would never come.

It seemed like hours had passed before Dante arrived. Kaiya had lain there alone, shivering from blood loss on the straw-covered floor. She had wet herself as well. Both of her wrists were still chained to the wall, restricting her movement. Being a servant himself, Dante was not a cruel man. He covered her with a blanket in an effort to preserve her modesty. The course fibers stung her back, and she groaned at the pain.

"Be silent, my dear. We must enter the house quietly. You don't want to draw the master's wrath again."

Upon releasing the shackle, he carried her out of the stable and laid her on the damp grass, pulling a syringe from his coat pocket and injecting it into the muscle of her exposed thigh.

"This will take your pain away. Now sleep." There was no argument from Kaiya who fell into a dreamless slumber.

She woke in a strange bedroom with no knowledge of how much time had passed, though it must have been substantial as the red sun was now high. She was on her stomach, afraid to move, while a woman cleaned her wounds. She felt the bulk and sting of an IV in her arm. As she stirred, the woman cautioned her.

"Don't move, child. I must clean the wounds. The nanocytes will speed your recovery, but you don't want any scars."

"I am no child," responded Kaiya. "But I have my share of scars."

"I can see that. But why should there be more?"

Kaiya saw no need to argue.

"What is your name?" she asked.

"I am Yasmine. Dante is my husband. He brought you to me for the healing. I see many girls like you. Our master is cruel."

Kaiya winced as Yasmine touched one of the more sensitive wounds with the gauze.

"The more cruel the man, the easier he is to control," she said, attempting to mask the pain with her words. "I have dealt with cruel men my entire life. Their cruelty betrays a lack confidence. It's exploitable."

Yasmine shook her head. "Don't be foolish, dear. Look what he has done to you. You are a child, but I have been here a long time. You must not draw the master's wrath."

Kaiya was moved by Yasmine's plea. She had long ago given up caring for others, but this woman's resilience touched her.

"As these nanocytes heal my wounds, you can't be so foolish as to think this is the first time I have received them from Flavius. I was born on this plantation, though I was gone before you arrived. I decided long ago to never be a slave again, and I will not be one now. I would appreciate it if you stopped calling me child. Do you think I had a bad day? Do you think I need your sympathy? I was raped from the age of thirteen and given the treatments to preserve my beauty so I could be raped again. What happened today was not an event. It was an inconvenience."

Yasmine stood up, horrified. She backed away from Kaiya.

"I don't know what to say."

"Then say nothing."

Silence passed between them, but Yasmine didn't fail to notice the rapid healing of the wounds.

"You were not lying, mistress. Only one with a history of the treatments could heal this quickly."

Kaiya, lying on her stomach, turned her head to view Yasmine for the first time. The age of the woman surprised her. Her hair was grey and wrinkles wracked her body. Kaiya stood, her wounds no longer painful, and removed the needle from her veins that was delivering the precious nano-treatments. Fully naked, she faced her nurse.

"What are you doing?"

"Tell me, Yasmine. Do you have natural children?"

"Two daughters. Dante and I didn't think we could get pregnant. I was forty when I had my first. They are fourteen and ten."

"Good. Hide this IV bag of nano-treatments for them, in case they are ever subjected to the same horrors this house offered me. My advice is to run, especially if they are cursed with beauty."

"Thank you, mistress. I don't know what to say."

"It's nothing, but I will need you to get me to the master's bedroom. If he trusts Dante this much, you must have access as well."

"I do have access, but not for you. What do you intend?"

"I merely need to make a call. I have powerful friends that can help us, and your family's prospects can change forever."

"I will see what I can do."

The following days passed with little fanfare. Kaiya was allowed to remain in her room. Flavius left her alone, assuming she would be healing for the next several days, and she was, slowly. She convinced Yasmine to store away her daily doses for her own children, were the need for them ever to arise. Still, it was not all a waste. Dante and Yasmine visited each evening, and she had promised them much.

Access to Flavius' qubit was the key. From there, she could contact Tiberius and find a way to set up her new allies as servants in Capitol City where they could build their lives in the Natural Born cities surrounding the dome. When Tiberius heard of her plight, he would help her. As always, her body would be the key that provided access, that and a little help from Dante and Yasmine.

***

It was a little over a week since the rape and Flavius was in his private bedroom, away from his wife. When Dante came to Kaiya, she was dressed seductively in light pink lingerie that both betrayed every curve of her body and showed nothing.

"Are you ready?"

"Dante, I promise you, after tonight, you will be free. Just do as we planned."

He grabbed her hand and walked her down the servant's corridor to the stairs that led to the master bedrooms. Pulling out an old key, he unlocked the door that opened to the stairs. They walked quietly, up the stairs and down the hall, past the rooms of the three sons of Flavius and then that of his wife. When they reached Flavius' bedroom door, Dante grabbed Kaiya by the shoulders. She flinched at his touch.

"Are you sure?" he whispered.

"I am. Just do as you promised."

"We will."

Kaiya knocked on the door, softly at first, and then hard, as Dante disappeared into the shadows. She heard grumbling on the other side of the door and then after some time, the latch lifting. As the door opened, they stood face to face, Kaiya with her rapist, and Flavius with his servant. He froze, taking in the beautiful specimen before him.

Realizing who she was, he demanded, "What do you want, girl?"

Kaiya placed her hand on his face and ran it down his neck and onto his chest. Flavius seemed confused.

"I can't stop thinking about when you took me in the stable," she said, her voice raw with sexuality. "I want you again." With that, he allowed her to push him into the bedroom and toward the bed. She closed and latched the door, untying her robe and revealing herself to him without letting the garment fall from her shoulders.

"I thought you would like it," he sneered. "You all do in the end."

She pushed him onto the bed playfully and climbed on top, kissing him. He was grabbing her roughly all over, but she steered him away from her back, where her wounds were still fresh.

"Slap me," she said, "like you did in the stable." He smirked, clearly aroused. He slapped her, softer than before. Kaiya slapped him back.

"Do you like that? Slap me again."

He smacked her, harder this time. His manhood was growing. He enjoyed this. Her body gyrated on top of him, driving him toward pleasure.

"Slap me again," she said.

She felt his hand hit her face. This time the blow fell harder. Her cheek tingled and her left ear rang from the impact. A flood of memories washed over her.

"Hit me," he said. "Hit me hard."

Pain and vengeance showed in Kaiya's eyes as she

reached her right hand to the back of her robe.

"You want me to slap you," she asked, seductively.

"Yes, bitch," he said between deep breaths, as if pleading. "Hit me. Choke me."

Kaiya grabbed his throat with her left hand and at the same time pulled her right hand from behind her back. In a seamless motion, as if the blade were part of her, she sliced through his carotid artery, esophagus, and trachea. Sitting atop him, she watched him bleed out. He choked a few times. It happened so fast she wasn't able to talk to him while he died. This was her only regret. Feeling hollow as the blood washed over her, she knew this was not the death Flavius deserved. The man deserved to plead for his life. Not knowing why, she stabbed the dead man's chest over and over, his gore and non-pulsing blood bathing her in a sick baptism that somehow made her free. She felt re-born, as if alive for the first time. Never again would she be a tool of men.

Standing from the bed dripping with blood, her heart raced. She wiped the blood from her eyes and looked for the qubit she so desperately sought. Others depended on her and she would not let them down. As she stood, she couldn't help but admire her body that was now covered in blood. She was more beautiful than ever.

Looking at the corpse of Flavius Decimus, she smiled to herself and said to it, "Men like you are always the easiest."

Finding the qubit on the bedside table, she typed in the private number of Tiberius Septus and listened as the transmission went through and then was denied. Unperturbed, she tried again with the same result. She knew now what she had suspected for some time. He would not answer because it was not prudent for him to answer. Kaiya had led Dante and Yasmine to their deaths. She exited the bloody scene into the hallway and found her compatriots. Dante, Yasmine, and their eldest daughter, Eppie, were all soaked in blood. They had done their jobs and executed the three sons. A scream rang throughout the corridor as Flavius' wife, Lucretia, ran out of her room, calling for her already dead sons. Dante caught her, first by the waist, and then by the throat. He held her as Kaiya walked to them.

"She has done nothing," said Dante. "She was a prisoner of Flavius, just as the rest us were."

Kaiya looked down at the scared woman. She was a prisoner of fate, but still, fate had put her on the wrong side. Kaiya plunged the knife into her chest without hesitation, killing her.

"Why did you do that?" Dante demanded. "She was innocent!"

"Innocent? Did you find her innocent when you picked me up in the stable? No one is innocent! Prepare your children. Tiberius will be here soon."

Dante ran down the hall, taking Yasmine and his eldest with him. Kaiya, fearing her actions had doomed the group, returned to the room of Flavius Decimus, looking at his now pale corpse on the bed, feeling no pity. His naked body was pathetic. She walked to the window that overlooked the grappa vines and tried to remember the wine she had enjoyed from these fields. As a peasant, they had merely produced, and as a consort to Tiberius Septus, the pleasures were never for her. She was part of the entertainment.

Kaiya tasted this wine with Arian at the Four Corners, ordering the dishes she longed to try for them both. When she later gave herself to him, it was the first time she had slept with a man for no gain. Even with Tiberius, it had been a sort of arrangement. Arian was the only man that had ever treated her with respect. Of course, that was all based on her deception, but once he knew the truth, he was unchanged. He wanted her. A solution to her predicament became clear.

Hearing the household stirring below, she needed to act fast. Sitting next to the dead body of Flavius Decimus, she typed the frequency that would connect to Arian's qubit. There was no answer, but her transmission was not cut off as it had been with Tiberius, and she was able to deliver a message.

"Arian, it's Kaiya. I'm in trouble. I'm in Avignon, but I fear my life is in danger. Please find me in Sikyon. Look for me at Angelica's Desires in the southern district. If you don't come, I will surely die."

She stood and exited the room. Yasmine was waiting outside the door with a clean servant's garment for her to wear. Dante was standing there with the two children who seemed afraid. They recoiled at the sight of Kaiya, still covered in blood.

"Don't worry, my dears, all of the evil in this house is gone now. Everything will be okay." Turning to Dante, she added, "We need to get moving. Our deeds will not remain unnoticed for long." He nodded in agreement.

"Were you able to contact your wealthy friend?"

"I was, and he is coming. We need to hide in Sikyon for a few days. I can protect us there."

Leaving all of their possessions behind, the five soon-to-be fugitives fled the house to the jeep that Dante had waiting. It was an hour's drive to Sikyon, and Kaiya hoped they could make it unnoticed.

# Chapter Twenty
# The Iris

Looking down at Arian, Ansley paused with curious interest. It had been so many years since he had known peaceful sleep, devoid of nightmares, that it was nice to witness it in someone else. He almost regretted waking him as he bent down to shake the kid. One would have thought he was dead had it not been for his intermittent snoring through the night. It was like sleeping in the same room as Jabari. Upon the third shaking, Arian stirred and woke, blinking and searching the room, confused by his surroundings.

"Get up Arian. Today is our big day."

Arian looked at him, disoriented and half asleep.

"Let me sleep a little longer." He pulled the covers over his head and turned away from Ansley.

"Who the hell am I trying to work with?" Ansley muttered to himself. "Wake the fuck up!" he shouted, grabbing the edge of the bed and tipping it, spilling Arian onto the floor.

"What the hell!" Arian moved his arms, removing the blankets that covered his face, awake now. Surveying the strange environment, he now saw that he was in a small room drilled within the cliff face. There were two beds, a small dresser with a mirror over it, and nothing else.

Running his hand through his hair and shaking himself awake, Arian looked to Ansley.

"You're an asshole."

"Just get ready. We have much to do today."

Arian walked to the dresser and looked at his reflection in the mirror.

"Damn. I look like hell. Is this what Desert Snake shots do?"

"It's what they do to amateurs. Now come on. I have a lot to show you."

"Don't I get to shower?"

"You aren't in the dome kid. You are in a hidden bunker in the Natural World. Make do."

"Or a bathroom?"

Ansley nodded. "Follow me."

They walked down a hallway dug out of the rock and entered a tiny restroom. As Arian moved to the stall and relieved the pressure in his bladder, he tried to remember how he had come to be in these rocky compartments. Washing his hands and splashing the lukewarm water onto his face, he heard Ansley speaking to someone outside. He walked out and found Ansley alone.

"Who were you talking to? You have no qubit."

Ansley laughed. "Ever heard of short-wave radio? Kid, we are in a different world. Perhaps you will meet a few other ghosts from the past as well. You are about to find out why I am considered to be a member of the so-called Centauri."

"I can't wait."

"That's funny," barked Ansley. "You will most likely die over this. Your mother did. Keep laughing, it's about to get real." The serious tone surprised Arian and had the desired effect of gaining his full attention.

At the end of the hallway was a steel door. Ansley typed in a code, and it unlocked with a loud thud, swinging ajar. He used his shoulder and body weight to push it inward. Arian jumped in to help. On the other side, they were met by the looming figure of Jabari Stoudamyre.

"Wake up, sleepy heads. It's time to go to work."

"Shut up, Jabari. My young friend here is hung over." He winked at Arian. "Is the Iris powered up?"

"It's getting there," replied Jabari. "The temperatures have lowered to near absolute zero. When I left, the magnetic field was becoming powerful. I could feel it in my blood."

"That's good. Let's give Arian a show." He took him by the shoulders. "I think it's time I give you a little more information."

"That would be nice," replied Arian.

"I assumed so. Would you believe that our friend Jabari is a physicist?" Ansley paused briefly. "I thought not. He wasn't trained in an Institute school. I trained him here, along with many others in this region. I'm sure you think no one born in the natural world could be a scientist on par with you, but I assure you, this is false. Your mother and I were born naturally, as were the Overseers. I found Jabari early on, when your mother and I first came to this place and began to develop it. He had talents far exceeding those he exhibits on the Patolli field, although I can't say I was disappointed when he developed into a behemoth. He has been very helpful to my expeditions outside the dome."

"Damn, dog, don't ruin my reputation with the kid," said Jabari, laughing. "Sometimes, being seen as an inferior is a strength," he added.

"I would never see you as an inferior," Arian avowed, reaching out to shake Jabari's hand. "I haven't had a chance to thank you for saving me last night from that lunatic."

Jabari squeezed Arian's palm. "It was nothing, but that man had reason to hate you. Your people have caused him to live his entire life with a boot to his neck. He found a way to vent."

"I understand," replied Arian, ruefully.

"No, you don't. But I appreciate the sentiment." He embraced Arian in a bear hug, lifting him from the ground.

"Are you girls done?" asked Ansley. "We have work."

Jabari led them to an industrial lift at the end of the hallway. Arian was nervous entering, as it appeared old. The platform moved down, jerking along the way, seemingly bound for the center of the planet. The change in temperature was evident as they descended. Despite their trajectory, Arian was struck by the increased humidity. He began to sweat and his stomach was queasy.

"Where are we going?" he asked, turning to Ansley.

"To see my baby," replied the old Professor.

The lift came to a rest and the doors opened. Arian didn't know what he was expected to see, but he found another narrow hallway carved in the rock, lined with incandescent lights framed in cast iron. Every fifty feet or so, emergency gas masks hung on the wall with white suits hanging beneath.

They walked a quarter mile, Ansley and Jabari taking long, purposeful strides, Arian following, wiping the sweat beading on his brow. He felt claustrophobic in the limited space so far beneath the ground, and was glad to see that even Jabari seemed affected by the environment. The man took shallow, intermittent breaths, as if not getting enough oxygen. Arriving at a fortified steel door, Jabari took a sharp left into a side room.

They were now in a small but well-lit office. Ansley motioned for Jabari and Arian to sit. Smiling at Arian, he reached into the desk and pulled out three oxygen tanks that had plastic form-fitting attachments for delivering gas to the nostrils and mouth.

"You look like you need this, kid," he said with a smile. He tossed one each to Jabari and Arian. Placing his own tank to his mouth, they sat for a moment, content to breathe in the rich and pure oxygen that was sparse in these ancient caverns. Jabari was the first to put his tank down. He was used to these levels. Ansley was second. Arian kept his tank to his face, unable to catch his breath.

"Well," said Ansley, "I'm sure you've realized that we have something big here. It's time I lay all my cards on the table."

"Let's hear it," said Arian.

"When Arameus began, your mother and I, along with Richard and a few others, were caught up in the movement. Everything was falling apart. Riots and wars were happening worldwide over the food and work shortages. Science was finally being used to improve humanity. Being the ones with the keys to immortality, we were amongst the first to be taken into the domes. We believed these were experiments on how to create sustainable living for the world. It was only later that we realized it had been a power grab. Our science was twisted to serve the needs of the rich."

"Padma wanted to leave, but I knew there was no way. They would never let us go in peace. We were too valuable, and we had the information they needed to maintain their control. We stayed, but began our work. Together we built the city under which you now stand. Your mother is long dead, along with many others but at long last, I have completed our task. Beyond those doors is the Iris. It is the largest particle accelerator ever constructed and is capable of creating energies previously unimaginable."

"You built an entire city to create a science experiment?" asked Arian.

"It is much more than a science experiment, my boy. Many of those marble statues in the National Mall are built in tribute to men who secretly contributed to this project, but it is my baby. Imagine a hundred years of collaboration between the greatest minds science has ever known. The Overseers have robbed us of many of these men, under the guise of fighting the Centuari, but I have persevered. I am the head of a group of refugee scientists that the Natural Born know as the

Council of Elders."

"And what exactly do you Elders do?" asked Arian.

"Are you dense, dog?" responded Jabari. "They make REVOLUTION." His fist shot into the air.

"Exactly," said Ansley, pleased.

"And how exactly does it make revolution? In my experience, particle accelerators smash things together and try to make sense of the chaos that comes from the massive energies created, searching for ghost particles that flash into existence in the interim."

"Ah, this is true, Arian, for a traditional accelerator," replied Ansley, smiling. "They try to create little big bangs in an attempt to understand the conditions at the beginning of the universe. But my accelerator is non-traditional."

"How so?"

"How does a man define time? There are only two true ways scientifically, since any measurement by a clock is relative to the observer and his own frame of reference. The first way we can define the flow of time is through thermodynamics and the law of entropy. Everything around you decays and thus you know time has passed. Of course, for us Nephites, our bodies persevere, but you understand the concept. The second arrow of time is defined by the universe's constant expansion from the Big Bang. Time began in that initial explosion and has continued since in the ever-constant expansion of the universe. We can measure the flow of time by tracing back all the known planets and galaxies to that original singularity that existed outside time and space and exploded us into existence."

"So how is your accelerator different?" asked Arian.

This time it was Jabari who responded.

"The Iris is the most sophisticated piece of machinery ever developed, notwithstanding the nanocytes coursing through your blood. However, they only function to keep your little body from being damaged. The Iris creates enough energy to reshape the very structure of space-time." Jabari leaned back, pleased, but Arian was unconvinced.

Looking at the two men, Arian shook his head. "I guess I am the tourist to this project so I will not argue. Just tell me what you're trying to do and what you need from me and this will go much smoother."

"Good," replied Ansley. "I grow tired of arguing with you. As Jabari said, we have created an engine so powerful it rivals the energies seen in the initial Big Bang that created our universe and the space-time continuum. However, space and time are not merely a stage on which a play is acted out. They are part of the play itself. As we began to approach the speed of light in the accelerator, with the help of the mineral from the Ursula moon, created secondary particles. These particles were known to physicists for some time, but as we approached 0.99999 times the speed of light, new particles sprang into existence, most notably, the Amasarsi boson, which, if you recall, we discussed on your balcony a few months ago."

"I remember," responded Arian, "vaguely."

"Well, then, you should also recall that this particle creates a mirror particle known as the Amasarsi singlet, which as a tachyon, is massless and exists outside of time. One could say that it goes backward in time. This creates an alternate field within the accelerator. For lack of a better term, we will call it an anti-matter field."

"I was under the impression that when matter and anti-matter fields came into contact, they annihilated one another in a blast of gamma radiation. I do know that much about particle physics." Arian smiled, pleased that he was keeping up.

"That is what we believed as well, but given our new ability to cool the magnet to near absolute zero, the magnetic field accelerates both of these phantom particle pairs on separate paths of increasing energies. The Amasarsi bosons, having mass and being within our own time dimension, accelerate closer to the speed of light and thus time slows for them. The Amasarsi singlets, however, being tachyons, increase in speed infinitely, shooting further back in time."

"Forgive me if this seems implausible," said Arian.

"Oh, we do, dog," nodded Jabari. "It makes more sense within the framework of the mathematics. You must understand that when we try to explain the quantum world in terms of our own physical experiences, we find ourselves in paradoxes. We didn't evolve to perceive these underlying realities. We are slaves to our senses. In the mathematics, we have no biases, and it works out on paper."

Arian looked at Jabari as if for the first time.

"I've underestimated you, Jabari, and for that, I was a fool. I will take your word for it."

"It happens," said Jabari with a shrug.

"I still fail to see how this leads to revolution or how I fit in?"

"We're getting there," answered Ansley. "You have much of your mother in you. I found this in my equations over a hundred years ago, though I didn't believe we would ever create it in practice. We never before had an energy source as powerful as the Ursuline mineral or the time to devote to such a project. In a traditional accelerator, the Amasarsi boson and the Amasarsi singlet are meant to annihilate within a trillionth-trillionth of a second but the fields we are generating allow them to persevere indefinitely. Linked independent of space and time, the particles in the fields are aware of one another and interact. This interaction is what separates the Iris from other accelerators."

"It violates the space-time continuum, ripping a hole in the fabric, like a small black hole, or wormhole, if you will. It is nature's way of conserving energy and matter." Ansley paced back and forth now, excited by his own brilliance. "The only way to do so is to do it back in time. By maintaining the field, we can determine where the tear will place us. The longer we maintain the field, the further back in time the particles will travel, maintaining energy conservation."

"This is where our 'revolution' as Jabari chooses to call it, becomes clear. I would not use so grandiose of a term," continued Ansley. "I consider this a redistribution of wealth. The big idea that I was able to sell your mother, Richard, and others on was this. Suppose we use this technology to send a signal back to ourselves within the cloud network utilized at Nanosoft, before the rise of Arameus. By our reasoning, if Padma and Richard shared their breakthrough with the greater community as opposed to Nanosoft, the world would remain free. We realized, however, that this would be of no help, as the only people with the money and power to develop and produce the nanocytes were those who became the Overseers, and they would eventually control them anyway.

"This is where you come in, Arian. The breakthrough you have stumbled upon is more powerful than you can possibly imagine. The attachment of the bio-bot to the telomere during S-phase of mitosis had long been a goal of Padma's, but she died before achieving it. We never could have predicted, however, that the bot would re-write the code in the DNA strand to which it attached, thus coding for a biological version of itself and creating a living network. This is precisely what we lacked: a sustainable way to create nanocytes. You have found a way for the body to create its own. There will be no need for continued treatments. We can make them for the sick as we would make an immunization. Now it will readily be available to the poor, and we can avoid this entire fiasco. We can hit a reset button, and reshape the world, not in the image of four rich men, but how the people wish."

"This is insane," declared Arian, standing. Jabari stood as well, adopting a defensive position in front of Ansley.

"Relax, Jabari. Let's hear the kid," said Ansley. Jabari stood down.

"Suppose we're able to send the technology for the bio-bots back, and suppose you are able to prevent the creation of Arameus. What then? I was created in Capitol City over two hundred years after its founding. What happens to me? If you were to succeed, have you not considered the paradox that if I never exist, I will not be able to create the bio-bots?"

"I have considered all circumstances," Ansley fired back, "much more and for far longer than you could ever imagine. This is a war, one that the Overseers started against the Natural Born long before your birth. It stretches back hundreds of years. As a Nephite, you believe yourself to be safe, but what will happen when you are no longer deemed necessary? Jabari, for one, and many others are willing to risk their entire existence to prevent the suffering that has been forced upon the masses by the Overseers' rule. Your mother understood this. You would be a severe disappointment to Padma."

"Who are you to judge how my mother would view me, you fucking asshole? She was dead thirty years before I was born. Your obsessions and loneliness have blinded you to reality and the luxuries you have been blessed with."

Arian sank back into his chair, not knowing what to do. He was deep within the hidden lair of the apparent rebel movement. It was not too late for him. He could easily go to Kaiya with this info and be done with this nonsense, his mother's allegiances be damned. He had never met her anyway.

Ansley looked at Arian and the empathy evident in his face was disarming.

"I didn't want it to be like this, but it's the only way. Wars require sacrifice, and unfortunately, in this war, we are fighting the nanocyte plague. They've used the treatments as a means to amass more power than any king or emperor in history. It's true, everything and everyone you have ever known must be sacrificed, but it is for the greater good of our world."

"Forgive me if I am less than enthused," said Arian.

"We do," answered Jabari. "You should at least see the machine before you leave us. I think it's time, Ans."

"That it is, but first, a small pick me up. I'm sure Arian could use it after all the Desert Snakes we took last night and our talk of blinking him out of existence. I could use one too."

Ansley pulled out a bottle of Tegave and three glasses from a nearby cabinet. After liberal pours, he passed them to the men. "To our future endeavors," he said, raising his glass with a wink to Arian.

Unamused, Arian drained his glass. He was ready to go home, and the sooner they saw the Iris, the better. As the brown liquor coursed through his veins, his mood softened. Perhaps this was Ansley's intent.

Ansley and Jabari stood.

"It's time, kid," said Jabari, giving Arian a nudge. Arian stood, uneasy about the machine. Exiting the office, Jabari led them back to the imposing steel door and its morbid implications. It was easily forty feet by forty feet, and Arian couldn't help but wonder how it had been transported so deep within these chiseled tunnels. Jabari placed his hand on a crystalline receptor, which glowed in recognition, opening a compartment in the rock wall to the side of the door that exposed a keypad. Jabari typed in a code, which Arian determined to be ten digits, and a red light flashed overhead as a buzzer sounded in short intervals. The door rose from the floor.

The change in atmosphere was instantaneous as hot air shot from underneath. The temperature was so high that Arian feared he would be burned. He now understood why the air had at first seemed cool but grew humid and muggy as they descended into the heart of the mountain. As the door lifted, Arian beheld a cavern so massive that he would not have believed it possible. They stood on the far edge of a central water reservoir, the end of which he could not see. Large pipes made of platinum, gold, silver, and copper expanded into the horizon. Some sort of polymer surrounded the pipes and reservoir, though he was not sure of its purpose. Scientists occupied various stations along the way, and every thousand feet or so, there were enormous photocells accompanied by computer stations. These were likely detectors.

"I apologize for the heat," said Ansley, turning to Arian. "The magnets must be kept near absolute zero so as to be superconducting. The heat must be siphoned out. The water itself does much of it. The waterfall that flows from the cliff you saw entering Beladero originates from this reservoir. It is superheated, near boiling, and provides all the energy used within the city."

Ansley moved away from the reservoir and machinery toward a door within the rock. Upon placing his hand on the recognition crystal, it slid open, gaining the three men access to an interior compartment. When the doors closed, the temperature instantly regulated to a cool 67 degrees and fresh oxygen flowed through the vents.

"Now that's better, isn't it?" asked Ansley.

Arian wasn't so sure. He had felt strange since entering this cavern. His blood felt constricted and his mouth dry. Even his bones and muscles ached. Perhaps it was the intense magnetic field Ansley and Jabari had spoken of, but these were strange sensations for a Nephite. The nanocytes regulated his body as long as he was in an oxygen rich environment, yet the effect lingered still in this compartment.

Jabari tapped a few buttons on a keypad and the room shot forward at a great speed. Ansley and Jabari, being prepared, grabbed onto leather handles hanging from the ceiling of the car. Arian, however, fell hard into the back of the vehicle, feeling his full inertial mass.

"Thanks for the heads up, assholes," he said, standing to his feet, now acclimated to the movement of the car. Jabari merely raised his eyebrow, turning to Ansley as if questioning. The scenery that shot by through the window of the transport was stunning as Arian was able to see the full breadth of the Iris machine. The many-colored blinking lights that blurred past were like galaxies. The accelerator and cavern were even bigger than he had first thought. People flashed by as well. There must have been thousands of workers within the cavern. He marveled at how they could withstand the heat.

Arian looked to Ansley and Jabari and smiled.

"This must be what it is like to be a particle in an

accelerator."

Ansley looked down at the floor and shook his head disappointed. Jabari let out a loud laugh.

"Ha. I feel the same way, dog!"

Ansley rolled his eyes, but a slight smile appeared on his face. These were both his children in some strange way, made possible by the rise of the ruling class he was trying to destroy. A pit grew in his stomach as he considered losing them both. The transport came to an abrupt stop. Again, Jabari and Ansley held the leather straps to steady themselves, and Arian, who had been content to stand free, adjusted to the velocity and lack of acceleration, took another spill, this time to the front of the car. The door opened on the other side of the car and they walked toward another security checkpoint.

"We are at the center of the Iris accelerator now," said Ansley to Arian. "This elevator leads us to the control room. I have some friends waiting above. Perhaps you will be interested in meeting a few."

This time, it was Ansley who placed his hand on the crystal, not Jabari, a distinction that was not lost on Arian. Entering a lift, they traveled much higher than he would have expected. Seeing the grandeur of the accelerator and cavern before him, he had not bothered to look up, but clearly the massive cavern was as tall as it was long. They traveled what Arian estimated to be at least fifty stories before arriving at the desired floor. Exiting the lift, they were now in a circular control room, enclosed in the same polymer that covered the pipes. Screens, computers, and lights flashed all around, but only a few workers occupied this space, perhaps six. Arian's eyes were drawn to four incredibly old people, three men and a woman seated in comfortable leather chairs in the center of the room.

"Arian Cyannah, please meet our Counsel of Elders," said Ansley, his voice demure.

As he got a closer look at the Elders, he could see that old was an understatement. They were older than the

Overseers themselves. Arian had never looked upon more wretched men. Their loose, papery skin, coupled with their thinning white hair and decrepit bodies made them seem skeletal. He had never seen men look this way and fought the urge to gag. One of the cachectic looking men, seated on the far left, spoke in his direction.

"My boy, I hear you have been occupying my former apartments. I hope you are keeping them up. They were beautiful if memory serves. Ansley claims he found my secret stash of Tegave."

Ansley and Jabari remained where they were as Arian walked forward. "I'm afraid I don't follow you, sir. I was born in Capitol City. We have never occupied the same apartments." Arian was aware of two men laughing from behind.

"Oh, but we did, my boy," answered the man before spilling into a fit of coughing. One of the apparent scientists rushed forward, revealing herself to not be a worker in the room, but instead a nurse. She held a towel in front of the man's mouth as he coughed, and when she removed it, it was covered in crimson. Arian was disgusted.

"You definitely got your looks from your mother," the man continued, laughing before breaking into a fit of coughing.

Once he regained his composure, he looked at Arian earnestly. "You might not believe it, but my name is Professor David Chandler. I am one of the founders of the Institute of Arameus as well as the field of modern statistical mechanics. The Overseers have long believed me to be dead as they did the rest of my friends here, but Ansley was able to save us. Unfortunately, he was not able to provide adequate treatments to preserve our youth, but who are we to complain? I have lived far past the life expectancy given to me at my birth. I would estimate I have stolen nearly two hundred years from death."

"I don't understand," responded Arian. "How can you be Professor Chandler? You died in the Blood Sun Day attacks that took my mother and father."

This time, the old man sitting to the left of Chandler spoke in his rasping voice.

"It is true that the attacks took your mother. However, your father survived, and I am embarrassed to say, sits before you now, although in my defense, you were fathered from my DNA, thirty years after I came under the protection of Ansley and the people of Beladero."

Time seemed to stop for Arian. He looked to the floor feeling nauseated. He hadn't felt right since he had entered this cavern, but this was something different. Not knowing why, the sight of his previously non-existent father filled him with rage and without fore thought, Arian turned and struck Ansley in the face, dropping him to the floor. Jabari lunged forward, grabbing Arian by the throat and holding him in place.

Standing to his feet and rubbing his jaw, Ansley placed a hand on Jabari's shoulder, signaling him to release Arian.

"I would think you would have informed me you were working with my genetic father who happens to be alive!" demanded Arian.

"Damn, kid. You pack a punch for a born Nephite. I thought you were all soft. I never deceived you. The Overseers and the government of Arameus deceived you. They systematically tried to murder all my friends and told you it was the poor people outside the city gates. They convinced you of a Centauri that didn't exist. I told you in the locker room before we came here that if it is a Centauri they want, they will have one. And let me add," he said, still rubbing his sore jaw, "it was him that didn't want me to alert you of his existence, and I can hardly blame him. The Counsel of Elders is our most closely guarded secret. I was made aware of your attempts to spy on me. How could you be trusted?"

Arian looked back to his father as if looking at a ghost. He stared for a moment, unable to speak. Finally, he found his voice.

"So you are Richard Cyannah?"

"Yes, I am," answered the old man.

"And you are my father?"

"Well, in a sense. I was considered long dead when they used my DNA to make you, and to be sure, I never had any affair with Padma. Ansley would have let me die had that happened. So while I may be your father in a genetic sense, I have no tie to you. Your mother and I worked together for many years to develop the nanocytes as well as your entire field of research. The man you just punched would be closer to that than me. He is the one who loved your mother as she loved him. In another world, he would have been your father, and rightfully so."

"I don't even know what to say. Obviously, I have no father. I was raised in the Institute hatcheries, proudly, I must add. I am better than you all. I need no father. I need no mother, yet here I stand, amongst men who would have me cancel my existence. My team was able to create a bio-bot in seven years of research that you men could not create in two hundred years."

"Ahem, ahem. Excuse me," said the old woman seated to the right of the three men. "So you believe you discovered your findings in some sort of research vacuum? I find that sort of ego insufferable."

Arian was taken aback by the vigor still present in the woman's voice. "And who exactly are you? Don't tell me. You're my long lost grandmother."

"At least he has a sense of humor," the woman remarked. "My name is Margaret Weaver. I am the head engineer of the Iris project. In my former life, I was chief designer of the hawk system used for personal transport in the domes. We have been well aware of your pursuits for some time. I'm sorry, my poor boy, but did you think it was coincidence that Ansley had an interest in your research and asked for your files? We knew what the Institute was after, even if you didn't."

"And what is the Institute after of which I am not aware?" demanded Arian.

"Well, clearly they are after the bio-bots, my dear. Surely you are not so foolish. They mean to use them to enslave all the Natural Born. They have already begun with Habimana Muteteli's Natural Born registration. All outside of the domes will be implanted with your work, and all will have receivers ready to upload any updates or controls that the Overseers wish, and at the cellular level, no less."

"That is absurd," replied Arian. "My work would never be used to such ends."

"But is it really your work?" responded the woman. "By our assessment, Matthew Conway had quite a bit to do with your recent breakthroughs. Can you vouch for his motivations?"

"I'm afraid I don't follow you."

"We have learned from our trusted sources that the Overseers plan on using the bio-bots as I suggested. The only remaining question is how is it that the rulers of Arameus have knowledge of the progress of a lowly assistant professor at the Institute? Surely someone has made them aware of your progress, and if it wasn't you, as your ignorance suggests, then who else could be informing them?"

Arian shook his head. "Supposing Conway was leaking our results to the higher-ups. What would be the motivations? Anyone from the Central Tower could easily contact me and achieve the same result."

"The Overseers didn't amass and maintain their power by revealing their plots to underlings," replied Margaret. "You are already serving the purpose of spying on Ansley to figure out what he has been working on all these years. It wouldn't do for you to know more and risk alerting Ansley, though our spies have done so nonetheless. Since their power is rooted in their control of the nanocytes, your field has always been closely monitored."

"It is true," chimed in Richard. "When they suspected your mother of plotting to share the nano-treatments with the world, they organized the bombings that killed her and were intended to kill the rest of us as well. Thankfully, Ansley was able to spirit us out of the city to Beladero. The government of Arameus is unaware of this cavern hidden in the mountain, and ignores this city. Motivated by Padma's death, Ansley vowed to complete the Iris. It has become a symbol of our revolution, closely guarded by the inhabitants who are responsible for its construction. They believe we can change the world and are willing to risk everything to do so. What are you willing to risk?"

Arian considered this. His mind had been made up since he heard about the Iris. He was going straight to Kaiya with this information to stop these lunatics from destroying the world with their machine. It was, however, a difficult spot because in order to get back to Capitol City alive, he would have to convince all present of his loyalty to their cause.

"You ask a great deal of me," he said after a moment. "This is a lot to take in in only a couple of days. Arameus has been great for me. The government created me, nurtured me, educated me, and gave me a position in the Institute. I live a very comfortable life. Yet you expect me to throw it all away and betray those who have given me so much? How can I justify this to myself?"

It was Jabari that answered his question.

"You justify it the same way that every soldier who has ever given his life for some stupid flag or political whim has justified it over the millennia. You justify by knowing you are giving your life for a cause greater than yourself."

Arian pondered this, turned to Jabari, and nodded in approval. "I will help you. I can provide you with the necessary information to create the bio-bots, but I will do so on one condition."

"And what is that?" asked Ansley.

Arian turned to Richard. "I'm not willing to sacrifice my existence for this cause. I will sacrifice my position, but not my life. If you are successful in sending a message back, it must include a complete mapping of my DNA signature, and you and Padma must create me, in the same way that the Institute did. The science is simple enough, even two hundred years ago. You must engineer me exactly as I am today, only this time, I will be raised by a family."

"I agree to these terms," said Richard, "provided Ansley agrees as well."

"Padma and I would be honored to raise you as our son. Even though we share no common DNA, I have always held you close in my heart as the offspring of Padma. It's decided."

Arian exhaled. They had bought the lie. True, the idea of a family appealed to him, but not enough for him to destroy his life. With any luck, he would be sitting back in his office a week from now, and all of these traitors would be imprisoned. He looked back at Jabari and gave him a smile. As it turned out, Arian was a soldier. He was a soldier for Arameus.

"Now that you are one of us, it is time I show you what my beautiful creation can do," said Ansley, walking up and clasping Arian on the shoulder. "Are you guys ready to power her up?"

Margaret, Richard, and Chandler shook their heads excitedly, while the fourth man sitting in the chair, who was unresponsive throughout the meeting, did not stir.

"Is that guy even alive?" asked Arian.

"Oh, don't mind him," replied Ansley. "That's Oswald Piperidge. I'm sure you have read about him. He developed the fusion technology that allows us to harness so much energy from the Ursuline mineral. He had a stroke ten years back and has been catatonic ever since. I didn't have the heart to remove him from the counsel. The nurse moves him back and forth. You've never missed a meeting, have you, Oswald?"

Oswald remained unresponsive.

"We have people sympathetic to our cause working in the medical nanocyte production facilities," Ansley explained. "We are able to smuggle out small amounts of the treatments deemed defective. This is how we have kept Oswald alive, along with the rest of the counsel. Still, we are not able to steal enough to preserve their health."

Arian was stunned. Perhaps two hundred years was too long for a man to live. All of these people seemed completely out of their minds. They had spent what had to be billions of credits that could have been used to relieve the suffering of the local people to build this massive accelerator with the express goal of changing the history of the world. It seemed like a waste of their money and talents on such an unlikely outcome. The intellectual gifts that allowed them to think outside the box and become great scientists had led them to an impractical solution. Perhaps this was why you never found scientists in positions of political power.

Arian followed Ansley, Jabari, Richard, Margaret, and Chandler through a door that led to the observation deck. Oswald, of course, remained in his chair.

"Don't leave Oswald," Ansley said to the nurse as they passed. "He won't want to miss this." The nurse wheeled the catatonic man's chair around and followed them out the door.

From the observation deck, high above the center of the machine, Arian was able to finally appreciate the true scope of the Iris. The amount of gold and platinum used to surround the pipes that encased the accelerator must have cost a fortune. The aquifer was central to its design, and the accelerator followed the outline of its banks, suspended over the water. A small city could fit within the cavernous expanse.

"Have we achieved absolute zero?" asked Ansley into a short wave radio.

"About ten minutes ago," came the voice from the other end.

"And the magnetic field?"

"We have just reached 100 Tesla."

"Fire it up." Ansley turned to Arian. "Get ready."

At first nothing happened. They stood, gazing down at the water fifty stories below. Then there was a loud noise, like a contained explosion. The water below started to move, slowly at first, before swirling violently and forming a whirlpool.

"The strength of the magnetic field generated as the particles accelerate pulls on the oxygen within the water, causing it to swirl. Oxygen is paramagnetic," said Ansley nonchalantly. Watching him, Arian saw a strange smirk on his face and a look in his eye that bordered on madness. It was disconcerting.

Another series of loud explosions startled him from his thoughts.

"These are the early collisions of the particles. As their velocity increases, the collisions will generate the energy needed to create the Amasarsi bosons and singlets that will be suspended in parallel fields."

The rising excitement was evident in Ansley's voice. He couldn't contain his exuberance. A loud boom echoed throughout the chamber, throwing the water below into the air. Were they not protected by the polymer, it would have reached their current height.

"That was the collision that generated the Amasarsi bosons and singlets. They will now accelerate to unimaginable speeds." Ansley's face took on a devilish demeanor, as if he were a man possessed. Suddenly, their faces were illuminated by a strange red and blue glow.

Looking down to the reservoir, Arian was shocked to find that he could no longer see the water. The parallel fields were interacting now, and the massive energies being generated were manifesting as a visible electric field radiating outward from a central point at the reservoir's center. It was as if red and blue lightning was shooting outward continuously from a central point. The brightness caused him to squint, though he knew the polymer would remove any harmful rays. Arian stood transfixed. A small black circle appeared in the center of the point from which the fields were radiating. It was no bigger than a Patolli ball at first, though at these heights, it was difficult to judge. It was starkly different from the bright lights emanating from its core. Its sheer blackness indicated nothingness.

It expanded, growing as the intensity of the light increased. Arian was frightened now and grateful for the protective cover of the polymer, though he wondered whether it could withstand these massive energies. The black nothingness was now the ominous size of a round table that would seat four.

"And now you have seen the nature of my creation," beamed Ansley maniacally. "Look at her in all of her beauty. This is the very essence of space and time. This is our blank slate from which we will repaint the future of our world. Look into the void that connects us to all of history. Padma is in there somewhere. Everyone who has ever existed is down there, lost in time and space."

Arian stared into the wormhole. He understood now why the machine had been named the Iris. The blackness at the center resembled a pupil while the colored bolts of electricity shooting outward gave the impression of an iris. It was as if some all-knowing sentient being was staring at him from across time. It made him feel insignificant. The power of this machine was clear to him. With this at their disposal, these men were god-like, able to shape the universe as they pleased, with or without his help. It wasn't right. The intensity of Ansley's gaze into the void was fiendish, devoid of humanity. He wasn't interested in the Natural Born or Arameus. He was only interested in Padma. This entire ruse, the Centauri and stopping the Overseers was merely his selfish quest to find his lost love. Arian was disgusted at this realization.

"Turn it off," said Ansley, breathless, into the short-wave transmitter. "We shouldn't maintain the field any longer until we're ready. We aren't sure we can contain the energy."

A final explosion echoed through the cavern as the matter and anti-matter fields were allowed to annihilate somewhere in time. Again, water shot upward toward the polymer surface and turned to a steamy mist from the heat. Arian watched as the chilling black hole shrank until it disappeared. And with its disappearance, an infinite number of potential realities slipped away from their grasps.

# Chapter Twenty-One
## A Better Life

Matthew Conway sat at his desk pondering his latest results. He had been working for months to replicate the success of the experiment in which he not only attached a bot to an actively replicating DNA sequence, but also succeeded in programming the body to recreate the bot on its own. It would be a feat worthy of the history books if he could show that he could do it again, and from the looks of the data in front of him, he had. Typically this would be a time to run to the office of his research advisor, Arian Cyannah, and proclaim his success, but Arian hadn't been to the laboratory for over a week.

He had grown to resent the professor over the last few months, both for his dismissive treatment of his work and his absence. After four years under Dr. Cyannah's tutelage, Conway seemed no closer to obtaining a doctorate. This groundbreaking work deserved recognition, and if he couldn't get that from his own advisor, he would seek it elsewhere, thus two months prior, he had approached the administrators of the Institute.

This was a breach of standard protocol since, Dr. Cyannah, as the graduate advisor, was the owner of the research. Given the work's potential to revolutionize nanocyte treatments, Matt was sure the Institute higher-ups would turn a blind eye to his betrayal. He had been proven correct beyond his wildest hopes. Not only had the administration been receptive, they referred him to the Head of Scientific Development at the Central Tower. For the first time in his twenty-four years of life, Matt had entered the Central Tower to meet with Tobias Fry, whose job it was to act as a liaison between the Parliament Science Committee and the Institute. It was he who alerted those who held the real power to the new developments in science on which they so depended.

Tobias seemed more than a little intrigued by his results and had his work sent off on the same day to his superiors within Parliament. Unbeknownst to Matt and even to Tobias, the results of his work made it all the way to the highest powers of Arameus, the Overseers themselves. That these men were already monitoring his research would forever remain unknown to him. They instantly recognized the potential of the bio-bots to firmly cement their power and had taken the necessary steps to begin production immediately.

Wishing to keep their true plans unknown, they chose a remote location outside Capitol City for production. They would then use Habimana Muteteli, under the guise of a representative of the Natural Born, to enact their new form of control. When choosing a scientist to manage the project, Arian was eliminated. He was too close to Ansley and thus could not be trusted. However, a graduate student who felt slighted by his professor and wished for something more was the perfect candidate. Tiberius, in his new role as facilitator of the Overseers' plans, would contact Mr. Conway and offer him his promotion.

Matt was unaware of this. Many nervous weeks later, he was contacted by a man named Thaddeus and invited to dine on one of the pleasure yachts cruising the Arymides, the river circling the Central Isle, for dinner and to discuss his new placement within the Institute. He was nervous about the prospect of getting a new professor. How could he be sure he would like this one any better? And would he have to start working toward his doctorate all over again? Time was a luxury Nephites had in abundance, but he was tired of being under the power of another man. He was ready to run his own research group. Regardless, anything would be better than his current absentee adviser.

He opened his qubit. "Hera, I'm leaving for the day. Have my messages forwarded."

"Of course, Matthew," came her reply.

He departed the labs, walking in the shadow of the East Tower toward his hawk. Though he was nervous about the meeting, he was excited about dining on a pleasure yacht. They were not open to the public except by invitation. High-ranking members of the Central Tower had passes and could extend invitations to others. His hawk was parked far from the entrance to the laboratories. He did not fail to notice Arian's empty space directly by the door. He walked almost a half-mile before he reached his transport, getting angrier by the minute. Straddling his vehicle, he typed in the coordinates for Dominiccio's Landing, named for the Overseer.

His hawk took off toward the interior of the isle, and the Central Tower, before descending to the North Tower, and finally the landing. This was an annoying and indirect route, but his low status dictated the path. Many higher-ranking Nephites would be traveling at this time of day, and this route would prevent any traffic stoppages. His hawk accelerated past the East Tower and to a ramp that led to the upper levels of the Central Isle. The four towers were located at the island's lowest level, but closer to the Central Tower, each block ascended a story, allowing for another visible street front for shops and restaurants as you neared the Central Tower's base. It also ensured that the Overseers and other high-ranking officials occupied the highest point in the city. It was yet one more assertion of their power.

His hawk traveled midway up the embankment before exiting the ramp onto a curving avenue. The Central Tower loomed above with the East Tower directly to his right. He passed restaurants and pubs where Nephites were gathering for after-work drinks. Many, he was sure, worked in the Central Tower. As he followed the avenue around, the North Tower came into view. His hawk shot to an exit ramp that led to the tower below. Passing the North Tower, he came to Arymides Avenue, which followed the river that surrounded the Central Isle. He parked at a charging station next to the bridge leading to the northern district. The yacht was docked, with many men and women standing around the entrance ramp waiting to board. It was a large boat, built to accommodate a hundred diners. Emblazoned on the side in bright red paint was the name of the boat, The Capitol Cruiser.

Not knowing what to do, or how to board, Matt eased off the bike and faced the crowd of people. A man approached him, dressed in a simple white shirt and black trousers. The shirt had a small eagle pattern on the right breast, indicating he was in the service of a consulate.

"Matthew Conway, I presume?"

Matt nodded.

"My name is Thaddeus Secundus. I am the head assistant to Consulate Tiberius Septus. I am glad you were able to join. My master awaits us inside if you will follow me." The man walked off, and it took Matt a moment to realize he better follow or be left behind.

As they approached the boarding ramp, the attendant saw Thaddeus and allowed the two men to bypass the line. They were greeted within by a host, a Natural Born man of about forty with a large, well-groomed mustache, his dark hair slicked back with some sort of grease. While Matt was sure the man felt he appeared elegant, in truth the man's style showed his lower class. They were led into an open dining area in the boat's interior. The walls were framed in glass to give the diners views of the city and river, while the floor was filled with circular tables adorned with white tablecloths, silverware, and empty champagne glasses. In the room's center was a small stage where a string quartet was readying their instruments. They continued to a spiraling staircase that led to the upper deck. Upon reaching the top stair, another attendant removed a velvet rope, allowing Matt to pass.

"This is where I must leave you, Mr. Conway," said Thaddeus with a slight incline of his head. "I hope you enjoy your dinner." With that, he hurried back down the staircase and out of sight.

Confused, Matt emerged on the top deck to find it devoid of passengers. The tables were unadorned, with no settings, save one, at the far end. From this distance, he could only make out the long white hair flowing from the man's head. He was seated alone. Perhaps it had been a mistake to go over Arian's head. This whole situation seemed wrong. Regardless, it was too late now. Taking a deep breath, trying to clear his head, Conway strode toward the man.

As he approached, he recognized the man to be none other than Tiberius Septus. He noted the tanned, lined face that went with the white hair and purple dinner jacket. Though he had never met the man, Tiberius was one of the most recognizable men in Arameus, and even young children in the Institute hatcheries would be able to identify his distinct features.

"Your honor," he began, slightly embarrassed, "I had no idea you would be here. Had I known, I would have dressed in a more befitting manner." He bowed as Tiberius looked on with a bemused grin.

"And how could you have known that which we did not share? You are Matthew Conway, I presume. Please be seated. I have much to discuss with you."

Matt awkwardly took the seat across from Tiberius, feeling every movement of his body being scrutinized. The mustachioed host he had met upon boarding walked up with an open bottle of wine and paused at the table silently.

"Your honor, if I have offended anyone by going above

my advisor, I apologize sincerely. I was upset and made a mistake."

Tiberius waved off these protestations with a flick of his wrist. "Fear not, young man, you have nothing for which you should be ashamed. You have done well. This is a celebration. I assume you will take a glass of wine? It is Sagittarian, grown in Avignon. It was bottled over forty years ago and is among the last left from that year. I am fond of the region and have spent much time there. Given my long years, perhaps I have even known some of those who picked these grapes so long ago. It makes me feel connected to the past."

"Of course, your honor. Thank you very much. It is a pleasure to be sitting with someone who has experienced so much. I have seen so little in my limited years."

"Don't worry, my boy. Before you know it you will be two hundred. No matter how much time we get, it seems to pass too quickly."

The waiter poured each of them a drink from the bottle. Tiberius shoved his nose into the glass and inhaled deeply, savoring the earthy odors. Drinking it, he swirled it around his tongue, enjoying every intricacy hidden within the wine. Conway, however, picked up his glass and drained half of it, wiping his mouth on his sleeve. With a look of slight offense, Tiberius grabbed his wrist lightly across the table.

"A fine wine such as this is to be savored and enjoyed, not shot down like some cheap Tegave. Allow your tongue to explore the earthiness and dryness. Feel a connection with the people who plowed that land forty years ago. Think of the children they had to provide for which led them to toil in the sun. Perhaps a little girl waited for her father to come home each day from his work. Perhaps that little girl has grown old now and this bottle is the last remaining connection to him."

Conway was beginning to realize that Tiberius had enjoyed a few drinks from the open bottle. Still, he picked up the glass again, this time taking a small sip and swirling it on his tongue as the Consulate looked on. He hoped he was doing it correctly, as he had no idea what he was supposed to be discovering in the wine.

"If it is not to bold, your honor, what is it that we are celebrating?" asked Matt, with some hesitation.

"We are celebrating the completion of your doctorate."

"I'm afraid I don't follow you, sir. I was under the impression I was being considered for a new placement within the Institute. I have not completed my doctorate. Dr. Cyannah has not seen it fit to grant me one."

"This is true," replied Tiberius, "but it is not Arian who grants doctorates. Arian only recommends them to the Institute. We have found much promise in your work, and your results have reached the ears of those who hold the ultimate power in Arameus, the Overseers themselves. They have granted you your doctorate and have a special position in the works."

Conway was dumbfounded. His emotions were a mix of joy, fear, and confusion. To hear that he had been granted the degree he had spent his life pursuing nearly brought him to tears, although he was shocked to hear that the Overseers knew of his work. He wasn't confident he was up to the task of meeting the expectations of ones so revered in society.

"So… my name is Dr. Matthew Conway?"

"From now until the day you die, should so unfortunate of an event ever occur."

"I don't know what to say," he said, a large smile spreading on his face that did not subside. He lifted his glass and drained the remaining contents without considering how this might offend Tiberius. The indiscretion was ignored as Tiberius motioned for the mustachioed waiter to refresh the glass.

"What about Arian?" It felt good to call Dr. Cyannah by his first name, now that they were equals. He would never again address the man by his formal title.

"Dr. Cyannah will no longer be in your life. We have a special task for you. The Overseers see great promise in your work with the bio-bots and want to begin commercializing them immediately. They began construction of an offsite laboratory, outside the dome over a month ago and you should have everything you need to begin producing the bots. You will have a team of well-trained Institute scientists at your disposal and unlimited funds."

"This is beyond anything I could have hoped for. I'll have my own research group? How do the Overseers plan to implement the bio-bots? They are still at the very early stages of development."

"That is their concern, not yours," replied Tiberius. "Just know that they will be used to cement peace and prosperity in Arameus and the world for generations to come. This project is classified. You can tell no one, at risk of death for treason. Gather your necessary belongings and a week from today, Thaddeus will meet you at your quarters and take you to the undisclosed lab. You will be there for some time. I would advise you to tie up any loose ends from a personal standpoint."

"I look forward to getting to work. Do I have any say in who is on my team?"

"Your team has already been selected."

Conway hesitated, but decided it was now or never. "Then I must make one small request. You ask me to tie up any loose ends, but there is a major one for me personally. Perhaps it would not be too much to add Alexandra De Rosia to the team. She is a top-notch geneticist and a wonderful scientist. I feel she would be an asset to my team and will allow me to work faster to achieve results."

Tiberius smiled across the table at the new professor. This was something he understood. Sipping his wine, he thought for a moment.

"So then, you are in love?"

"Since I was twelve. She was seventeen and a graduate assistant to my intro biochemistry courses. She has always been above me and would never have considered me before. But now, as a professor in charge of a team carrying out the direct orders of the Overseers, she cannot ignore me. I am no longer that child."

"This, I understand," said Tiberius thoughtfully. "But this sort of thing can make a man weak, blinded by his passions and unable to carry out his duties. All men must struggle with this on their path to greatness. The successful ones always make the right choice, which is the difficult choice. Your duties come first. Still, I will take your request into consideration. If it tickles my fancy, then she will be with you next week when you enter the compound. I have not decided."

"Thank you for considering, your honor."

"It is nothing. Now go," replied Tiberius.

"Go? The yacht just launched. It will be cruising for two hours. We haven't even eaten."

"I prefer to dine alone. Don't worry. You will eat. Thaddeus has a table for you downstairs. You won't mind his company. Enjoy the view of the Central Isle. It is quite beautiful this time of day."

Matt looked at him, puzzled, before standing, bowing in respect, and walking toward the staircase from which he came. Though he still felt the sting of the slight he had just received from Tiberius, his heart was beating twice as fast as normal in his excitement. Not only was he a professor, he also had his own research group funded by the Overseers. They had even sent a high-ranking Parliament member to inform him. All of his dreams were coming true and he would not disappoint. He only hoped that his plea to get Alexandra placed on his team would not be ignored. In truth, she was a mediocre scientist, but she had a body that drove him crazy. She would not be able to resist his advances while working under him for this project.

As the young man disappeared from view down the spiral staircase, Tiberius motioned for the waiter.

"Get rid of this cheap wine and bring the real bottle."

As Tiberius sipped the vintage, forty-year old Sagittarian wine, his thoughts went to Kaiya. He wondered if she had been old enough to run through the grappa vineyards when this crop was harvested. He hoped so. It made him feel close to her to think that her father's fingers may have picked the very fruit that went into this bottle, and she may have played beside the vine, imbuing the fruit with energy from her unmistakable charisma and magnetism. He pondered this as he looked out over the Central Isle while the yacht moved slowly past. Fixating on the top of the Central Tower, he focused on the offices in which he knew the Overseers were now residing. It could all be different for him soon. If he could usher in the age of bio-bots, he would be free on his own private island to find and reunite with the woman he loved. For the second time in his life, he was alone. He had first lost his wife to the horror of death. Now he was alone because the woman he chose to love was not born into the proper family. Though she was lost, Tiberius had not forgotten his love and he would do everything in his power to earn the right to Kaiya.

# Chapter Twenty-Two
# The Spring Festival

*Bodies were thrown through the air with hellish force. Charred flesh smoldered, falling off the bones of fresh-made corpses. All sound was gone except for a persistent ringing. Stumbling, his body was numb. Palms finding pavement, he steadied himself, eyes open, yet only seeing the white light burned into his retinas. Choking on black smoke and reaching for her hand, his hearing returned, and the sound of the afflicted was horrendous. Explosions in the distance punctuated the crash of falling marble. Feeling around the immediate area for her body, his hand found hers, and the ash that had been her flesh fell from bone. Following the path from her hand to her chest, he felt no movement. Blinking rapidly to restore vision, the white light faded and was replaced by a bald, blackened face.*

*"Padma," he whispered, cradling her smoldering head in his arms. The heat emanating from her burned his skin, yet it was nothing. He stroked what remained of her face, the charred flesh falling away.*

*"I love you, Padma. Please don't leave me alone. I can't do this without you."*

*She was silent. He sat there rocking her. Her breathing diminished until it ceased, her heart too weak to beat again, leaving the burned shell of his former lover.*

*He heard a muffled scream and, regaining his composure, he searched the area for survivors. Movement under some collapsed shelving caught his eye. Removing the debris, he discovered the bodies of Richard and Chandler, badly injured, but alive and seemingly unburned. Mustering all his strength, he hoisted Richard onto his shoulders and carried him out of the ashes. Emerging from the ruined laboratory onto the cobbled street, he looked around for help. As if by providence, he heard the buzz of a hawk approaching. It was Margaret, arriving late to the meeting. Her face was horror-stricken as she approached the wreckage in the burgeoning light of the Red Sun.*

*"What happened!?"*

*"No time. Take him," said the man, hoisting Richard's motionless body onto the back of her hawk. Take him to Eduardo at the Devonshire Pub. He will know what to do." The woman nodded and without a word, her hawk launched down the Avenue. The man rushed back into the inferno, to where Padma lay. Kneeling beside the corpse, he cradled her body in a loving embrace.*

*"You will always be with me, my love," he whispered to her. "I will find a way to be with you again." He kissed what was left of her destroyed cheek and reached into her pocket pulling out a silver cigarette case. Warped by the heat, the initials P.L. were engraved into the side. After one last longing look, he rushed back to Chandler. Hoisting him onto his shoulder, he hurried to his hawk, throwing the body on the back and fleeing the horrifying scene.*

Ansley awoke, his body drenched in sweat. His breathing was erratic, and he searched the room for signs of the explosion. As always, there were none. He breathed deep breaths trying to calm his nerves, his eyes wet with tears. Padma seemed so close. He longed to hug even her corpse one last time. He had come far, but an infinite distance still separated them. Ansley could not forget his last promise to her and had devoted his life to bridging that insurmountable barrier. The only way to live with her again was to prevent her death from happening. He cared not for the Overseers, the Centauri, the Natural Born, or Arian. He cared only for her and would destroy the world to find her again. Such dreams would shatter most men, but they only made Ansley's resolve stronger. He rose from the bed. There was work to do.

Ansley met Arian in the restaurant they had come to when arriving in Beladero three nights before. They were to have breakfast with Jabari and Daniella before heading back to Capitol City. Arian was already seated with the couple when Ansley arrived. Still reeling from the vivid dream, an obvious symptom of his post-traumatic stress from that fateful night, Ansley had little appetite. He contented himself to sip on a mimosa.

"Damn Ansley. You're an alcoholic, dog," commented Jabari.

Arian laughed. He had been silent to this point, pushing his eggs around his plate with his fork. Something was troubling him. He had said little since seeing the Iris. This was worrisome to Ansley given Arian's connection to Tiberius through the girl, but there was no way around the risk. They needed the bio-bot technology. Eventually the risk had to be taken.

"I can't be an alcoholic," responded Ansley. "I don't have any kids. Only people with kids are alcoholics. I'm merely a swinging bachelor."

"You are one old ass bachelor," returned Jabari. He laughed, slapping Arian on the back. "This water is pretty refreshing. You should try some."

"I'm just annoyed that they put all of this wretched orange juice into my champagne." Ansley winked at Arian, who didn't respond. His mind was elsewhere, though Ansley was sure he was contemplating the full gravity of the Iris and his role in the affair. Hoping to break through the ice, he spoke directly to Arian.

"We have much work to do when we return to the city, my boy. You need to create a step-by-step blueprint for the production of the bio-bots and have a student follow the instructions to prove the results are reproducible. We have to ensure that when Richard and Padma receive the message in the past, they have the necessary information to create the bots. I know it is a heavy burden to bear, but the freedom of our entire species is at stake."

"I know what is required of me," answered Arian, still looking down at his plate. "I will carry out my end of the bargain. Just make sure that you uphold your end."

"Prepare a blood sample. We will map your DNA sequence and include it in our message to the past. When you are born again, it will be into a free world, where everyone will have the opportunity to flourish according to merit. I will raise you as my own son."

Arian narrowed his eyes. "You do realize how astronomically small the chances are that this plan will actually work? Supposing you can send a message to the past, how can you be sure they will receive it and follow it? It will seem a ridiculous proposal to them as well. And what happens if it does work? We just walk out of the caverns and the world is different all around us?"

"If it works," responded Ansley, annoyed, "we will never know. This timeline will be eliminated. It will be as if the last two hundred years were nothing more than a negative feedback mechanism for the world to self-correct. We won't even have knowledge of this world other than that which we communicate in the message. And if it doesn't work… we will know right away."

"If it doesn't work," added Jabari, "young Arian will be the newest member of the Council of Elders."

Daniella shot Jabari a stern glance. "Don't frighten the boy," she cooed. "If it doesn't work, the people of Beladero have long been prepared to execute Order Omega."

"He doesn't need to know about that," grumbled Ansley.

"Just know this, kid," said Jabari. "We can take down those old men Ansley's way, with no bloodshed, or we can go to plan B. But I assure you, your precious domed city will fall before this year ends."

"What the hell is Order Omega!" demanded Arian.

"Enough. If it becomes necessary, you will learn then. For now, leave it alone." Ansley's face was red with anger. "We need to get moving. People will begin to notice your absence from the city, Arian. You are still a professor, and I have a commitment I cannot forsake today."

Jabari nodded and stood, indicating an end to breakfast. Daniella hugged him and began to clear the dishes from the table.

"It was lovely as always," Ansley said to Daniella heading outside with Jabari and Arian, where Jabari's all terrain cruiser was waiting.

"We need to make one stop on the way out of the city," Ansley told Jabari. "We need to go to Sharie's house."

"Are you sure that's a good idea, Ansley? I'm not sure her family really wants to see you right now."

"I have a promise to fulfill."

They drove away from the center of the city and the waterfall spilling down the cliff face. Knowing what he now knew, the nearly boiling water spilling out of the cliff bunker took on a much more sinister appearance to Arian. He watched it disappear from view in silence. He needed only to get back to Capitol City alive and he could contact Kaiya to end this insane chapter of his life, securing Arameus in the process. He would be a hero. For now, he would remain silent and go along with the two men.

They drove toward the outskirts of the city. The

homes built within the walls of the surrounding mountains disappeared and were replaced by poorly constructed wooden shacks. Barely dressed children with dirty faces played in the desert sand. Old women with faces turned to leather by the sun washed linens in the stream that flowed outward from the city. Jabari brought his cruiser to a halt in front of one of these hovels.

"Wait here," Ansley said to Jabari. Jabari raised an eyebrow in question but said nothing, allowing Ansley to exit the vehicle. Taking a deep breath, Ansley walked to the makeshift piece of plywood that served as a door to the shack. He knocked three times. A small girl dressed in a long dirty shirt that covered her to just above the knee opened the door.

"And you must be Mia," said Ansley, bending down to his knee so that he was eye level with the small girl. "Your mother told me much about you. Is your father around?"

Without a word, the girl disappeared into the shack, leaving Ansley to wait. Back in the cruiser, Jabari adjusted the mirror so that Arian came into his view.

"I really appreciate what you're doing for us, dog. We all do. We're willing to sacrifice our lives so that the people of this world can be free. Don't think for a minute that you are the only one."

"Is it so bad, though?" asked Arian. "Would you risk your very existence to be free of the power of Arameus?"

"In a second. You accept your servitude because you are given the gift of vast wealth and immortality. Out here, we scrape out an existence as your waiters, farmers, and miners. I kill myself in the Patolli ring to entertain you, but nothing will ever be mine. We have no aspirations to sell to our children. How do you tell a small girl that she will never learn to read? How do you tell her that if she is lucky, she can work as a sex slave to a wealthy Nephite, being immunized so that she will never accidentally bear a child. There needs to be a shift in this world. There needs to be a re-balancing of power. If we must sacrifice ourselves in order for this to happen, then we are willing."

"You're a brave man, Jabari," said Arian. He looked at his feet, wishing to avoid eye contact with the large, dark-skinned man. He hated that Jabari would fall along with Ansley when he reported the bunker in Beladero to Kaiya. He hated that Ansley had convinced these impoverished people to join him on his foolish and misguided quest, dooming them all. How had he ever allowed himself to be involved in this? It was too big for him. The guilt weighing on his conscience was overwhelming. He looked back to the shack just in time to see a smallish, brown-skinned man punch Ansley in the jaw, the second time he had been punched in as many days.

"What the hell!" shouted Jabari as he jumped out of the jeep and ran to Ansley's aid. Struggling to his feet, Ansley waved him off, stopping Jabari in his tracks.

"How dare you show up to my house after what you did to my family!" demanded the man. "You stole everything from us. She was my life." He punched Ansley again, this time, sending him flat on his back, leaving him motionless. Jabari ran up and threw the man to the ground. He struggled but was no match for Jabari's size and strength. Ansley came to after a few seconds and sat up, rubbing his cheek and jaw, his head still ringing from the blows. It took him a moment to realize where he was.

"Damn it, Pedro, will you stop fucking hitting me? I'm here to help." Ansley slowly got back to his feet, still unsteady.

"Let him up, Jabari. I probably deserved that."

Jabari got off Pedro's back and lifted him to his feet, still keeping a firm grip on him. The man glowered at Ansley.

"You promised you would protect her," he shouted at Ansley. "Instead, you left her to die alone in your wretched city."

"I'm sorry, Pedro, from the bottom of my heart, I'm sorry. I thought I could protect her and I failed in that regard. But she died for your people, a hero, and she was not alone. I held her hand as she passed into the void."

"You... you were there?" Tears were streaming down

the man's face. Despite Jabari's tight grip, he wriggled free and fell to his knees sobbing. The small girl, Mia, ran to him from within the house, wrapping her arms around him in an attempt to comfort her father.

"I was there," confirmed Ansley, placing a sympathetic hand on the man's back. "And in her last moments she spoke of you. She had a final request. I could not protect her, but I can honor her last words. She asked me to take care of her family."

Pedro looked up at Ansley through his tears, hatred still evident, but also a hint of the question going through his mind.

"And how do you propose to take care of our broken and ruined family?"

Reaching into his pocket and fumbling around, Ansley pulled out a golden ring in which the largest diamond Jabari had ever seen was set.

"This is the Mardonian Diamond. When my father won the National Medal of Science over three hundred years ago, he used his prize money to gift this to my mother. It is my most prized possession, and it will make you a rich man. Take it, sell it, and move as far away from here as you can. Beladero is no longer safe. Find a free city and raise your daughter there. It will never replace Sharie, but it will fulfill my vow and protect your daughter."

Pedro took the ring, looking at Ansley, but saying nothing.

"We should be going," Ansley said to Jabari. They headed back to the vehicle. Ansley took one last look back at the grief stricken man clutching his mother's beautiful ring. There had been a time when he had intended to give the ring to Padma. His long years had led him to many unexpected twists, but all would be irrelevant soon. He would either be dead or with Padma. Regardless, one nagging burden had been lifted from his conscience.

Entering the cruiser, Ansley sat in silence. Jabari started the vehicle and began the journey back to Capitol City.

About five minutes passed before Arian broke the silence.

"That was the family of the woman who died in the casino, wasn't it? She was the woman with the flash drive."

"It was," said Ansley stoically.

"You knew her well?"

"Very."

"Death follows you everywhere. You destroy everyone around you, and for what? To get back a woman who died fifty years ago?"

"That woman was your mother," said Ansley quietly.

"But at what point in this quest of yours did your motives become selfish? Do you even know why you are doing this anymore? Is this really about freeing the people of the outside world or is it about Ansley Brightmore getting even with the Overseers for killing his girlfriend?"

"If we do our jobs, these deaths will be wiped away. We will have a clean slate. People will be able to live and prosper without the bombings and fear. Sharie died doing something she believed in. We should all be so lucky."

"That's what you call the scenario that just played out? Was that little girl lucky to be without a mother?"

"Her mother died the same way as yours. And I killed neither of them. You better figure out who the enemy is, kid, because we have no room for your misplaced doubts."

Arian leaned back in his seat, crossing his arms and closing his eyes. The rest of the journey passed in silence. He napped, comforted by the warmth of the unblocked yellow sun. When Jabari awoke him, he could feel his face burning, and taste the saltiness of his sweat on his tongue. They were at the locker room entrance for the Capitol City Gliders, and the dome rose high above.

"Wake up, sleepyhead," said Jabari. "Your mansion awaits."

Arian stretched and exited the vehicle. Ansley was already on the ground, standing next to the driver-side door.

"Thank you, Jabari. I will be in touch." He embraced the hulking man.

"Keep this one safe, Ans," said Jabari as they released one another. "We are very close."

"Let's go, kid," Ansley said to Arian.

They walked to the entrance and punched in Jabari's code. As the massive doors creaked and began to open, Ansley cast one more glance at Jabari who smiled broadly at him. Dust covered from the journey and all muscle, he was a heroic figure. Had Ansley known it was to be the last time he would ever meet with Jabari Stoudamyre, who had been like a son to him, he would have hugged him longer. But he would always remember the Jabari he knew, the statuesque, grinning man, standing in the desert, a beacon of hope for his entire class.

Ansley and Arian continued the trip to the city in silence. Arian contemplated whether he had it in him to betray Ansley to Kaiya, while Ansley's mind focused on Anabelle. He had treated her poorly and felt obligated to show his contrition before it was too late. They moved through the dark, musky tunnel toward the locker room. When they arrived, Raul was waiting to let them in.

"You're late, Professor," said Raul. "I was beginning to think you weren't going to make it back."

"I always make it back," returned Ansley. "Somehow."

"Your qubits," said the short, balding man, "and the Patolli ball you requested."

Ansley took the items, handing Arian his qubit, which was flashing red, indicating an urgent message. Before Arian could check it, Ansley tossed the ball in the direction of his face.

"Heads up, kid."

"What the hell, man," cried Arian, dodging the hard ball.

"Pick it up," said Ansley with a sly smile.

Leaning down to pick up the Patolli ball, Arian could see that it was covered in signatures. He looked back at

Ansley, bewildered, but the young man within him couldn't hide the smile lighting up his face.

"The team signs balls for kids all the time. I felt a little bad for making fun of you, so I contacted Raul from Beladero to see if he could dig up a ball. You even have Jabari's signature. Lucky you."

"You're a strange man, Ansley, but thank you," was all Arian could say.

"Well, Raul, I appreciate your help," said Ansley. "Are we clear to leave?"

"Yes Professor. Everyone is celebrating the Spring Festival. There has not been another person in the building today. They have all likely been drinking since the morning."

"I hate amateur hour. We should get going. I have somewhere to be."

Ansley hugged Raul and turned to look at Arian, who reached out his hand to the old man. The two men shook hands as equals.

"You Natural Born are all much braver than I."

"No choice, my friend. No choice," was Raul's reply.

Arian turned and strode away, but Ansley caught up to him.

"Take a few days, kid. I know this is a large burden to consider. I don't want you to be involved if you are not completely behind the cause." He reached his hand out and gave Arian's shoulder an affectionate squeeze before turning and heading across the National Mall toward the southern district of the city, where the sounds of music and large crowds beckoned.

Arian sat on his hawk, pulling his qubit from his pocket. Skipping over the inevitable messages from students and colleagues, he went directly to the urgent message. It was from an unknown residence. The soft and barely audible voice was filled with fear and apprehension. He pressed the qubit closer to his ear and still had trouble making out the words.

*"Arian, it's Kaiya. I'm in trouble. I have been in exile in Avignon, but I fear my life is in danger. Please find me in Sikyon. Look for me at Angelica's Desires in the southern district. If you don't come, I will die."*

His heart palpitated as he replayed the message again and again. There was a wild quality to her voice that frightened him. Arian had never been in love or emotionally connected to another person in his engineered life. As strange as it seemed, Ansley, the man he was planning on betraying, was his best friend. He had rationalized his feelings for Kaiya as merely lust, but upon hearing her voice for the first time since the night they shared, he knew now that he must love her and could not imagine a life in which he never looked upon her beautiful features again. Turning, he saw Ansley walking away in the distance. Dropping the signed Patolli ball and jumping from the hawk, he broke into a sprint. He didn't know why she was back in Avignon, or what had happened between her and Tiberius, but she needed him, and if there was any man in Arameus that could help him find her in Sikyon, it was Ansley. He was out of breath when he finally caught the man.

"Ansley, I need you."

Seeing the state of the kid, Ansley was concerned.

"What's wrong?"

"It's Kaiya. She's in trouble. Something has gone wrong. She's hiding in Sikyon and needs my help."

"She is no concern of mine," replied Ansley. "Or yours, if you are truly with us. She is one of Tiberius' many spies. She was using you to get to me. This is a trap, kid, forget about it." Ansley turned to walk away, but Arian caught him by the shoulder.

"Please, Ansley. I love her." The words caught in his throat as he began to choke up. "I love her, Ansley. Please, please, help me. I can't live without seeing her again. If anyone can understand this, it's you."

Looking at Arian, Ansley couldn't help but see the

genetic traces of Padma in his face. It made him want to comfort him, even though this was bad business. It was too risky. Tiberius was again playing Arian.

"My answer remains no. We can't smuggle you into Sikyon to save the spy recruited by our enemies to destroy our cause. Please tell me you understand this."

"I slept with her, Ansley," said Arian, sobbing now. "We opened up to one another. She is as much as a slave as every other Natural Born you purport to want to save. You've asked much of me, and I agreed. If you can't grant me this one, then I will no longer help you. You can't just be this shell of a man. There has to be compassion left in you. What would you do if it were Padma?"

"But it's not Padma!" screamed Ansley.

"But…" stuttered Arian, "but what if it were Padma. I have to go to her, with or without you! Nothing will stop me."

Arian turned and walked away determined, though he had no idea how he would get to Sikyon without help. Inter-dome travel required express consent from the government. He was sure that whatever forces had placed Kaiya in Sikyon would not be willing to grant him a travel pass.

Ansley stood, considering Arian as he walked away. It was dumb, suicide even, but the kid's romantic streak had touched Ansley, not to mention that he needed Arian alive. How could he deny Padma's own son the very connection that he still sought himself? He would help him, but he would have to go through some very unsavory avenues to do so.

"Hey, kid," Ansley shouted after Arian. "Come back here. I'll help you."

Arian stopped and all of his anxiety melted away. While he could not be sure he would find Kaiya safe, at least he could guarantee he was doing everything within his power to help her. He walked back to Ansley.

"Getting you into Sikyon without the government's knowledge is no easy task. The price will be high. I hope you're willing to pay it."

"I'll do anything, Ansley, and be forever grateful. Thank you."

"When Don Gravano gets finished with you, you may not be so grateful. Now walk with me. I have an uncomfortable task ahead of me tonight. If I am to risk our entire operation to get you to a government spy, the least you can do is hang out with me."

"I will go wherever. When can we get Kaiya?"

"When can you get Kaiya," Ansley corrected. "It will take me a week to organize the details. This man Gravano is as dangerous as the Overseers. The two of you are likely to die by his hand."

"Then why should we enlist his help?" asked Arian, walking beside Ansley across the mall.

"Because Don Gravano responds to only two things, money and power. We can offer him both. Just hope that no one else offers him more."

"I'm willing to risk everything for Kaiya."

"Of course you are."

"Thank you, Ansley. I can never repay you. So what is this commitment?"

"We're going to a fashion show, Anabelle's to be exact. I've done some things I'm not proud of, and think I should at least be there to help her set up."

Arian frowned, then shrugged his shoulders and followed across the mall. His mind was too preoccupied with Kaiya to question this more. The two men traversed the area quickly, Arian having to double his normal pace to keep up with Ansley. The sounds of music and raised voices became louder as they approached the Arymides.

Using a pedestrian tunnel that went underneath the river, they emerged on the other side in the South District. The change in scenery was evident, as masses of revelers roamed chaotic streets drinking ale from plastic cups. Patriotic songs sporadically sprung from the crowd, praising the founders of Arameus and welcoming the spring. It was an old ritual, passed down from the older generations, the true meaning long ago lost upon the citizens of Capitol City. Scantily clad women became even less garbed, as they bared their breasts to passing men in hopes of acquiring golden Spring Festival tokens. The tokens, produced by the Parliament, featured the faces of the four Overseers and could be cashed in for prizes at the end of the festival. Given the vast wealth and luxury the inhabitants of the city enjoyed, the prizes were meager at best, but that never stopped the women from engaging in more and more risqué behavior.

After all Arian had seen in Beladero, the Festival took on a more sinister tone. Kaiya's fate weighed heavily on him, as did Ansley's request. For the first time, he understood the old Professor's negative views of the Empire. His thoughts were an odd juxtaposition to colored floats and alcohol-fueled revelry before him.

Ansley stopped abruptly and grabbed Arian by the arm.

"Even with extended years, Arian, life is short. These may be our last days. We might as well enjoy them." With that, Ansley ordered two ales from the street vendor.

"You don't know how much I need this beer," said Arian. "I think spending time with you is making me an alcoholic."

"Never let people make you feel bad about embracing your character enhancers, my boy. No one remembers chaste people fondly. It is the drinkers and the gamblers that people spread stories about."

Drinks in hand, the men slowed their pace, dodging between the masses of people. Even with the climate controls set at a cool and breezy 65 degrees, the heat from the bodies caused them to sweat. The air was thick with the pheromones and smells of the thousands of intoxicated Nephites dancing to music that filled the air over loudspeakers. As they walked, they heard a shrill voice call out from a distance.

"Arian!"

Turning, Arian nearly dropped his drink as Alexandra

de Rosia jumped onto him, embracing him and wrapping her legs around his waist. She was clad in a short skirt and a bikini top. Her hair was styled in a tight bun, and a sparkling green mask covered the top of her face, just above the nose. The green from the mask accented her brilliant green eyes. She was drunk, and at this point, Arian was wondering why he had chosen not to sleep with her after the Patolli game.

"I was hoping I would see you here!" she exclaimed, as he set her back on her feet. She surveyed him. "You look so much darker than when I last saw you. Have you been using bronzer?"

"Yeah," answered Arian, glancing to Ansley. "I was going for a new look."

"Well, I love it!" she responded. "Are you heading to Anabelle's fashion show? We have become best friends. She is so talented. She even did my hair. Do you like it?"

"It looks great," answered Arian. "We were just headed that way. Would you like to walk together?"

Seeming to notice Ansley for the first time, Alexandra's look soured. "You have a lot of nerve showing. Anabelle told me about the last time you were together. You promised to help her prepare. She's really hurt."

"Something came up that couldn't be ignored," answered a stoic Ansley.

Seeming to forget about Ansley altogether, Alexandra turned back to Arian. "Well, let's go. I want to help set up."

The trio walked the crowded streets, stopping as Alexandra ran into colleagues and friends along the way. Ansley visited five more ale stands as well as a couple of stands that served chilled Tegave shots. Arian could see that he was apprehensive about meeting Anabelle and wondered what had transpired between them. Ansley seemed so devoted to Padma that it didn't fit in with his view of the man to consider that he was carrying on an affair with Anabelle.

As they walked, Alexandra chatted with Arian about all that had been happening since they last met. She had taken a new job offered from the highest levels of the Institute. She was vague about the professor she would be working with and the research in general. With all that was on his mind, Arian found it difficult to care.

When they arrived at the storefront of the boutique, it was roped off, with security standing outside the door. Already there was a line forming of elite Nephites, likely friends of Anabelle's influential father, as well as fashion buyers searching for the season's next big trend. Their attire stood out from the street revelers, fully clothed in fashionable spring dresses with expensive shoes and bags to match. If they acknowledged the Spring Festival, it was only in their choices of colors, which were overwhelmingly pastel. Walking to the front of the line, Alexandra spoke to the security guard, a Natural Born man, who eyed her fashion choices with a skeptical eye.

"We are here to help Anabelle set up. I am Alexandra. I should be on the list."

The man removed the rope, allowing the three to pass, not bothering to check the two men. As he passed, Ansley slapped the guard on the arm.

"Good to see you, Roberto. How's your wife?"

"Good, Professor. She wanted to thank you for helping us when our child was ill last year. We can never repay you."

With an easy wink, a buzzed Ansley replied, "It is nothing between friends, Bertie. I hope to talk to you before I leave tonight." With that, he entered the boutique behind Alexandra and Arian.

The interior was transformed from the last time Ansley had seen it. The clothing racks were removed, replaced by ordered rows of chairs and a makeshift runway. Natural Born servers chilled champagne and cocktail shrimp on tables to the side while fashion photographers readied their equipment. The entire store was bustling with activity, as Anabelle barked orders at those surrounding her, attempting to make the final preparations before the doors opened. Alexandra went to her and whispered something. Anabelle's gaze shot to Ansley, icy cold and filled with derision. She marched up to him and slapped him hard on his right cheek. The blow stung, though not in a physical way.

"You decide to show up after a month without contacting me, and on the day of my show? Who do you think you are?" she demanded before storming off.

Arian grinned and shook his head at Ansley. "People sure seem to want to hit you today. I can't say I blame them."

Ansley muttered something unintelligible under his breath and moved to one of the side tables. Grabbing a bottle of champagne, he popped the cork and began drinking. With the champagne bubbling over the top and overflowing his mouth, he was forced to cough up half of what he drank as the contents of the bottle spilled over onto the floor.

"Sir, that champagne is for the show!" a concerned server screamed as he ran over to confront Ansley.

"There is plenty more for the others," replied Ansley, annoyed.

One of the nearby photographers came up and began shooting pictures of Ansley as he tried to contain his spill and wipe off his clothes. Ansley smacked the camera out of the man's hand, sending it shattering to the floor.

"That was a 10,000 credit camera!" exclaimed the photographer.

Anabelle rushed up to see what the commotion was about.

"Are you okay, Jeffrey? My father will replace your camera, I promise."

Turning to Ansley, she glared. "I will not have your drunk ass ruining my show. Now come with me. I have to get into my dress, and we have much to discuss."

Grabbing him by the hand, she led him past the runway to the backstage area. They passed a plethora of models dressing for the show and entered Anabelle's private office. There was a dressing mirror set up within, and a tailor was making the final preparations to her evening gown.

"Leave us, Giovanni," said Anabelle. "I will dress in private." Shutting the door behind him as he left, Ansley was alone with her for the first time. Nervous, he paced in front of the door.

"Honestly, Ansley, of all nights to show back up in my life, and drunk at that, you have to choose this one?" She was almost imploring him to explain himself.

"I...I... don't know what to say," stammered Ansley. She remained unmoved, staring at him. "I just don't think I can ever be the man you need or the man you want me to be."

"And what man do you think I need you to be?" she asked, incredulous. "We have sex, on occasion, when drunk, nothing more. It's just that last time, you promised me more. Last time was different. I expected you to be here for me, at least as a friend."

Ansley looked down at the ground, trying to hide the tears he knew were forming in his eyes, hoping that somehow she wouldn't notice.

"I'm just broken, Bella. I should have died long ago. I should have died with... I don't even know. I'm a ghost, wandering the world for the last fifty years, and I hate it. This is not the world I was born into. This is not how man was intended to live. This... this life... it..."

"Stop, Ansley," interrupted Anabelle, her own eyes tearing up. "I don't want to hear anymore. I've heard enough of your drunken rants and your feeling sorry for yourself. Get out!"

He looked up at her, shocked, and saw in her eyes, beyond the tears, a firm resoluteness. He knew they had come to a point where it was better for him to just walk away, and it made him sad. Selfishly, however, he was most sad that he would never be able to redeem himself in her eyes. Her words hurt him, but there was no other way. He had chosen his path, rightness be damned.

"I do love you, Bella," he said, then turned and exited

the room. He wanted to look back, to see her one last time, but thought better of it. He left the boutique through the back door and walked through a deserted alley reserved for garbage pickup. He heard the revelers in the distance, but they seemed as if from another world that would soon be no more. He walked past the phantom people and felt no pity for them, continuing all the way home.

Sitting on his sofa, he contemplated the massive events that fate or his own stubbornness had placed in his path. Picking up his qubit, he dialed a code that he used sparingly and always with great apprehension. A gruff, uncouth voice responded on the other end.

"This better be good, Brightmore."

"Gravano, I have something for you. It will be dangerous, but the payment I can offer is beyond even your greediest dreams."

# Chapter Twenty-Three
## Sikyon

The rendezvous point was an out of place hill overlooking the barren desert outside Beladero. The desolation of the environment matched that of Arian's soul. Here he awaited the shadowy character that would be his transport to Sikyon, though it had taken more time than he hoped. It had been two weeks since Ansley had made a fool of himself at the fashion show. A few days passed after that night before Ansley contacted him. It was for the best, it turned out, since Arian had come down with the first illness of his life. This was due to the inertness of his nanobots due to the Iris' intense magnetic field. The medics at the nano-center had been at a loss to explain how his bots had suddenly been destroyed.

Some unforeseen factors had arisen, which Ansley neglected to explain, involving the payment to Don Gravano, leading to the delay. When finally contacted, he was instructed to meet Jabari outside the Patolli locker rooms as before. They drove for nearly three hours, far past Beladero and into the mountains before stopping on a hill that seemed ready made to be a landing pad. Jabari stood beside him now, a reassuring presence in this harsh environment. It was past five and the yellow sun's heat was diminishing. Gravano was already an hour late.

Arian looked at Jabari, nervous. "Do you think he'll show?"

"He'll show, dog," answered Jabari. "Although I'm not sure you want him to."

"If he's that bad, why would Ansley choose him for this task? Who is he?"

"Gravano is a crime boss, a war lord. His crime family, like many others, seized power in the vacuum left when the greater wealth and leaders of the world formed Arameus. They rule their cities with absolute power, much like your Overseers. It is nothing like Beladero. Gravano doesn't recognize Arameus as an authority, but he has no problem selling coal to your cities and taking care of certain tasks your leaders may find unseemly. He can never be trusted. His allegiance is only to money and even if your government has no idea about this venture, or if Ansley outbid them, he is still just as likely to kill you after receiving payment."

"He sounds charming. I can't wait to meet him."

"Just watch yourself. You will rendezvous back with me and a few of our men when the time for payment comes, so we will be able to provide some protection, but seriously dog, have you ever even fired a gun before?"

"Come on, Jabari, I'm a professor at the Institute. I had never even seen a gun until I met you."

"Take this," said Jabari, handing him a switchblade. "Just push the button and stick him with the pointy end. You'll be searched upon boarding, but they aren't likely to notice that in your waistband. It may come in handy if you feel threatened."

"Thanks," said Arian, feeling unsure about what he, who had never been in an altercation, would do if confronted.

He didn't have long to consider this as they heard the thunderous sound of approaching engines. The hulking black

Capitol Raven came into view, its thrusters maneuvering to first slow the ship and then set it down onto the hill five hundred feet from where they were standing. This was a ship of the Imperial fleet, not the ship of a gangster.

Noticing Arian's change in posture, Jabari reassured him. "Don't worry. Gravano deals with all levels of the Aramean government. The Raven is your ticket into the loading docks within the dome of Sikyon."

The landing ramp descended from the main door. Eight heavily armed guards emerged, garbed in green and black camouflaged clothes, a testament to their life of strife beyond Arameus. The guards walked out, in groups of two, followed by a fat older man dressed in a suit of white, his completely bald head spotted by years of sun damage. Even from this distance, his gaudy jewelry gleamed in the afternoon sun. In his hand, he held a dark mahogany cane, tipped with a gold sculpture, the details of which Arian could not make out.

"Drop your weapons and show your hands," demanded one of the guards in the front. Jabari placed his automatic rifle on the ground and put his hands in the air. Arian followed his lead, apprehensive. Once the men were contained, Gravano approached, walking with a limp, though not using his cane. His stench was sickening to Arian as he came close, surprising due to the pristineness of his suit.

"So you are the lover boy who wishes to get in and out of Sikyon unnoticed?" he began.

Arian wasn't sure whether he should answer, but Gravano continued, saving him the trouble.

"Many fish occupy the sea, my friend," he said, chuckling. "Perhaps I could introduce you to a few." He laughed, showing his yellowing teeth.

It was Jabari who answered. "You don't get your payment unless you deliver Arian and the girl, alive and unharmed."

"Jabari... a giant of a man and a true Patolli hero, you're in no position to make demands of me."

"I'm not sure your men and all their weapons would be able to stop me before I snapped your neck," shot back Jabari.

"This mission must be very important to Ansley if he chose to employ me and sent you to deliver the boy. And the payment he has offered, almost unbelievable. Hard to imagine he would offer such a treasure to one he despises so."

"He will pay what he promised. You have my word. Just meet at the allotted time and get my guys out. You will have your prize."

"Of that, I have no doubt. We should be going then. The docks close for the night in a few hours. We will meet at this time in two days. Make sure your men are ready to obtain my payment."

With that Gravano returned to the Raven, his men following. Jabari grabbed Arian by both shoulders. The man towered over Arian to such a degree that he had to strain his neck to look up at him.

"Be safe, dog. Do not trust this man for a moment and when in doubt, push the damn button on that blade."

"What does he mean about having your men ready?" asked Arian.

"It's no concern of yours. Just know that the cost of this venture is very high. I hope she's worth it."

"She is," replied Arian. He had never intended to put others in harm's way. Filled with apprehension, he followed Gravano's men into the Raven. Jabari stayed, watching until the door closed and the ship lifted from the ground, disappearing into the horizon. Shaking his head, he got into his cruiser. It would be a long drive home and he ached to be with Daniella on what may be one of his last nights alive.

Arian was shocked by the luxury of the Raven. This was not the traditional model he visited on field trips as a child. Gravano had outfitted it with all the amenities of a comfortable home. Couches lined the walls, and there was a bar in the corner, complete with a bartender. The guards removed their guns and lounged about the aircraft. An impressive screen replayed Patolli highlights and discussed upcoming match-ups. Gravano took Arian aside to the bar.

"Let me get you a drink from the old world," he said, and called the bartender. "Two gin martinis, extra dirty."

While they waited, he looked Arian over. "You seem a bit young to be caught up in all this. Are you sure you have chosen the right side?"

"I have no side," replied Arian, still nervous. "I only want to save Kaiya."

"My little lover boy, so caught up in his amore. Still, you have placed your faith in Ansley Brightmore. I know of him and his endeavors, and I don't see a way for him to come out on top. Have you ever seen him gamble? You are a young professor of the Institute. You can live forever. Why trouble yourself with this desperate man when you have knowledge that is far more valuable? You could be powerful beyond your dreams. Why not share these bio-bots with me? I will give them to the world, and you can have it all."

"What do you know of my work?" demanded Arian, adopting a defensive tone.

"Foolish boy, I know much more than you arrogant Nephites think. You can have it all, power, wealth, your life, and the girl. I can offer all of this to you, along with my protection. The world is much bigger than you know."

The drinks arrived. Gravano raised his glass to Arian, adding, "It's something to think about, no?"

Arian raised his glass to his lips. The bitter taste of salt and flowers washed over his pallet. He nearly spat the drink out, but forced himself to swallow.

"Perhaps this is a drink for a man and not a boy," said Gravano, his tone mocking.

Arian picked the drink back up and drained the contents of the glass, barely suppressing the urge to gag as he swallowed the last bit. His head was spinning and not from the drink. Of all of the scenarios presented to him in these tumultuous months, Gravano's offer was the only one that allowed him to preserve his life, maintain a good position, and be with Kaiya. Perhaps this was the way to save them both. Still, the thought of this wretched man having bio-bots and preserving his life further held no appeal for Arian.

"You are the only man who has offered me a deal that allows me personal gain. I will consider it. Don? Gravano? What should I call you?"

"You can call me Christoph, my boy. It is my given name. I only ask that you consider. Still, seeing your dire circumstances, I cannot imagine another way. We will ignore business for now. Another drink, perhaps?"

"Sure."

"Good. I will leave you to relax now. The journey will take four hours. Anything you need, just ask Isaac," he said, motioning to the bartender. "And take this," he added, handing over a qubit. "Function 1 will call my contact in Sikyon. She is aware of our venture, and will guide you to your girl when we arrive."

With that, Gravano walked to the front of the cabin and disappeared into the cockpit of the Raven.

Taking his fresh drink from the bar, Arian walked to a part of the cabin devoid of guards and took a seat on the couch. He raised the drink to his lips, before thinking better of it and setting it aside on an end table. The drink was disgusting, not to mention that he needed to be fresh when they landed. He discreetly pulled the blade from his waistband and placed it into his pocket in a pointless effort to feel safe.

He sat, thinking, before deciding to call the woman Gravano had mentioned. Typing in Function 1, the qubit beeped twice in his ear before connecting. A silky voice answered. Her name was Serenity. She explained that the extraction from a brothel called Angelica's Desires would be difficult given Kaiya's fugitive status, though she gave no details regarding how this had come to be. She was brief, stating that she would meet the Raven upon its arrival and escort Arian to the brothel. That was all he was able to ascertain from the conversation before she hung up. Dealing with the underworld would be a less than straightforward task, and the thought that Kaiya was somehow a fugitive concerned him. He wasn't sure how, but he must have fallen asleep, lulled by the roar of the engines. The next thing he saw was Gravano standing over him, shaking him to consciousness.

"We are landing, lover boy, it is time for you to carry out your task. Remember to trust no one in the dome other than my contact. You are safe with her. And do not forget my offer."

"You are kind, Christoph. I will not forget your generosity."

"I have been called many things in my life, but kindness and generosity were never associated with me," replied Gravano.

Arian stood and walked to a window. The Raven was circling the dome in a landing pattern. As they approached the Northwestern end of the city, the aircraft slowed and hovered, its engines directed downward. An unseen hinge in the dome opened, sliding inward as if it were a door, allowing the Raven to enter the city. The aircraft eased downward until it rested on the landing pad. City workers rushed around to meet the sizeable foreign ship. Arian worried how they would get past customs. They were bringing no cargo and had no reason to enter the dome. His fears were unfounded. Gravano greeted the city agents as if they were old friends. After a brief hug, the captain of the custom agents laughingly asked Gravano what business he had in the city. The question was met with a large wad of bills placed in his hands, the money of the outside world. The captain would use it for illegal trade. It would be untraceable by the consulates who ruled the city.

Arian was ushered off the ship by the custom agents to a four-man transport hawk. A thin, dark-haired woman with piercing blue eyes met him. Her appearance was meek, yet there was a fierceness within her that made Arian uneasy. She introduced herself as Serenity, a name that was far from fitting to her demeanor.

"You seek a woman at Angelica's Desires called Kaiya?" the woman asked in a stern rasping voice as he entered the hawk.

"Yes. Thank you. Is she okay?"

"I know nothing of this woman, other than that she is the most wanted woman in the region. She is charged with the murder of plantation owner Flavius Decimus and his family. The Decimus family was close with our Lead Consulate, Sergio Mondavi. If she had been apprehended, I would know."

"Kaiya could never do such a thing," responded Arian, his voice heavy with doubt.

"Never pretend to know the true nature of a woman. It will lead you to trouble. Still, we could all become wealthy by the knowledge of her whereabouts. Perhaps we should revise our goals."

"Gravano said I could trust you."

"And as long as he sides with you, you can. You must be paying him a substantial sum."

"Exactly. Let's get going," answered Arian. He was tired of knowing less than those around him. It was a situation he vowed to remedy in the future.

Serenity typed the coordinates into the hawk.

"Angelica's Desires is in the southern end of the city. It will take half an hour to get there. Take this," she said tossing him a duffle bag. "Your Capitol City garb will attract unwanted attention in Sikyon. We wear muted tones here, and are far more casual."

Arian caught the bag and changed, feeling awkward as Serenity watched from across the cab. She continued to stare in silence as the hawk sped through the city. Not knowing what to do, Arian averted his eyes, choosing to take in the sights of Sikyon as they passed. Its set up was different from Capitol City. There was no Central Isle or towers. The design was random and Arian assumed this was due to the uneven landscape of the region, which had long been the heart of wine country. They passed an ancient yet elegant structure constructed from stone. A towering spire rose from the top, equipped with a bell. It reminded him of the old world churches he had seen in books during his schooling.

"What is that building?" he asked, breaking the silence.

"That is the Aristides Monastery. It was a church, built long ago for pilgrims and travelers the world over to come and give thanks for a good harvest. It fell into decay after hundreds of years of nonuse but the foundation was strong. The Mondavi are a family of Nephites, related to Pierre de Medici. They made their wealth working this land. They preserved the historical landscape when this dome was constructed.

"Who built the cathedral?" asked Arian.

"The Order of the Red Sun. They are a cult devoted to preserving the true history of the world, unaffected by politics or popular opinion. They have done this for tens of thousands of years, since the beginning of recorded history. That building is used as a library, preserving the great works. It is rumored that in an airtight vault underneath the church, texts outlining the entire history of our world are kept, unknown even to the Overseers themselves."

"There is much I don't know of your city," responded Arian, "but I think I would like these Mondavi."

"As an outward lying dome, we are only loosely governed by the Overseers and Parliament of Arameus. They like our wine, which I believe, is our only purpose in the Empire. It allows us certain luxuries you do not have in Capitol City. For instance, I'm sure you have no brothel."

"The idea is offensive to me," answered Arian. "The thought of Kaiya being there gives me trouble. Sadly, our leaders do keep their whores, even in the Capitol."

"Not to pry, but how much do you know of this woman to risk so much? Angelica is not a woman who would harbor a stranger."

"You do pry, and this is no business of yours."

"As you wish," replied Serenity.

The rest of the ride passed without words. Arian

contented himself to watch the rustic, old-world architecture pass outside the window. The view slowly changed, from grand buildings to pubs, and finally to lower income homes. The streets were crowded with Natural Born merchants and vendors. The transport hawk came to a stop outside a nondescript building, with no visible entrance or sign in the front. It was the size of a small country inn, containing about eight rooms by Arian's estimate.

"We have arrived," said Serenity. "I'm sure Christoph has warned you, but trust no one in Sikyon. You have no friends here. Take this money," she added, handing him a crumpled wad of bills. "Credits will do you no good here, but this will get you by."

"Thank you," said Arian. "You have been kind to me."

"I have done nothing," she replied sternly, "but do as Gravano asked. I will be here in two days to bring you back to the Raven. If you are alive, then you will meet me at noon. Gravano will not wait. My master has one more piece of advice for you. When the time comes to choose, make sure you choose the Black Rose. All other choices will lead to an ill met fate. Now go."

Wondering at Serenity's cryptic words, Arian stepped out of the hawk and into the heart of the Sikyon underworld. He took the hood of the dark jacket he was now wearing and placed it over his head. Walking to the old façade of the red brick building, he searched for an entrance. An aging Natural Born man called him from the corner.

"You have unfulfilled desires, young one? You seek Angelica?"

"I do," responded Arian, his voice filled with apprehension.

"Down the alley around the corner," said the man, motioning with his head. "Tell them Garbo sent you."

Arian nodded and entered the dim alley. He found three stairs descending to a wooden door, lit only by a flickering light hanging from overhead. Cautiously, he walked down the stairs and rapped on the door three times. Receiving no answer, he knocked again. He was startled as the doors to an unseen cellar to his right flung outward, revealing an armed man standing five stairs below.

"What is your business?" the ill-tempered man asked.

"I'm here for companionship," replied Arian, pulling down his hood and exposing his face.

The man eyed him for a long moment, causing Arian to question whether he had made the right decision coming here. His fears were alleviated when the man stepped aside, motioning him with a gun toward the entrance below. Moving past without a word, he came to an iron door, which creaked as he opened it. Vibrant reds filled his vision along with the sounds of laughter. The warmth and welcome of the room stood in stark contrast to the grimness of the alley and guard outside. Rich velvet couches, occupied by beautiful women and expectant men lined the room, while an ornate circular bar occupied the center. Two hulking fireplaces at both ends of the room offered an orange glow and shed an ambience that made Arian relax. The air was thick with the smell of jasmine, citrus, and musk, likely from the perfume of the women. Arian walked to the bar, sat, and ordered an ale.

The beer slid easily down his throat, easing his weariness from travel. Surveying the room, he found it difficult to imagine that the elegant woman he believed he loved could be in such a place. The bartender served him, asking no questions. He sat alone for at least ten minutes before a pretty though world-weary woman approached. Imposing, she was dressed in an emerald green evening gown with a diamond necklace glittering across her wrinkled olive skin. Her dark black hair was dyed, with grey roots showing, and it matched darker eyes. Her racial heritage was difficult to place, but she must have come from the Islands. She sat next to him. Seeing her close up, she was no less than seventy, and her eyes betrayed her colorful history.

"I haven't seen you here before, stranger. What brings such a handsome young man to my establishment?"

"I'm looking for someone," Arian spat out.

"Well, I do believe you have found someone," replied the woman. "Perhaps you can give a bit more detail as to what you are looking for. That will help us to meet your," she leaned forward, whispering into his ear, "desires."

Looking her over, Arian was unsure how to proceed. He decided to introduce himself as a way to keep the conversation going.

"My name is Maxwell," he lied. "To whom do I have the pleasure of speaking?"

"Such manners in the young man. I am the Madame of this house. If you have the money, we will make your dreams come true. What kind of woman do you fancy?"

"I've heard things," replied Arian after a pause, "about a woman known as the Black Rose. I hear she's the best you have. I wish to meet with her."

"Oh," responded Angelica coyly, "a man with high end tastes. Our Rosey does not come cheap. Are you sure I can't offer you one of these other tarts?" she said, waving her hand in a motion that encompassed the room.

"I want the Black Rose," answered Arian, attempting to sound resolute and not betray his nervousness.

"Very well," said Angelica. "I shall fetch her; provided our money is good and she will have you. Marcel, please escort this young gentleman to Room #4."

Arian followed the imposing man down the hall and into the room, wondering just what the hell he was getting himself into. The room was cozy, with a four-post king size bed, soft carpet, and a fire already blazing. The man closed the door as Arian entered. Slightly disgusted by the bed and not wanting to sit on it, Arian walked over to a sink in the corner. Splashing water on his face, he surveyed his reflection in the mirror. He looked terrible for a Nephite. The strain of travel and the stress of this endeavor had left dark bags around his eyes. How had he come to this? His life had been so perfect before. Now he was in a brothel in Sikyon, traveling unbeknownst to the government with an outside world gangster, all organized by a traitor to Arameus. His thoughts went to his laboratory and students. He had neglected both for weeks now, and he was fearful to think of the disarray his projects would be in when he returned, though it was a long shot he would come out of this unscathed.

The door opened behind him. Looking in the mirror, he watched as a tall black-skinned woman entered. She was beautiful, dressed in pink lingerie that contrasted starkly with her skin, with bright red lipstick and hair fixed in a tight bun on the top of her head. All of her wardrobe and design choices were made to accent her elegant lines and stunning features. Arian toweled off his face.

"It is two thousand Lyra for the full girlfriend experience. Do you have the money?" Her voice was rich and raspy, full of musical tones.

Arian pulled the wad of bills from his pocket and held them up for her to see.

"Good baby," she responded seductively. "It is so good to see you again. I've missed you so much. Promise me you won't be gone this long again. I can't stand to be without you. My body craves you."

She walked behind him, wrapping her arms around his stomach, rubbing it while she kissed the back of his neck. Arian forgot himself for a moment, lost in her feminine spell before he came to. Only Kaiya had ever touched him in that way, and he was here for her. Opening his eyes to view the stranger in the mirror, he jerked his shoulder to the left violently, pushing her away from his body. She seemed frightened, but quickly returned to character.

"Oh, my baby is jumpy today. Perhaps my baby wants it rough?" She swayed back and forth seductively, eyeing him like a cat.

Pulling all the money from his pocket and throwing it on the bed, Arian spoke his true intentions.

"You are very lovely, but I am not here for the reasons

stated. That is all of my money. I know nothing of Lyra, but I assume this is a substantial amount. My name is Arian Cyannah. A woman named Serenity on behalf of Don Gravano referred me to you. I have come for Kaiya."

Rosey stared at him for a moment before walking to the bed and grabbing the wadded up Lyra. Unfolding it and counting it out, she exclaimed, "You have over twelve thousand Lyra here!"

"It's yours if you can help me. I have traveled far and at great personal risk. Please… help me if you can?"

"Even if I could help you, what do you want with Kaiya?" asked Rosey, staring hard into him.

"I received a message on my qubit two weeks back from her. She needed help. I have come for her."

Eyeing him suspiciously, Rosey backed toward the door.

"If you are who you say you are, you are most welcome. Wait here." With that, she disappeared down the hallway. Arian sat on the bed finally, forgetting his previous aversion to its likely history. His heart raced in anticipation. He was so close. All he wanted in the world was to see her alive one more time. All he wanted was to tell her he loved her.

The sound of footsteps echoed in the hall. Three men armed men entered, pointing the muzzles of their guns at Arian. Behind them followed Black Rose and Angelica, looking on with cold expressions.

"Maxwell?" asked Angelica from the rear. "I believe you have been untruthful in my household. This is something we do not tolerate. Now state your true business."

"I was only untruthful out of necessity and for fear for the one I wish to save. I have come at the bequest of Kaiya. She told me she would be hiding here. She said she was in trouble."

"That's an interesting story. The only thing I am having trouble with is that Kaiya told us nothing of you. Doesn't that seem a bit odd?" She made a swift motion with her hand. The last thing Arian saw was the butt of the gun of the man standing closest to him flying toward his forehead. Everything went black.

***

His head pounded such that he didn't want to open his eyes, though he was conscious. He felt the bed beneath him, the blankets, and something else. He felt the warmth of a small, soft body, cradled in his arm. He felt her head on his shoulder, felt her breath on his naked skin. She was rubbing his chest, whispering something. He tried to focus, but the aching in his skull made it difficult.

"I'm so sorry," she whispered. "I'm so sorry they hurt you. They were only trying to protect me. Please forgive them."

Even in a whisper he recognized Kaiya's voice. He forced himself to open his eyes. Daylight rushed through a nearby window, blinding him and increasing the pain in his head. He tried to focus, his body jerking.

"Are you awake, Arian?" she asked, her tone sincere and full of concern.

"I am," he thought he muttered. He wasn't sure whether the sound had been audible.

She squeezed him, cradling his body to her own, embracing him in her warmth. He felt dampness on his left shoulder by her head. She had been weeping.

"You are a tough woman to find," he tried to joke.

She laughed, squeezing him tighter. "You came for me, Arian. You came for me."

He started to chuckle, but the pain in his head was too much, stopping him short.

"Relax, baby," she comforted. "Try not to move." She rose, leaning over him, and planted the softest kiss on his forehead, where his wound was still fresh. "You came for me," she whispered again, looking down at him with such love and concern that he forgot his wound and his pain.

"I had to come for you. I couldn't bear the thought of never seeing you again. I am enamored with you."

"So is that it?" she whispered, her voice seductive. "You just want to fuck me again?"

"No, Kaiya, not at all. I can't explain it. I just wanted to see you again. Have you ever desired to be around another person so much you can't stand it and you don't know why? The way you left me, I had questions."

"Ask me anything."

"That night you came to my apartments, it was amazing. I've never felt closer to another person. Then you were gone. I wanted to… no, I needed to know, why you slept with me that night. Was it just to serve Ansley up to Tiberius?"

"Shhh," she whispered, calming him. She rubbed his cheek and kissed him again, this time on the nose. "My life is not as easy as yours. I have had to make my own way and difficult decisions in the process. I opened up to you for the first time in your den, telling you where I was from. Then, that day in the park, on the bench, I came for the drive, it is true, but… I opened up to you again. I told you my history. And you apologized to me. You said you understood. No Nephite has ever treated me with such respect. No Nephite has ever treated me as anything other than trash that they could fuck and then throw away. You looked at me. You really looked at me, and saw me. I wanted to give myself to a man who saw me for me and not as a possession. I know I used you, but the night you speak of was not part of the game. That night was as special for me as it was for you."

Arian looked at her. He wondered if he did truly see her. Her beauty was blinding. It was a handicap for her in reality. No man would ever be able to see her as she was. She would always be this unattainable treasure. But now, she was in his arms.

"I came for you," he said, through heavy breaths,

"because I am in love with you."

Kaiya looked at him, eyes glistening with tears. Staring deep within them, Arian could sense her true age and the depth of her struggles. Pinning his arms down, she straddled him. For the first time, he realized they were both naked. She eased herself onto him, connecting them carnally. Though her movements were rapid, experienced, her gaze never wavered from his. All thoughts of injury were lost in the pulsating stabs of pleasure. It was short. As he climaxed, she fell back to his shoulder, cradling his head in her arms. They fell asleep in the fading afternoon light as lovers.

They awoke a few hours later to heavy rapping on the door. It was early evening, as evident by the rising of the red sun. Arian's headache had receded, his thoughts clear. He looked at Kaiya, still resting in the crook of his shoulder. He watched her as she opened her eyes, and blinked, trying to reacquaint herself with the surroundings. The knocking came again.

"Who is it?" she asked, her voice raspy from sleep.

"It's Dante," the voice replied. "Angelica says to wake up. Our evening meal is ready. Get dressed and come down."

"We will be there shortly," replied Kaiya. They heard his footsteps disappear down the hall.

"You must be starving," said Kaiya. He could feel her breath under his chin. "You were unconscious for nearly ten hours. Let's go get you some food."

It was true. Arian was hungry, but if he had a say in the matter, he would stay in this bed with Kaiya forever. He wondered if there was some way that they could forget about Gravano, Ansley, and all of Capitol City. They could stay in Sikyon and work for Angelica, never making their presence known to the Mondavi. These thoughts were short-lived, however, as Kaiya stood from the bed, sliding a purple silk robe around her body. Arian followed suit and stood, dressing in the same clothes that had been removed on the previous night.

Looking at Kaiya's skimpy attire, he mused, "Are you really going to dinner like that? You're barely covered."

"I was sent to this brothel at the age of fifteen, Arian. There is nothing on me they haven't seen. Angelica is like a mother to me. Don't tell me you are going to be one of those possessive, jealous types."

Arian relented, trying to ignore the strange feelings in the pit of his stomach at the revelation. He wasn't sure how he felt about it, or these strange new feelings, so he sat them aside. There would be time to return to them later.

Seeing the uncomfortable look on his face, she added, "Not all of us were born into the luxury of the Institute. When my father passed, I had no protection. I was victimized again and again by that monster Flavius. His wife was jealous of his affections to me, or more accurately, my childish frame. She forced him to sell me into Angelica's service. Fate granted you a genetically engineered brain. It granted me this body."

"I had no idea," said Arian, horror evident on his face. He regretted the way he felt. She was the victim here. "Let's go eat."

He guided her toward the door, sliding his hand down her back and allowing it to linger there affectionately. They walked down a hallway he didn't recognize, passing room after room filled with girls chattering and joking with each other. Witnessing the living quarters of the brothel, it was strange to see the women lounging and talking easily to one another. It was as if they were a family.

"Do you know these girls?" asked Arian.

"I have been hiding here for a few weeks, so I have become acquainted. All of the girls who were here when I was are long gone. Many are dead. I have been in Capitol City for nearly thirty years. Tiberius, as you know, allowed me to have treatments so that I could maintain my youth. There is no use for an aging concubine."

Arian swallowed, again trying to ignore that feeling in his stomach. She led him down a flight of stairs and through a corridor that opened to a dining hall. It was large enough to seat forty, which was likely the number of workers at the brothel. There were only about six people in the hall currently. Angelica sat at the center of the table, elegantly dressed, her long grey hair falling onto exposed shoulders. The Black Rose was seated to her left. Arian was shocked to find a middle aged couple and two children across from them. The table was set with a pot of roast with carrots and potatoes. The smell of the food awakened Arian's ravenous hunger. Kaiya and Arian took the seats to Angelica's right.

"I'm going to have to beg your forgiveness for your treatment at the hands of my guards," said Angelica politely. "We were only trying to protect our beautiful Kaiya. She is like a daughter to me."

"All is forgiven," answered Arian. "I appreciate you hitting me with the gun instead of shooting me with it. I might not have been here to accept your apology." The others around the table laughed. "Thank you for helping Kaiya and allowing her a haven. I have arranged for transport back to Capitol City. I will be able to protect Kaiya there and we will get to the bottom of why she was framed for these murders."

The others at the table glanced at one another. Kaiya placed her hand on his shoulder. In a voice that was almost a whisper she said, "I wasn't framed, Arian. I did commit those murders." The youngest child across the table cried out, and was comforted by her father.

"But how could you?" stammered Arian. "How could you commit these crimes?"

"I assure you, young man," said Angelica, adopting a defensive tone, "that the world is a much better place without the Decimus family. He molested half of my girls before his wretched wife would send them here when they came of age. May she rest in peace," she added with a wink.

"And you keep them as sex slaves."

"I give them a place to live and sustenance. We have to pay for all of this somehow. They are free to leave whenever they wish. I ask them to do nothing that I did not do myself. At least here they are safe and can choose whom they sell their services to. Do you have a better way for these girls? Perhaps they can get a job at your Institute." This drew a chuckle from Black Rose.

"This complicates things," said Arian, his tone serious. "Exonerating Kaiya would have been much easier than hiding her forever. Can we appeal to Tiberius for help? How did you come to be in Avignon in the first place? Is he aware?"

"Tiberius is the last man on the planet who would help me. His position has risen. The Overseers could no longer overlook him keeping a Natural Born woman as a mistress. I was taken by force from a hotel in Pathos. I must have been drugged, because I awoke under the control of Flavius, who soon went back to his old habits. There is nothing like being raped and beaten in a horse stable to make you feel at home. At least that's how my home always was. Tiberius knows where I am. He has abandoned me to satisfy his greater lust for power." Arian could see the tears welling in her eyes and felt his own throat tightening.

"And I am afraid," she continued, fighting through her emotion, "that I am not the only one you must hide." She nodded across the table at the family. "This is Dante and his wife Yasmine, and these are their children. The youngest is Chloe and her elder sister is called Eppie. It was they who helped me escape from my nightmarish homecoming. Unfortunately I had to involve them in my crime, and they are no longer safe here."

"Please," plead Yasmine. "Please help my daughters. I will be forever indebted to you."

Dante rubbed her back, staring across the table at Arian, his eyes filled with desperation. Arian chewed his bottom lip as he thought. Capitol City would no longer be an option for them. The path to their safety was clear. He would have to take them to Beladero. Coming here had saved Ansley and his rebellion. He would no longer be able to inform on the people of Beladero if he wanted to protect Kaiya. He searched his mind for another way, but no option presented itself. He hated what he had become, but Kaiya was all that mattered now. He would do anything to protect her.

"I think I can help all of you, but not in the way you expect," said Arian after a moment. Yasmine, who had been waiting nervously, let out a relieved sigh.

"What do you mean?" asked Dante.

"I mean that I know a place you can go where you will be safe and outside the reach of Arameus. The domes are no longer an option for you. This is a free society, where you can flourish with others born in the Natural World. It so happens that I've acquired a few friends who are influential in the community. And…"

He turned to Kaiya, gripping her thigh under the table, "if I can finally trust you and that this isn't an elaborate ploy to turn my new friends over to the government of Arameus, I would be more than happy to escort you there. My friend Jabari, who seems a bit scary at first, is a good man and will help you to integrate into society there. Your children can grow up free."

In the back of his head, he felt a twinge. He hadn't worked all of it out yet. He knew he could not return to his former life, this much was clear. But if he continued on this path, it still ended with the Iris and possibly erasing this timeline. He pushed these thoughts aside, leaving them to fester next to his apprehension at his newfound knowledge of Kaiya's past in the brothel. He had difficulty envisioning a way in which all of them came out of this alive and well.

"I have a pick-up scheduled for noon tomorrow to take Kaiya and I back to Capitol City. Dante, your family is welcome to join us."

"We accept," he replied, rubbing Yasmine's shoulders.

"Good," said Angelica, "it's settled. Arian will take you all to his magical city, and my girls will be safe. Harboring suspected murderers would likely be frowned upon by the Mondavi." She smiled at them.

"Now we can eat," interjected the Black Rose. "I

want to thank you Mother Angelica for providing this food for the sustenance of our bodies." Arian watched as everyone around the table nodded their heads in agreement. Angelica was clearly a powerful force in the lives of her underlings. Arian surmised that everyone at the table would do anything to protect her. The matron rose to serve the food. She served the children first, cutting succulent pieces of roast before adding carrots, potatoes, and gravy. Kaiya poured refreshing lemonade drinks from a nearby pitcher. It was strange for Arian to see the woman he had idolized acting in a servile domestic role. He thought he might like it. He imagined this would be what a family with her would be like. It was a strange thought for him, who had never known a family.

When Angelica finally placed meat on his plate, Arian wanted more than anything to rip into the charred flesh, but politeness dictated that he wait for everyone to be served. Once the aged woman seated herself, everyone's attention shifted to the wonderful meal. Arian grabbed his fork and knife and began to saw at the slightly pink meat. Just as he stabbed the chunk of flesh with his fork, ready to engulf it, three men burst into the room.

"City Patrols have entered the premises, Madame. They know that the fugitives are here. They will be here in moments," said the man who had allowed Arian into the brothel the previous evening.

Angelica stood calmly, in complete control of the situation.

"Men," she said to the guards, "discard your guns. They will be perceived as threatening. Leave the way you came, locking the door behind you. Lock the door to the stairs as well. We will leave through the back entrance. Say nothing of us. I will be there to meet them soon. Now go."

The men followed her instructions without question, leaving their guns and departing. Arian could hear the clink of the metal lock as they fastened the heavy oaken doors.

"We must part now, my friends," said Angelica ruefully. "I wish you the best in all of your endeavors. Now follow me. This was once a safe house for the Order of the Red Sun. There is a passage known only by me to their Cathedral. Go there now."

They stood and followed her toward the hearth at the end of the room, opposite the doors. Arian's mind raced. There was no way out. Ansley was thousands of miles away and Gravano had double-crossed them. Still, he followed the old Madame. She was the only hope for salvation. She ran to the fireplace and lifted an ornate rug before it. To his happy surprise, as she lifted the dusty carpet, the outline of a cellar door appeared in the dark wood of the floor. Unlatching it, she pulled the cast iron handle, but was unable to lift the heavy door. She implored Dante to help. Grabbing the handle, he pulled with all his might. The old trap door creaked and groaned as it opened, likely for the first time in hundreds of years. Ancient dust shot out of the crypt within, filling the room and causing them to cough. Still attached to the inside plank of the door was a survival pack. Angelica ripped it off and opened it, revealing an old style torch, a lighter, and a map.

She handed the torch to Kaiya and the map to Arian.

"This is an old tunnel that leads to the cathedral at the center of the city. Back when the Order of the Red Sun was more powerful, in the days before Arameus, they were a group of monks dedicated to recording history. They were also the central church for their society, engaging in ancestor worship. In times of trouble, people would come to them seeking protection in their walls. They had a system of tunnels constructed that emerge at various points in the city of Sikyon. This building was one of those safe houses. Follow this map to a secret passage into the cathedral. From there you can contact your escort and inform them of the changes in the plan. I wish all of you the best."

She turned to Kaiya and embraced her. Pulling back, she gripped her shoulders and examined her face.

"You are still so beautiful, my darling. I am so sorry your life has come to this. When you came to me as a broken little girl, I wanted so much more for you. When Tiberius took you away, I thought I had succeeded. Still, you retain your unmatched fire. Go with peace, my love." She kissed Kaiya on the mouth and gave her a push toward the entryway in the floor. "Go!" she demanded more forcefully.

With that, Arian, Kaiya, Dante, Yasmine, Eppie, and Chloe entered into the cavern below. The cellar door slammed behind them, leaving them in darkness. A flicker of light flashed as Kaiya tried the old lighter. A few more tries and it beamed with light. She lit the torch she held in her other hand, illuminating the tunnel. There wasn't much to see. It was made of red brick, faded by age, with puddles of standing water punctuating the area, having slowly seeped down over the years. The air smelled of a mixture of butane and sewage. Surveying the map to get his bearings, Arian determined their location, and pointing the direction to the others, began walking toward the cathedral. The crypt was deep and they could hear nothing from above, only the echoes of their footsteps. Arian hoped the old Madame was okay. Kaiya inched forward, the light illuminating only a few feet in front. Chloe, the youngest child, was afraid.

"I'm scared daddy. Let's go back up."

"Quiet, my love. We must go forward. Be brave." Dante leaned down and scooped up the little girl, small, despite her ten years. "Are you alright, Eppie?" he asked his other daughter.

"I'm fourteen, dad," she answered.

Arian was moved by the exchange. There was something so simple and pure about the conversation that made him long for the childhood he would never have. But maybe he would. Perhaps Ansley was right. It was wrong that these young children were fumbling through the dark in an abandoned tunnel, running from the supposed utopic government of Arameus.

The cavern resonated with the sound of their feet splashing in the grime. Large rats darted from the recesses, startling the children. They walked through hundreds of years of cobwebs and animal excrement, batting insects from their shoulders. At one point, even Kaiya jumped at a movement, dropping the lantern, leaving them in darkness. She picked it up, and happily, it was re-lit, the oil canister unaffected.

They came to a junction in the tunnel, leaving them with the decision to continue forward, or go to the left or right. Arian turned the torch, illuminating the possible paths. The flickering light showed that the way to the right had long ago collapsed, leaving them with only two options. Luckily, Arian realized as he studied the map, that their destination lay to the left. It added, however, an air of desperation, as he hoped that they would not stumble upon a similar scenario in the dark passages beyond and wind up trapped within the crypts.

They passed petrified torches hanging on the walls, intended for use in the distant past. They would be of no help in the present. Continuing forward, Arian's nervousness and claustrophobia increased, though he hoped to not betray his fear to the other members of the party. Unlikely as it was, he was the leader of this group and needed to appear unfazed. The air in the sculpted cavern was becoming more and more stale, filled with sulfur and hanging heavy above them. He longed for a passage out into the filtered and cooled air of the dome.

Finally, after what seemed like an hour, they came to a wall. Painted on it, in what was once red, was a rusted brown impression of the cathedral he had passed with Serenity in the transport hawk. A rusted ladder, rungs lost by age, led to a latch in the ceiling. Arian wondered how they would manage to open the cellar.

"Well," he mused aloud, "I guess we will see if anyone is home." He climbed the old ladder and knocked hard on the door above. It was hollow, clearly, which was a good sign, but he had little confidence about whether he would find a reply on the other end. The group waited. He knocked again, then again. Still there was no response from above.

"There is no one there, Arian," Dante yelled from below. "We are lost."

Not wanting to give up, though agreeing with Dante's assertion, Arian beat on the door, again and again for nearly a minute, until he was breathless. Still, there was no response. Defeated, he descended the ladder, standing back on the wet ground, looking up.

"What now?" asked Kaiya, looking with patient calm.

"We go back to Angelica's" replied Arian, "and wait out the soldiers. They know nothing of this passage. We will be safer there. We have the children to consider."

Just as they were turning to leave, they heard a heavily accented voice on the other side of the door.

"Hello? Helloooooo?" said the voice, fear and curiosity evident in the tone.

"Hello!!" responded Arian, Dante, and Yasmine in unison.

"Hello!" Arian yelled again. "We are trapped down here. Please let us up. We have young children with us."

There was a pause on the other side.

"Do you come in peace?" asked the voice.

"Peace? Yes, peace!" responded Arian. "We come in peace. Please let us up."

Again, there was a pause, this time longer. Arian feared the man had left to alert the authorities and was about to instruct the group to flee, but after a long moment, he heard the sound of a latch being unfastened and an old door being sprung open. Relief and joy washed over him. He gathered his party and looked to the opening.

"Well," said the voice again, "what to do? Are you coming up or what?"

"We are coming up now. Thank you," replied Arian. Wanting to be the first man up, in case of an ambush, Arian climbed. He emerged into a dimly lit stone room, occupied by hundreds, if not thousands, of shelves filled with books. Each evenly spaced row had an attached ladder on wheels so that browsers could reach works on the top shelves. The short, brown skinned man, the source of the voice, watched him suspiciously.

"How is it you come from the ground?" he asked.

"How is it you open doors in the ground?" replied Arian.

"This is actually a fair question," responded the man. "I was reading a tome on the roots of languages. Then, suddenly, I hear a knock from the ground. Then it continues. I went to investigate, lifting the rug, and I find a door, with you on the other end. You say you come in peace, so I opened the door. This is all."

"Well, I thank you. I will bring my friends up now. You seem to be harmless enough." Arian called down to his group below. They quickly filled the room, with Dante coming last.

"You were not lying about the children, I see. This is good. Underground is no place for children. My name is Sanjay Patel. I am chief science officer on a space voyage leaving very soon on order of the Overseers. I am here combing the archives to study the root of languages. My captain believes it will serve us well. And who are you, who comes in peace?"

"Thank you, Sanjay, we appreciate your help. My name is Arian Cyannah. I am an Assistant Professor of Bio-cybernetics at the Institute in Capitol City. I was escorting my friends here back to Capitol City, but we ran into some trouble we would rather not discuss. We were told we should seek shelter from the Order of the Red Sun and sent here in that underground tunnel."

"Hmm. I am merely a guest here, allowed to browse the many texts, and have no power to offer you sanctuary. However, I can take you to Fez al-Sun, the head of the order and keeper of the archives. It is he who can make such a decision. Follow me upstairs, Arian. The rest of you can wait here in the vaults."

Arian followed Sanjay in silence past the bookshelves, to the other end of the massive stone vault. They came to an aging staircase, worn from over a thousand years of feet shuffling up and down it. As they reached the top, Sanjay unlatched a trap door, which opened in the floor above. Arian exhaled audibly as he entered the Cathedral of the Red Sun. He had seen nothing like it in all his years in Capitol City. The only thing that could possibly compare in scope would be the Iris.

The floor was made of smooth marble, covered in intricate and colorful mosaics depicting scenes from times long past. The ceiling was hundreds of feet high, supported by stone arches extending far into the distance. The cathedral was much longer than it was wide, allowing the arches to provide the proper support for the heavy building materials. The stonemasons had decorated every inch of the walls with various statues, likely representing important figures of a long lost religion. The ceiling was as colorful as the floor, painstakingly painted, though from his vantage point, Arian couldn't make out the pictures.

As the two men walked, their footsteps echoed, giving their journey a foreboding feel, as if they were entering somewhere holy where they should not tread. Sanjay guided him toward the center of the structure, where precious metals had been shaped to form a sort of designer gate around a raised central platform. They walked to the doorway of the gate, finding a mysterious figure dressed in brown robes, with a hood covering his head.

"What is it you need, my son?" asked the figure.

"A party has come from below the vaults seeking refuge in your walls," answered Sanjay. "They say they come in peace. I have brought their leader to see Brother Fez al-Sun."

"If he comes in peace, then he may enter these gates in peace," answered the mysterious man. He moved aside, allowing Sanjay and Arian to pass.

Arian walked slowly, surveying the interior of the choir. Carved oak made up the seating on either side of him, which was filled with similarly dressed monks, poring over ancient looking texts, many of them scribbling notes. None of the men paid them much notice. They continued forward, toward a raised alter made of gold. Behind it, standing and chanting softly from a large book, stood the man Arian assumed was Fez al-Sun. He was wearing the same robes, though they had been dyed a bright red. His hood was down, revealing a white head that was shaved bald. As they approached, the man stopped his activity and looked to them.

"Sanjay, I trust you have found some information that will be useful in your endeavors?" he asked politely, his voice having an almost ethereal quality.

"Yes, brother, and I thank you kindly."

"Good. And what business do you have with me now? Let your new companion explain, if you don't mind."

"Um," stammered Arian, intimidated and unsure how to address this impressive looking man. He chose to use the formal methodology of Capitol City.

"Your Grace, my name is Arian Cyannah. I was sent here by Angelica, the Madame of an ill-reputed house within this city. I have traveled here from Capitol City in secret to retrieve some Natural Born friends who have found trouble within this dome. We were betrayed, unfortunately. Angelica sent us through the tunnels underneath your vault to seek refuge within your walls."

"We are all Natural Born, young Arian," answered the Fez al-Sun, calmly, betraying no emotion or intention. "Do you think yourself any less natural because you were made in a laboratory? I assure you, my son, you were made by natural humans, and nothing unnatural can come from something natural."

Arian wasn't sure how to respond. He was spared having to come up with an argument when Raz continued.

"Now that we have established we are all born of this world as equals, tell me, how is my old friend Angelica?"

"I'm afraid I can't say, Your Grace, as we were forced to flee. I hope we have not endangered her," responded Arian.

"I have no grace, young Arian. Please call me brother. I would not fear for Angelica. She has many high friends within the governing circles of Sikyon. I am sure she will be fine. She came here as a child, seeking refuge for some past trouble of her own. I, being a young monk at the time, took her in. We donated the building she currently occupies, as she promised to make a place safe for the women in this region born of less fortunate means. She has done much to help them, though their means of sustenance is unfortunate to be sure. Still, they do what they must to feed themselves. It is difficult to not be one of the so-called Nephites during the plague of Arameus."

"Then you have no love for Arameus?" asked Arian.

The old man chuckled, as if amused, but with a hint of sadness in his eyes.

"The four dictators that sit in your gilded city have destroyed tens of thousands of years of history and human culture. They have left hundreds of millions to fend for themselves and starve outside their domes while they re-shape our world in their own image. The populace has forgotten where we came from. Our Order exists independently, protected by the Mondavi family, who, with all of their allegiance to your rulers, never fully gave up the superstition associated with their old religion. Our order is no longer allowed to practice worship, but nearly three hundred years ago, we decided to chronicle and preserve the history of our great world, so that one day, when this storm has passed, the survivors may use the wisdom of their ancestors to rebuild."

"Then you will help us?" asked Arian. "Aren't you even concerned with why we are hiding?"

"It is of no consequence to us what you have done or plan to do. And it is no coincidence that you are here. Time and history are circular. You are in a loop. This is a sanctuary, and once you enter these walls, all transgressions are forgotten and forgiven. We are here to serve humanity, not to judge it. You may stay here as long as you require. Go get the rest of your party. Brother Groza al-Sun will show you to your lodgings upstairs. I pray that you find them to be adequate."

"If you don't mind my prying, why would there be tunnels leading into this place?"

"The tunnels were dug long ago, when my pre-cursors in this Order held much power in the region. They developed multiple escape routes so that they would be safe if the city were attacked."

"Thank you, brother," said Arian sincerely. "Your benevolence and charity will not be forgotten in all of my days. You are doing a great thing."

With a slight bow, Arian and Sanjay turned to leave, escorted by Brother Groza back to the vaults to retrieve their friends. Arian breathed a deep sigh of relief as they walked. Finally, they could relax and regroup. He felt they would be safe here.

That night, Arian sat in the barren room that he shared with Dante. It was a small room, carved into the stone, outfitted with a few cots and a dresser on which sat a pitcher of water and a stale loaf of bread. He imagined that all of the brothers kept similarly barren quarters. They were located on a circular hallway that ran around the base of the dome that rose far above the cathedral floor, directly above the high alter. The children had struggled to climb the steep, winding stairs. Arian wondered how the older monks were able to travel this path every evening.

To his displeasure, Arian had been separated from Kaiya. The women were sharing a room on the opposite side of the dome. No matter how much he pleaded, the brothers would not acquiesce to men and women sharing rooms, and he would have to respect that. He sat on his cot, glancing down at the qubit Gravano had given him on the Raven. Dante was lying on the cot adjacent to Arian, looking up at the ceiling. He began to speak.

"I haven't had a chance to thank you properly, Arian," he said, still looking upward. "Thank you for taking us with you."

"It is not my doing," answered Arian. "I came for Kaiya. Your gratitude belongs to her."

"Still, the thought of bringing my daughters up in a

brothel was unfathomable. Thank you for taking us with you, and at least giving them an opportunity to be raised free in the city you spoke of."

"I am happy to help, Dante," said Arian truthfully. "A few months ago, I despised all non-Nephites. I thought of the Natural Born as if they were another species, savage and uncivilized. Now I have been shown otherwise and am embarrassed by my previous behavior. The Overseers have purposefully created this class warfare to further place a wedge between all peoples and cement their power."

"We are all victims of our upbringings and the notions conceived therein," Dante said. "You as a Nephite are as much as a victim of the propaganda as I, though your path has likely been much easier than mine."

"May I ask you a question, Dante?"

"Of course. I will answer anything," he replied.

"If you had a chance to sacrifice your life to overthrow the current rule in the land and ensure that future peoples would be born free, without titles or restrictions on their positions, would you do it?"

"Arian. I would sacrifice myself, my wife, and my own children in order to free the people of this world from the tyranny of the Overseers."

Arian nodded his head. "I thought you might say that."

"What do we do now," asked Dante. "How do we get out of Sikyon?"

Feeling safe in the Cathedral under the protection of the Mondavi, Arian pulled a slip of paper from his pocket. It was the contact info for Gravano that Ansley had given him when they had departed. Fingering the qubit and pondering for a moment, he decided to type in the code, consequences be damned.

Gravano answered immediately.

"I see you have found trouble, my young friend," Gravano's chilling voice came over the qubit.

"Fuck you, Christoph. You set me up."

"Relax, my friend," came his cool voice. "I'm glad to hear that you are alive. Serenity proved to be untrustworthy. She will be dealt with harshly. I will not have my good named sullied. Consider her dead."

"So you had nothing to do with the men that showed up at the brothel?" asked Arian.

"No, I did not. I heard about it from some men loyal to me within the City Patrol. I had to leave Sikyon upon the news. It was all too risky."

"What are we to do now, then?" asked Arian. "Will you just abandon us? I have Kaiya. We need passage out of the city."

"And you will have it. My sources tell me you are at the Cathedral of the Red Sun. You will be safe there. Stay there, and do not leave its walls, you are only protected as long as you remain within. The people of Sikyon are a superstitious bunch. They would never enter those walls against the wishes of the brothers. I am arranging a pickup in seven days' time. I talked with Jabari, and we have re-negotiated our terms."

"How can I trust that you will honor this agreement?"

"I assure you, lover boy, my payment is worth far more than the trifle of turning you in. I will pick you up. The brothers will come and get you at the time of my transport's arrival. Be ready."

Arian thought for a moment. Something didn't add up in all of this. He voiced his concern.

"You said you re-negotiated with Jabari. Why not, Ansley? Has something gone wrong?" He was met with silence. Don Gravano was gone, leaving him with nothing to do but wait with his party until the transport arrived seven days from now.

Instinctively, he dialed Ansley, hoping to get to the bottom of all this. His call was met with Esther's voice, beckoning him to leave a message. He had learned much of himself in this recent journey and re-evaluated many of the views he once held. Strangely, he found himself fearing for the friend he had only a couple of weeks ago been planning to betray; this was not a good sign.

# Chapter Twenty-Four
# Facility One

Looking down from the second level balcony, the man now known as Dr. Matthew Conway found it surreal to see hundreds of workers laboring under his control. He had taken to leadership well, as if it were a natural progression. Tiberius had given him his instructions, indirectly from the Overseers, and he would see them carried out. Still, he felt some guilt at having gained his new position in a manner that was less than honorable, but if he were able to deliver the bio-bots to Habimana on time, he would be able to achieve all of his most ambitious dreams. No need to trifle with moral concerns; he would worry about practical matters for now.

The work itself mandated a certain proficiency and competence that required the workers to be Nephites, trained in biological sciences and cybernetics. At each station, men and women clothed in white used the most delicate instruments, employing super-powered microscopes to attach artificial bots onto protein receptors within petri dishes. It seemed strange for Matthew, looking from above, that sterility was always associated with white. In his previous life, he had worn the white without questioning. Now, however, garbed in Imperial purple, he noticed these minute differences. He surveyed the room, searching for Alexandra. His new position had yielded him no more interest from his object of desire. She agreed to join the lab as a volunteer for the Overseers, not that it was an option. He had hoped his new position as Director of the laboratory would impress her, but she remained unmoved. Watching her now, checking the work of the low level scientists attaching the bots, he couldn't help but notice the supple curve of her back and the bulge of her breasts. As she labored below, the heat generated by the PCR machines around the room caused the sweat to drip from her brow to her shirt. Even this was beautiful to him.

He hadn't heard the man approach from behind, but he could feel his eyes on him.

"My employers would like to know if you're on schedule. It would be unfortunate if you were not."

Matt turned around and faced Siva. The man was short, but his eyes were icy, betraying nothing of his inner thoughts. The man was emotionless, mechanical, and his presence was intimidating.

"The first batch of bots will be ready, just as I promised. I still don't understand why you need to be here to watch over me. I am meeting my deadlines. Just look at what I have created," said Matt, with a sweep of his arm over the laboratory.

"You are nothing," answered Siva coldly. "Just deliver what you have promised. Those above you do not even know you exist, and I can make that a reality."

"I understand," Matt said, fear evident in his eyes. "What do you want from me?"

"I only want results," replied Siva. "You are to deliver the bio-bots to Habimana, I am to ensure that this happens. Our tasks are simple, really."

"Simple for you, maybe. I assure you, mass-producing a targeted nano-bot meant to hijack a cell during DNA synthesis is no easy task. This thing should really still be in the testing phase. We can't be sure that by uploading data in the parent bot, it will then be communicated to the second-generation cells and influence thoughts and feelings. Yet you tell me we need enough for a small city?"

"For now. We have our test subjects pre-selected. If we are successful, you will need enough for the world," replied Siva.

Shaking his head, Conway tried to wrap his brain around the sheer scope of what was taking place and the magnitude of the task ahead. He would single-handedly be re-shaping society, and delivering the masses under the direct control of the Overseers, if their theories were correct. It was monumental, really. He felt proud to be a part of this new chapter in the rise of Arameus. It would be the perfect Empire, an actual utopia, the likes of which had been dreamed of and written about by men since the dawn of time.

"And who will be the lucky test subjects?" asked Matt.

"Not that it's any of your business, but the Overseers have identified a Centauri outpost just to the east of here. Some village called Beladero. It is amazing that they have eluded us for this long, being right under our noses. It is they who will first be registered by Habimana. They will be led to believe that are being injected with a sophisticated tracking device meant to root out terrorists. Instead, they will be injected with your creation. We will then have the ability to upload whatever thoughts and feelings we wish. Imagine it, an entire population of anarchists who are instantly imbued with a patriotic love of our dear leaders. All doubts and subversive thoughts instantly cleansed and replaced with the harmonious purpose to work for the betterment of Arameus."

"I doubt the people of this city will be keen on the idea of receiving an injection from representatives of the Empire," said Matt.

"Ah, my friend, but you don't give our leaders their due credit. The injection is a package deal. Flu season will again soon be upon us, and the tracking device comes with an immunization against this season's virus. They will feel like regular Nephites, being protected and not having to worry about losing their young ones. It is a small price to pay for the safety of their children. Impending death has a way of weakening principles." Siva laughed coldly.

Matt looked at him, suspicion evident on his face. "Even the Natural Born can't be so foolish as to believe we already have an immunization against a virus that has not yet presented itself."

"Don't be so foolish, boy," said Siva with disdain. "The flu was eliminated generations ago, long before Arameus. Each year in your summer nano-treatments, all Nephites are inoculated with a new and more deadly strain of the virus, created in our labs. We are all protected from it by our nanocytes, but we pass the strain to the Natural Born workers within our cities, and they in turn, bring it to those outside the domes. It is yet another way for us to keep those in the natural world weak, afraid, and unorganized. Of course, with the bio-bots, there will be no need for this primitive control."

Conway looked at Siva, horrified. He had never imagined that the rulers of Arameus could stoop so low or be so cruel, even to the Natural Born.

"This is unacceptable!" he exclaimed. "How can they knowingly infect and kill innocent children? It's monstrous!"

"Choose your words carefully, boy," replied Siva. "I will end your life now if you say another negative word toward my masters."

Frightened, Matt looked back to Siva, muttering, "I apologize. I was just a bit shocked, I guess."

"It is a good deal for them," continued Siva, backing off a bit. "Take the transmitter, guarantee you aren't a terrorist, and you never have to fear for the health of your children again, at least during flu season."

"I understand. It is a reasonable offer. I appreciate your honesty."

"I'm sure you do," answered Siva, the chilling tone

returning to his voice. "See that your workers produce at least two thousand more doses today. Our time is short, and I am anxious to leave this hell hole and return to the city. I will be in my quarters. I have an important call with Consulate Septus. A major strategic move is being planned. If I understand it correctly, those of us here are to play a large part in it." With that, Siva turned and walked away, his footsteps resonating throughout the metal corridor.

Left alone to ponder all he had just heard, Conway couldn't help but feel concerned. It wasn't so much that the Overseers had been creating flu viruses to keep the Natural Born in check. This actually inspired him, given that his bots would end this practice. He was more concerned about the covert inoculation of Nephites with these viruses. If those in power accepted these practices for the lowborn, what was to stop them from going one step further and injecting the bio-bots into the Nephites? This would offer the Overseers complete control of the world population. It was something to consider.

Still thinking on this unpleasant scenario, he walked down the stairs to the main floor of the laboratory. It was lined with benchtops where dozens of Nephite scientists were working. The floor was divided into three distinct groups. Alexandra headed the cytology group. They were responsible for producing the healthy cells and getting them to the correct phase of mitosis. Another group was responsible for engineering the alpha bot and upgrading them with the proper software, as well as the secure channel that would link to the supercomputer currently being constructed in the Central Tower. The computer would be the control center and source of communication with the bots that would eventually occupy every cell of the host's body. The third group was made up of biomechanical engineers whose job it was to attach the alpha bot to a host stem cell and suspend it in a small injectable dose.

To date, Conway's lab had produced over ten thousand individual doses. At a rate of nearly two thousand per day, they would reach the goal of twenty thousand by the end of the week. If he met his deadline, Tiberius had promised that the Overseers would build another ten facilities to ramp up production.

Walking up and down the rows of scientists, he felt it was important to make sure he was a constant presence on the floor. If he had learned anything from his experience working under Arian, it was that he wanted to always be available. There was nothing worse than an absentee advisor. He stopped here and there to examine more closely the work of some of his colleagues, offering advice where he felt it was needed. The lab was running at an 85% acceptance level, which was unheard of when trying to attach a cybernetic organism to a living cell. He was shocked that so few of the cells were dying.

As always, he found his way, unconsciously, to Alexandra. She looked beautiful, bending over and gazing into a microscope. Her hair was in a ponytail, but a few stray dark strands had found their way out of the binding and were falling gently onto her shoulder. Dressed in all white, she looked as pure and virginal as he imagined her.

He placed his hand on her back to get her attention. Startled, she jumped upward, bumping her nose on the ocular lens of the microscope.

"I'm sorry to scare you. How are things going today?" he asked, in his coolest voice.

"Oh, they're going," she replied. "PCR-3 has been down all morning. It has set us back quite a bit. We have a technician working on it right now."

"And how are you?" he asked. "Are you comfortable in your quarters? I got you the best room of all of the scientists. I wanted to make sure you were happy."

"You did, did you? Because the way I see it, if you wanted me to be happy, you would have left me to run the research laboratory I spent my entire life working toward and to guide the students who depend upon me for their doctoral work."

"It wasn't like that, Alex. The Overseers specifically

requested you due to your expertise in this field. What we are doing is very important. It is going to bring peace to the entire world. We will be remembered as heroes."

"Oh, I'm sure you had nothing to do with my recruitment. I don't know the true purpose of these bots we are creating, but I have difficulty believing they will be used for peace," she replied.

"I don't know why you have such animosity toward me, Alex, but I am no longer that young boy following you around the Institute. I am the director of a top-secret project developed by the Overseers themselves. I would think you would show me a little more respect. We would make a good match."

"And do you mind explaining to me how it came to be that you are running this project and not Arian?" she asked.

"It always comes back to Arian with you, doesn't it? What does he have that I don't? This is my discovery and mine alone. Arian hasn't been around the lab in over two months, and he left me in charge," he lied, defensively. "The Overseers chose me, not him."

"Not one of their better choices," she said, looking back into the microscope.

He stood there for a moment, wondering how to proceed. Finally, he summoned the courage to speak the words that were in his heart.

"Look, perhaps in another setting, you could get to know me better. I know the food you guys are being served down in the mess hall is far below the cuisine you are accustomed to in Capitol City. Come to my quarters tonight and dine. We are served fine wine and excellent selections of gourmet food. Here is the key card to my room on the upper level. We eat at seven. I hope to see you there."

When she failed to respond, he slid the key onto the lab bench next to her microscope and slunk off defeated. He wondered to himself why he had chosen to love a woman who would never love him back.

# Chapter Twenty-Five
## Checkmate

Tiberius felt a mixture of excitement and pride sitting on his outside patio and looking across the river to the Central Isle. It was evening and the lights emanating from the five towers reflected on the water, blending with the dull red rays cast by the night sun. Marco Luccio was to visit his private quarters this night. The Overseers rarely ventured out of the Central Tower and into Capitol City. Typically they left their secure quarters only to visit their palatial island estates at undisclosed locations all over the world. However, given the recent developments in their plans, Luccio had chosen to honor him with a visit. Perhaps soon Tiberius would be visiting his own palatial estate. Perhaps soon he would be with Kaiya.

Tiberius' own massive household was situated just above the embankment that descended into the Arymides River. The back gate of his estate opened to a ramp that led down to a dock on the river. His private boat was tied there now. He had instructed his servants to light the torches leading up the ramp to his patio before sending them home. A meeting with an Overseer required discretion. Only Gallia remained, standing away from the table, to provide the men refreshment when his guest arrived.

After some time, he saw the Imperial vessel coming up the river toward his home. It was more of a battleship than a cruiser, heavily armored and outfitted with imposing guns. Even from this distance, he could see the golden eagle of Arameus shining in the light cast by the Central Isle. Pulling up to the dock, it dwarfed his own boat, and Tiberius felt a stab of nervous anxiety as he mentally prepared himself for the meeting.

Marco Luccio appeared on the landing ramp with two-armed Formaddi. The Overseers went nowhere without their trusted assassins. He was dressed in his purple robes, much more formal than their lunch meeting, and seemed in good spirits. Tiberius stood and nodded at Gallia to open the gate. Gallia kept her head down and gaze averted as Luccio and the two Formaddi entered the patio. She closed the gate behind them and rushed back into the house to gather the serving tray.

Tiberius dipped his head low. "Welcome to my humble household, your grace. You honor it and me with your presence."

The Overseer nodded and seated himself, flanked by the Formaddi.

"Be seated, Tiberius," said Marco, motioning to the chair across from him. "We have much to discuss."

As Tiberius took his seat, Gallia approached with a tray containing a bottle, two rocks glasses, and an ice bin.

"Your grace, I am honored to present to you a bottle of Tegave aged 40 years in a charred oak barrel. It was handed down to me from my father. He always told me to save it for a special occasion. I can think of no more special event than having you as a guest in my home. May I offer you a drink?"

"Ah," answered Marco, clearly pleased, "it is you who do me an honor. Your father was a great man. It is unfortunate that he passed before we were able to triumph over death. We shall drink to his memory."

Gallia placed the two glasses in front of the men and,

using tongs, placed three ice cubes into each. She then set the bottle down in front of Tiberius, allowing him the honor of serving the Overseer. Tiberius picked up the bottle, looking at it sentimentally. Pulling the cork, he poured into Marco's glass first before filling his own. Marco picked up his drink and breathed in deeply, savoring the aromatic odors before exhaling loudly. Taking his first sip of the dark brown liquor, Tiberius saw a visible chill run the length of the old man's body.

"They don't make them like this anymore," he said, pondering the flavor. "I believe the last 40 year vintage was produced twenty years before your father died. This bottle must be upwards of three hundred years old." He took another drink, a strange look coming over his face. "Just imagine all the lives that have come and gone since this spirit was placed in the oak barrel all those years ago. It's as if I can taste the history and the toil of those men. And yet, here I remain. This is what power is, Tiberius. Power is the ability to survive and to thrive where others fail and fade away. Hopefully you saved another bottle. Perhaps three hundred years from now we will open it and contemplate our shared history."

Tiberius was flattered, and sipping his own Tegave, his thoughts went to his father. He could barely picture the face of the once great man after so many years. Pictures and records of the pre-Arameus past were forbidden within the domes. He knew that if his father existed somehow in the cosmos, he would be proud. How could he not be?

"Enough reflection on ghosts, my boy," said Marco. "We must now focus on the battles of the present. I came here tonight to hear the new developments that you promised me. I pray that this trip will not be a waste. What news do you have of our project?"

"I have important news on two fronts," replied Tiberius, pride evident in his voice. "We have had a breakthrough in analyzing the hard drive Arian was able to acquire from Professor Brightmore. It was difficult, but our best men were able to retrieve echo information. We have a complete record of the Centauri's illegal monetary transactions. It was just as you expected. The woman at the casino, Sharie, was running a money laundering and embezzlement operation under the direction of Ansley Brightmore. We have the entire history. The money was being funneled to her hometown, a small Natural Born village called Beladero. The amount of money stolen from our city is staggering, spread out over fifty years. We don't yet know the purpose of these transactions, but it must be something big. All of your instincts about there being a Centauri were correct."

"You sound as if you doubted yourself," replied Marco, coolly.

"I just wasn't sure, seeing as some of the bombings," he cast his eyes downward, feeling both embarrassed and ashamed, "were perpetrated by us."

Marco cackled, the guffaws turning to that horrible cough.

"We did what was needed to eliminate enemies of the state, thieves, who were robbing our good citizens of their wealth and distributing it to those who wish our destruction. We have always known of a powerful element of resistance from those on the outside, who are jealous of our prosperity. In order to fight this invisible enemy who wished to rob us of our rightfully earned positions, it was necessary to create an evil face for the public to latch onto. This is what the Centauri was. It is just a happy circumstance that this fool, Ansley Brightmore, has chosen to make our scapegoat a reality. We could not have planned it better." His loud cackle again echoed over the river. Tiberius wondered whether the other Overseers were up in the Central Tower laughing at their triumphs as well.

"You truly are a wise and great man," said Tiberius with deference, though in his head, he was fighting off doubts about the validity of all his investigations.

"And what will you do now?" asked Marco, looking across the table at his subject pointedly.

"That is my next piece of news," answered Tiberius, pushing back his doubts. "As we speak, Ansley Brightmore is being arrested. I was informed just before you arrived that my men had found the old Professor drinking at a pub in the Southern district. He will cause you no more trouble."

"Good. Very good," hummed Marco, pride evident in his voice. "You have done exceptional work, my boy, and earned the status we shall bestow upon you."

"I'm not finished," beamed Tiberius. "Your man Siva informed me today that the bio-bot production is proceeding on schedule. We will have twenty thousand doses by the end of this week. I hope this wasn't too presumptuous of me, but I have implemented a plan. Of course, if you disagree, I will cancel it right away."

"No, tell me," answered Marco. "Any man who has performed as admirably as you deserves to be heard. I didn't get to where I am by not utilizing the talent at my disposal."

"I was discussing the plan with Siva, just hours ago, and he seemed to agree with the direction. I think we should start the bio-bot inoculation in Beladero itself. We will strike at the heart of whatever organized resistance there is and eliminate the threat. If the money was going there, it must be key to the resistance. You will gain control of their thoughts and crumble the terrorist cell from within. Beladero should be City Zero."

"Ha! I love it," exclaimed Marco. "You think like Vladymir, my boy! I couldn't have scripted that better myself. Everything is coming together nicely. And now I have news of my own that may be helpful in your interrogations of the criminal, Ansley Brightmore."

"Of course, your grace. What is it?" asked Tiberius.

"Pour us another drink of your father's fine vintage and we shall discuss these new developments. I am allowing you information to which only the highest members of Arameus are privy. You have earned it." The strong liquor was altering Marco's judgment, making him more open to talk to the man before him.

After refreshing the drinks, Tiberius sipped his in silence, listening.

"I'm sure you remember our operation in Pathos a few months past. I know it wasn't comfortable for you, but we showed you how serious we were about fraternizing with the Natural Born. We saw much in you, and I assure you, it was a shame that your friend had to lose his life for us to get your attention." Tiberius felt the acid rising in the back of his throat but controlled his anger, seeing the two Formaddi surrounding the old man.

"However," continued the Overseer, "we never conduct an operation of that variety without there being a more far-reaching goal. There is a gangster in the region outside Pathos that has a sort of power over the peasants who work the coal mines. He has proven useful in the past for operations we found... distasteful, but we do not trust him. He carried out the murder of your philandering friend for the price of a few low-grade weapons and for the acquisition of an Imperial Falcon. What he did not know was that it was outfitted with our newest and most sophisticated tracking technology, undetectable to any means he may have of de-bugging. We have been tracking and monitoring his in-flight conversations for some time. You won't believe the sort of things we discovered. There have been some shocking developments to be sure."

"What have you discovered?" asked Tiberius.

"What we found out was of a personal nature to yourself. Are you sure you wish me to continue?" The old man grinned, his bright white teeth shining in the patio lights.

Nervous now, Tiberius wasn't quite sure whether he wished to hear.

"Well," continued Marco, "our Falcon happened to end up traveling to the far province of Avignon and landed in the dome of Sikyon."

Tiberius' heart raced in nervous anticipation. If Avignon was involved, that could only mean one thing. Kaiya. He thought back to when he had blocked the transmissions from Avignon. In spite of his best efforts to cut her off and do as he was told, it seemed his former lover could still come back to undermine his plans for them. Surely she would understand when they were safe together on the island he had been promised.

"As it turns out, you were a good little Nephite and did as you were told. Unfortunately for you and your future plans, the spy you enlisted to get Ansley, Professor Arian Cyannah, hired the gangster to take him to her in a whorehouse in Sikyon. Apparently she was ill content with her new surroundings. She murdered the entire family of the owner of a well-known winery. The victim was a close friend of the Mondavi who govern the dome, who happen to be cousins of Pierre de Medici. It has caused quite a headache in my circles as you may imagine. These are the reasons we forbid co-habitation with Natural Born outside of private isles. They are barbaric. Obviously she did more than enlist Arian into our plans. A man would not risk his entire life to save a woman he was not sharing a bed with. She is a manipulative bitch and was dangerous for you. You made the right choice in leaving her there."

Tiberius was shell-shocked, unable to move or speak. He felt as if she had stabbed him in the heart. All his work, all his plans for them collapsed in his mind. Marcus looked on, amused at the inner turmoil he saw on man's face. Tiberius remained silent, his mind replaying their history, wondering if she had ever cared for him. Crestfallen, he wanted nothing more than to run into the house and bury himself in his bed, anything to stop the dark thoughts that were plaguing him. His mind flashed between wonderful memories he shared with Kaiya and false visions of her sharing her most intimate feelings in bed with Arian. Reaching for the bottle, he poured much more liberally.

"I see you are upset," Marco chuckled. "My boy, I told you to stay away from the Natural Born whores. Trust me. I've been around. All great men must come to this point in their lives. We must realize we can trust no one and that women are only for pleasure, nothing more. If you require companionship, purchase a dog. Feed it and clean its shit. It will love you for it."

And as had always been true in his life, anguish became anger, and then cold detachment. Tiberius was not a man to be played for a fool. The only way to save face was to finish the job. And if that meant destroying Kaiya, the Centauri, and all those who sympathized with the wretched souls beyond the domes, then so be it. The name Septus would strike terror in the hearts of the Natural Born, his pain a whetstone to sharpen his focus. He knew he needed to compose himself and keep a stern face before the Overseer. A great man must be capable of separating personal feelings from business.

"I owe you a debt of gratitude, your grace," he said after a moment. "You were right about Kaiya and all of the Natural Born. I'm sorry that I ever doubted you and that I tried to hide her in Pathos."

Marco laughed a triumphant laugh, lifting his glass and savoring his drink.

"It is only natural that you reacted that way, Tiberius. You are but a man in a long line of men who have been deceived by the beauty of a treacherous woman. This is why you were forgiven. While this news may cause you some discomfort," the Overseer continued, "it is not all bad. The mistakes made by both Arian and Don Gravano have yielded better results than you may realize. Gravano does nothing for free, and a man raised in Capitol City would have no ability to contact or know of a man such as him. Our interrogations of Gravano have led us to a discovery that may unravel this entire conspiracy once and for all."

"What did you find?" asked Tiberius, anxious to know. He wanted Kaiya's betrayal to be beneficial in some way.

"As it turns out," replied Marco, "Arian did not fall under the spell of the Natural Born whore alone. Apparently, our young, weak professor has also allowed his allegiances to be turned by Ansley himself. It was Ansley who negotiated the terms for Don Gravano to extract Kaiya from Sikyon. Apparently Brightmore has his own spies and has become aware of our plans to use Arian's bio-bots for a measure of mass control. There is little doubt he was alerted, to some degree, by Arian himself. We are currently unaware of how Gravano would benefit from the bots, but apparently Ansley convinced the man they would offer a measure of extended life similar to our current nano-treatments. We don't see this as a possibility but it would be unwise to not take note of the ideas of a scientist of Brightmore's caliber."

"But how could Ansley get his hands on the bio-bots? They are being produced in a secure facility, overseen by Siva himself. He doesn't have the manpower to infiltrate a place such as that."

"This is where you are wrong, my friend," answered Marco curtly. "A man doesn't spend fifty years funneling money to an obscure city outside the dome without commanding a high level of loyalty. Whatever he is doing there, it is substantial. According to Gravano, he has been building a sort of Natural Born army. The deal was to rendezvous just outside Facility One, where a contingent of this force would be waiting, led by none other than our own Capitol City Gliders star, Jabari Stoudamyre. As it turns out, his injury is not as serious as advertised. This force would then infiltrate the facility, extract a few bots for payment to Gravano, and destroy everything else. The gangster gets his payment, and Jabari delivers Arian and Kaiya to Ansley at an undisclosed location."

"Well that won't happen," said Tiberius, smiling at his contribution to this whole scheme. "And what is the plan now, given these new developments?"

"Oh," responded Marco, unable to contain his smile, "this is my favorite part. Now, the plan goes as Ansley envisioned, with a slight kink. Gravano, who has been 'convinced' which side he is on, will extract Kaiya and Arian from Sikyon as planned, only a week later. He will release them to Jabari upon landing and the raid will proceed, only now, a legion of our best men will be awaiting them. We will crush this ridiculous band of rebels and send a message to the rest. Your injections in Beladero will soon follow. That was a very fine idea, my boy."

"So where are Kaiya and Arian currently?" asked Tiberius, trying to not let the concern for his former lover be evident in his voice.

"Upon apprehending Gravano, we got to his messenger who escorted Arian to the whorehouse where Kaiya was hiding. They believe they have escaped, but we know they currently reside in an old cathedral within the city. Gravano has convinced them it will take a week to extract them given an unforeseen double-cross. This will give us time to plan and mobilize a force to execute the ambush at Facility One."

Tiberius shook his head slowly from side to side then sipped his drink. It was astounding to witness one of the Overseers going over his plans and showing his inner workings. It wasn't by accident that they had taken over the world. Their genius was unparalleled, and with the bio-bots strengthening their power, it was difficult to see a time in the future that they would not control Arameus. A strange feeling came over Tiberius, a mix of fear and pride. On one hand, he was horrified by their methods and their wish to control humanity, but on the other, he was proud to be able to live in the era of these four great men and to be able to work side by side with them.

Anticipating the next move of the Overseer, Tiberius beat him to it.

"So what is it you need from me now?" he asked.

"This is why we like you so much, Tiberius. When I speak to you, I feel like we are collaborating. You have no idea how many blank stares I receive from those lower than yourself. It is as if we have collected an entire city of idiots." He laughed again, that cold, dead laugh. "We had knowledge of your impending arrest of Ansley. It should not surprise you at this point, but we have intelligence on everything and everyone, with one glaring exception."

"What is it, your grace?" asked Tiberius.

"Why would Ansley risk everything to deal with a gangster like Gravano so that Arian can get this Kaiya out of Sikyon? Does that bring anything to mind?"

"I'm afraid it does not," replied Tiberius.

"A man who builds a rebellion over fifty years would not take such a risk lightly. He needs Arian for something. For what, we have not been able to determine, but it must be important."

"Could it be the bots?" asked Tiberius.

"We have considered this, but it can't be that simple. They do not have the ability or the infrastructure to implement them in any meaningful way, but your arrest has given us an option. I am giving you this key and badge," he said, sliding the objects across the table. "These will give you all the authority you need to go to the holding cells below the Central Tower and interrogate Ansley Brightmore. I want you to make him suffer. Extract every detail you can about his operation, and when it seems he can take no more, inject him with this."

Marco pulled out a small silver vial from within his pocket. Tiberius instantly knew what it was, though he allowed the Overseer to explain.

"This is a sample from one of our batches of bio-bots being produced at Facility One. Inject Ansley with this. Be mindful to gauge his reaction upon injection. Perhaps it will allow us an insight into how he perceives they can be used for his own purposes. After that, we will provide the software that will make him Patient Zero. We will upload our own programming into the bots and test their ability for thought control. Ansley has brought about his own downfall trying to protect the Natural Born and will fittingly be the test subject for our future plans. The entire thing is quite elegant, don't you think?"

Tiberius took the vial from the Overseer, rolling it between his fingers, slowly comprehending the power he held in his hands. Without the old Professor and his traitorous plots, Kaiya would never have met Arian.

"I will make him suffer," he replied, a twisted grin forming upon his face.

## Chapter Twenty-Six
## The Dance of the Desert

*GONNGGGGG!!!*

"Son of a bitch," thought Arian. "It's too early."

*GONNGGGGG!!!*

He had come to hate the brothers and their rigid ways. It had been a week since he had seen Kaiya, the woman he had risked everything to save. The brothers of the cathedral had very strict rules against the mixing of sexes. Arian opened one eye, unwilling to give up his treasured slumber without a fight. He saw Dante bound out of his cot. The man had adapted to the life of a monk with ready ease. Arian imagined that after spending the last twenty years with his wife and then his two daughters, the life the brothers led was a welcome repose.

GONNGGGG!!!

"I'm going to kill these bastards," he said to himself.

Dante was already dressing. He was no doubt rushing down to meet Sanjay in the crypts. This was something Arian could understand. Dante, having never been taught to read, gravitated toward the visitor in the library, and Sanjay was a willing teacher of the wonders of the written word. Dante's reading lessons were progressing slowly. He wasn't much past the alphabet, but he enjoyed hearing Sanjay read about the ancient world. Arian wondered whether he was aware that seven days had passed, and soon their transport to the Raven and Beladero would arrive.

Educated men like Jabari and the others, who had learned under the tutelage of Ansley and his mother, would help to continue his education, along with that of his wife and children. Still, this newly found academic freedom would be difficult to leave. In this last week of living with a Natural Born servant, Arian had been astounded at the number of things he had taken for granted in his former life. Life was much less complicated here. He only lacked one thing. Kaiya.

GONNGGGG!!!!

Kaiya rose upon the fourth chiming of the bell. She had been awake since before the first, waiting to hear the telltale signs that Chloe and Eppie had risen for the day. She loved jumping out of bed and surprising them as soon as they awoke. She had become like a third sister to the girls, fitting right in with their talk of boys and giggles in the night. Knowing her past and the fact that she was older, Yasmine had been upset by this at first, but Kaiya's genuine affection and obvious immaturity won her over in the end. It was strange, but Yasmine could see that the broken woman was benefiting from this reprieve from the opposite sex, and the girls were fond of her as well.

"Kaiya, watch this!" screamed Chloe, adopting the demeanor of a horse and galloping around the room.

"You are such a dork," said the older Eppie, rolling her eyes and looking to Kaiya for approval.

"Oh, let your sister have her fun, Eppie," responded Kaiya, in her soft, high girlish tone. "Come here. I will fix your hair. A beautiful woman should have beautiful hair."

She pulled Eppie to her, running a brush through her long blonde locks and styling it while Chloe galloped on all fours. Yasmine watched all this from her bed, a bit disturbed, but happy nonetheless. She had slowly come to look at Kaiya and her deceptively young face as another daughter. The prepubescent tone of her voice aided in this.

"Doesn't she look beautiful, Yasmine?" asked Kaiya, as she finished styling the hair, turning toward the largish woman.

"You always make her hair beautiful, Kaiya," responded Yasmine. "I hope you still have time for them when we reach this new city. They have grown fond of you."

"I wanted to talk to you about that," said Kaiya, a hint of somberness in her tone.

"What is it my dear?"

"It's just that I haven't had a family since I was much younger than Eppie. I was wondering if I might join you in Beladero. I could earn money and help with the kids. I wouldn't be a burden."

Yasmine was touched by the sentiment. "Of course you can come with us, dear. We would be happy to have you. But what of Arian?"

"What of Arian?" replied Kaiya sternly. "My life has been dictated by the wants and desires of men since the death of my father. I have no need for them anymore, whether for protection or for love. I am content with you and the girls. I'm happy here. I feel safe."

Yasmine walked from her bed and embraced Kaiya. Eppie and Chloe joined her.

"We would love for you to be with us. But without the treatments, you will get old. Your wonderful beauty will fade. You will die like us."

"Good. My looks have brought me nothing but pain. I desire nothing more than to be with your family."

"Then you shall be my beautiful child," responded Yasmine, meaning every word.

GONNGGGG!!!!! GONNGGGG!!!!! GONNGGGG!!!! GONNGGGG!!!!!!

"I've never heard that before," thought Arian to himself as he stood and walked to the door. Before he could reach the handle, the door flew open from the other side. Fez al-Sun was standing in the hallway, breathing rapidly.

"Your escort has arrived, professor," he said, catching his breath from rushing up the steep spiraling staircase. "The monks are gathering the others."

Arian took a deep breath. It was time. He was both nervous and excited. He wanted nothing more than to see Kaiya again but was anxious about what awaited them outside the cathedral wall. Was it another double-cross? He just hoped that somehow, after all this, he could return to his previous life. Perhaps there was a way to save Kaiya, his career, and even Ansley.

He followed Fez al-Sun down the staircase. At the bottom, he saw that Kaiya, Eppie, Chloe, and Yasmine were already there. He tried to catch Kaiya's eye, but she avoided his gaze. She seemed dismayed by his presence. Just then, the trap door to the crypts opened in the thick marbled floor and Sanjay and Dante emerged. Dante rushed to his family, hugging first his girls, then his wife. All thoughts of learning to read temporarily vanished from his mind.

Turning to them all, Fez al-Sun said, "I'm afraid it is time for us to part. Your transport is outside the front doors. We do not allow men such as these within our walls. Know that you have refuge here as long as you desire, but if you choose to go, we wish you the best of fortunes." He moved toward Arian, leaning in close to whisper, "Time is as a river, ever changing, unfixed, yet the current need not be unidirectional. Should the need arise, the vault of this special cathedral can be quite informative." With this, he bowed and walked past them toward the choir of the cathedral where they had met the first day.

As the group turned to leave, Sanjay rushed after Arian, cutting him off and grabbing his hand in a firm shake.

"If you must go, I hope that you go in peace my friend," he said in his heavily accented, cheery voice. "Hate gains one nothing in this life."

Confused, Arian embraced the brown-skinned man.

"Thank you for opening that door for us, Sanjay. We would have been lost without you. I hope to meet you again in the future."

"The future? Oh I wouldn't expect that, my friend. My travels shall take me very far from here indeed. But I wish you the best. I expect your journey will be quite eventful. No matter what, you can always return here. This temple is a constant sanctuary. You hear me? Constant, my friend. A special place indeed."

With this Arian and the others headed for the arched oak doors at the front of the cathedral. Two more monks were waiting to open the doors for them. Yellow light held back by stained glass streamed into the building, washing over the white marble, creating an awe-inspiring impression. The group walked out into the blinding light to a waiting transport. Arian was happy to see that Serenity was not there. Perhaps Gravano had been telling the truth. They entered an eight-man transport, greeted by an unknown man.

"Are you with Don Gravano?" asked Arian.

The man said nothing, contenting himself to type a few coordinates into the console and look away from them all.

"Okay," said Arian aloud. He leaned back in the transport, deciding to relax. Whatever happened from here, it was out of his control. He had done everything he could to rescue Kaiya. He just hoped that Ansley's payment would be enough.

Travelling through the streets of Sikyon, there seemed to be no other drivers on the road. They approached and passed every intersection they came to without incident. Arian surveyed the horizon but could see no evidence that they were being followed. Perhaps Gravano would come through. The girls played and chattered together as if they had no care in the world. Arian followed Kaiya's eyes and could see that she was jealously watching them. Dante was humming the Alphabet song to himself. It was pathetic, yet touching. He haphazardly put his foot out in an attempt to touch Kaiya's leg, only to have her yank it away without so much as a look. In almost no time, they began to pass the familiar sights Arian had witnessed upon leaving the landing pad with Serenity. Moving past the last of the buildings on the main avenue, the Raven loomed into view.

The transport was waved through each security checkpoint, a fact that was not lost on Arian. Whatever deal Gravano had worked out with the dome agents, it was allowing them to pass unimpeded. Just inside the final security gate, the transport stopped and its doors opened. The group exited, standing on the runway. The escort finally spoke to Arian.

"Here are your belongings," he said gruffly, tossing a black duffle bag out the door as his transport pulled away. Picking it up from the ground and opening it, Arian was shocked to find as he shuffled through his Capitol City clothes the small switchblade that Jabari had given him. Something didn't add up. Arian's instincts told him they should run.

Dante looked to Arian, observing the nervousness on his face.

"I didn't expect the plane to be here. Thank you, friend." Yasmine and the children moved forward and hugged their father. Even Kaiya seemed excited by the Raven. She walked over and embraced him, adding a light kiss on his cheek. He lost himself in the feeling of her body on his and her scent. He ignored his unease.

A walkway descended from the Raven. Arian watched with relief as he saw guards, not Imperial guards, but those he had previously seen with Gravano walk down the ramp. Gravano himself appeared in the doorway.

"We made it," said Arian.

The others looked to him for the next move, so in a fit of triumph, he grabbed Kaiya's hand and rushed toward the entryway. Dante, Yasmine, Eppie, and Chloe followed at a slower pace. Arian pulled Kaiya behind him, rushing them to their escape. They stopped at the top of the ramp, before Gravano.

"Thank you, Christof," Arian declared, grateful.

Strangely, Gravano didn't deign to respond. He merely looked in the distance, as if undaunted by the presence of those he had come to save. Arian felt the strong arms of the closest guard ripping him from Kaiya and locking around his neck, while the other restrained him. As they dragged him inside, he searched for her with his limited vision, and saw that she was being similarly manhandled and carried inside. Once they were past the Don, the guards held them so that they faced the opening, and could see the family ascending the ramp. Dante froze, realizing something was wrong, though his daughters continued to gallop forward.

"Men," was all Gravano uttered, as a chorus of gunfire sang out from the other guards along the ramp. Arian watched helplessly as bullets riddled the bodies of the young girls he had brought here to begin their new lives. Chloe screamed wretchedly, until a bullet tore through her neck and rendered her forever mute. Dante rushed forward to cover Eppie. The guards shot until he was clearly dead before walking forward and callously tossing his body aside. He had succeeded in protecting her until this moment. Arian could hear Kaiya's blood curdling scream as the guard placed the barrel to Eppie's temple and blew her brains, memories, and consciousness to oblivion. Only Yasmine remained. She kneeled, huddled and afraid in the blood and gore of what had seconds ago been her family.

"Let her go," said Gravano, with an air of benevolence. The guards stood down.

Yasmine looked up, whimpering and confused.

"Go!!!!!" shouted Gravano.

Yasmine turned and ran down the ramp, running away from the violence and the hate and the destruction of those she had loved. Running away from her shattered life. She made it halfway down the runway toward the security checkpoint before Gravano pulled a pistol from his pocket, aiming it at the fleeing woman.

"Watch this, boys," he said with glee as the barrel flashed.

Yasmine dropped instantly, never to rise again.

The landing ramp withdrew and the doors closed, leaving Arian with a last image of the bloody scene that burned into his retinas like the after effect of staring for too long at the sun. Wherever he looked, he saw the girls' dead faces, staring ahead lifeless, imploring him to provide a future that would never come. He would never forgive himself for letting them down.

The guards twisted their bodies and threw both Arian and Kaiya to the ground as the Raven took off. Arian sprung to his feet and lunged at Gravano. He was only inches from the old man's fat neck before the guards caught him and again shoved him to the ground, this time, holding him there. Gravano leaned down and looked into his eyes. His harsh face seemed to soften upon seeing Arian, wild-eyed and in despair.

"I admire the fight in you, lover boy, but you must understand our agreement was only to pick up you and the girl. Anything else is an added risk and is something I am not being paid to accomplish. You were foolish to assume they would be safe with me. Their deaths, I'm afraid, are on you."

"Fuck you!" screamed Arian, fighting the men who held him. He looked over to Kaiya and saw her struggling to resist restraint. He forced himself to relax his demeanor. He could still save Kaiya. As he softened, so did the hold on his body. The men lifted him to his feet, training their weapons on him as he stood to face Gravano. Out of the corner of his eye, he could see that Kaiya was also brought to her feet, tears streaming down her cheeks.

The thugs shoved them together. Arian had no fight left. His soul had been destroyed by the event he had just witnessed. He felt as an empty cavity, understanding for the first time why Ansley had asked of him what he had. Before this moment, Arian had been naïve. Ansley wasn't asking him to sacrifice his life so that he could be with a deceased lover. Ansley was asking him to deliver the world from tyranny. He wished he was strong enough to help fulfill that dream.

"I'm sorry for your loss, truly, my friend," said Gravano, "but it was unavoidable."

"How was shooting an entire family of unarmed people unavoidable?" whispered Arian.

"You understand very little, my young friend. Everything has always been handed to you. You are part of the system you now pretend to hate. It is quite unbecoming. Come. Let's have a martini together and talk. Perhaps I can enlighten you on the intricacies of being born outside of the dome."

Having no choice, Arian followed him to the bar in the corner of the Raven, where what seemed like months ago he had tasted that dreadful concoction. Kaiya also followed, taking a seat on the stool beside Gravano. Arian tried to read her face. All of the blood was drained from it, leaving her with a white pallor, but other than this, her expression was stony, betraying no emotion. He found her behavior odd.

"And what will you be having, my lovely lady?" asked Gravano. Arian was forced down into the stool on the other side of the fat man, the guards remaining as a menacing reminder of their allegiance to Gravano's ruthlessness.

"A glass of wine would be nice," answered Kaiya sweetly. Arian was stunned by her nonchalance. It was as if none of the murders had just occurred. She even seemed demure, as if flirting with the Don.

"Very good," responded Gravano, his voice cheery. "At

least someone here knows how to accept my hospitality. And for you, lover boy? Perhaps another dirty martini?"

"I'm fine," replied Arian coldly.

"Suit yourself. But you must understand that my predicament has been precarious since your arrival. We were betrayed. I barely made it out of Sikyon after leaving you. It took over a week to acquire the proper permits to return. You and Kaiya are outlaws. Removing you was possible, but escaping with another family of outlaws would have attracted too much attention. Their deaths were an offering to those in charge. They were a sacrifice to ensure our safe passage, not to mention that we are not fueled to support the extra weight. We never would have made it to our destination. I never would have received my payment."

Arian was unconvinced.

"That was not a mere sacrifice. You took pleasure in murdering Yasmine. You toyed with her life before you destroyed it. No mother should have to watch her children die."

"Let me educate you a bit about the life I have led, boy, before you presume to lecture me. I was born in a poor coal-mining town outside of Pathos. After the collapse of the world governments, our region was dominated by warlords who forced my people to labor, while becoming wealthy from our toil. To this day, our coal heats your luxurious homes. I was forced into the mines at age twelve. I worked alongside my older brother Cornell. He was sixteen. He had a crush on the daughter of a neighbor and wanted to buy her something nice, so he stole a bit of coal from the mine and sold it to get the money. When the lord of the region, a gangster named Don Raphaelli discovered this, he sent a group of thugs to my home, dragged my brother into the street and murdered him in front of my mother. She was taken by the flu less than a year later."

Kaiya shocked Arian by rubbing Gravano's shoulder sympathetically.

"I'm so sorry," she said. "I lost my father and two

siblings to the flu."

"Don't fret dear, this story has a happy ending," answered Gravano, patting her leg. He continued.

"I gathered a group of friends from the ghetto where we lived, and one night, we snuck into Don Raphaelli's house and slit his throat while he slept. I enjoyed every second of his last gurgled breaths. For good measure, I left the knife planted in the belly of his wife. From this point on, I had the respect of the neighborhood, and when I grew to manhood, it was I who became the new Don, and our region has flourished ever since. I have dealt with, backstabbed, and fought with your Overseers, taking care of tasks they find unseemly and providing them with cheap coal when their space ore becomes scarce. I have fortified and strengthened our defenses and even negotiated access to seasonal vaccines so that none of my people need die as my mother did. My methods have been brutal but effective. It is your government that abandoned us to a lawless land and a harsh environment requiring harsher leaders. When it comes to being a ruler, power is not only important, it is everything."

Arian was unimpressed and expressed his contempt for the man. "A leader should inspire people. He should be kind and just. You use your hardship as an excuse for your actions while at the same time continuing the same cycle of violence. You have embraced the very methods that took your brother from you. You have become Don Raphaelli," said Arian, his voice calm and steady. He no longer cared what happened to him. He had lost all appetite for life after watching that eager family be shot like animals.

"You have a lot of balls lecturing me, lover boy, you who has never known want and will never die." Gravano nodded to one of the guards, who cocked a handgun and placed it to Arian's temple. "I should say 'will never die naturally'. I can end your life on a whim." He laughed to himself, seeming to consider something before snapping back.

"And now we arrive at the crux of the matter," continued Gravano. "I want something that your people can get me, and you will use this to bargain for your life. We all do what we must to survive. For some of us, this entails reading science books and living in lavish apartments. For others," he added, turning to Kaiya, eyeing her lithe body from head to toe, "it involves living as a whore. For me, it has been a life of violence and intimidation. Each of us has done as they must, and none of us can judge the other."

Kaiya smiled at this sentiment. Arian could not determine whether it was in agreement or whether she was in survival mode, making sure not to draw the ire of this terrible man. One fact Arian could not get over was that the Don did have a point. None aboard the Raven were innocent, not any longer. Whether or not Kaiya agreed with Gravano's reasoning he could not know, but he hoped for the sake of his love for her that she found him as disgusting as he did.

"Do you mind removing the gun from my head?" asked Arian. "It makes it a bit difficult to continue this conversation, Christof." Gravano again nodded at the guard, who removed the barrel from his temple, thumbing the safety. "Thank you. So what exactly is this payment that you negotiated with Jabari? I feel I'm entitled to know."

"With all your advantages and intellectual gifts, Arian, I feel sorry for you in all this," replied Gravano in a slow and measured tone. "You are the epitome of a man with no power. Your role has been that of a pawn, manipulated by Ansley, by Tiberius, and even Kaiya. You have failed to understand the politics and forces that swirl around you, sweeping you up in their wake."

Kaiya giggled at this, and Gravano shot her a quick wink. Arian was both hurt and furious by Kaiya's strange and callous behavior in the presence of the Don. It was as if nothing they shared at Angelica's had occurred. Following Arian's gaze, Gravano interrupted his train of thought.

"Fret not, my boy. The girl behaves as she must and the way her life has taught her. She is a survivor. She adapts to the situation. At present, I am the most powerful man in the room. I assure you, she despises me."

"And what is it that I do not understand?" asked Arian.

"You don't understand that in your secret dealings with Ansley and your quest to save Kaiya, you have neglected your duties as a professor, and one who was once below you has brought his findings to the attention of those in the Central Tower. Apparently they saw much potential in the bio-bot technology. They not only raised your student to the status of professor, they gave him control of a secret lab constructed outside Capitol City, whose sole purpose is the mass production of these bots."

"Conway?" demanded Arian, knowing the answer before the name left his mouth. "But how could he go over my head? This goes against all protocol. It is against the law!"

"He had faith that those in charge of the Institute would see the value of the research, even if you didn't, and take it to the Central Tower. He understood the politics and was correct on both assumptions."

Of all the revelations that Gravano could have given him, this one hurt the most. His pride was wounded at a student stealing work carried out under his supervision, as well at the thought of being surpassed by one so limited as Conway. No matter how he dissected his future, he knew his career at the Institute as well as his place in Arameus was lost forever. He was now a fugitive, no different than Kaiya, who, in their current situation, seemed indifferent toward him. He only hoped that Ansley could help him when they landed.

"I still fail to see how this figures into your payment. I understand that I have been played as the fool, but there is no way a lab run by Arameus would turn over the bot technology to you. And what benefit would they be to you anyway?"

"It would seem a small victory to one such as yourself, but it has been determined by those in charge of your world that the bio-bots will revolutionize extended life. Controlled by a central computer whose A.I. is always evolving, they will make continued nano-treatments unnecessary. I don't ask much. I only want what you have, and what every man wants. I want to preserve my life and what vigor I still retain, and why should I be denied this? It has always been impossible for a man such as me to receive the treatments, though I have found them here and there. With this new technology, I will be on the same footing as your Overseers, and can use my long life to gain power and lead my people against yours. I don't understand why they would risk their power over extended life and the nanocyte supply chain. Leaks are inevitable, and it only takes a few to undermine their control."

"Trust me, where the Overseers are concerned, very little is overlooked. It would be unfortunate if you played into yet another power grab," answered Arian, amused at the ignorant confidence of this uneducated brute. "If they are giving them up, they come with a hefty price."

"They aren't giving them up, you foolish boy. You will be stealing them. Why do you think we are dealing with that beast of a man Jabari? When we land, Jabari and a team of his men will be waiting for us. You will accompany them on an assault of the lab. You will go to ensure they obtain a useable form of the bots. Upon the delivery of my payment, we will take you and Kaiya back to Beladero and release you."

"This is insane. You can't expect us to directly attack a lab sanctioned by the Central Tower. It's suicide."

"It's a science lab in the desert, not a damn military base. If Jabari and his men can't infiltrate a facility so lightly defended, then their reputation far outweighs them."

Arian considered this. If there was one man he trusted in all of this, it was Jabari. If he thought that they could get the bio-bots from the lab, then Arian had to have faith.

"Very well, Christof, I will do as you wish. If you double cross me, Jabari will not be so easily threatened as that unarmed family."

"Oh, I'm sure," replied Gravano. He turned his back to Arian, now facing Kaiya, ordering her another glass of wine, which she gladly accepted. Defeated, Arian stood and walked to the other side of the Raven, finding an empty couch. He laid on it, closing his eyes, meditating on all that had transpired, using his analytical brain to envision the different ways in

which the rest of the day might unfold. They had at least
four hours of travel before they would reach the other side
of Capitol City, so he had time to think. He often found his
thoughts interrupted by Kaiya and Gravano's loud laughter
echoing through the cabin.

The hours were slow in passing as Arian lay with
his eyes closed, feigning sleep. The laughter died away and
Gravano left the cabin. She must have approached silently
for he was startled when he felt her hand upon his shoulder.
Opening his eyes, he saw her looking down at him, concern on
her face.

"What happened to your date?" he asked, embarrassed
as soon as the question left his lips.

"Stop it, Arian. You have your bots to trade. I have my
looks. I am only trying to secure survival for us."

"For us?" he asked, a bit confused.

"If it comes to it, yes. No man can refuse me."

"I see," said Arian, closing his eyes again, attempting to
block her out.

She sat on the couch beside him.

"I only want to get out of here alive. Did you see
what his men did to the girls? Like it or not, we are under his
control for now."

"Until I deliver him the bots, and possibly eternal life,"
returned a miserable Arian.

"We will do what we must. I do care for you Arian.
You're unlike any man I have encountered. You are kind,
where they are cruel, sensitive where they are hard, and you
believe in and speak of a life of substance and righteousness
that we have never known."

"We?"

"Like it or not, Gravano and I are both Natural Born
and share experiences you could never understand. But you
have to be strong now, for both of us. You have to get those
bots and get me off this ship. I will not be a slave to a man
again. You see the way he eyes me. Stay alive, and we will

361

escape together. Our lots have become the same. We will leave Beladero and find a town far away from Arameus and Gravano and Ansley."

Arian sighed. He had no other choice. All options were closed to him. He would go along with this ploy and at his first chance find Ansley and then the Iris. None of this would matter if Ansley's theories proved correct. It was difficult to grasp how much his opinions had changed over the past several weeks.

"Very well," he replied. "I will get the bots and get us to Beladero. From there, I can guarantee nothing."

"Thank you," she said, kissing him on the cheek. Despite his reservations and resolve, he felt butterflies in his stomach as her body came into contact with his own. He had no power to resist the raw sensuality exuded by this woman. One touch from her and he would follow her anywhere.

"I will let you rest now," she said, as she laid beside him on the couch, slipping her head into the crook of his shoulder and wrapping her leg around his lower torso. He closed his eyes again and mentally prepared for whatever was to follow, trying to ignore the feeling of her heartbeat and her intoxicating smell. He may have even fallen asleep briefly, for as he came back to consciousness, his ears were popping due to the changing pressure as the Falcon hurtled toward the ground below. The first thing he noticed was that Kaiya was no longer in his grasp.

As they landed, it was all a blur of sound and motion for Arian. Guards were again surrounding him, guns aimed at his head. Gravano had reappeared and was standing, clutching Kaiya by the shoulders.

"It's time for you to uphold your end of the bargain," shouted Gravano over the noise, the twisted pleasure of control evident in his voice. The door to the Raven opened and the exit ramp descended, washing the dim interior in the bright light of the noonday yellow sunrays, made more blinding by the refection from the red desert sand. He was forced into the light, unable to see anything as his eyes adjusted, unable to hear due to the sound of the engines, and scarcely able to breath due to the dust in the air. His eyes began to focus by the time he was midway down the ramp. He saw Jabari standing in the passenger side of a cruiser loaded down with six other heavily armed men. There were at least seven other similarly outfitted cruisers beside him. Jabari's face wore an intense look.

"Yo dog," he yelled. "Where the fuck is the girl?"

"You will get the girl upon the Don's payment. She's safe," called out one the rear guards.

Jabari shook his head in disgust.

"Fucking gangsters," he screamed back. "We'll deal with you. Don't worry."

Arian was shoved in his back, sending him tumbling down the remainder of the ramp. Jabari jumped out of the cruiser and rushed forward to him, as the landing ramp was drawn back up, sealing the Raven. He helped Arian to his feet.

"I'm glad you're okay," he said, patting him on the back. "Now it's time to pay for your journey. We will lose men today. Ansley believes your cooperation is worth it. I hope you prove him correct."

"Where is Ansley?" asked Arian. "I need to talk to him."

A look of sadness flitted across Jabari's face and was gone.

"He couldn't make it. We need to move."

Arian reached into his pocket and pulled out the switchblade he had received the last time the men had met, handing it over.

"You keep that, dog. It was a gift," said Jabari. "Actually," he added, removing a pistol from inside the back of his pants and cocking it, "take this as well. You might need it." Arian took it, unable to fathom how it could be of use to a man like him.

He escorted Arian to an empty seat in the cruiser next to his own. Without a word, he returned to his and ordered the men to drive. The vehicles turned around and drove away from the Raven in a caravan formation. It wasn't long, perhaps only a quarter mile, before the sparse, barrack-like three-story façade of the laboratory came into view. This was nothing like the laboratories in Capitol City, which were architectural masterpieces. This was constructed with the intention of not drawing attention. They drove up an embankment in the sand that overlooked the structure, stopping just before their cruisers would come into view by those below. Jabari jumped down, signaling one of his men, obviously a trusted comrade, and Arian to follow on foot. They trekked the final few meters to the top of the embankment. Jabari lifted a pair of binoculars from his chest and surveyed the scene below. After a moment, he handed them to Arian and pointed in the direction for him to look.

Through the binoculars, Arian saw a driving ramp descending into a loading dock. Two guards flanked the door, automatic weapons hanging from their necks.

"We've been watching this entrance for a few days," said Jabari's comrade. "Twice a day, convoys come from Capitol City to deliver supplies. Each time, the guards swipe ID cards at the same time to open the doors. We take down the guards, swipe the cards, and we're in."

"By the way," added Jabari, "this is my second in command, Francisco Dominguez. If there was ever a man to entrust your life to, he is that man."

Francisco nodded.

"We will bring twelve men in to secure the building," Jabari told Arian. "Me and two others will follow you and act as protection. You need to find useable bots to pay Gravano. You are the only one who can identify what we're looking for."

Arian nodded in apprehensive acceptance of his fate.

"Then it's simple," said Francisco, an expectant grin spreading over his face. "Let's go kick these doors in, shoot some Nephites, and get what we came for."

"I hope you're right," answered Jabari.

The three men walked back down the embankment to the cruisers. This time, Jabari escorted Arian to his own cruiser along with Francisco and two other men. They were flanked on both sides by vehicles outfitted with six men each. Jabari shouted an order for the remaining cruisers to follow them up the embankment and remain there guarding the perimeter and awaiting further instruction. With everything in place, the three vehicles moved down the hill toward the laboratory.

Jabari and Arian were in the back, with an unnamed driver and Francisco in the front. Arian's heart raced, and he felt as if he might be sick as they traversed the uneven landscape. Jabari gave him a sympathetic squeeze on the shoulder, although it did nothing to calm his nerves. As the two guards came into view, Arian saw them freeze with surprise at the approaching vehicles. They had very little time to do much else as Francisco stood in the cruiser and, with the trained hand of an experienced assassin, dropped them both in two quick, successive shots. They were entering the ramp and exiting the vehicle before the bodies of the men stopped quivering. The two other vehicles stopped at the top of the ramp and the men exited, running down to join the assault.

Arian felt uneasy as he watched Jabari and Francisco reach into the pockets of the deceased men, both Nephites, and extract the key cards. Just as the two men were about to swipe the cards, an explosion in the distance shook the ground, causing Arian to stumble. Turning, he saw two of the cruisers left on the embankment engulfed in flames, the men flailing and screaming as they burned.

"That mother fucker!" shouted Jabari, rage shaking his core. "He led us into an ambush."

Arian could see the unit of Imperial infantry approaching from the left of the embankment, pounding the men with heavy artillery. He froze in fear. Jabari grabbed him by the back of his shirt and threw him toward the now open door.

"Let's go, dog, we have to complete the mission."

"The mission is done," yelled Arian. "We've been

deceived."

"Gravano's mission is done," replied Jabari, continuing to shove him forward.

"We have the Iris. Ansley is counting on you. Now let's go!"

As he was rushed through the door, Arian cast one last look back toward the embankment. The remaining men had exited their cruisers and were returning fire to the Imperial infantry. The high ground gave them a strategic advantage now that the trap had sprung. The other twelve men followed them into the lab.

Sirens were already sounding as they entered the dim, narrow hallway. A few of the men rushed forward from the rear, throwing flashbangs ahead. When the bright light subsided, Arian saw lab guards rush forward into the smoke. A chorus of gunfire from Jabari's men signaled their deaths. Rushing past the bodies, they came into the open expanse that was the ground floor of the lab. Confused by the sirens and gun blasts, the Nephite scientists seemed frozen in place. As they entered the floor, one brave scientist jumped off a lab bench at Jabari. Francisco scoped the man's chest, the bullet creating an exit wound in his back five times the size of the entry wound.

"There won't be any fucking heroes here today," he screamed. "I shoot any man or woman who isn't on the ground."

Every person in the building dropped to the floor. Flashes of gunfire rang above them and Arian nearly emptied his bladder as a bullet whizzed by his ear, shattering an Erlenmeyer flask nearby. Jabari trained his gun to the balcony, and a single bullet to the head ended the threat. Francisco ran forward with six of the men leading them from wall to wall, placing explosives in key structural positions.

"We have to get every support," he yelled to his men, as Arian heard the beeps of the timed explosives coming to life.

Jabari grabbed him by the collar.

"This is all you, man. You've got to lead us to the

useable bots, dog. And real fucking quick."

Arian tried to ignore the chaotic sounds and the fear inside him as he surveyed the lab. He saw the PCR machines, as well as the electron microscopes used for nano-robotics. He rushed toward the PCR tables, hoping that these would lead him to a successful implantation. He couldn't help but empathize with his fellow scientists cowering on the ground, men who were just like him. With no time to dwell, he focused on the task and getting out of the facility alive. He ran to a microscope adjacent to a PCR machine, Jabari and two men following behind. From his experience, this was the last stage of development, though he had no idea how the leaders of Capitol City would have implemented the process. He looked through a microscope, hoping to be lucky enough to see something promising. As he looked, he felt a soft squeeze on the back of his ankle, and heard a scared voice.

"Arian?"

Looking down, Arian was shocked to find Alexandra, her face contorted in terror and streaked with tears, clutching his ankle. He leaned down to her, taking his old friend into his arms in a feeble attempt to comfort her.

"What are you doing here, Alex?" he asked, surprised at the fear he heard in his own voice.

"That asshole Conway requested that I be made part of the team. I had no choice. I was sent here by the Director of the Institute himself."

"We have to get out of here, Alex. Imperial troops are outside. There is a battle going on, but we can't leave without useable bots. Can you get us some?"

They both jerked as gunfire erupted above them. Looking up, they saw smoke rising from the barrel of Jabari's gun as a laboratory guard fell lifeless to the floor.

"Let's get moving, dog," shouted Jabari. We don't have time for a reunion!"

Alex gasped and her words tumbled out. "I know where we can get some. For every shipment we send back to

Capitol City, a few samples are sent to Conway's office for Quality Control purposes. I have a key card to his office. I am certain we will find them there."

"Great, let's fucking go," shouted Jabari. "Lead the way. Guitierrez, Rodrigo, come with us," he called to two men who were close by. Arian lifted Alex to her feet, and she led them toward a staircase at the far wall. The three men formed a protective circle around the two scientists, but there was little action in the main lab, as Francisco's men had the area secured. It was promising that the Imperial troopers had yet to enter the facility. The small group of Beladero men outside must be holding their ground. They followed Alex up two flights of stairs to the third floor of the building, running around the perimeter balcony that overlooked the main floor. They stopped in front of an unassuming door at the far corner.

"This is his office," said Alex, looking back at Jabari, recognizing who was in charge.

She handed him the key card as his men readied their weapons. Jabari swiped the card and kicked open the door before jumping aside as the other two men rushed in and discharged their weapons at two unfortunate guards.

"All clear!" they heard one of the men shout from inside.

Jabari looked at Alex sympathetically. "Time to find the bots, girl. This will all be over soon. We will keep you safe."

Alex looked up at the hulking man and nodded. She and Arian entered the room stumbling over the two guards who had fallen to the ground on top of one another. The office was large, lined with bookshelves, with a rectangular meeting table in the center. At the very back, beside the window, was Conway's desk console.

"They have to be here somewhere," said Alex, searching frantically for clues.

Arian knew where he would keep the bots if he were in charge of the project; locked in his desk, close to him. The desk was bathed in yellow sunlight from the window and as he approached, he could see the vast desert beyond. They were on the opposite side of the building from where they had entered, so he could not see the battle, but it gave him hope to know they were not surrounded. Picking up a notepad on the desk, he heard the slightest whimper, followed by rustling.

Arian started, jumping backward.

"Jabari," he yelled, "someone is here."

Jabari and his men rushed over to the other side of the desk. His two men leaned down, and when they came up, they held between them a petrified-looking Matthew Conway. In his hands, he clutched a box of syringes.

"Those are the bots," exclaimed Alexandra.

Arian held Conway in his gaze as he took the box. Examining the contents, he could see that it was meant to hold twelve doses, but one of the syringes was missing.

"Always thinking of you," said Arian, shaking his head. "I'm disappointed, Matt. You had so much promise, but your ambition has led you here."

Matt looked at Alex, imploring her to help.

"Alexandra, please don't let them hurt me. I was only doing what I was asked, just as you were. What makes you different?"

"I could never be with a cowering man like you," she answered coldly. All of his will seemed to drain from his body at her words.

"The way I see it," said Jabari, closing in on him, "this entire facility is just one more way for your people to control mine, and unfortunately for you, you happen to be in charge."

He sprang forward and in a swift and fluid motion, grabbed the frightened man's jaw and the back of his head, snapping his neck. Rodrigo and Gutierrez allowed his corpse to drop to the floor.

While the others dispersed, Arian stood over the body, contemplating the gun in his hand. Though he had never fired a weapon, he was pretty sure all he had to do was pull the trigger. Aiming it at the center of the forehead, he fired, sending pieces of skull and brain into the air.

"Damn, dog," said Jabari, raising an eyebrow.

Arian shrugged. The men around him nodded their approval, though Alexandra looked horrified. He should have felt guilty, but there was no time for that. They had to keep moving.

Jabari got on his radio and called to Francisco.

"We have the bots. What's your status?"

After a moment of white noise, Francisco's voice came from the other end. He sounded frantic, even frightened.

"We have to get out of here now. Our men are being routed outside. The Imperial troops will be here soon. We can't escape the way we came."

Jabari muttered under his breath before responding. "Have Cooper drive the cruiser to the entrance on the opposite side of the building. We can escape that way."

After a longer pause, Francisco's voice came again.

"He's on his way. You need to get the fuck out of here. This building will blow in less than four minutes. I will try to hold them from entering through the front and following. If I can, I will allow them to enter just as the building explodes."

"It's been an honor fighting beside you," said Jabari, his voice thick with emotion.

"I'm not dead yet, my friend," replied Francisco with a laugh. "I plan on having a lot of fun in these next four minutes. Now go! Save our people."

"You heard the man," shouted Jabari at the others. "We don't have much time. He will not sacrifice his life in vain. Yo girlie, show us out that way," he said, pointing to the empty desert outside the window.

They followed Alex in a full sprint back down the corridor on the perimeter to the stairs. Glancing down to the main floor, Arian saw the remaining ten men with Francisco concentrating their fire on the hallway leading from the loading dock. The Imperial infantry had arrived. He only hoped their transport cruiser had escaped in time.

He heard Francisco shout to the scientists who were still on the floor covering their heads, "Anyone who is in this building in four minutes will be dead. Exit through the loading dock if you want to live."

In a mad rush, hundreds of white-coated scientists rushed toward the very door through which the Imperial infantry was trying to enter. The unfortunate front-runners were gunned down by their own Imperial saviors who did not yet realize who was rushing toward them. Upon realization, they stayed their fire, as the frightened Nephites overwhelmed them, halting their progress and buying time for Arian and his cohorts to escape.

On the main floor, Alex used a key card to open a door leading to the rear exit. Jabari looked longingly back across the lab to his friend, who was commanding the troops of Beladero in a suicidal last stand. For a moment, Arian believed he would join his friend, but Jabari shook his head and rushed after them, allowing the door to close and lock. They sprinted down a well-furnished corridor, meant to house administrative offices. The light spilling through the glass doors leading to their freedom was visible ahead as they ran from the violence and carnage. It was only fifty feet away now. Forty. Thirty. Ten. Arian never knew that fresh air could smell and taste so sweet as it did when they burst through the doors.

Running into the hot desert air, the cruiser came into view, only twenty feet away. Arian felt Jabari's hand clamp his shoulder like a vice, bringing him to a stop. The others in the group followed suit, with only Jabari walking cautiously ahead. It was only now that Arian saw what had stopped the man. The scene before them was grim and efficient. Four bodies were sprawled around the cruiser, bleeding from trauma to their necks. Cooper was still seated at the wheel, his head rolled back over the seat, only attached to his body by skin and a few remaining tendons. Arian heard motion from behind and turned around in time to see a man emerge from the shadows by the door. Like a predator, he leapt forward, in between

Rodrigo and Gutierrez. Arian saw the flash of bloodstained silver blades as the man, not bothering to look behind him, shot his arms backward, shoving a blade into the throat of each man, leaving them lodged deep within. Before the men had fallen and Arian could lift his gun, the man was upon him, unarmed now, though no less deadly. Arian felt a brief intense pain ripple down his spinal chord as the man connected a precise blow with his hand, which felt as sharp as a knife, between his throat and collarbone. He lost all control of his body and fell to the ground, unable to move. The gun dropped beside him.

Jabari reeled around, but before he was able to fire his weapon, the man kicked the gun out of his hands and struck him in the throat, sending him to his knees. As Arian watched the man from the ground, still unable to move, he could see the cold and steady precision of the assassin. The man moved with speed but did not rush. He had no fear. He was in complete control of the situation. Shooting a quick, cat-like look back to Arian, who was now being tended to by Alexandra, he was convinced they posed no threat, and now picked up Rodrigo's automatic rifle, pointing it at Jabari.

Jabari stood and surveyed the man, clutching his throat and trying to catch his breath. Arian watched, helpless in Alex's arms.

"You killed my men, dog," said Jabari between gasps for air. "What are you waiting for? Shoot."

"Jabari Stoudamyre. Capitol City's greatest athlete. I never took you to be an enemy of the state. I'm a big fan. Still, I don't believe I have had the honor of killing a man of your physical prowess. I'm excited by the challenge."

"Not much challenge here," answered Jabari. "Just got to pull the trigger."

Arian could see from the way Jabari was positioning his feet that he was readying himself to spring at the man. His eyes burned with hatred. The two could not have been more different physically. Jabari, with his dark skin, 6'6" heavily muscled frame, and imposing demeanor starkly contrasted with the slightly built, tan-skinned man, with thinning blonde hair.

"Shoot you?" replied the man. "I'm not going to shoot you, unless, of course, you choose to follow through with your ill-conceived plan to rush me." Arian saw Jabari's posture relax a bit. "It would be such a waste of a chance to test my skills against an elite specimen such as you. There are so few of you left. I would like to settle this like men. Hand to hand."

Jabari laughed in an exaggerated gesture.

"You want to fight me hand to hand? I welcome that challenge. I will destroy you, you pathetic assassin."

"Silence your tongue, beast, or I may not choose to allow you to die as honorably as I intend."

"Like you honorably attacked my men from behind?"

The man smiled. "They are but pawns. I assure you, had they been facing me, the result would not have varied. I'm afraid I have been rude. I know your name, but you do not yet know mine. They call me Siva. I am the first and head of the elite group of assassins known as the Formaddi. For my diligent services to Vladymir Romanov, I was awarded the extended life. I have been killing for the Overseers since the beginning of Arameus. You will fall, just as all others have before."

"There's only one way to find out, dog. Drop your gun and let's do this, you pathetic murdering piece of shit."

Siva squinted at him and nodded in a gentlemanly acceptance of the challenge. He tossed the gun aside as Jabari rushed forward, letting his fists fly loosely, reigning down blows on the small man, though none landed. Siva dodged, left, right, in and out, playing with the distances and not allowing Jabari to find his range. Jabari finally landed a blow to Siva's left cheek with the sickening thud of knuckle on bone, but instead of falling, the man moved into Jabari's body, deftly removing two small blades from within his vest and in a flurry of motion, stabbed him in the back and kidneys at least six times. This act repeated again and again, with Jabari landing blow after blow on Siva's face, splitting the flesh and pulverizing the meat, while his adversary, instead of falling, jumped forward, stabbing his opponent in the back, ribs, and chest with the knives.

Jabari seemed to slow, and as his fist found Siva's mouth, the smaller man spat a mixture of saliva and blood back into his face. Jabari staggered backward, weary and weakened by loss of blood from his now numerous wounds. He lunged forward again, this time, his punch finding only air. Siva laughed manically, his face swollen and cut, mangled by Jabari's massive fists, yet still moved with ease. Arian watched Jabari throw a slow and lumbering left hand. Siva used his own left hand to catch the strike at the forearm. As Jabari attempted to follow it up with his right hand, Arian could see the development of his friend's demise. Predicting the punch, Siva readied his knife in his right hand, re-positioning his grip on the handle. As the overhand right rained, Siva relaxed his grip on the forearm and ducking under the punch, executed a spinning backhanded blow, lodging the blade firmly and deeply into Jabari's throat. The giant, undefeatable hero of Arian's youth fell to the ground, his face in the sand.

Siva stood over Jabari, looking down at his latest conquest. He spat on the body of his fallen foe, before leaning down and pulling out the knife, allowing the warm blood from the wound to wash over his arm.

He stood again, stretching his back and popping his neck. Taking a deep breath to regain his composure, he heard the gun cock. Wheeling around, he found Alexandra standing with Arian's pistol aimed at his chest.

"Come on, child," he chided, his battered and swollen face unable to show emotion. "We both know you aren't going to fire that gun. You are a beautiful woman, caught up in a very bad thing. I will make sure no harm comes to you."

He stepped toward her and the gun fired, ripping a hole in the center of his chest. His legs collapsed under him, and he fell backwards to the ground, face-up. Alexandra rushed forward to stand over him. Concerned, Arian mustered his strength and popped his shoulder back into the socket. He felt a rush throughout his body as feeling returned. He ran to her side, clutching his injured arm. Alex stood over Siva, aiming the gun at his head, though she was not sure why. She was a Nephite, just as he was, but there was no sympathy in her soul. The powers of Arameus would view this as self-defense, but she had made her own arrangements with a little help from family. She began to weep as Arian came to her side, taking the gun from her trembling hands. Siva lay below them, twitching in the dirt, still alive, but not a threat.

"We have to go," said Arian in a hushed tone, clutching her around the waist. "He doesn't deserve a swift death."

Alex nodded to him. Arian walked to Jabari's motionless body. It took a massive effort to roll him over. He was shocked to hear choking sounds coming from his friend. Jabari was alive, though barely.

"Alex, get over here!" he yelled. "He's still alive. Give me your coat."

Removing her coat and using the switchblade Jabari had given him, he cut off one of the sleeves. Tying it around Jabari's throat, he was careful to make it just tight enough to stop the bleeding but not tight enough to strangle the man. He took a deep breath and grabbed Jabari under his arms, dragging him toward the cruiser. Alex joined in, easing the load. They were just a few feet away from the vehicle when they saw the Imperial troops exiting the door from which they had come. Arian watched as the men in front dropped down and aimed their weapons at him and Alex. He closed his eyes, waiting for the bullets to enter him, but instead felt an intense heat wash over him as he was thrown backward off his feet in a deafening explosion. It took him a few seconds to regain his bearings. He searched around and found Alex getting to her feet beside him. What had been the laboratory was now a massive fireball. Everyone who would have been pursuing them was now trapped inside, burning and dying. It gave him a strange feeling of satisfaction.

"Let's go," he yelled at Alex. "Help me get Jabari."

They dragged Jabari the rest of the way, with Alex helping maneuver him into the back of the vehicle. She remained there, tending to him and applying pressure to his many gaping wounds. Arian ran to the driver's side of the vehicle. Tossing the body of the man he only knew as Cooper onto the desert floor, he put the cruiser into gear and sped away from the nightmare of what had only an hour ago been an operational laboratory.

Arian drove into the desert, trying to put as much distance as he could between them and the traumatic scene they had just witnessed. Pulling the box of syringes from his coat, he tossed them into the empty passenger seat. A few of the syringes spilled out. He grabbed three and placed them back into his coat. He had a decision to make. For the first time since he had met Ansley and Kaiya, he was on his own. He could just drive into the desert and keep going, away from it all. He and Alex could have a life together. They had been together since birth. But what of Kaiya? He would not abandon her to Gravano. And all of those men who had died today, they believed in Ansley. They believed in a better future for their people. He would not abandon them either. He had learned much from Jabari, and devotion was foremost. He turned the vehicle and headed back to the rendezvous point.

Taking a wide trajectory to circumvent the burning building on the horizon, he hoped that the main force had been destroyed in the explosion. All involved in the battle would be assumed dead. No one would be looking for them. They drove as the yellow sun began to fade and the first rays of the red sun began to show. They passed what had been the lab without incident. As they sped up the embankment from which their force had originally descended, Arian could see the smoking husks of what had been their force. The remaining Imperial infantry had moved away, occupied by putting out the fire and searching the lab. They drove by, accosted by no one. Arian headed toward the Raven, hoping it was still there.

"Arian," came Alex's voice from the back. "He's waking up. He's alive."

Jabari coughed, spitting up blood. He tried to speak but was taken by a more violent fit of coughing. He was choking.

Alex lifted his head and shoulders slightly, letting his upper body rest on her, allowing the blood to drain down, away from his respiratory system.

He tried to speak.

"What is it?" asked Alex.

He tried again, this time with more success.

"You have to get to Ansley. He is the key. You have to get to Ansley and destroy all this." His body went limp and he was silent.

"Jabari," shouted Arian from the front. "Jabari, you have to stay with us. Try to stay with us. Where is Ansley? Jabari. Where is Ansley?"

Alex could barely hear Arian over the noise of the motor and repeated what she heard to the dying man. Jabari coughed fresh blood onto his chest and again tried to speak.

Arian couldn't hear him this time, but Alex leaned in close and listened.

"He says that Ansley has been arrested for treason. He is being held below the North Tower under the care of Tiberius Septus. You need to find Eduardo, within Capitol City. He can help you."

"Tell him to rest," Arian yelled back to Alex. "We will find him help soon."

Arian drove, unsure of what help they would find. Given Gravano's treatment of the last people he had tried to help, he didn't expect much, not to mention that the man had just led them into a trap. Still, he knew the type of man that Gravano was. He would do anything for a payment and Arian happened to have a payment that Gravano wasn't likely to turn down. It was only ten minutes more before the outline of the Raven came into view. There were no troops. This was the first of many victories that Arian would need in order to come out alive. He had no idea how he could get Ansley out of the North Tower, especially without the help of Jabari. They drove until they were only twenty yards from the Raven. Arian brought the cruiser to a halt. He had a plan.

The door opened and six soldiers exited the ramp, two by two, with Gravano himself coming to the door and stopping at the top of the ramp.

"I have come for Kaiya," yelled Arian, to the fat, disgusting man.

"Oh, Arian," said Gravano, "I'm so happy to see you survived. My lover boy is full of tricks."

"You led us into a trap, Christof, but I'm here. All of the Imperial troops are dead. Check your scanners if you don't believe me."

Gravano nodded to one of his men, who entered the Raven.

"You are most surprising, lover boy. You have much fight in you. Do not judge me too harshly. I did what I had to do to survive. Still, I have something you want. I have the superior position. Do you have my payment?"

"I have what you want," replied Arian. "Bring me Kaiya and you shall have it."

Gravano laughed his disgusting laugh. "My boy, you have made a mistake. Why should I not just take what I want from you, now that I know you have it? My men could just as easily kill you and take it from your lifeless body."

"The Imperial soldiers are all dead, Christof. We destroyed them. I have over thirty cruisers surrounding this perimeter, many with anti-aircraft guns. I can have you destroyed with nothing more than a word."

"I see. You are an interesting Nephite aren't you? Growing a pair of balls all of a sudden. Very well. Walk the bots to me. You give me my payment, and I will give you that which you desire to possess."

"How do I know she's alive?"

Gravano motioned to an unseen guard. Kaiya was thrust forward, squirming, yet held tight by the two men.

"Arian!" she screamed.

"I'm coming forward, Christof," yelled Arian, "with your payment. If you harm either of us, then your Raven will be destroyed, rest assured."

Arian put the cruiser into park, leaving the motor running. Trying to ignore the bloody remnants of the previous driver, he grabbed the box of syringes from the seat beside him and exited the vehicle. As he crept forward, he heard Alex's voice from behind.

"I'm coming with you."

"Stay in the vehicle. You aren't safe with me."

Alex laughed.

"You were safe with me when I killed that Formaddi. Who are you to deny me? I'm coming with you. Perhaps a pretty face will be of some use."

Arian shrugged, walking forward, Alex by his side. As they began to walk up the ramp that led to Gravano, the guards that flanked it glared menacingly. Unperturbed, Arian and Alex moved forward, stopping five feet from Gravano. Arian held the box containing the bio-bots in his hands.

"Give them over, boy, and you will have the girl," demanded Gravano.

"You are in no position to negotiate, Christof. We are being monitored. One wrong word and we all die here in this wretched desert. I don't think either of us wants that."

"I tire of your games, you fool. You're bluffing, and you will die today at my hand."

"Now boys," said Alex from his side. "There is no need for all the testosterone." She turned to Arian and took the box of syringes from his hands. He stared at her, shocked. "Trust me," she whispered.

Walking forward, she handed the box to Don Gravano.

"Here you go, Uncle. Is this what you wanted?"

"Alexandra," he said kissing her lightly on her cheek. "If your father were alive, he would be so proud of you. I see my purchase of your station has not been entirely in vain."

"Of course not, uncle. Please, just don't hurt Arian. I care for him."

"For you, my dear niece, anything." He hugged her tightly to his body before announcing to his guards, "Get on board, boys. We're leaving. There is no threat here."

Arian rushed forward, attempting to enter the Raven, but a kick to the chest from Gravano sent him tumbling down the ramp, back to the desert. As he looked up, he could still see Kaiya being held by the guards. They released her as the Raven began to rise from the ground. The last he saw of Alex, she was shoving Kaiya forward before the doors closed, sending her tumbling to the sandy floor below. She landed with a soft thud, and Arian watched as the Raven disappeared into the early evening sky.

# Chapter Twenty-Seven
## The Die is Cast

Arian scrambled to his feet and rushed over to Kaiya, who lay motionless on the desert floor. When he saw her tiny rib cage rising and falling as she inhaled the dry air, he was overjoyed. She was alive. He hadn't yet dealt with what had occurred. The thought that Alex was the niece of Don Gravano was too much for him now. It was enough that Alex had thrown Kaiya from the Raven, returning him his obsession. Leaning down, he turned her over. Her eyes opened and she smiled sweetly before reaching up and kissing him lightly on the cheek.

"You did it, my love. You saved me." He embraced her.

"A lot of men died today, darling, for us. No matter what, I can never go back to what I was. Dante and his family, the people of Beladero, they can't have died in vain." Arian paused, steeling himself for the admission he knew was forthcoming. "From here on, I will do what I can to undermine Arameus. Will you come with me?"

Kaiya stared ahead, her chameleon eyes changing

emotion at will. "I will follow you anywhere, my love."

"You may regret that," replied Arian, lifting her to her feet and guiding her to the cruiser, "because we are going to Capitol City to free Ansley."

Kaiya stopped in her tracks. "You can't be serious. Arian, even if we could get into the city, we are the most wanted people in the Empire. You promised we would go to Beladero and be safe."

"I assure you, we will be going to Beladero, only it will not be to hide, and we will not be safe. Beladero is the center of a well-organized resistance. And Tiberius was right all along. Ansley has been planning something big… something that will change the world. Get in the cruiser and I will explain on the way. Sit in the back and look after Jabari. We need to keep him alive."

"Jabari? The Patolli player?"

"He doesn't have much time."

In the cruiser, Arian was surprised by how nonchalant Kaiya was toward the gravely wounded man. She lifted his head and allowed it to rest on her lap, applying light pressure to the sleeve tied around his neck. Blood covered her forearms and soiled her tunic. Arian put the cruiser into gear, checked the compass on the dashboard, and turned the vehicle north, back toward Capitol City. Kaiya sat in silence, calmly observing the man dying in her arms. Arian found her keen interest in the macabre situation disarming.

"So how are we supposed to get into the city undetected?" she asked.

"There is a hidden entrance into the city that leads to the Patolli stadium. The players use it to enter the dome without going through customs. Your task is to get Jabari to wake up and give us his clearance code."

"And once we're in?" she asked, unconvinced.

"Jabari says we need to seek out Eduardo. I believe you are familiar with him."

"Eduardo! Have you lost your mind? Eduardo is one of Tiberius' paid informants. We will be in the custody of the city guards within an hour."

Arian shook his head. "Tiberius has been played a fool by Ansley and Eduardo. If Jabari says we should find him, then that is what we should do."

"Ansley also trusted Gravano to deliver us safely and we see how that turned out."

"He did so grudgingly. I put him in a tough situation to save you. I used the fact that he needs me. I just hope we can find him and make it right."

"We need to be going the other direction, Arian. We can make a life outside of Arameus. You don't need to be caught up in Ansley's crazy quest. It was never your fight."

"Well, it's my fight now!" snapped Arian. "I've seen how the people outside the domes are treated. I have witnessed the Overseers' cruelty and their unquenchable thirst for control and I no longer wish to be a part of their machine. We have no time to argue. I came for you and you owe me. Tonight we are destroying Capitol City. Now try to wake up Jabari and get us the code to the fucking arena!"

In the rear view mirror Arian could see Kaiya's eyes narrow menacingly at his outburst of anger before her impassive gaze returned. For a second, he thought she was going to attack him. Instead, she shifted her gaze back to Jabari. Over the hum of the motor, he heard her whispering to him. She shook him and he began to stir. He was alive. Beyond all reasonable expectation, with his many wounds and massive blood loss, the giant man was alive.

"Jabari," she whispered, in her girlish voice. "Jabari, you need to wake up."

His eyes remained closed but he began to mutter something that Arian couldn't hear. Kaiya leaned in closer.

"Daniella. I need Daniella."

"This is Daniella," Kaiya whispered seductively in his ear. "You're home with me, baby."

"I'm not going to make it, Danny. You need to get out of Beladero. Go far away." Jabari exhaled slowly, and Kaiya was unsure if he would ever breathe again.

"You can't go yet, my darling. I need one more thing from you. Baby, I need the code to the secret city entrance. I need this one last thing from you, and then you can die, here in my arms."

"Danny," he muttered again, this time, much more feeble, his voice breathy and bereft of its former baritone.

"Jabari, I need the code. What is the code to enter the city?"

His dark skin had taken on a dull, ashy luster and his eyes were unfocused, yet she could see tears forming in their corners. Summoning his remaining strength, he spoke his last words.

"The code is 1-4-3-6-6-6. Danny, I love you," he said, his lip quivering.

"I love you too, darling," she whispered into his ear as she untied the makeshift tourniquet from his neck allowing the blood to again pump liberally from the ruptured artery. Jabari took three more shallow breaths before he exhaled for the last time, an extended death rattle. His eyes remained open, gazing forever upward toward Danny. Kaiya sat transfixed, returning his gaze the remainder of the drive, whispering into his ear the entire time. Arian never knew what she said.

By the time they reached the player's entrance to the dome, the red sun was high in the sky, and all traces of yellow light were gone. Kaiya retied the tourniquet around Jabari's neck. Arian shut down the engine and turned back to her.

"How is he?" he asked, but one look at his fallen comrade was all he needed to ascertain the answer. Kaiya shook her head from side to side.

"He died peacefully."

Arian exited the vehicle and walked toward Kaiya. Helping her out, he could see she was covered in blood, as was he. This would not be a good way to enter the city.

"Were you able to get the code?"

"With his dying breath."

"Good." Arian leaned down into the vehicle and pushed Jabari's eyelids together, closing them for eternity.

Instinctively, he pulled the switchblade from his pocket, folded it in the dead man's fingers, and crossed his arms on his chest.

"Goodbye, my friend. You deserve much better than this, but we still have work to do. I will tell Daniella of your heroism today." With a sigh, he steadied himself and turned, ready to face the challenges ahead. He would complete Ansley's quest and die for the cause, this much he knew. He had one more night, and he would spend it fruitfully.

"Who's Daniella?" asked Kaiya, with too much cheer.

"His wife," he answered blankly. Kaiya's charms were lost to him after all he had been through. He could feel the weight in his eyes. His energy was waning and he was in desperate need of a nano-treatment. "Let's go. The key pad is this way."

He led her to the pad and, after lifting the metal covering, allowed her to enter the code. The hydraulic system deep beneath hummed to life and the door lifted, exposing the hallway leading into the underbelly of the great city. The fluorescent lights that guided the path from overhead flickered to life. As the bulbs reanimated, they illuminated the tunnel, which seemed more foreboding than it had on his previous re-entry. Behind them lay a field of death and destruction and they were running toward more of the same. The path before them was set, and now it was time to see just how well Ansley had organized this resistance.

As they walked in silence, Kaiya slipped her hand into his. Her presence and touch calmed him. They were in this together now, and it felt good to know that he had someone on his side. After a half hour of not speaking, her voice came as a surprise to him.

"So what exactly is in Beladero?"

"I guess there's no reason for secrets anymore," Arian replied. "It's a particle accelerator. The largest and most powerful ever built. It can generate energies similar to those during the creation of the universe."

"And how is this supposed to change the balance of power?" asked Kaiya.

"It will sound a bit crazy, but it can generate enough energy to warp space and time itself, opening a wormhole. Ansley has been entertaining a crazy idea that through this wormhole, we can send information back to the time before the rise of the Empire and somehow prevent it. He was romantically involved with my mother, you see," he said, stopping midstride and dropping his gaze to the cement floor as if embarrassed. Kaiya looked up at him.

"The thing is," continued Arian, "my mother and her partner Richard developed the nanocytes that allow extended life. Ansley's idea is that if we can prevent Nanosoft from gaining this technology and giving it to the Overseers, they will die naturally, and all of this will be prevented."

"That is a ridiculous idea," responded Kaiya. "And I don't understand," she continued, "why you figure into this plan at all. He took a huge risk that ultimately led to his arrest. What was the purpose?"

"His secondary purpose was to have me give instructions for the development of the bio-bots that were being created in the lab we destroyed today. With the bots, no continued treatments are necessary and their production cannot be controlled. Were we to give the people of the past this knowledge, it could be shared with the world, and the Overseers would lose their power."

Kaiya moved closer to him. "So what you are saying is that with this machine, we could go back and fix the mistakes of the past?"

"It's possible in theory. However in practice, there is much more to consider. You would not understand the subtleties."

"I guess not. But imagine it, Arian. Imagine having the power to change all the wrongs in your life. Imagine having the ability to go back and anticipate the political movements and take control. If this machine does what you say, we would have this power. We could be the new Overseers and rule justly, with empathy for the people."

Arian chuckled, his weariness evident.

"I don't think people could travel back, my love. The radiation alone, not to mention the gravitational forces, would destroy them. Replacing one Overseer with another doesn't sound like much of a change anyway. We will get Ansley and proceed with the plan."

Kaiya grinned and stood on her tiptoes, craning her neck to kiss him on the mouth. He looked down at her, taking in her beauty. She was so small and lovely. He was overwhelmed with the need to protect her.

"Of course, baby," she chirped. "And what happens to us if this plan is successful?"

"It doesn't matter. Nothing matters now. This Empire cannot be allowed to continue. Look at our lives - you a sex slave, me a puppet. We aren't being the people we were meant to be. Somewhere in the cosmos, we will exist again, in a better world and with a better outcome. For now we will be the tragic heroes. This place needs one."

"Then lead on, hero," she replied, irony heavy in her tone.

They traversed the remaining distance without a word. At the clearance pad, Kaiya entered the code that Jabari had given her with his dying breath. The door opened, revealing the Gliders' locker room, and against all odds, they were back in Capitol City. Arian reached into his pocket and fingered the qubit Gravano had given him upon setting off for Sikyon. After everything that had occurred, it was still there. He hit a button on the top, and the qubit buzzed with life. Being an unofficial and off the grid qubit, it had no AI host. He could use it as he needed with no need to worry of being tracked or recognized as being other than Gravano.

"The Devonshire Pub," he said into the speaker.

Within seconds, the line was ringing on the other end and he was connected.

"Devonshire Pub, this is Carlos," said a thickly accented voice.

"I need to talk to Eduardo," Arian demanded.

"Umm… He's busy. Can I take a message?"

"Is he in the pub?"

"I'm not at liberty to say," replied Carlos.

"It's about Ansley!" screamed Arian, losing patience. "Get him on the fucking phone."

Silence followed. The seconds stretched into minutes and just as Arian was about to end the call and seek out another option, a familiar voice came from the other end of the line.

"Who is this? What do you want?"

"Eduardo, it's Arian. Jabari told me we could trust you to help us. I'm here to free Ansley."

"We have this under control. You are nothing," came Eduardo's reply. "Ansley was a fool to trust you. I warned him. You are nothing but a tool of Tiberius' concubine. I saw it at the Four Corners and again with your irresponsible trip to Sikyon. You are not a part of this movement. You are a liability. If this is a ploy to arrest me, then come do so. You know where I am. You will find we don't go quietly."

"I have no quarrel with you, Eduardo, and you were right about me all along. But things have changed. I have seen what Ansley and you are fighting for, and so has Kaiya. I'm here to get Ansley and fulfill his mission. I will do it with or without your help."

"Why should I believe you? I have heard nothing from Jabari. It was he who was to determine your true allegiance."

"Jabari is dead, Eduardo. He was killed by a Formaddi assassin. He died saving us, and I will not disrespect his death by failing in the task for which he gave his life. I am ready to sacrifice myself for the cause. The walls are closing in on all of us, Eddie. We can make a stand now and see this through or fall to the Overseers like all those before us. You choose."

There was silence on the other end of the line. Then Eduardo spoke.

"I don't like you or trust you, and if you have a gun you should put a bullet in Kaiya's head right now. We have a plan in the works to save Ansley, but it's suicide. We are rebels, and we will die as such. We have tracking systems in all of our cruisers, and our elite men carry microchips in the skin so that we can track their movements. I see that you are not lying. Jabari's body lies next to the western entrance of the dome. No amount of torture would have caused him to give you the code. I assume you will be exiting the South Tower. We will have a man pick you up in ten minutes to bring you here. You were correct about the walls closing in. We must move tonight."

The call ended. Arian and Kaiya moved though the locker room and into the back hallways of the stadium under the South Tower. It was late now, and everyone had left for the day. They walked through dark hallways, Arian remembering the path they had taken with Raul. Exiting the tower into the cool climate-controlled air of the dome, they saw a man standing beside a cab.

"Arian and Kaiya, I assume," said the man. "I was sent by Eduardo to transport you. Let's go. We don't have much time."

They stepped into the light and approached the cab. The man recoiled from them in disgust. Arian looked to Kaiya and saw the dark crimson that stained her arms and shirt and then looked down to find the same on his own being.

"I guess the war has started," said the driver, attempting to laugh.

"It will be a short war," replied Arian, pulling Kaiya past the man and guiding her into the cab. "Let's go."

They drove through the streets in silence to the outskirts of the Central Isle, away from the tower, across the bridge, and into the Southern pub district. Arian was surprised by how few people he saw walking the streets. It had to be no more than eight at night.

"Driver, why is there no one out?" he asked.

"Because it's Monday. Do you go to bars on a Monday night?"

Arian had lost track of the days since he had been gone, but the driver must be correct. This was even better for their endeavors. No one, not even Capitol City guards, work hard on a Monday. His thoughts went to his lab. He ached to see it again and to talk to his graduate students that he had long neglected, but he knew that this was a privilege that was forever lost to him. Even if he had not engaged in today's traitorous activities, Conway's actions would have sealed his fate. And now Conway lay dead, charred in the ruins of the tomb he had built for himself. It was just as well. Arian was not the same man he had been when he left Capitol City, and he no longer desired what he had before.

They passed Ansley's favorite casino, now rebuilt and open, and passed the Devonshire as well, where he had first conversed with his imprisoned friend. Not two weeks ago, he would have felt that Ansley's imprisonment was justified, but now he wished for nothing more than to free the man and alleviate the guilt that gnawed at his soul. The cab took a hard left down an alley, followed by another, and then stopped at the rear entrance to the Devonshire. Exiting the vehicle, Arian guided Kaiya toward the screened backdoor, but as he moved to open it, the driver yelled for him to stop.

"Not that way, Señor. This way." He tossed aside some empty garbage cans to reveal a hidden cellar door. "We meet below."

Shrugging his shoulders, Arian followed the man, along with Kaiya, as he unlatched the doors and led them down the stairs to the space below.

The ceiling was low, so low that Arian had to duck his head. The room was unfinished with drainage water puddling on the ground, and the air was thick with humidity, betraying poor circulation. His nose filled with the putrid smells of sewage, and he fought the urge to gag. As he looked to the far end of the room, he found a group of five men who seemed frozen, as if interrupted by unexpected visitors. Feeling Kaiya's grip on his shoulder, Arian froze as well, as for the first time he noticed that four of the men were Imperial guards, surrounding a man who could only be Eduardo, weapons in hand.

"I told you we couldn't trust him!" shouted Kaiya. As they turned to exit, they found themselves face to face with the barrel of a gun, held by the man who had driven them to the

Devonshire.

"Why in such a hurry, my friends?" Eduardo asked from across the room, an air of laughter in his voice. "I thought you came to visit. Come. Join us." He seated himself at a table across from two chairs to which he now beckoned.

"Please, friends, have a seat."

With no other choice, they obliged. Arian was tense, aware of the gun pointed at his back, along with the guns of the Imperial troops.

"Would you like a drink?" asked Eduardo, with no hint of sarcasm.

When they both shook their heads, he seemed offended.

"No! I insist. How about Sagittarian Wine? We will wait to begin. Raphael, please fetch us a bottle." A man emerged from the corner and ascended the staircase to the pub. They waited in silence, Eduardo seeming to relish in the situation, the guards looking down menacingly, and Arian unsure of what to say or do to get out of the situation. He wondered how Kaiya felt. Her expression, as always, was unreadable.

Raphael arrived with the wine and three glasses, popping the cork and pouring into each. As he placed the glasses in front of the people seated at the table, no one moved. Eduardo sat smiling.

"I guess my humor is lost on you, friends. I apologize sincerely. I thought it would be good to celebrate our first meeting at the Four Corners. It was Sagittarian Wine if I am correct?" He looked at Kaiya, his smile never wavering. She smiled back politely, saying nothing.

"Drink, please. I beg of you," continued Eduardo.

"While I do appreciate the wine, Eduardo, I find that its intricacies will be lost, overwhelmed by this disgusting sewer you inhabit," said Kaiya, her voice full of disdain.

"You have lost none of your charms, my dear, but I think perhaps it is not the sewer that chafes you, but the fact that it is not I who am serving you. You are here as my guest."

"Looks like you finally learned to speak properly,"

replied Kaiya.

"I've played my part as the dumb Natural Born servant. And I know you have played yours. I have no hate for you, Kaiya. Just disappointment in how you turned your back on your people when confronted with luxury."

As Arian stood, five bullets entered their respective chambers with their owners' barrels aimed at him.

"You've won, Eduardo. We took the bait and you caught us. We've been through too much today for your gloating. Just know that Kaiya was never a part of this. She doesn't deserve to be brought before the Security Counsel. I brought her here, and it is I who wished to save Ansley. I beg you to please spare her. Let her go. She's no threat."

Eduardo leaned back and studied Arian, struggling with something. Finally, he broke into laughter, followed by the guards and the driver behind them.

"Shit, kid, you really are scared of these guards. You're a regular rebel now, aren't you? I would have never thought it in a thousand years. Maybe Ansley was right about you."

The guards backed down, and Eduardo stood, reaching his hand across the table to greet them. Arian took it, still confused. Kaiya abstained, refusing to look at the man.

"You know?" Eddie continued. "I was sure you were working for them. The guards were a good touch, huh? They told me everything I needed to know about your motives. You guys were depressed as hell when you saw them. That's when I knew. Damn, man, take a drink of this wine. Let's not waste it. Pardon the smell!"

Kaiya abstained, sitting in the same position, leaving her wine untouched. Arian, however, grabbed his glass and stood in a celebratory toast with Eduardo.

"You have no idea how much better I feel right now," said Arian. "From the beginning of this day, I have been waiting for the hammer to fall, and it has, over and over again, on the men of Beladero, on Jabari, but I held out hope that somehow we could save Ansley. When I saw the guards, I felt all the deaths were for nothing, but now, I feel like we can actually do it. How much good luck does a man need? A whole fucking lot… Give me a gun and I will shoot my way through."

Primal screams erupted from every man present as they drank and postured with fake bravado, immune to the inevitable fate that lay before. Only Kaiya sat in silence.

"So how are we going to do this?" asked Arian.

"This is the purpose of the guards, you see. We have acquired these garments over many years. Luckily, nothing ever changes in Arameus. Our plan was to come to the North Tower as a guard change and once inside, work from there. The challenge is to get past the initial security and into the dungeons. Without a passcode, we will be vulnerable, and I believe it would be unwise to assault the front guards to gain entry. We will likely be stopped long before we reach Ansley, yet we need to move tonight. The Overseers' next move will be on Beladero."

"Exactly," replied Arian. "Many of the City Guard will be at the bot facility, searching for survivors and salvaging what they can. Tonight is the night to act."

"Then you are with us, death be damned?" asked Eduardo.

"Death be damned."

Kaiya laughed from her seat at the table.

"Do you have something to add, my dear?" asked Eduardo.

Kaiya stood, her blood-drenched tunic tracing the curves of her body. Grabbing the wine glass by the stem, she sipped its contents. All eyes in the room were now on her.

"You must want to die," she said, sipping the blood red liquid. "But I assure you dumb boys, there is an easier way. Perhaps none of you brutes need to die today. However, if you want to rush the North Tower in your costumes, then by all means, be my guest. I will wait here alone for word of your… success."

Arian, furious at her demeanor, grabbed her by the arm. "If you have another way, then now is not the time to be coy!"

He threw her arm down violently.

Rubbing the spot on her forearm, Kaiya gazed at the floor before again addressing the room.

"All I'm saying is that if Ansley is being held in the North Tower, then it's under the authority of the new Chief Security Officer of Capitol City. As it happens, I have lived in his household for the last twenty years and am well acquainted with the servants. Suppose we went to his home, absconded with his qubit, and walked into Ansley's prison, along with these 'guards', as expected guests?"

Eduardo shot across the room before Arian could react, and shoved a handgun into Kaiya's cheek, grabbing her hard by the back of the neck to secure her in the process.

"And what if you just deliver us all to your former lover in an effort to regain your place in the city? Once a whore, always a whore. Why should we trust you?"

"If I am merely a whore," she replied, looking up at him with large eyes, "then I have no master. Perhaps I am your whore now?"

Arian stepped in, shoving Eduardo aside. "She's with us, and you will not disrespect her again! Her plan sounds a lot better than yours. Kaiya, can you get us into Tiberius's house and gain access to his qubit?"

"Without a doubt, my love."

Eduardo rolled his eyes.

"Then that is what we'll attempt. Will you help us?" he asked, looking at Eduardo.

Glancing around the room and seeing the nods of solidarity from his men, Eduardo agreed.

"Then our path is clear," continued Arian. "We accompany Kaiya to Tiberius' place, and she gets us the qubit. From there, we enter as interrogators on behalf of the Consulate. His automated assistant will pave the way for our entrance. The guards will make us seem more official. We retrieve Ansley on behalf of Tiberius and bring him here."

Eduardo eyed Arian and then Kaiya before calling Raphael to him and whispering into his ear. They spoke back and forth for a moment, before Eduardo looked back to them.

"We will do it Kaiya's way, as it seems to give us the best chance of success, but keep this in mind," he added, focusing his gaze on Kaiya. "We have men and women all over this town and this resistance goes deeper than even Ansley could imagine. If you double cross us, you will die tonight." He was looking at Kaiya now. "I almost want you to give me a reason."

# Chapter Twenty-Eight
## A Prisoner of Fate

Pulling up to the front gate of Tiberius Septus' household, Arian was nervous, not just because Kaiya would be entering the home of her former lover, but also because he was not convinced of her loyalty. His experience with Eduardo's men had done little to alleviate the doubts. Stepping out of the car, she looked back at Arian, as if to reassure him. As the transport moved to a safe distance, over a block away, he watched her walk toward the black iron gates.

Kaiya stared at the keypad, knowing the number that would gain her entry, but choosing to bypass this method. Instead, she pushed the intercom button. After some static, she heard a voice on the other end.

"Consulate Septus' house."

"Idalia, this is Kaiya, I need to see Tiberius."

"Oh my! Where have you been? We were so worried about you."

"Can you let me in, Idalia? I really need to talk to him."

"I need Gallia to override the security, let me get her."

Kaiya waited for a few minutes by the gate. Looking down at herself, she wondered why she hadn't thought to change out of her blood soaked clothing at the Devonshire. She hoped in her heart that Idalia would not alert Tiberius but only Gallia. After a moment, her fears were allayed.

"If this is Kaiya, then what are the names of my three children," came Gallia's voice.

"Well," answered Kaiya, "there is that precocious little devil Miguel, that beautiful bastard Petrov, and that trouble maker Pieter." Kaiya placed her hands on her hips. "And I know you guys can see me, so let me in. I need to speak with Tiberius."

The gate opened and Kaiya entered, walking straight to the front door of the mansion to meet Gallia. The door opened and the two women embraced.

"Oh, mistress," said Gallia, "he will be so happy to see you. He has been a shell of himself without you."

Looking Kaiya over and seeing for the first time her blood-soaked garments, her mouth dropped and she looked as if she would scream.

"Shhh," said Kaiya, raising her finger to her mouth. "I will explain later. I want to surprise my love."

"Of course," replied Gallia, taking two steps back from the petite woman.

Kaiya walked through the kitchen and the dark empty dining room, stopping before a hutch that held the fine silver of the house. Rummaging quietly through its contents, she selected a carving knife, used to cut the meat from large birds when they hosted dinners. She slid the knife carefully into the leg of her black leather boots so that only the very top of the handle was visible. Who looked at Kaiya's shoes? She found the stairs and walked up, cautious so as not to make a sound. This was unnecessary. Tiberius would be happy to greet her, in spite of the fact that he had left her to rot in Sikyon. It would be rectified soon. She knew the man as well as she knew herself, and regardless of how he felt about her, he would be no issue.

She walked down the hallway past the bathroom where he showered and prepared for the day. She had watched him get ready for the Parliament in that room a thousand times, yet she felt nothing but disdain for the man as she approached his room. Twenty years together in luxury and she had been tossed aside as if nothing. As her footsteps sounded throughout the oaken hallway, she hoped he would hear her and as she turned the corner to the atrium that led to his quarters, he did.

"Gallia? Have you brought my tea?" came his voice, once seductive, but now terrible.

Kaiya moved effortless across the white marble. Looking down at her bloodstained white blouse, she shed it, along with her bra. Continuing to walk and noticing the blood on her skirt, she shed it as well, along with her underwear, so that she stood at his door, naked and ready to confront him, made more beautiful by the fierce gaze in her eyes and Jabari's crimson red blood, now dried on her forearms.

He opened the door. "Gallia, what the…."

The words froze in his mouth as he took in her beauty. His Kaiya had returned, and everything else was meaningless.

She stepped forward, throwing her body into his. "Did you think I would go away so easily? We had a life together."

"My love," he stuttered, pulling her close in jubilation. "You came back to me. I have done everything for you, my dear. I have it all worked out with the Overseers. We can be together. I am to be given an island. You will be my princess there. I love you so much, my Kaiya."

She guided him toward the bed.

"You promise, honey? You would do all that for me?" she asked, as she unzipped his pants and dropped them to the floor.

"I would do anything for you, my love," he replied, breathless, allowing her to disrobe him and push him backward toward the bed. "I only want to be with you."

"And I with you, my darling," she replied as she shoved her lithe naked body forward, knocking him onto the bed. As she worked her nude pelvis up his body, she nestled her face to his and could hear him speaking, and at the same time, felt his arousal.

"I was going to come and find you," he said, as he shoved himself into her. "I missed you so much."

"I missed you, too," said Kaiya, as she reached to her boot, to the grip of the hidden blade, still enthralling Tiberius with the passion of her body. He hardly noticed as she thrust the silver knife downward, into his heart. The blade eased into the chest cavity, slicing past the ribs and sternum just as easily as it carved a roast duck.

He coughed, spitting up blood. For her, it was as if he had climaxed. She looked into his glassy, dying eyes and spoke to him, as she had wanted to for years.

"Oh... now that is interesting, isn't it? You can die, you pompous motherfucker. And a Natural Born can kill you. I hope you have a miserable afterlife in whatever terrible utopia you dead assholes can dream up."

She leaned down close to him, feeling his manhood shrinking inside of her. "My darling," she whispered into his ear, removing his disgusting member from her, "Nice means nothing."

Tiberius continued to stare forward, a stunned look on his face, but he never again spoke. As his last breath rattled out from his unmoving diaphragm, she moved away and stood looking down, examining his frozen features in the same odd way in which she had watched Jabari as he died. A change in the lighting snapped her back to attention, drawing her gaze to the door. There, a frightened and shocked Gallia stood, unmoving. The two women, longtime household companions but never friends, looked at one another for a moment, as if sizing up the situation. Finally, Kaiya broke the awkward silence.

"Well, Gallia, your choices here are simple. You can

either alert on me, or you can help me. Tonight the Natural Born will strike back at all of those who have oppressed us."

"I will not alert on you, my dear. I'm not sure the master deserved that death, but I am also not sure that he did not," came her reply.

"Then I need one thing from you, Gallia. A last request, and then you and Idalia must leave Capitol City and never return."

"What can I do to help you?" asked Gallia. She seemed distracted, and unable to ignore the dead man in the center of the bed. Kaiya stood, naked, covered in blood, a terrible and beautiful huntress. She would do anything this woman asked of her.

"I am assuming you still download Tiberius' notes from his qubit every night?"

"I do."

"Then you have the access codes to Pandora."

She nodded her head in acknowledgement.

"And do you have the access codes to the Central Tower security database? Surely you must prepare notes for his Security Council meetings. Can you access the dungeons of the North Tower?"

Again, Gallia remained silent, but nodded her head in affirmation.

"Perfect. Fetch me his qubit and write down the access codes for me. I must shower and dress. Leave the qubit in here for me and then let my friends enter and have them wait in the parlor downstairs. I will be down shortly."

She followed Gallia out of the room, stopping to pick up her bloody garments. Walking into the shower room, she locked the door behind her. Finally alone, she closed her eyes and allowed herself a moment to calm down, taking deep breaths. From the pants in her hand, she removed the short-wave transponder that Eduardo had given her back at the Devonshire. Pressing down on the talk button, she informed her companions of the current situation.

"Tiberius is away for the night. The servants believe he is at the bio-bot lab, searching the ruins. I have his qubit and access codes. Gallia will let you in. She has no love for him or Arameus. We will take his personal transport to the North Tower. It will allow us entry without question."

"Are you sure it is safe?" came Eduardo's hesitant reply. "I would hate to think you would double-cross us at this point."

"If I were going to double-cross you, would I invite five armed men into a house with three women and a Consulate? What purpose would that serve?"

"I hope for your sake that it is only you women," said Eduardo, and Kaiya heard brief static as he released his talk button.

Rolling her eyes, she couldn't help but think how much better the world would be if all men were removed from it. She walked down into the basin of the shower, which, triggered by her motion, rained down hot water and soap, scrubbing her body clean of the blood, dirt, and gore from the day's activities. There was no telling what the night would hold. She cleared her mind, allowing herself to enjoy the first hot shower she had had in weeks. The water stopped and the hot vent kicked on, blowing her body dry. She exited the basin and walked to the corner of the dressing room that Tiberius had reserved for her dresses, happy to see that they were still in place. Selecting a short, purple evening dress, she slipped it over her head, and wrapped her hair in a purple lace ribbon, fixing it in a sort of loose bun that was the style at the time. Purple was a good choice, as it was the official Imperial color. She would look right in place next to her guards. Glancing in the mirror, she couldn't help but notice how beautiful she looked. It was a shame a gown like this had to be wasted on a prison break and flight into the desert.

Walking away from her small portion of shelves that lined the circular room, she looked through Tiberius' clothes, searching for something for Arian and Eduardo to wear. Neither of the men had guard uniforms and would stick out in their group, particularly Arian in his bloodstained outfit. Since Arian and Tiberius were close to the same build, she settled on a dress military uniform. Tiberius had never been a military man, but dignitaries were expected to observe such formalities at patriotic parades and the like. This was the perfect outfit for their task. Eduardo, with his hulking frame and awkward disposition, was another matter. There was no way he could pass for anything other than a Natural Born, and the Natural Born did not enter the North Tower holding cells. He would have to wait in the transport. Bringing him along was not worth endangering the mission.

She sat at a dressing table and put on a fresh pair of high black boots retrieved from her closet. Opening a drawer, she pulled out her old bottle of perfume, spraying it liberally on her neck. The air around her was filled with the scent of lavender, grapefruit rind, and animal musk. She stood, glancing one last time in the mirror, before exiting the bathing area and heading back to Tiberius' room, where he was unceremoniously holding a visitation for no one. The qubit and a notepad filled with access codes were on the bedside table. She examined both, and was pleased with Gallia's work.

Tiberius had been dead for over half an hour, and the loss of blood along with the weakness of his dead-eyed stare made him appear much less imposing than he had in life. His long frost-white hair, which had once given him a distinguished quality, now made him seem frail and elderly. In the reality glimpsed through death, he was an old and feeble man.

She reached down and yanked the knife from the dead man's thoracic cavity. It didn't come out nearly as easily as it had entered as rigor mortis had set in and caused the muscles to tighten around the knife. She wiped the blood onto the white linen sheets and carefully placed the knife back into her knee high boot, the top of which was just obscured by the purple dress. She walked down to meet her companions in the parlor below.

Entering the room, she gasped at the sight of Gallia and Idalia on their knees, each with a gun to the back of their head.

Eduardo stood in the rear, looking on in a silent challenge. The two gunmen seemed uncomfortable threatening the helpless servants, and threw repeated glances to their leader, imploring him to rescind the order. Arian himself was frozen by the tension in the room. The possibility for violence was tangible.

"What the hell? They're helping us!" screamed Kaiya, beside herself with rage.

"This is how you re-pay them?"

"I just want to be sure of one thing," said Eduardo, stepping forward. "Why would Tiberius Septus leave his household to inspect the bio-bot lab, yet leave his qubit behind? It doesn't add up."

Kaiya was caught, unable to speak.

"I would hate to think you are lying to us," continued Eduardo. "Well... What is it?"

Accustomed to stress, she relaxed and answered. "What do I need to do to make you trust me, Eduardo?" asked Kaiya.

"I guess you need to earn that trust," he answered.

"I see. Follow me. I have something to show you. Just you."

Eduardo glanced at his men. "If you hear anything from upstairs, execute the two women and set off the charges in your packs. No one will leave here alive." He looked stonily at Kaiya and followed her up the stairs to the remains of Tiberius Septus.

Kaiya sat on a clean part of the bed, beside the body, patting a leg that was growing colder by the minute. She looked to Eduardo seductively and patted a place on the bed beside her.

"Well, what do you think big guy? Want to join me?"

Eduardo was horrified. He had been in battles and had killed men, but never in so callous and hateful a way. His struggles had been out of necessity. Surveying the brutal scene, it was obvious the killer had enjoyed the act, and observing her now, he could tell that she still did.

"Shit, woman, you are one crazy bitch," was all he could utter.

"Do you trust me now?" she asked, batting her eyes ironically.

"Hell no, but I know you aren't on his side."

"Good. Then let my friends go. They are good women and innocent victims in this. We have the qubit, the access codes, and Tiberius' transport. We can succeed tonight if you will get out of the way."

"Perhaps I underestimated you," said Eduardo, shooting another glance at the corpse. "I will do so again at my own peril."

"One thing, Eduardo. Don't mention a word of this to Arian. He doesn't need to know."

"I see," the man replied, though by his expression, he was unconvinced. "Let's go. We have much to do."

As they re-entered the parlor area, Arian looked to Kaiya, seeking some sort of explanation. She shook her head, brushing him off.

"Release the women," Eduardo ordered. "They are free to go." The men lowered their guns and the two women stood. Kaiya rushed to them, hugging them each in turn.

"I know we haven't had the best or most fair relationship, but I wish you both nothing but the best," she said. "Go to your homes, get your families, and get as far from here as possible. It may not be safe for the Natural Born surrounding the city after this night."

Both women nodded and rushed out the door, not bothering to look back at the six men inhabiting the room. Kaiya watched from the window as they exited the house and wondered what would happen to them. Even if they were able to make it to safety, what would be the implications of Arian and Ansley's overall designs for them or any of the others in the room? She shook off her thoughts and typed in Pandora's access code, the angelic female voice filling the room.

"What do you need, Tiberius?"

Knowing Tiberius had removed the voice recognition software so that his staff could handle his daily tasks, she was confident her commands would be accepted.

"I need you to alert the guards at the North Tower and those within the cell block that I am sending two trusted associates to interrogate the political prisoner Ansley Brightmore," said Kaiya in a commanding voice that Arian had never heard. "They will be accompanied by four of my personal security detail. This is to be done with the utmost secrecy, at the bequest of the Overseers."

"Of course, Tiberius, I just need the North Tower security code," came Pandora's response.

Finding the code on the notepad Gallia had prepared, she typed it into the qubit's graphical interface.

"Thank you, Tiberius. Is there anything else that you need?"

"Bring my group transport to the front of the house and direct it to deliver my men to the secure entrance to the North Tower."

"Your vehicle is on its way. Estimated time of arrival to front of house: two minutes, estimated time of arrival to North Tower: eighteen minutes. Have a good night, Tiberius."

As Pandora's voice faded, Kaiya looked up at the shocked faces staring back. Arian in particular beheld her with a mixture of surprise and respect. She was earning both their trust and esteem.

"Well, I guess there's only one thing left to do," said Arian, hope evident in his voice.

"Two things for you," said Kaiya, smiling at his confidence. She found the set of clothes she dropped upon finding the servants in harm's way and tossed them to him. "It wouldn't do for you to show up to the North Tower covered in blood."

While Arian changed in the parlor, Eduardo seemed to notice his own garb for the first time.

"I'm afraid you will have to wait back at the

Devonshire," said Kaiya, her voice seeming deeper. "You could never pass for a Nephite and you're not dressed to enter the building. Your friends, however," she continued, motioning toward the other four men, "well, they could almost be Nephites."

"We are Nephites," answered one of the men, stepping forward. "My name is Conrad Percy, and these three men are my brothers. This is Chase, Connor, and Callan. We've been in Capitol City since the beginning and are amongst the oldest men in Arameus. We were all in our thirties when the nano treatments were introduced. Our deceased father had business dealings with Marco Luccio, allowing us to enter the dome, though we have no love for this totalitarian regime."

Noticing the shock on Arian's face, Conrad was bemused.

"You didn't think Ansley was the only Nephite fighting for the Natural Born cause did you? The man is brilliant, but he couldn't have smuggled all that money to Beladero alone."

"Then I'm glad to have you with us," replied Arian.

"We would all give our lives for Professor Brightmore," Connor chimed in. "He has fought for the freedom of the world at great personal loss."

"And you may well give your life tonight," said Kaiya flatly. "And the fact remains, the Nephites shall accompany us, and Eduardo will not."

"I will wait in the transport for you then. I need to be there to help."

"You'll only attract attention from other guards. We can't have a hulking, dark-skinned Natural Born sitting outside. Do you want to blow this entire operation? We can execute this smoothly as an act of espionage and no one will be aware, or we can continue to do things your way by stumbling around with guns."

"I will not be marginalized by you," retorted Eduardo. "These are my men whose lives you will be risking. I will see that they are safe."

"And you will.  When we retrieve Ansley, we still need to get out of the city.  It will be up to you to find us a way to Beladero.  I hardly see that as a marginalized role.  We will reconvene with you at the Devonshire.  Make sure you have us a way out."

Eduardo looked as if he was going to argue but relented.

"I will be at the Devonshire.  Bring them there safe and I will get you to Beladero."

"Then we are in agreement," replied Kaiya.  "Arian, the brothers, and I will go to the tower.  You go back to the transport and await our arrival."

"Good luck, men," said Eduardo before leaving to prepare their escape route.

"We're now expected at the detention block," she said.  "Let's not keep our hosts waiting."

The four brothers filed past her toward the transport.  As Arian followed their lead, she placed a hand on his chest stopping him.  When he looked at her, she saw in his eyes that same mixture of surprise and respect she had noticed before, as if he were seeing her for the first time.

"You look amazing in your uniform," she whispered.

His fingers smoothed the fabric of Tiberius' former dress uniform.  He felt distinguished.

"You're amazing, my love," he said.  "I didn't know you had this in you."

"I am capable of much more than you realize, Arian.  Just know that I'm doing all this for you.  I only want to get you out of here safely.  You came for me, so I am helping you go to Ansley.  I still say we should run as far from here as possible."

"I can't do that," replied Arian.

"I know," she said, as she straightened his collar.  "There.  Now you look like a true dignitary."  She patted him on his chest.  "Let's go get your friend."

"Hold on," said Arian, reaching down to his bloody,

discarded shirt and removing the three remaining bio-bot injections. Kaiya eyed him, but said nothing. He slipped them into a pocket in his shirt, below Tiberius' ceremonial robe.

They followed after the guards and took their seats in the official transport of Tiberius Septus. The vehicle, being outfitted for a high-ranking government official, was equipped with bullet proof armor and blast proof glass that was tinted so that riders could see out while no one outside could see in. As Kaiya entered with the qubit, Pandora again began speaking.

"Is your entire party in the car, Tiberius?"

"Yes," answered Kaiya.

"Then we will get under way. There are 18 minutes to your destination."

The transport shot off at a high speed on the track network that connected all the streets in Capitol City. All over the grid, transportation was stopped for he passing of a high-ranking official.

Arian was nervous, and he could tell by the faces of the other men that they were as well. He could read nothing from Kaiya. It was disconcerting to know she was so peaceful in these circumstances. Tiberius' transport drove itself through the streets unimpeded until they came to the security checkpoint at the West Bridge that led to the Central Isle. As the transport hawk slowed, everyone in the vehicle sat upright and put their hands on their guns, but Pandora communicated the proper codes and they passed without question, ushered toward the North Tower. The hawk docked in front of two Imperial soldiers.

"Be cool, boys," said Kaiya. "We're expected. I'm the interrogator, you all work for me." The men nodded as the transport opened.

The soldiers came to the door. The larger of them spoke.

"You are here on behalf of Tiberius Septus?"

"I'm here to interrogate the prisoner," Kaiya said. "According to Consulate Septus, he is a Centauri. They have been working him toward a confession. I will get this confession."

Her bravado had an effect on the guards.

"Well," said the larger one, "I hope you can get it out of him." He made an exaggerated motion to allow her, Arian, and their four escorts into the North Tower. He followed, leading them into the building and guiding them to a security station situated by an elevator.

"Stop there. We need your passcodes to allow you to advance." The captain seemed peaceful, but the men around him were heavily armed.

"Are you kidding me?" demanded Kaiya. "I was informed by Consulate Septus that you fools were aware we were coming. I am here to interrogate Ansley Brightmore. What more do we need?"

"We were informed, just doing our jobs. I apologize for any inconvenience. Please don't tell the Consulate of this." Her mind flashed to his corpse.

"See that it doesn't happen, captain. I have no desire to go after a man who is doing his duty. Just take us to the prisoner."

"Right away, Madame." The captain of the guard station walked down from his perch and led them to an adjacent elevator.

"You'll find the traitorous bastard at basement level C." The captain placed a small object on a keychain over a scanner, which registered the floor. "He will be there, but I must warn you, he is very weak. The Overseers themselves have been to see him and I'm afraid that Brightmore was less than forthcoming with information, to Overseer Romanov's great dismay. He has been severely tortured." A strange look of guilt and shame was obvious on the guard's face. "I wish you better luck than they had."

"I assure you," answered Kaiya, "I will achieve results. Luck is fanciful and foolish."

"I hope so," replied the captain, handing her the key

card to enter the cell as the elevator closed. They were again alone, descending into the depths of the tower.

The group was silent as the elevator dropped. Arian was afraid but would not show it to his companions. Arriving at C-level, Arian watched Connor pull out the same egg-shaped device Ansley had used to block spying in his apartments. As the door opened, Kaiya stormed out, past two cell guards who hurried after her. Connor activated the egg.

"I thought the guards in this prison were a well-oiled machine, but clearly I was mistaken," she said as she hurried down the hall. "Tiberius will have much to tell the Overseers about the lack of security and competence in the lower levels."

She stopped abruptly, and the two guards following ran into her, knocking her 5'2" frame to the ground. Connor ran to her aid, while Conrad and Chase drew their firearms and aimed them at the two guards. Arian hung back, taking in the scene as if in slow motion.

"This is how you treat an interrogator for Tiberius Septus!!!" she screamed at the bewildered and frightened men.

"No, Madame," answered one of the guards, helping Connor pull her to her feet. "We didn't know it was you."

"So you were not aware that we were coming tonight? Tiberius informed me that Pandora had announced our presence."

"She did, Your Grace. We made a mistake," stammered the guard. "You shot out of the elevator and we reacted. Please don't let this get back to the Consulate. We will do anything."

"I know that you will," replied Kaiya coldly. "Which cell houses Ansley Brightmore?"

"Cell Four," replied the frightened guard.

"Open it and leave us, please. I need to interrogate the prisoner alone."

"Of course," murmured the guard, rushing down the hall and unlocking the fourth cell. Chase and Conrad lowered their guns, though they did not holster them.

"We apologize for any inconvenience," said the other

guard.

"Is there anyone housed in Cell Three?" asked Kaiya.

"No, Madame," replied the guard.

"Open it and show me." The guard opened the cell. At a nod from Kaiya, Chase struck the man in the back of the head with the butt of his gun, splitting his scalp and sending him to the floor, where he lay motionless. The second guard reeled around, but Conrad already had him covered.

"You can either go in the cell like your friend there, or you can walk into the cell willingly," said Conrad.

The frightened guard nodded and said nothing.

"Give me your qubit and get in the cell."

The man handed over his qubit and entered. Chase and Callan dragged the other man, who was either unconscious or dead, into the cell behind him, removing his qubit as well.

"Take a break, gentleman," Conrad said snidely as he closed the cell door. "I'm sure they will have you guys out of here in no time, although you may not get a very good performance review."

With the guards secured, they were alone in the hallway. Arian walked forward and pushed open the heavy steel door to Ansley's cell. He took a deep breath, nervous about what he would find on the other side. After the guard's recap of his friend's interrogation, he knew that it would not be pleasant. As Arian entered the dark cell, sensors signaled the overhead lights to flicker on, bathing the room in white fluorescent light. He was horrified by what he saw.

The room was almost bare, save for an exam table in the center, an IV stand, and a monitor registering the rhythmic beats of Ansley's heart. Ansley was restrained on the table, strapped from head to toe, allowing him minimal movement. Fresh, pink scars covered his face, arms, legs, and chest. Arian was puzzled by their rapid emergence. At first, he didn't appear to be conscious, but as Arian moved closer, the once great man spoke in a weak and pitiable voice.

"I've told you everything I know. I can't do this

anymore. You have to find a way to kill me. Please. The pain is unbearable."

Emboldened by his friend's agony and the need to comfort him, Arian rushed forward, grabbing the Professor's hand.

"It's Arian," he said in a soothing tone. "We are here to rescue you."

Ansley opened his eyes and turned his head as far as the restraint would allow, squinting at the brightness.

"I couldn't resist them. The pain. The torture. They know of our assault on the lab. What day is it? We have to warn Jabari's men."

"I'm afraid it's too late for that," said Arian in a somber tone. "But we were able to escape and have come for you."

The four brothers approached the table and stood looking down at Ansley, their faces full of compassion.

"Do you think you can walk, old friend?" asked Conrad, unclasping the restraints.

"I can walk, but you must leave me. This body is no longer my own."

"I'm afraid I don't understand," said Arian.

"They tried to break me and get me to give up our plans. They cut me and beat me and broke my fingers and ribs, but I wouldn't crack. Five days ago, Vladymir Romanov came with a team of doctors who injected me with the bio-bots they've been producing in the desert. The bots, they wrote themselves into my genetic code. Once the bots hijack the machinery of DNA synthesis, they code themselves into your very being. I can feel them. I can communicate with them. It's as if they're alive. They used me as a test subject, just one more humiliation, but then something unexpected happened. Knowing now that the bot injections would not destroy the host and frustrated with my lack of cooperation, they had no more use for me. Vladymir cut my throat in a fit of rage. I bled to death on this very table. But the bots didn't die. They repaired me, using my body's chemical energy stores and medical records downloaded from the same transmission system the Overseers will use to control the Natural Born. I was returned to homeostasis. You see, they are me now, and they don't want to die."

Arian exchanged confused looks with the brothers and then glanced back at Kaiya, who was studying Ansley intently.

"Don't worry about those things now, my friend," Arian said. Let's just get you out of here. We will find a way to get those things out of you. We were able to destroy the lab. The bio bots are no more, but I was able to save a few samples. We can still carry out the plan. We just need to make it to the Iris and you can alter history and bring down this regime."

"You don't understand," said Ansley. "When they saw that my body had healed, they cut me. They forced me to die over and over again, but I kept coming back. I couldn't tell what was real and what was fantasy. I didn't know if I was alive or dead. I just wanted it to stop, so I broke. They broke me. I told them everything. I told them about the assault on the lab, about Beladero. Everything. And I was a selfish fool." Ansley closed his eyes and single tear rolled down his scarred cheek. "It was never about the Natural Born, and it was never about the regime. It was always about Padma. All the men that have died, all those that have sacrificed to create the Iris, it was all for me and me alone. I needed to somehow go back, to find her. I couldn't deal with the fact that she was gone forever. I couldn't just sit there and allow her memory to fade into oblivion, so I began to build the accelerator, a fool's quest to warp time and space to find my love. I purposely misled the people of Beladero with promises of sending a message back before the rise of the Overseers, but I knew it would not be possible. How can one send a message through space and time and assure its arrival?"

"The wormhole was for me. I was going to enter it in a selfish attempt to find her again. And I knew I would die doing so. The gravitational forces would surely tear me apart. But then I met you." His eyes met Arian's. "I had watched you since your birth, as you were my only link to Padma. I followed your research. I saw you speak at the Institute six months ago on the progress of your research, and I was struck by an idea. Even though you yourself were unaware, I saw the potential for the bots as a self-sustaining source of health and youthfulness. Without control of extended life, the Overseers would lose all power over the world. Unexpectedly, I found myself believing that we just might be able to change the world after all, and for a time I forgot my own selfish desires. I thought if we could somehow deliver this technology before the rise of Arameus, we could eliminate their power."

"But we still can... I have three syringes of the bots. We can send them back," implored Arian. "Ansley, we can still win this!"

Ansley got up from the table, and Arian, aware of his nakedness, removed his outer robe and placed it around his shoulders. The Professor tied the robe and stood taller. He seemed to be growing stronger by the minute. Searching the room, he found a cabinet in the corner and, opening it, he sighed with relief.

"I thought I had lost these forever," he said, more to himself than the group. Arian watched as he removed a gold watch and the damaged silver cigarette case that he carried everywhere.

"I apologize for my weakened state," he said, a half smile showing and a bit of his familiar arrogance returning, "but I was stabbed in the heart just this morning." The other men looked with shocked expression at the pink scar on his chest that showed this to be true. "They seemed to never tire of killing me."

Ansley shot a glance at Kaiya, frowned, and turned back to Arian.

"I see you found her," he said.

"Without me, you would still be chained to that table," she shot back.

"I'm sure I owe you a large debt of gratitude," responded Ansley dryly. He embraced Conrad. "It's good to see you old friend," he whispered. The other three brothers surrounded him and embraced him in turn.

Ansley addressed the group. "I have learned a valuable lesson from my imprisonment and it is this. We need to die. I have descended into that dark crevice of death more than any man in the history of our world now, and I must tell you, I have always been disappointed to return. The source of the Overseers' power is their unending grip on people's fears of the unknown. They keep their equals in line with promises of extended life and dominate those who have nothing. No matter what we do, it will always be the same. If we destroy the Overseers, others like them will rise. If tyrants can't be controlled by the people, then at least we should be able to count on nature to rid us of them."

"Then what do you propose?" asked Arian.

"Strangely, enough, with my newfound… prowess for survival, I might just be able to survive a trip through the wormhole."

"Then we should try," insisted Arian. "I have three doses of the bio-bot injections that I was able to save from the lab. We can at least try."

"No. We can't try. It's wrong. Padma lived her life, and now she is dead. I have lived two hundred years longer than I should have, as have the Overseers. Death is nothing to fear. It is eternal rest, and we will deliver the Overseers to their long overdue naps. All nano-treatments are produced in Capitol City, and the technology is jealously guarded here. All knowledge of the bio-bots is here as well. You remember the explosion that occurred when we shut down the Iris and closed the hole, right?"

"I do."

"The longer we allow the hole to remain open, the further back in time the particles must travel to annihilate their anti-particle couplet. This entire region sits on top of the largest cave system on the planet. If we leave the Iris running long enough, we can create an explosion large enough to collapse 100 square miles, including Capitol City. Let's see these bots survive that. Our deaths will be our parting gift to the world. The Overseers will be destroyed, and all knowledge of extended life lost. The Natural Born will re-build a free world."

"I didn't sign up for this," interjected Kaiya. "This is suicide. How can you expect these people to follow you after you just admitted to deceiving them?"

"You signed your death warrant when you took up with Tiberius," retorted Ansley. "Do you expect the Overseers to allow you to survive? They sent you back into servitude. What will they do now that you have illegally infiltrated the North Tower?"

"We will follow him because he is right," said Conrad, placing a hand on Ansley's shoulder. "Regardless of his previous motivations, his current ones are correct." His brothers nodded in agreement. "We have all lived too long. And we have lived most of that time as slaves. We aren't even allowed to have children. It isn't right. We are still with you, Ansley."

Arian cast a glance at Kaiya, who seemed incredulous, but he shrugged her off.

"I am with you too, Ansley. I have seen too many men die today for the freedom of their children to just walk away. I will not allow the world to be enslaved by a creation from my own research."

"Then it's decided. We destroy Capitol City," said Ansley. "Now how do you propose we get out of here?"

"Leave that to me," said Kaiya. "We entered under the guise of Tiberius' interrogation team. We will leave as such. These guards are fools. They will not notice one more member of our party, especially one garbed in an Imperial robe."

"Let's go," said Ansley, raising the purple hood to cover his face. "Perhaps we can beat them to Beladero. If you really were able to destroy the lab today, they will be busy there. We shouldn't be naïve, though. They will have Imperial brigades marching on the city. I was able to hold off telling them of the Iris, so they will feel no need to hurry. To them, it is merely a rebel city that they can destroy in their own time. Let's hope their arrogance is as extreme as I believe it to be."

They exited the cell into the empty hallway. The egg was still holding. Kaiya walked in front with Arian trailing close behind. Ansley walked between the four brothers in an attempt to blend in. They entered the elevator and Kaiya scanned the key card pushing the button for the ground floor. Connor deactivated the egg. They rose in silence, the mood tense. When they arrived at their destination floor, Ansley placed his hand over the button that kept the doors closed.

"We are about to take a leap that none of us will come back from," he said looking at the group. "I look at you all and I see brothers," he nodded to his guards, "I see a son," he nodded to Arian, "and perhaps now, another friend to our cause," he added, acknowledging Kaiya. "We have had our differences, and all have made mistakes, but if all of you were willing to risk your lives to come to this, the heart of the Overseers' stronghold to save me, then I am sure you are willing to go one step further and give your lives so that the world can be free. When we leave this lift, we will do so as the true Centauri, the fictional band of rebels the men in power have used for so long to murder our families and keep us under control. Whatever waits ahead, I am committed to the cause of helping those who can't help themselves, and I know if you join me that you are as well. Let's send a message to the world that tyranny, no matter what it offers, be it riches or eternal life, will never be tolerated in our world. Let's send a message to those looking for a beacon of hope that we are the bringers of death to those who oppose hope, to those who ignore the abandoned. We are the justice that those without a voice dream of in their sleep. Hope is real. And we will make it so."

No one in the lift said a word as Ansley finished his speech, but he could see in their eyes their commitment, everyone but Kaiya. Her expression, as always, was unreadable. Her head tilted as if studying the man before her.

418

Ansley released the button and the doors opened. The four brothers split, allowing Kaiya to march ahead.

As she walked by the guard station, she nonchalantly tossed the electronic elevator access key onto the counter of the captain's station.

"We were able to get what we needed from the prisoner. Tiberius will be pleased," she said brusquely as she continued past.

"Wait," said the captain, standing to his feet. "Is everything alright? We lost the camera feed to the cellblock." The concerned captain surveyed the group trailing behind her. He noticed the extra man at once.

"Stop them," he yelled to his three companions, who rushed to head off Kaiya, keeping their weapons holstered, not wishing to threaten a representative of the Consulate.

"Is there a problem, captain?" asked Kaiya sweetly.

"I'm afraid there is, Madame. Six of you went down but seven have come up. You in the hood, show me your face."

Ansley, his face lowered to avoid detection looked to his left and right, nodding his head and whispering something before responding.

"As you wish," he replied in a calm and measured tone. Lifting his head, he threw back his hood, revealing his once famous and now infamous features. The shock was evident on the captain's face as he realized what was happening. He jumped backward in a defensive posture as his men went for their guns. Arian lunged at Kaiya, tackling her to the ground, and Ansley lowered himself to his knees, as Conrad, Chase, Connor, and Callan stepped forward and unloaded their weapons on the surprised guards. The confrontation was over before it began, and the hallway was filled with smoke as the captain and his three men lay dead before them.

"We've got to run," shouted Ansley. "That's not going unnoticed."

Leaping over the bodies, he rushed ahead, down the corridor toward the entrance along with the four brothers.

Lifting Kaiya to her feet, Arian followed, pulling her behind him as she struggled to keep up with his longer stride. They were halfway down the corridor when shots rang out ahead. Ansley felt his shoulder explode in searing pain and was knocked to the floor. Connor and Chase dropped to the ground and returned fire. It was the two soldiers guarding the entrance. Within seconds the gunfire ceased and the guards lay dead. Arian went to help Ansley.

Leaning over his injured friend, he could see blood pouring from a gunshot wound to the shoulder.

"Are you alright, can you walk?"

Painfully pushing himself up with his good arm to a seated position, Ansley surveyed his wound. "It is of no consequence," he replied. "It will heal." Arian and Kaiya helped him to his feet. "We have to keep moving," said Ansley.

It was then that they noticed three of the brothers surrounding a body on the ground. Callan lay dead from a bullet through the forehead. Conrad's voice shook with a mixture of anguish and rage.

"We must leave him. We have a mission to finish. If we succeed tonight, we will all join in his fate, along with the Overseers. We must go, now!"

Without a look back at their fallen brother, Chase and Connor and the rest of them were again sprinting down the hall, this time Ansley falling behind, running awkwardly from his wound. They made it to the entryway and burst out into the night. With no other soldiers in the immediate area, the path to the transport was clear. Kaiya removed Tiberius' qubit from her dress and instructed Pandora to open the doors. They entered, with Arian helping Ansley.

"Pandora, we need to go to the Devonshire Pub in the Southern District. Go now!"

"A strange choice for you, Tiberius. Estimated time of arrival, 10 minutes."

"We need to get into contact with Eduardo," said

Ansley through labored breaths and gritted teeth. "I assume from the destination he is working with you?"

"He is awaiting our arrival at the pub and planning our way out of the city," replied Arian.

"We may need to improvise," said Ansley. "Can you contact him?"

Kaiya tossed the short-wave transponder to Ansley.

"Just press the button to talk."

The transport began moving, driving through the curved avenues surrounding the Central Tower toward the main route to the Southern District. Using his good arm, Ansley picked up the transponder and pressed the button.

"Eddie, are you there?" Static… A few seconds passed before he tried again. "Damn it, Eddie, you better fucking be there."

After another few seconds, he heard the accented voice of his old friend from the other end.

"Professor, is that really you? Shit! I can't believe this! Then they succeeded?"

"Not yet, Eddie," replied Ansley. "We're in trouble. Can you get us out?"

"I have a plan. Just get to the Devonshire."

"I don't think that's going to happen, Eddie. We made a mess back there. There is no way we are getting through this check point."

"Ansley," interrupted Arian. "Ansley…"

"What!" fired back Ansley, annoyed by the disturbance.

"We have a cruiser outside the Patolli players' entrance to the city. We're going right by the South Tower. If we can gain access, we can make it to Beladero before the Overseers realize we've left the city."

Ansley nodded in acknowledgement.

"What time is it, Eddie?" he said into the transponder.

"Nearly midnight, professor."

"Good. Raul should still be in the tower cleaning,

correct?"

"He works all night on Mondays. He'll be there."

"Good. Contact him and have him stand by at the service entrance. This is going to be close."

"What's your plan?" asked Eduardo, concern in his voice.

"I'm going to do what you always wanted me to do, Eddie. I'm going to take down this whole city. If I leave the Iris on long enough, I can create enough energy destabilize the outer crust of this entire region. Those in the remaining cities can rebuild this world. If you want to live, I suggest you go west and as far away from here as the next few hours will allow. Everything within a hundred miles of Beladero is going to collapse into the subterranean cave system."

"I think not, Professor," answered Eduardo, pride and respect evident in his tone. "I will not run while our comrades die. I look forward to dying tonight as we ring in a new era of freedom. I will alert my fellow Natural Born, however, and give them the chance to flee."

"Eddie, if you can, contact Anabelle. I would see her safe."

"I will do my best. I'll see you on the other side, my friend."

"And I you Eduardo," replied Ansley. "Now get ahold of Raul and get him to that fucking door!"

Ansley threw the transponder back to Kaiya and surveyed the men in the transport. The brothers were somber but resolute. Arian returned his gaze, prepared to meet his fate. Ansley moved his wounded shoulder. The bleeding had stopped and the pain was already subsiding. He noticed Kaiya studying his movements and shoulder intently. In spite of her efforts on his behalf, he still didn't trust her. Ignoring his misgivings, he spoke to the men in the vehicle.

"By now they know what happened in there, and they know precisely where we are on the grid. That checkpoint at the Southern bridge is a death trap waiting to spring."

The others in the car nodded.

"We need to get to the South Tower without them following. I'm afraid we have some tough decisions to make," continued Ansley, making eye contact with Conrad, who seemed to understand.

"There is no tough decision, old friend," said Conrad, answering Ansley's stare and reading his thoughts. "You, Arian, Kaiya, and Chase will exit as we pass the South Tower and meet this Raul. Connor and I will continue forward to the checkpoint. They will assume we are all in the vehicle. Connor and I will give them hell and buy you time to escape. They will never suspect that you would have gone to the South Tower."

"No!" interjected Arian. "You can't just give yourself to them. Come with us. We will all run for it."

"We all die tonight, my new friend," replied Conrad, repeating the words he said over his brother's corpse.

"He's right," said Ansley. "They can buy us enough time to get into the tower before they realize we're no longer in the vehicle. We'll leave the city right under their noses while they search the streets above. With luck, we can make it to Beladero before they realize we're gone and end this tonight."

Though Arian still seemed uncomfortable with this scenario and unconvinced of its necessity, he said nothing else. Chase and Connor both nodded in solemn agreement with Ansley.

"Then it's decided," said Ansley. "Kaiya, tell Pandora to slow the transport to five miles an hour when we pass the National Mall by the South Tower and open the left door. We'll jump out and she will continue forward at that speed with the door open. This will give you both the advantage of being able to leap out and open fire as soon as the vehicle stops at the checkpoint before they can surround you. Use the vehicle for cover. You need to buy us as much time as possible."

Conrad and Connor nodded while Kaiya instructed Pandora as to how the transport was to behave. They rode in silence for the next few minutes, each man and woman nervously contemplating what they would have to do. Arian prayed that the South Tower, looming in the distance, would never arrive, but against his best hopes, it rose larger and larger in the window. As they neared, the transport slowed, and they knew it was time. Chase, the brother chosen to accompany Kaiya, Arian, and Ansley, embraced each of his brothers who would soon sacrifice themselves so that they could make it to the Iris.

"It has been an honor to be your brother and serve with you in this resistance," he said, his voice choking. "I don't know what awaits each of us in death, but I hope to meet you again in the halls of our ancestors."

Ansley, Arian, and Kaiya said their goodbyes as well, shaking the hands of the men who would give their own lives for them. As they came even with the National Mall that led to the South Tower, the door to their left slid open.

"Now is the time," shouted Ansley, leaping from the vehicle and hitting the ground in a jog. Arian and Kaiya followed, with Kaiya nearly falling before being lifted back up by her companion. Chase was the last man to exit the vehicle. He stopped, watching the transport move forward carrying his brothers and friends of over two hundred years to a violent death. With a pained sigh, he turned his back and joined the others. The park was empty, with everyone who didn't work there home for the evening. The four of them sprinted across the green to their destination.

They ran past the marbled monuments to the men who had built the Empire of Arameus, the very empire they were trying to destroy. Arian couldn't stop his thoughts from drifting to that day that he and Ansley had attended the Patolli game, the day they cemented their friendship. It had all seemed so innocent, drinking at the Devonshire with Alexandra and Anabelle, before walking across this very mall to the Patolli stadium. Anabelle would be dead by the end of this night, along with them all, while Alex was somewhere far away with her cruel gangster uncle. At least she would be safe. Despite her betrayal, this gave him comfort. It was nice to know that someone he cared for would survive. Ansley must have known it would end like this. Nothing had been innocent for him. He understood now why his friend was always brooding, drowning himself in alcohol. That knowledge must have weighed heavy on his soul for a long time. He tricked himself with thoughts of saving Padma and stopping the war, but the war was always necessary.

Then a troubling thought came to him. Gravano had bio-bots and would be far from the blast radius. This was all futile. They would not be able to destroy the technology. It would continue, now controlled by a man potentially more dangerous than the Overseers themselves. Coupled with Alex, they could continue production. No matter what they did tonight, his work would live on and the oppression might continue. He opened his mouth to call out to Ansley and warn him about the flaw in their plan, but was interrupted as gunfire sounded just to the south of them.

They froze to listen. Seven shots fired in succession before a brief pause. Then four more shots rang out. Still, they listened, unable to continue on. The red night erupted in hundreds of shots fired without interruption for a full minute. They ceased. Ten seconds later, two solitary shots echoed over the Central Isle and Ansley knew it was over. The brothers would have been incapacitated in the final flurry. The last two shots were the kill shots, executed at close range. After a sustained silence, Ansley reached out and gave Chase's shoulder an empathetic squeeze. The man looked devastated but raised his head, looking Ansley in the eye.

"Let's make sure they didn't die in vain."

With a solemn nod, Ansley raced for the tower along with the rest of the crew. As they ran, they heard a siren wail over the Isle. Their absence had been discovered. It wouldn't be long before a full patrol was canvassing the area. They rushed onto the tower pavilion, Ansley leading the way past the main entrance and around the corner to the custodial entrance. He knocked hard, three times. Within seconds, the door opened and Ansley was never as happy to see Raul as he was at that moment.

"I thought you guys would never get here," he said. "What the hell is going on out there? It sounds like a war zone."

"No time," said Ansley, between heavy breathes. "You have to get us to the tunnel from the locker room."

Ansley stepped aside, allowing Kaiya, Arian, and Chase to enter first. The last thing he saw as he closed the door behind him was a Raven circling the green with a spotlight shining down and a full brigade of guards entering the mall. Raul led them down the corridor to the elevator and then to the entrance of the locker room. Entering, Ansley stopped, turning to Raul and grabbing him by the arm.

"You have saved us once again, my friend, and I thank you. Now get out of the city and as far north or west as you can. Go now!"

With that, Ansley, Arian, Kaiya, and Chase left, descending to the tunnel that would lead them from the city.

*** 

Eduardo sat at the bar of the Devonshire Pub, contemplating the diminishing glass of bourbon before him. It wasn't often he sat on the patron's side, but the doors were locked and he was alone, so what the hell. He lifted the strong spirit to his lips, feeling the burn of the alcohol wash over his body, giving him a chill, as the aromatics shot through his sinus cavity. He had always enjoyed fine bourbon. He breathed in deep to appreciate the subtle vanilla and caramel notes tracing his pallet. His thoughts went to Juanita. He had loved her. She was another victim of a curable flu. He would be with her again soon. For now, he would drink and appreciate the good things he had left in his life. It gave him solace to know that no matter how much power the Overseers gained and how much they had controlled, there were still good men in the world, both Nephite and Natural Born, who were willing to give their lives to protect the most basic right in the world: freedom to pursue your own happiness.

He was proud of his friends. A lot of good families would die this evening on both sides, but when time allowed for healing, he knew the world would be better because of their sacrifices. This gave him hope, in spite of the fact that he was staring in the face of his own death. He laughed. It was too bad the Overseers' media directors would perish as well. Otherwise, this would be known as the Blood Monday attack.

His transponder buzzed with static and Raul's voice came from the other side.

"They made it to the South Tower, Eduardo, and I have delivered them to the locker room. They will be out of the city in no time."

"You did great, Raul. Thank you. Now get your little ass out of the city and as far away as possible."

"I don't think so, Eduardo. I still have some cleaning to finish. I was never one to leave a job unfinished that I've been paid for."

"You're a good man, Raul."

# Chapter Twenty-Nine
## Into the Iris

The tunnel seemed different to Arian this passage. The flicker of fluorescent lights above seemed sinister. The dank muskiness of water leaking down from the city gave the impression of a tomb. Arian realized it was the feeling of impending doom. This time, he would not be coming home. None of them would be. Capitol City, the only city he had ever known, was now shut off to him forever. If they were successful on this night, they would all be dead and the city he had once loved would be obliterated, along with the seat of power that held Arameus together. If they were unsuccessful, they would be dead all the same. There was a sense of finality that left him unsettled, but there was also a certain poetic beauty that could not be denied. His life would be of consequence after all, though in a far different way than he could have imagined.

They pushed forward, their initial speed slowed to a jog by the miles that stretched to the edge of the city. Ansley lagged behind the farthest. Kaiya was faltering as well, though Arian kept a firm grip on her hand, pulling and urging her forward. Chase, in the best physical condition, took the lead. They were in a race to Beladero against the forces of Arameus, and they had to get to the Iris first. Under torture, Ansley had laid out the defenses of the city for the Imperial troops, and it would only be a matter of time before Beladero was taken. Arian hoped the assault would be delayed until morning while the Imperial soldiers focused on canvassing the city in search of the fugitives. They needed the Overseers to make one more arrogant mistake.

"I can't keep running," said Kaiya through labored breaths. "We have to stop. We haven't eaten since this morning in Sikyon. I need to rest."

Arian and Chase stopped, looking back. Ansley caught them and paused briefly.

"Anyone who wants to rest is welcome to stay here. I'm going to the Iris."

He took off again, jogging awkwardly to avoid jostling his injured shoulder.

The other three looked at one another. Chase shrugged and followed Ansley. Arian studied Kaiya, who tossed up her hands and exhaled in an exaggerated manner.

"Easy for the man to say with bio-bots coursing through his body," she observed. With that, she gave Arian a resigned look and held out her hand, which he took again, leading her forward.

It was another half hour before they reached the vaulted door that led to the outside world. Ansley typed in the same access code that Kaiya had only hours earlier retrieved from Jabari, and they held their collective breath as the door rose, hoping they would not find an armed brigade of Imperial troops waiting for them. Ansley was pleased to find nothing but the desert, bathed in the red light of the night sun, the cruiser exactly where Arian had left it.

"Let's go," commanded Ansley, rushing to the vehicle. In the instant before he got there, Arian realized what awaited him, feeling pangs of guilt in his chest.

Ansley stood before the cruiser, frozen in place, unable to remove his eyes from the broken body of Jabari Stoudamyre. Chase came forward and placed a hand on his old friend's shoulder.

"There's nothing you can do for him now, Ansley."

"There's so much I would change," said Ansley, stifling a sob. "Had I not been selfish, I could have saved us all. There is always a more elegant solution, and I've had two hundred years to discover it. Instead, we go down the familiar barbaric paths of our ancestors, wasting the lives of men to accomplish goals that should be self-evident to those in power."

"We need to get him out guys," Arian said, hoping his words would not offend Ansley.

Ansley opened the door to the rear of the cruiser and grabbed Jabari under both shoulders. As he hoisted him out of the seat, the head rolled backward, revealing the deep wound in the neck. Carefully laying him on the ground, Ansley stroked the cheek of the friend who had been like a son. He remembered first meeting the large, gangly boy who took such an interest in the strangers and the machine they were building. Seeing himself in the boy, Ansley had encouraged this curiosity, eventually taking the boy on as a student. He had been bright, and, in the world that Ansley had grown up in, would likely have been a well-respected physicist. His skill at Patolli had been a happy accident that had provided him with a way in and out of the city. The fact that Jabari was now dead lay squarely on the old Professor's shoulders.

Crossing his arms on his chest, he noticed something clutched in the man's hand. Ansley pried open Jabari's fingers, removing the knife from his grip. Noticing the questioning glances exchanged between Arian and Chase, he decided to explain himself.

"Jabari was not a man of the knife. He was a loving husband and a scholar. The violence he did was out of necessity and duty to his people, but it was not the defining quality of the man."

All remained silent, respecting the brief eulogy.

"Goodbye, old friend," whispered Ansley, leaning down and kissing Jabari on the forehead. "I'll be joining you soon."

Ansley stood and without looking back opened the driver's side door and took his seat. The keys were still in the ignition so he fired up the engine. Chase took the passenger's seat, while Kaiya and Arian took their places in the back, trying to ignore the semi-dry pools of blood on which they sat. Ansley sped off over the barren land toward Beladero and the inevitable fate awaiting them all. The drive to Beladero was close to thirty minutes and they were silent for a bit, each contemplating the job ahead. Arian looked up at the red night sun. This entire week had been one improbable task after another, yet here he was, Kaiya and Ansley safely in tow, headed toward the Iris. It was as if something was guiding them, helping them to accomplish the impossible, yet Arian was not a superstitious man. He found Kaiya's hand and she allowed him to grasp it, a small comfort.

Halfway through the drive, Ansley was roused from his reverie by a poke in the back. He found Kaiya's eyes in the rearview mirror.

"There's an exit hole in your shirt. The bullet must have gone clear through you," she said over the hum of the motor, her tone flat.

"It would appear that this is the case," responded Ansley.

"But there is no longer a hole in your back. It's already closed and scabbed over."

"Get to the point, girl," said Ansley.

"My point," continued Kaiya, unperturbed by Ansley's tone, "is that there are three of us in this car who do not have the luxury of the treatments, and Arian has three vials of useable bots in his possession. Why send us into harm's way unprotected? We don't have to die tonight. If we can accomplish this task and possibly survive, why not take that chance?"

"Kaiya!" shouted Arian.

"Shut up, Arian. You know I'm right. We are pawns in all of this. Between Tiberius, Ansley, and the Overseers, this has all been forced on us. Why should we die? Ansley can turn on the damn machine without us, and we can get as far from here as possible."

"You are welcome to leave at any time, my dear, but you will not be using the bots," responded Ansley with conviction. "Have you learned nothing? No one should have the power over mortality. As long as these bots are in existence, they will find themselves in the control of those who wish to oppress and dominate. The bots will die with us."

"But that's the thing, isn't it? They won't die with us. Gravano escaped in a Raven with an entire box of syringes, along with Alexandra. Destroy Capitol City, and you will replace the Overseers with a gangster."

Ansley's dismay was evident to Arian. He was silent for five minutes as everyone in the vehicle waited for his response. He sighed and closed his eyes, defeated.

"Yet another mistake adding to my litany of failures," he said, his voice quivering as if he was on the verge of tears. "I should have anticipated this. It was I who negotiated the trade with Gravano. For delivering you to and from Sikyon, he would receive the bio-bots as payment. Jabari was instructed to kill him after destroying the lab. At the time, I believed the bots would merely make Gravano another slave to the Overseers. I didn't anticipate their true power."

"What's our play?" asked Arian.

Ansley considered for another moment, examining the many possibilities that could unfold from here. Finally, he made up his mind, and was resolute in his decision.

"We continue forward with the plan to destroy Capitol City."

He reached forward, grabbing the short-wave radio from the console. Dialing in the coordinates, he spoke into the handheld attachment. A woman's voice came from the other end.

"April, inform the counsel that the time has come to finish this. Fire up the Iris. We will be there soon."

"As you wish, sir," came April's reply, her voice filled with apprehension.

"What?" Kaiya protested.

"Gravano is just one man, without the wealth, power, or the infrastructure of Arameus. We can strike a crippling blow to the Empire tonight. We can wipe out all production of nanocytes and bio-bots in one blow, along with the Overseers and the Parliament. Certainly the power vacuum will need to be filled, but the power of the Natural Born, if they come together, will dwarf anything Gravano can amass, and without the infrastructure of the Institute, he will be years, if not decades from producing the bio-bots, even if Alex has the capability to reproduce the science. We will take our chances against this one man. Maybe Alex will prove an ally in the end. She didn't seem the power hungry type to me."

"I agree," said Chase, resolute.

"As do I," added Arian. "We set out to free the world. Let's give it a chance."

"So we throw our lives away on a chance?" asked Kaiya.

"Yes, Kaiya, that's precisely it," Ansley replied. "It's possible this will be unsuccessful and we are only prolonging the inevitability of another ageless despot, but what if we succeed? Remember who you are. We are doing this so that little girls born in Avignon can be anything they wish."

"Then let Arian and me get out. We will take the bots with us and you can destroy the city. We will disappear. Gravano has the bots, why should we not survive as well?"

"You can leave if you choose Kaiya, but you will be doing so without the bots," answered Arian. "I'm with Ansley. We should destroy as much of this as possible. If those left behind need to face Gravano one day, then it will be on them.

We will have done our part."

Ansley nodded in agreement. "It matters not anyway. You won't make it far on foot. Bots or not, we will all be incinerated."

Defeated, Kaiya relented, leaning back in her seat and staring into the distance. Ten minutes later, the cliffs of Beladero came into view on the horizon. Arian thought he saw a flash of lightning in the distance, followed by the sound of thunder. Looking to the sky, he didn't see any above the city. As he puzzled over the strange flash, he saw another one, followed by an explosion of orange, the air filling with thick black smoke.

"They have already arrived," observed Ansley. "The attack on Beladero has begun."

"What do we do?" asked Chase.

"We stick to the plan," replied Ansley, his voice firm. "They will have formed a perimeter around the city. If I know the people of Beladero, they will have set up their defenses around the city square, in front of the central reservoir. They probably have destroyed the footbridges over the irrigation canals. We will have to drive up the center street and hope to find a friendly face."

"But how will we get through the Imperial lines?" asked Arian.

"We're all dressed in Imperial attire. If Kaiya stays low and Chase shoots his firearm like a madman, with a little luck, we may just pass as one of them. After that, I have no idea."

"Sounds like a great plan," said Kaiya, rolling her eyes.

"Shut that bitch up, Arian," barked Ansley. "We have no need for her incessant commentary."

Arian gave her a pleading look, urging her to trust him, even though he had no more faith in the plan of action than she.

From to the city's edge, they could see that it was embroiled in a fierce battle. Three Ravens hovered in the air, firing missiles at the larger structures and raining down bullets on the populace. The heart of the ground forces pushed forward toward the square, with no attention given to the rear. Chase seemed frightened, focused on the Ravens looming overhead. Against such firepower, the city was doomed. With a flash of light, a projectile launched from the ground and into the underbelly of one of the planes. The explosion shook the surrounding area, sending the Raven down into a row of houses. They could hear disparate cheers from the defenders of the city.

"They have no idea what they're in for!" exclaimed Ansley. "These people have some fight, my friends. AHHHHH!" The primal scream escaped unexpectedly and had the unintended effect of giving hope to those in the vehicle.

"These bastards underestimate everyone," yelled Chase, the fear in his eyes replaced with a violent determination.

They pushed through the main gate, which remained open. The Imperial forces were still concentrated far ahead, toward the square. As they passed the many hovels on the outskirts of the city, they could see Imperial soldiers moving from house to house, pulling entire families into their yards and executing them, including the women and children.

"Make a show of it, Chase," screamed Ansley, barreling ahead.

Chase pulled a pistol from his belt and tossed it to Arian. Both men stood, Chase with his automatic rifle and Arian with the pistol, firing with abandon, careful to aim at nothing significant. As they passed, many of the Imperial soldiers turned and aimed their weapons at the cruiser but upon seeing an Imperial guard and dignitary firing into the crowd, returned to their own tasks.

"It's working," shouted Ansley as a bullet ripped through the windshield of the cruiser. This bullet had come from the front. He hadn't considered the idea that their ruse made them vulnerable to friendly fire. Still, he pushed down on the accelerator, gaining speed. The Imperial troops made no effort to contest them. They were likely confused by the all-terrain vehicle inhabited by two men with the robes of Aramean dignitaries and an Imperial guard madly firing into the crowd.

Arriving behind the Imperial force's main line, the crux of the Beladero forces came into view. They had constructed a crude barricade around the square and reservoir. A wall of furniture, old vehicles, sandbags, and other various odds and ends formed a barrier. Behind the barricade, militiamen were perched, firing on the encroaching force. The citizens of Beladero flung homemade bombs, scattering the forces attempting to advance. The two remaining Ravens, now out of missiles, concentrated their fire on the city's defenders. From the cliff dwellings surrounding the square, citizens of the city fired back at the Ravens. A rocket took down yet another of the ships, sending it crashing into an Imperial brigade that had been advancing to the left flank of the barricade. Their threat was now neutralized. Those who were not crushed by the wreckage burned to death when the fuel ignited, their piteous screams contrasting darkly with the rebel cheers. The people of Beladero were fighting valiantly, but they were outgunned and outmanned. The line would not hold for long.

"We have to do something," shouted Arian from the back. "We can't go ahead. We have to find another way in. If we aren't killed by the Imperials, we'll be killed by our own. There has to be another way!"

"I'm done sneaking around," responded Ansley, pushing the accelerator all the way to the floor. "Brace yourself, kid."

The cruiser accelerated, dropping Arian back into his seat with great force. When they reached eighty miles per hour, the turbo kicked in, accelerating them to over one hundred and twenty miles per hour. Chase now concentrated his fire on the Imperials in front of him. Men fell en masse before the onslaught of bullets. The remaining soldiers barely had time to turn. The cruiser obliterated them, body parts and blood splattering the windshield. Arian estimated they had run down twenty men. Finally realizing what Ansley intended, he jumped on top of Kaiya, covering her with his body. Fire came from all directions as they approached the barricade.

Chase was riddled with bullets in his chest before a well-placed shot entered his head, exploding out the back, his brain raining down in bits on his fellow passengers. Ansley suffered multiple shots to the chest as the barricade came closer, filling his vision.

They hit the makeshift wall with unimaginable force, the heavy reinforced vehicle smashing through with a bone jarring collision. Foam and airbags deployed, and Ansley was thrown from the vehicle. Kaiya and Arian, huddling on the floor in the back were protected, but the buckling of the vehicle's infrastructure left them trapped, breathless from the oppressive force of the deployed bags and the stench of gasoline. Chase slumped forward against the passenger airbag, a hole where his face had been.

Arian felt Kaiya's small body below him as he struggled in vain against the protective cushions.

"Kaiya, darling, are you alright?" he whispered. There was no response. The weight of the foam was driving his body into hers. He felt as if his ribs would soon break from the strain. If she was still alive, the pressure from his body was suffocating her. As if through water, he heard shouting from above the cruiser. The voices sounded unfriendly, murderous. Arian felt the pressure from the bags release as the soldiers of Beladero stabbed their bayonets into the vehicle, degassing the protective layer, both exposing him and allowing his diaphragm room to expand. His first instinct was to jump up and relieve Kaiya of his weight. This proved a terrible mistake, as his face was met with the butt of a rifle, breaking his nose and knocking him backward, dazed and bleeding, though conscious. The ravenous defenders of the city pulled him from the vehicle, and he could see in his periphery they were doing the same to Kaiya. As two men lifted him to his knees, he felt the muzzle placed against the back of his head. He knew it was over and internally welcomed the reprieve of death. He wanted to hear the click of the hammer that would signal his end.

The click never came.

A frantic man entered his vision, waving for

his executioners to stop. A faint twinge of recognition. Arian struggled to focus his vision and noticed the uncharacteristically large diamond on the man's hand. It was the Mardonian diamond. It was Pedro, Sharie's widower, now defending himself from yet another assault against his family. He had not sold the ring. He had carried it as a badge of honor, a testament to his late wife's bravery. The muzzle of the gun remained on Arian's head.

"Stop!" Pedro shouted. "They are with Ansley. They've come to help."

"Ansley!" shouted one of the men from behind. "He is dead, along with Jabari. We are on our own. They were the empty lies of the Nephite."

"No, you fools. You are mistaken. Ansley has come to deliver us, just as he promised. I saw him myself. He gave me this ring." He flashed the diamond to the men. "He was thrown from the car. Our men have carried him to Daniella in the restaurant. If he brought these people, then they must be important. Take them to her."

The men behind Arian relented, dragging him to his feet without apology. He understood. They were at war. A few harsh shouts brought Kaiya from around the cruiser and to his side. He was happy to see that she was alive, though not surprised. He and Kaiya were pulled away from the barricade, which the fighters worked frantically to repair. Arian could see they were being ushered toward the restaurant where he had first met the people of Beladero. Inside, the violent noises of the fight were replaced by the heart piercing screams and moans of wounded men and women. Hatred for the Overseers raged in his heart and Arian felt validated in his suicidal quest.

He was led, along with Kaiya, past the wounded to the kitchen, where Ansley lay covered in blood, his chest riddled with the same friendly bullets that had killed Chase. Daniella leaned down beside him. She wept, a heart-wrenching cry, deep from within her gut, her anguish alerting Arian that she had ascertained everything of significance from Jabari's absence. Her thick, desperate tears fell on Ansley, and Arian felt a deep sense of loss. He had only recently, given his upbringing, considered the dark oblivion, but he knew in his heart that no one would ever know of Jabari or the brothers and all they sacrificed. And no one would mourn him either. Everyone who was close to him was here. It gave him a sense of life and its importance that he had never known. This was his family, and no one would mourn them either. This, more than anything, drove him to act. No one would remember any of them, but he had to do right by his friends.

"Lift him up!" he ordered the medics.

"Sir, he will die if we move him. His wounds are grave."

"Daniella, I've come to help end the struggle Jabari died for. We have a mission to complete. Ansley will survive and we don't have time. Now lift him the fuck up! We have to make it to the Iris. It is what your husband died for."

A faint voice came from the background, almost unnoticed.

"So you are Daniella. You are as beautiful as described. He spoke of you as he died. I could only dream that a man could love me such as he loved you."

Daniella seemed to gain strength from these words and stifled her sobs. "Carry him on a stretcher," she ordered the medics. "We have to get him to the Iris. Fifty years of building better be worth something."

"Thank you," mouthed Arian to Daniella, who moved away to tend to the other wounded. She was strong like her husband. Four men came and lifted the field stretcher on which Ansley lay unconscious.

"You know the way to the Iris?" asked Arian.

The men nodded.

"Good. It's time to start a new chapter."

The men carried the stretcher out of the kitchen and through the restaurant's main hall. Arian tried to ignore the desperate cries coming from his periphery as he and Kaiya followed, but it was impossible.

At the back of the restaurant, a secret door led to the tunnels. Arian had been drunk the last time he had traversed this path, and half formed memories flooded his mind. They followed the men and Ansley's bullet-ridden body into the mountain to the Iris. The air was hot as they descended into the cave. The machine was operating, warming the underground lake and changing the ambient climate. They marched deep into the mountain, past the office where Jabari and Ansley had offered Arian a drink to steel his nerves before exposing him to the shock of the machine. All the possibilities, only hinted at previously, would now come to pass. Arian felt at peace. He thought this must have been what soldiers felt in battle: an inevitability of the grim outcome, yet a resolve to do what was necessary. At last they came to the vaulted iron door that led to his future.

"Set him down there," Arian instructed the men. "He is the only man who knows the code to enter. We need to rouse him."

The men obliged, gingerly setting Ansley's stretcher on the ground. Arian gazed down on his injured friend. He hoped the bio-bots were as good as advertised.

"What the fuck are you waiting for?" came Ansley's voice, his left eye opening. "Help me up."

"Are you sure?" asked Arian, kneeling down and placing a sympathetic hand on his shoulder. "You don't look good. We have bought some time."

"I'm afraid time is a luxury I have exploited to its limit."

Ansley thrust his arm out and Arian grabbed hold, lifting him to his feet. The man winced from the pain, struggling to remain erect. Kaiya moved forward to aid and steady the injured man.

"First the shoulder, now the chest, you're indestructible," said Kaiya as she guided him. She shot a long look at Arian.

The two of them held Ansley as he lumbered toward

the keypad. Arian could feel the pull of the magnetic field on his blood. The Iris was almost charged. Ansley reached a shaky hand to the recognition crystal and, as before, the patch of false stone lifted, exposing the keypad. It took him multiple attempts to find the right code, but as he returned to lucidity, he typed the proper digits and red lights flashed as the large iron door rose, revealing the main cavern that housed the Iris. A rush of warm air washed over them as the heat removed from the magnets rushed into the corridor. Ansley turned and looked to the four men who had carried him to this point.

"Go now, friends. Be with your families and make peace with whatever gods you hold. This is your last night."

The men, though not understanding the full meaning, grasped the gravity of the words. They nodded in unison and rushed off, back down the tunnel toward whatever life they had left.

Kaiya gasped as they stepped forward, still supporting Ansley, frozen in awed silence as she beheld the sheer massiveness of the spectacle of science, engineering, and the immense fortitude of humans when working together on a singular task. In spite of his previous experience with the Iris, Arian was equally entranced by the complex system of gold, platinum, and copper tubes connecting the great photocells and computer stations surrounding the aquifer. The Iris was a monument to the ingenuity of his species.

They were already sweating from the intense heat given off by the machinery. Ansley was weak, and supported by his two companions. He knew they wouldn't maintain consciousness for long in the oppressive humidity. They had to keep moving.

"You can marvel at its beauty from the control deck," he barked gruffly. "Let's go."

Arian guided the trio toward the clear polymer door leading to the shuttle that would transport them across the reservoir to the control deck. Ansley placed his hand on the recognition crystal and the doors opened. Arian was relieved as they entered the climate controlled compartment. They placed Ansley on a seat within. He was weak, but some color reappeared in his cheeks. The blood had stopped seeping from his wounds. The bio-bots were performing their tasks. The same could not be said for Kaiya. She was pale and her body swayed as if faint. Arian could relate. The magnetic field's strength and the extreme heat wreaked havoc on their bodies. Arian steadied Kaiya.

"Your body will adjust soon, my dear. Bear with us."

She frowned, returning his gaze. "He seems to be improving," she said, bitterness in her voice, motioning with her eyes to the slumped Ansley. If there were an implication behind her words, it was lost on Arian. He turned back to Ansley.

"What are the coordinates to the control deck?"

"0-4-3-8-4. Your mother's birthday."

"Hold on to one of the straps," he called to Kaiya as he typed in the code. The shuttle shot forward at a great speed, the inertial force tugging them back. They hurtled toward the center of the Iris, arriving at their destination less than two minutes later. As he recalled from his previous trip, not even Jabari could access the final recognition crystal leading to the control room and living quarters of the Counsel of Elders. This was the heart of the Centauri. Whether Ansley had known it or not, he had been leading the rebel movement the entire time. The Overseers were not wrong in sensing a plot against them.

The old Professor stood on his own volition this time, slowly walking to the recognition crystal. Passing Arian, he placed a hand on the young man's shoulder and gave it a gentle squeeze.

"You led us here today, my friend. You are as much a part of this now as your mother, Richard, or even me. I would have been proud to call you my son."

Placing his hand on the crystal, the polymer casing opened the elevator leading to the control room. Ansley lumbered inside. Arian stood at the door waiting for Kaiya. She seemed afraid. He had never seen fear in her. She had always been so controlled and hard to read. Reluctantly, she walked forward and entered the lift. The doors closed and it began to rise. Ansley seemed tranquil, almost content, as if he were coming to the end of a long and arduous journey. He had earned his rest. He had lived long.

While Arian should have been frightened or even bitter at being cheated out of his own enhanced life, he found himself feeling only pride. Pride at Ansley's words, and pride that he had found courage he never knew existed within him. His life's story had been written in the past week and he was content with that.

They reached the 50th floor of the control tower, and as the doors opened, Margaret Weaver, head engineer of the Iris, met them. Her grey hair was frazzled, coming loose from what had been a tight bun.

"Oh my!" she exclaimed seeing Ansley's blood-soaked shirt. "We need to get you medical attention."

Ansley waved her off with a sheepish smile. "I will be fine, Margie. Trust me. Is the machine operational?"

Trying to ignore the blood, she looked away, replying, "It's ready. Do you have the bots? We have the calculations completed for the precise coordinates we discussed. We need only scan the bots, and we should be able to deliver the data to both Richard and Padma's Nanosoft cloud network at the appointed time."

Arian looked at Ansley, wondering what he would do. The old Professor stepped forward and placed a sympathetic hand on Margaret's shoulder. He didn't have the heart to tell her the truth. He nodded to Arian. "Give her a syringe."

Arian obliged, reaching into his pocket and removing one of the three remaining injections. As he handed it over, Ansley continued his instruction.

"Commence the scan immediately and load the data into the transmitter. When the Iris has been operational long enough to reach the proper time coordinate, begin transmission. Once this is accomplished, we will maintain the field."

"But Ansley!!" protested Margaret.

"I understand the implications, Margie," he replied. "Either we're successful or we aren't. I'm assuming it will be the latter, and in that case, we all die today no matter what. At least we will take down the entire Aramean infrastructure with us."

Margaret grasped his meaning and rushed away without another word. The three of them stepped through the polymer door and into the circular control deck. As before, the room was abuzz with flashing screens and workers tending their various tasks. With Margaret being off on her errand, only three of the black chairs were occupied. Eyeing Richard's decrepit body, Arian nodded at his biological father, feeling foolish about his reaction at their first meeting. The two men shared only a chemical connection based on circumstances beyond either's control. There was no history between the men and nothing to be said. Richard returned the gesture with a feeble nod of his own.

Ansley addressed the Council.

"My friends, we have now arrived at the end of a journey that began over fifty years ago. There is no going back from here. Our cover is blown and Beladero stands in battle against the Imperial forces of Capitol City. None present shall leave this room."

Richard and Chandler gave knowing smiles, while Oswald gazed catatonically at nothing. It was unclear whether he had understood anything in ten years. None of the men had any future to speak of anyway, so this news was of little consequence to them.

"Margie is scanning the bots as we speak. We will attempt to deliver the signal to the Nanosoft cloud network. Regarding the prospect of that being successful, I have little hope. If it happens to be, by the time we reach the present we now occupy, we will either be long dead by natural causes, or perhaps the nano-treatments will have been made widely available to all inhabitants of the world, in which case we will have no memories of this and will have gone on whatever path our past selves chose." Ansley paused and cast an uneasy glance at Arian, who he knew grasped the implication. " Upon initializing the transmission, we will let the Iris run its course to the inevitable annihilation of the parallel particle fields. We all know what happens then. It will be up to the survivors to rebuild a world without the Overseers and the Empire. It will be for them to create a more just world. Are we in agreement?"

Again, the two sentient members of the Council nodded, this time joined by Arian. Kaiya's face had lost color.

"Good. Margie is in agreement as well. Then it's settled. Regardless of what happens tonight, it has been an honor working side by side with you these past two hundred years. It has been a pleasure matching wits and challenging one another in the completion of this project. If I lament one thing tonight, it is the loss of this collaboration."

Ansley removed an unopen bottle of Tegave from the shelf and dusted it off. Popping the cork, he raised it to the others in the room.

"We have saved this bottle for the time when we would implement our design. I guess it's time to drink it. To times past."

He took a long, somber draw off of the bottle and passed it to Richard. Each man, excluding Oswald, repeated the ritual in turn. Ansley became emotional at the ritualized close of his long life, all his triumphs and recent sorrows summed up in this final toast.

The moment of reflection was fleeting as Margie re-entered the control room.

"Our scans are complete. All pertinent data pertaining to the specifications of the bio-bots have been uploaded to the transmitter. The magnet has achieved 100 Tesla. It's time."

"Let's watch from the observation deck," said Ansley, the finality of it all evident in his voice. "I want to see my baby operate one more time." He helped Richard and Chandler to their feet and guided them to the door before wheeling Oswald out.

Arian grabbed Kaiya's hand, interlocking his fingers with her own. She was trembling.

"C'mon, my love, he whispered. "If we are to die, let's die together, gazing into the mysteries of the universe." He pulled her toward the door, though she strained slightly against the inevitable. She was not prepared to die like this. Still, she followed. Ansley, Richard, Chandler, and Margaret all stood against the railing looking down to the center of the aquifer against the stunning backdrop of the platinum and gold wiring that circled the cavern. Oswald remained seated beside them. It was a beautiful sight, full of melancholy and resoluteness. Arian and Kaiya joined them at the rail. Ansley moved over to make room for them, placing his arm around Arian's shoulders.

"Fire it up," he said, almost in a whisper. Margaret communicated to the workers still occupying the control tower and they heard the great accelerator buzz with life below.

Just as on his previous visit to the Iris, the strong magnetic field began to accelerate the particles at increasing speeds around the circular cavern, and the pull of the particles on the water created a vortex in the aquifer. Then, there came a series of loud cracks as the first particle collisions generated secondary particles, which continued to accelerate. The electricity and increasing heat was evident in the room even from behind the protective polymer that separated them from the main room. Their hair began to stand on end from the static electricity building up. Kaiya screamed and threw herself into Arian's arms as the loud explosion and burst of super-heated water indicated the creation of the Amasarsi bosons and their singlets, which would now be accelerated to unimaginable speeds in the parallel tachyon field further and further backward in time.

The room was illuminated in bright red, green, and blue light as the massive energies manifested in visible fields generating from the central focal point. Finally, a small black dot appeared in the center, barely noticeable at first, but growing with each passing second, until the reservoir resembled a massive eye, with the swirling waters and colorful electric fields forming the iris while the darkness in the center formed the pupil. The machine had been aptly named. The water itself seemed to disappear as they stared into the ever-growing black void.

Arian moved himself from Ansley's grasp and embraced Kaiya, who was shaking with fear.

"Don't be afraid, my love. Look down below into space and time and our entire history. Somewhere down there, your mother still lives. Somewhere down there is a young version of you, before your troubles. Maybe there is a time line where we were able to be together, without strife. The universe is a mysterious place. Don't fear your destiny."

The structure around them began to shake as the newly created worm-hole continued to grow, pulling at the surroundings in nature's attempts to collapse the parallel fields and balance the energy.

"How far are we from transmission?" shouted Ansley over the roar below them. Already, he knew the termination of the fields would be sufficient to collapse complex system of caves, destroying the region.

"We've never been this far. I don't know how long the infrastructure will hold."
Margaret was frantically tapping at a hand-held computer. "We are almost to the proper coordinates," she screamed in response. "I will initiate transmission."

From a platform suspended from the cavern's roof, Arian could see a diamond shaped transmitter lowering to a position a few hundred feet above the growing void, which was now the size of a small café table. It anchored into a reinforced steel structure, which was rooted deep within the surrounding granite walls.

"The pressure locks are now engaged," shouted Margaret. "Beginning transmission." The diamond structure lit as if with a million lights, as the crystals within activated in unison. In spite of the now deafening roar from below and the nearly blinding light, Arian marveled as he realized that, for the first time in history, humans were actually sending a signal into a tear in space-time. The sheer irresponsibility of the endeavor overwhelmed his amazement.

"And now, we wait to meet our fates," shouted Ansley, that same madness Arian had seen during his first visit to the Iris again evident in the old Professor's eyes, transforming his features.

Kaiya's grip on Arian strengthened as the blackness below them grew. The humidity was stifling as the climate control mechanisms began to fail. Water condensed on the protective polymer that separated them from the chaos below. Arian wondered what the implication would be for the rest of the galaxy if they accidently created a black hole in the region inhabited by their bi-solar system. It would take billions of years, but he imagined it would eventually join with the super-massive black hole at the center of the galaxy, with terrible results for the surrounding star systems. He was shaken from his morbid musings by a strange and sickening sound. Looking up, he could see that Ansley and the others were also disturbed. Releasing Kaiya, he turned toward Ansley to find the root of the noise. Before he could speak, it occurred again, as a massive crack formed along the protective polymer. Ansley's eyes were wide, as if even he had not expected this new wrinkle. Arian could read in his face that he was now also having doubts about whether the fields would self-annihilate.

With Arian's back turned, Kaiya, frightened by the prospect of the polymer giving way to the swirling forces below rushed back to the control room. She desperately tried to open the door, anything to escape the certain death that awaited her in this accursed cavern. It was to no avail. The workers were under strict instruction to not open the doors for any reason. She searched her surroundings for another escape. This was not a valiant death. This was hell.

At the far end of the observation deck's back wall, she

spotted a brightly painted box. She rushed to it. It was a slight lever encased in glass. Above it were the words, "Emergency Magnet Quenching." It was so simple it could have been a fire alarm in an office building. The same calmness that always came over her in times of adversity washed over her, and her path was clear. Whether it was being raped in a stable or draining the life from a former lover, it was always the same. Kaiya was a survivor, and she knew what she had to do.

She didn't rush to Arian. She walked. He and the others anxiously watched the growing weakness in the polymer, which creaked and groaned under great stress. She grabbed him, turning his body and pulling him close.

"If we're to die, my love, I must feel your lips on mine one final time."

As he leaned down, she thrust her mouth to his, before parting his lips and swirling their tongues together. For a moment, Arian forgot their imminent death and allowed himself to be enraptured by Kaiya's smell, her taste, her softness. He didn't notice when her right hand moved to his breast pocket and removed the two remaining syringes. It was only when he felt the sharp jab in his deltoid muscle that her spell was broken. He jumped backward wincing.

"What the fuck!" he exclaimed as he removed the syringe with his right hand and realized what had happened.

Surveying him with her cold, expressionless gaze, Kaiya said nothing, as she injected herself in the left bicep with the remaining syringe, giving no indication of pain. Without a word, she returned to the emergency quenching mechanism. Ansley's attention was drawn away from the cracking polymer by Arian's exclamation. He noticed the used syringe in his hand, and looked to Kaiya. Her intentions were obvious. Futile as they were, her life now beyond saving, he had to ensure that enough energy was built up to destroy not only Beladero, but Capitol City as well. He moved to intercept her. Seeing him approaching, she rushed for the emergency lever. As she was about to reach it, he dove at her, throwing her small body along with his own into the railing just below. Her ribs hit the top of the railing with a thud, breaking the lower two, as Ansley hit his head on the brittle metal, still managing to wrap his arms around one of her legs. Just then, the polymer that had been shielding them gave way with a shattering explosion, sucking the air and glass into the growing void of the wormhole.

The outward supports suspending the platform buckled under the gravitational pull and the floor collapsed, swinging downward as if on a latch and slamming into the wall below. As the floor disappeared beneath her, Kaiya wrapped her arms around the top rung of the rail, feeling pain in her newly fractured ribs. Ansley, still gripping her leg, grabbed the bottom rung of the railing. Arian fell backward toward the void, landing on the iron bars he had just been standing behind, nearly losing consciousness from the impact but managing to grab hold to prevent from being drawn into oblivion. He watched helpless as the frail bodies of the four Council members were flung into the great pupil of the Iris. With a sickening feeling in his stomach and a strange sensation in his blood, he turned his gaze to the platform that was now against the wall to find Kaiya and Ansley far above, hanging on to the railing that had been at the back.

Kaiya struggled against the forces drawing her downward and Ansley's one-handed grip on her ankle toward the lever, as her diaphragm struggled to expand and draw in the dwindling oxygen supply in the cavern. If she wasn't able to rid herself of Ansley, she would not be able to hold for much longer. She felt the full force of his body as he used her ankle to lift himself up toward her, clamping his right arm onto her thigh. She was surprised she was able to hold his weight. Perhaps the injection was already paying dividends. As she looked down at him, her eye caught a slight shimmer coming from the top of her boot. Wrapping her left arm around the rail so that both of them were supported by her chest and shoulder, she plunged her right hand down between his chest and her boot. Grabbing hold of the silver handle, she pulled the carving knife from its place of concealment.

"I will not die for you or any man!" she declared as she reversed the motion of her arm, stabbing the knife deep into Ansley's chest.

Brief shock registered on his ageless face before his eyes glossed over and he was no longer staring at her. He was not seeing anything anymore. His body went limp and his grip released as he dropped into the unknown that had claimed his oldest friends. Kaiya had little strength, and dangled by two hands, with the quenching mechanism still two feet above her. Mustering everything she had left, she pulled her body up, put all her weight on her right arm and, using her left, struck the glass protecting the lever, shattering it. She nearly lost her grip and fell back down into a hanging position. Not believing she could make it, she knew that she had to try. She pulled with all her might, throwing herself at the now exposed lever. As she wrapped her fingers around the warm steel, she knew she had made a mistake. Even as she pulled the lever down, initiating the quenching mechanism, her body was being pulled away, toward the center of the room. When she tried to find the railing, it was already out of reach as she hurtled downward, disappearing into the black.

Arian held to the railing, his legs and arms wrapped around it in a bear hug as the gravity grew stronger and stronger, sapping his strength. He had watched helplessly as Kaiya stabbed his friend and mentor Ansley, sending him to his death. They had all known the score when they came to the Iris. None would survive. Still, as he saw the only woman he had ever loved tumble out of this world, he lost most of his will to hang on. The pull upon his body began to lessen and the swirling pupil of the Iris shrank, spiraling inward upon itself with a dazzling array of light flashes emanating from the center. Soon it would collapse and obliterate the surrounding terrain as it rebalanced the energy of the universe. Arian, ever the scientist, was grateful that Kaiya had succeeded in quenching the magnet, thus debilitating the accelerator. For a moment, he had feared the wormhole would keep expanding and swallow the entire world. The weakening pull and the dissipation of the space-time tear told Arian this would not be the case.

As he looked through the portal of time and awaited the blast that would incinerate him, he pondered the fates of the only two people he had cared for in his life. Where were they now? He had never considered the possibility of an afterlife, but could they be there now? Or were they forever lost in the dark void? He wanted to see Ansley again. He wanted to be with Kaiya forever. He lamented that it had all come to this. As the pupil of the Iris shrank, he wondered if Ansley would find Padma, somewhere out in the cosmos, in another life or universe. Were they together now, in a passionate embrace, with no more life and death to keep them apart? He had no faith in the message sent through time. If they were together, it would be through some other unknown metaphysical means.

His muscles tightened as his body tensed for the explosion. He didn't want to die alone in this cavern separated from his friends, but death was inevitable and he would not wait. Without hesitation, he relaxed his arms and legs and let the pull take him. Whatever was on the other side, he would follow them into the black. Relaxed and at peace, Arian closed his eyes and fell, crossing the void just as it disappeared and the fields annihilated.

\*\*\*

In the heart of Beladero, the battle raged on, no one aware of what was happening within the great cliffs that surrounded the city. The Capitol City force was advancing, and the lines were broken. All hope was lost within the rebel ranks. The intense flash of light briefly blinded all present just before their bodies were turned to ash. None would bear witness to the thunderous noise as the entire mountain chain exploded from within.